Inspector Abberline
and the
Gods of Rome

Inspector Abberline

and the

Gods of Rome

SIMON CLARK

ROBERT HALE · LONDON

ISBN 978-0-7198-1084-8

Robert Hale Limited
Clerkenwell House
Clerkenwell Green
London EC1R 0HT

www.halebooks.com

2 4 6 8 10 9 7 5 3 1

Typeset in 10.5/13pt Sabon
Printed in Great Britain by Berforts Information Press Ltd

Who is Inspector Abberline?

IF A MAN could ever be described as a rival to the legendary Sherlock Holmes then the real-life Inspector Frederick Abberline is that man.

Frederick George Abberline (1843-1929) rose to fame in his search for the serial-killer Jack the Ripper in 1888. He was widely featured in national newspapers, which portrayed him as a heroic figure who tirelessly fought crime. Although Abberline never did catch the notorious Whitechapel 'Ripper', he was an enormously successful policeman, receiving eighty-four commendations and awards, as well as earning the loyalty and respect of his colleagues. He retired from Scotland Yard at the age of forty-nine, yet continued to work as a private detective. At various times, he was based in Monte Carlo where he investigated the most sensitive of cases before being appointed head of the European office of the Pinkerton Detective Agency. Inspector Abberline's legendary stature grew as he solved crimes on the international stage and without doubt became the most famous detective in the world.

WHEN THE GODS FLED ROME

408 AD: THE glory that is Rome is already being consigned to history. Roman legions leave Britain to fend for herself. Caesar's vast empire is collapsing. Barbarians sweep from the north into Italy to plunder its towns and slaughter its people. Alaric, King of the Visigoths, lays siege to Rome, attempting to starve an already decaying and impoverished city into submission.

Emperor Honorious knows that soon the barbarians will swarm through the capital's streets to loot what remains of its treasures, so he orders his bodyguard to carry away seven golden statues, known as the Gods of Rome, and hide them until the fortunes of the empire are restored.

At the dead of night, the Gods of Rome are smuggled out through secret catacombs beneath the barbarian army's very feet and are taken to a place of safety.

The Roman Empire continues its long, slow decline. By 476 AD this once mighty civilization will be gone forever. And so, it seems, will the fabulous treasure known as the Gods of Rome – until, that is, a mysterious photograph is found in the most strangest of circumstances.

BIZARRE DEATH

SIR ALFRED DENBY, 63, of Fairfax Manor, East Carlton, has been found dead in a workshop adjacent to his home. Sir Alfred continued the custom of his late father by signalling the start of the working day to estate staff by the firing of a cannon at seven o' clock in the morning. The gentleman's last words to his manservant were, 'Edward, the lock of the workshop is sprained. See that it's repaired today.' Sir Alfred then went to the workshop where a considerable quantity of gunpowder was stored for use in the cannon. Witnesses report that a violent explosion occurred at 6.30am. Mr T. Barstow, coroner, believed that Sir Alfred placed a candle too close to an open barrel of gunpowder, resulting in its detonation.

The gentleman was found in the debris of the workshop, quite dead, and in a shockingly injured condition.

Sir Alfred Denby makes the fourth brother in the same family on whom an inquest has been held.

From *The Todworth Chronicle*, 9 February 1890

CHAPTER 1

THE JOURNALIST WITNESSED the dramatic incident from the window of the White Horse Tavern on Charing Cross Road. A large, red-faced gent in a grey coat roughly pushed aside a small boy who'd crossed his path. The boy carried a jug, which splashed its contents across the front of the man.

The man reacted with fury. He grabbed hold of the boy's wrist so fiercely that the jug flew into the road where it shattered. The man's face grew even redder as he shouted at his captive, while pointing at what appeared to be milk dripping down the front of his coat. Hardly anyone glanced in the direction of the angry man shaking the distraught boy. Nor did passers-by react when the thug raised his fist. Such occurrences were commonplace on these streets. Clearly, the child would be beaten for an accident that wasn't even his fault in the first place; for it was the man who had roughly pushed the boy aside, causing the milk to be spilt on his clothes.

Such is life in London, thought the journalist. Violence is every-where. The cab driver who whips his horse, the thief who knocks down a woman to steal her purse, the master who beats his servants; even rats fight one another in the sewers for scraps of food. Not only the River Thames flows through the city, there's also an ever-present current of violence, too. The journalist liked the line about the River Thames and *an ever-present current of violence* and decided to use it in the article he was writing. As he jotted down the words, he heard an indignant shout. Before the thug in the grey coat could strike the child, another man had intervened. The newcomer had grabbed the bully's sleeve at the cuff. Now both men were standing toe-to-toe. The individual with milk still dripping down his coat bunched his large fist and held it just an inch or so from the other man's chin.

The journalist quickly rose to his feet, slipping the notebook into his pocket as he did so, then he ran across the busy road just as the fight started. The gentleman who'd intervened had protectively moved the boy behind him while looking his opponent in the eye. Grey Coat appeared to be the vile type who settles disputes with his fists.

What happened next proved the journalist right. Grey Coat threw a punch. The other man stepped back, moving the child as he did so. The bully punched a second time, and a third, each time missing his target. With growing frustration, he launched himself forward while swinging his fist at the boy's protector.

The smaller man had appeared to be flinching back in terror from the punches. Now, however, he rather neatly turned the tables. As Grey Coat almost lost his balance, due to the violence of the missed blow, the other man seized the lapels of the milk-spattered garment and gave a sharp tug. The brute toppled forward. He struck the pavement belly first with a resounding smack that could be heard above the rumble of carts. Swiftly, and with such an air of quiet confidence, suggesting that he'd done this many times before, the smaller man seized Grey Coat's hand, bent it back against the wrist then placed one foot on the side of the fallen man's neck.

The journalist stepped forward. 'Can I be of any help, sir?'

'He will lie there quite calmly now.' The victor added a few words that Grey Coat was clearly intended to hear, '*Otherwise, if the gentleman struggles, I shall break his wrist.*' The man applied just enough pressure to make the thug squirm in pain.

At last, pedestrians and cart drivers alike were taking an interest, and they stopped to find out what would happen next. This, after all, was quite a spectacle. A middle-aged man, softly spoken, of modest stature, and with the appearance of a bank manager or country solicitor, perhaps, had toppled Goliath. Now this 'David' stood there, resting one foot on Goliath's neck, while gripping his hand in such a way that left him unable to fight back.

At that moment, a pair of constables, immaculate in their dark-blue uniforms and crested helmets, moved through the growing crowd.

'Hey, you there,' barked one of the constables to the victor, 'let go of that gent immediately.'

'Not until the boy's safely away from here.' The man who'd defeated the thug spoke to the child. 'Best be on your way home. Explain to your mother that it wasn't your fault about the jug. A clumsy, ill-mannered gentleman barged into you.'

Without a second's hesitation, the child vanished into the crowds.

The man who'd saved him from a beating shook his head and sighed. 'Though I suspect the boy's mother will thrash him for spilling the milk, so he probably won't escape unscathed after all.'

One of the constables put his hand on the man's shoulder. 'Sir, you must release him.'

'Indeed I will, and I release him into your custody.'

When the man turned to face the constables they immediately took a step back and saluted. 'I'm sorry, sir,' said one, with a genuine note of apology. 'I didn't recognize you for a moment there.'

Grey Coat had, at last, climbed to his feet. Before he had time to decide whether to resume his attack or run away, the constables gripped an arm apiece. With a uniformed officer at either side of him, he realized the time had come to surrender. He stood there quietly with his head lowered.

'What's the charge, sir?' asked one of the policemen.

'A breach of the peace is sufficient, Constable.'

After that, one of the constables noted down details of the incident then they led the rather despondent-looking Goliath away. Meanwhile, the crowd quickly dispersed now the excitement was over. Within moments, London returned to its timeless melody: horses clipping smartly along, drawing hansom cabs; the ponderous rumble of carts laden with flour, coal, bales of cloth, kegs of ale, and all the other essentials that kept Londoners fed, clothed and warm. Threading themselves through the noise of the seemingly eternal traffic were human voices: children calling to one another, the shout of an old man selling apples from a barrow – all mingling with the chirpy whistling of delivery boys, and the long, booming call of the newspaper vendor.

The journalist remained a short distance from that singular individual who, for a few moments at least, had stopped London's traffic. When the man looked the journalist in the eye, he tilted his head to one side, clearly expecting to be spoken to.

Stepping forward, the journalist nodded politely, and held out his hand. 'Inspector Abberline, please allow me to introduce myself. My name is Thomas Lloyd. I'm a journalist, and I've been hired to tell your story.'

CHAPTER 2

AFTER INSPECTOR ABBERLINE had shaken the journalist's hand, they left Charing Cross Road for a narrow street lined with shops. Small flakes of snow fell, leaving white speckles on the inspector's hat. Even though it was April, winter showed no sign of yielding to spring. People hurried by, eager to finish errands and get out of the cold. A man in a leather apron stirred a simmering vat. Thomas Lloyd could smell the hot liquor from the other side of the street – clearly some potent concoction of oranges, cinnamon and sugar boiled up with water and plenty of gin.

The man in the leather apron barked out to passers-by, 'Good for all that ails thee. Cures colds, bronchitis and lumbago!'

'More likely to send you blind than cure you,' muttered Thomas, as the raw fumes of hot gin prickled his nose.

Abberline smiled. 'I'm more of an ale man myself.'

Thomas nodded in the direction of a snug-looking tavern. 'Can I buy you a pint of something, Inspector Abberline?'

'Thank you, but no. I devote as much time as I possibly can to walking. One of the tools of the policeman's trade are his feet ... together with eyes, ears, and a nose for trouble, of course.'

Thomas noticed that the man had quickened his pace. He realized that Abberline had a restless need to cover a good deal of ground, and see and hear as much as he could. What's more, the detective didn't simply gaze on a general London street scene of people, shops, horses and taverns – he noticed precise details. The way a man might slouch on a corner with the brim of his hat pulled down over his eyes to conceal his identity, or the way a woman carried a bundle of linen while constantly glancing back over her shoulder as if she was being followed.

Inspector Abberline didn't say anything more, or even question what must have been a surprising statement that Thomas had uttered a few minutes ago: *I'm a journalist, and I've been hired to tell your story.* Eventually, Thomas decided to break the silence.

'What you did back there was remarkable.'

'Really?'

'The boy would have taken a savage beating from that thug.'

'The policeman's duty is to protect the lives and property of everyone. Beggar or aristocrat – or even a journalist come to that.' He paused by a factory as its gates opened and hundreds of women poured out in their long skirts, with shawls over their heads, and carrying baskets. When they joined the crowds in the street it was like watching a pair of rivers in flood merge. Inspector Abberline's brown eyes calmly regarded this deluge of humanity.

'Mr Lloyd,' he began, 'London is one of the biggest cities in the world. Its population has increased to more than six million. Most of the people you see here weren't even born in London. They were raised in villages; they once picked apples in orchards; they tended cattle and sheep. These people escaped poor, rural communities in order to earn enough money to prevent their families from starving. Men and women have poured into this, the capital of Queen Victoria's empire, not to become rich, but in order to survive. The problem that confronts them is that there aren't enough houses, or jobs, or even space to walk without being pushed and jostled. So people become angry. They find the noise and clamour oppressive. Sheer pressure of human beings in this town becomes explosive. Ordinary men and women find themselves doing terrible things that they would never have even dreamt of doing when they lived in the countryside. If people don't find work they're driven to prostitute their bodies, or forced to steal in order to stay alive. Those individuals occupy the bulk of the police officer's time; however, there is a new breed of wrong-doer that I've never encountered before until much later in my career. It's my belief, Mr Lloyd, that in the most evil and oppressive conditions found in cities, there are certain human beings who cannot remain fully human. Their minds shatter, and then they commit murder. What I fear above everything else is that such murders will become an epidemic: that they will upend society and lead to a state of anarchy where law and order cease to exist.'

That was an extraordinarily powerful statement – a heartfelt one, too. Thomas hesitated for a moment before broaching what he knew would be a sensitive subject. 'Sir, I know that you investigated the slayings in Whitechapel two years ago.'

'It's all right, Mr Lloyd, I won't take offence. You may safely use *that* name: Jack the Ripper.'

'I didn't want to cause any embarrassment.'

'I'm not embarrassed, Mr Lloyd, I am ashamed. That monster, the so-called Jack the Ripper, murdered and butchered at least five women. I failed to catch their killer. That failure is a stain on my professional life. And far, far worse than making me appear incompetent there is a danger that the monster might start killing again ... all because I failed to catch him ... or her ... or them.'

He began walking again.

'Inspector Abberline, I've clearly made you angry.'

'No, you've reminded me that I can never be complacent. If there's any anger it's directed at myself. Whatever newspapers might write in praise of my work, I know that I will always be found wanting in respect of the Ripper atrocities.'

'Inspector, I told you that I've been hired to write your story. We have an appointment to meet tomorrow at Scotland Yard, but chance brought us together today. Yet I fear that I've failed before I've even begun.'

'Far from it. Your editor told me that you will write about the daily toil of the modern investigator.' He smiled. 'Is that so?'

'Yes, it is, Inspector. Allow me to tell you something about myself.'

'You are Mr Thomas Lloyd, aged thirty-seven of Pimlico. Just this week you went to work for The Pictorial Evening News ... and you were engaged to a young lady by the name of Miss Emma Bright. Are my facts on target?'

'Yes, sir.'

'I spoke to you during the Ripper Case when you reported for the *Wimbledon Herald.*'

Thomas did not hide his surprise. 'That was two years ago. I don't believe we spoke for more than five minutes at most, and you still remember me?'

'You told me that you were meeting your fiancée that afternoon in order to hear a lecture on botany – something to do with the nutritional merits of breadfruit, I believe. Perhaps Miss Bright is now Mrs Lloyd?'

'Ah, not yet, sir. However, Emma is still my fiancée.'

'Oh.'

'She's helping her father in Ceylon. He's cultivating tea plants that are resistant to disease.'

'But she will become your wife one day?'

Yes, sir.' Then Thomas added with some heat, 'As soon as she leaves those blessed tea plants and comes home.'

'In that case, I hope you won't be kept waiting much longer.'

'If I may ask, how do you know so much about me, sir?'

'Ah ... in my class at school there was a boy who grew and grew. When he was thirteen years old he stood fully six feet and seven inches tall.' The inspector paused to allow a butcher's cart to pass by before he crossed the road. 'I didn't grow a great deal in physical stature, but my memory grew and grew in what I daresay is an abnormal way. This isn't a boast but a fact, Mr Lloyd: *I remember.* That's the long and the short of it: I remember faces, conversations; I remember the physical detail of the killer's knife, the sound of a victim's scream.' He touched his head. 'All goes in here ... it never leaves. Though sometimes I wish it would. Memory can haunt as doggedly as a ghost, is that not so? I recall speaking with you outside McCarthy's shop in Whitechapel, on the tenth of November, 1888, the day after Mary Kelly had been murdered by the Ripper. You wore a red scarf with a pale-brown coat, and I remembered an especially striking feature.'

'What feature, sir?'

'You weren't like other journalists. You weren't falling over yourself to ask whether the poor woman was found naked, or whether she'd been violated sexually. No, what struck me was that you cared about those poor women. You have a humane heart.'

Presently, they joined a road that led toward the Houses of Parliament. Thomas Lloyd took the opportunity to scrutinize the man who would feature in his newspaper articles. He mentally noted the brown herringbone pattern coat, the wisps of fine hair emerging from beneath the hat. He especially noted the broad, open face, with its thick moustache, and a pair of clear, brown eyes that appeared to record every detail of human life that surrounded him.

Thomas cast his mind back to the start of the week when he'd been hired by the The *Pictorial Evening News* to write a detailed account of Inspector Abberline's work. Thomas had spent an entire day reading an enormously thick file devoted to newspaper clippings and reports of Abberline's life and career. Thomas learnt that Frederick George Abberline had been born in Dorset in 1843. His father, a saddlemaker, died when Abberline was six years old. Thereafter, his mother opened a tiny shop and raised her children all by herself. Life was a constant struggle for Hannah Abberline: poverty and hunger were never far away.

The young Frederick Abberline was a sharp-witted boy. He was sensitive to the feelings of others, too. The harm and distress inflicted upon innocent people by criminals never failed to anger him, and probably that's what prompted him to join the police force when he was nineteen years old. His knack for catching wrong-doers, and sheer talent for giving evidence in court that lead to a high conviction rate, impressed his superiors so much that he quickly rose through the police ranks. By the age of thirty, he'd been promoted to inspector and assigned to a station in Whitechapel before being promoted yet again to a senior position at Scotland Yard. However, a grim twist of fate took Inspector Abberline back to Whitechapel a few months later when he investigated the murder of several women by a shadowy figure known as Jack the Ripper.

Thomas read every document in the file: he felt as if he'd got inside the skin of the man himself and had begun to understand his nature. Inspector Abberline did truly believe that the police must not discriminate on the grounds of wealth, poverty, race or religion. Abberline investigated cases of theft, kidnap, common assault, homicide, as well as internationally famous cases of a highly sensitive nature. Abberline also understood that the loss of a simple possession could have profound consequences. One newspaper carried this telling statement of his: *'The theft of a duke's gold watch is undoubtedly a crime. However, I am more inclined to be occupied by the theft of a coat from an impoverished man or woman. For in winter, the possession of a warm coat is of absolute importance. After all, someone without a roof over his head and with no coat will almost certainly die.'* If Thomas had gained a sense of the man's virtuous character by reading the file, that sense had crystallized when Inspector Abberline had saved the child from violence just thirty minutes ago.

As they walked, Thomas asked, 'So you won't resent my presence, if I shadow you for my newspaper article?'

'With all my heart, I shall welcome it, Mr Lloyd, because if we're to be successful in waging war on crime it's vital that we have the understanding and support of the public.'

Once again the journalist held out his hand. 'Then, if we are working together, I would like you to call me Thomas, if that is acceptable to you?'

The inspector shook the journalist's hand. 'That is most acceptable, Thomas, thank you. I'll leave you to decide what you call me.'

'If I may, I'd prefer to continue with Inspector Abberline.'

'As you wish.'

'So, please consider me to be your very own shadow, Inspector. I go where you go.'

'Then meet me at Fenchurch Street Station tomorrow morning, seven sharp; we'll be taking a train to East Carlton.'

'East Carlton?'

'The name must ring bells, surely?'

'The Sir Alfred Denby accident? He was killed in an explosion.'

'According to Sir Alfred's brother the death was no accident. It was murder.' Abberline touched his hat in a gesture of farewell. 'Now I must detach myself from my shadow. I have an appointment in that building over yonder. Good day, Thomas.'

With that, Inspector Abberline crossed the road, passed over the threshold of the Houses of Parliament, and vanished into that Gothic palace where a few hundred men created laws that were enforced by individuals like Inspector Frederick Abberline, and which governed the lives of millions who dwelt within the British Empire.

CHAPTER 3

ON A COLD, frosty April morning, with bright blue skies, Thomas Lloyd entered Fenchurch Street Railway Station to find Inspector Abberline already standing by the ticket office. The detective spoke to three constables in uniform. After carefully listening to what Abberline told them, they saluted smartly before walking across to where men and women queued to pass through a turnstile to a station platform. One of the constables seized a young man by the collar. The youth reacted with surprise, struggled a little, but the six foot constable easily bundled him away through a door.

Thomas watched the other two constables continue their patrol of the station. Like most policemen in uniform they were former soldiers – large, powerful men with straight backs, and a talent for deterring potential troublemakers with nothing more than a stern glance. Thomas knew that as well as being armed with ebony sticks, which they called truncheons, the men had lead weights sewn into the hems of their capes. Thomas had seen plenty of thugs sent crashing to the ground with just a flick of one of these formidable garments.

The station clock stood at three minutes to seven when Thomas greeted Inspector Abberline.

'Good morning, Thomas. All set for adventure?' Abberline held out a piece of card. 'I took the liberty of buying your ticket.'

'Do you really think we are faced with adventure? After all, the coroner ruled that Sir Alfred Denby's death was an accident.'

'All I can do is examine the facts surrounding his death. Then see if those facts suggest that there has been foul play. Ah, our train leaves in ten minutes.'

'But there is more to detective work than accumulating facts, isn't there?'

'You mean intuition? The policeman's sixth sense that allows him to divine when there is a criminal nearby, plotting mischief?'

'Indeed so.'

'It's remarkable how criminals do give themselves away. They develop tell-tale traits that visibly advertise their guilt. You only have to learn to read the expression in a man's face, or the way he'll slope his shoulders, or turn away when he sees a constable.' They passed through a turnstile. 'You might have seen the arrest of the young man in the queue. Most people standing in line gaze forward as they await their turn. That particular man, however, repeatedly glanced back at the constables standing by the entrance. When the constables' attention was fixed on the street the man picked the pocket of the gentleman in front of him. The important thing to note, if you write about this incident, is that the young man's movements and his manner betrayed him long before he dipped his fingers into his victim's pocket. After you, Thomas.' Abberline opened the carriage door.

Thomas took his seat in the carriage with Abberline facing him. A little while later, the guard sounded a whistle. After blasting out torrents of steam, the locomotive eased its way out of the station, the carriages swaying gently from side to side. Thomas Lloyd glanced at the man opposite, who'd investigated some of the most famous crimes of the century, and felt shivers of excitement. Inspector Abberline had spoken about the policeman's sixth sense when it came to detection, now Thomas's own journalistic instincts told him loud and clear that this would be the start of a remarkable day, and that the best was yet to come.

They had the carriage to themselves as the train rumbled southwards. Every so often, smoke from the engine would find its way through a chink in the window and the carriage would fill with a faint, blue haze. Thomas tried to suppress the tickle in his throat until he couldn't any longer and coughed. Inspector Abberline, meanwhile, sat with his eyes closed. Thomas suspected the man hadn't fallen asleep, but that he had, perhaps, entered that formidable memory of his to review the facts of the case they were investigating today.

Thomas made good use of the time. Taking a pencil and notepad from his pocket, he jotted down a description of Abberline, which he'd use in his article. *Abberline, age 49, moustache, side-whiskers, four parallel scars on back of right hand – knife wounds? Smaller scars above left eye possibly inflicted during days as a constable. Remember to ask about his time in uniform.*

The train sounded its whistle as it clattered over a road crossing.

There were hardly any hansoms here in the suburbs; traffic mainly consisted of delivery carts. Thomas marvelled that although they were fully ten miles from the heart of the city the suburbs still appeared limitless. Most of the houses were new; their brickwork shone a brilliant orange in the sunlight. In every available acre of land yet more homes were being built.

Without opening his eyes Abberline said, 'The city has doubled in size since I arrived here over twenty years ago. When I think of London, I picture a bottle of ink that has been spilt on a green carpet – the stain keeps spreading outwards as if nothing will ever stop it.'

'I daresay when it reaches the coast it must stop there; although I wouldn't be surprised if one day they drain the English Channel, so more suburbs can be built.'

Abberline opened his eyes. 'You're not a born Londoner, so all the noise and sheer immensity must have been as alien to you as it was to me.'

'Indeed it was. My parents were schoolteachers in a small village between Leeds and Bradford in Yorkshire. I grew up seeing green fields and forests.'

'You'll see less and less of those. London is devouring every blade of grass in her path.' He nodded at the scene beyond the window. 'How many men do you suppose are employed to put up all those new buildings? Ten thousand? Twenty thousand?'

'I would imagine that they are beyond counting, Inspector.'

'And with money in their pockets they'll be preyed on by thieves and tricksters given half the chance.'

'Then it's my duty to write about your work, Inspector, and inform all and sundry that you and your colleagues are doing your utmost to protect the public.'

'We try, Thomas, though we aren't guardian angels by any means, so never portray us as such. We're damned mortals. And our conscience then damns us when we fail ... which is more often than we'd care to admit.'

'The police force should be championed. I will endeavour to do exactly that.'

'That sounds like a compliment, Thomas.'

'Then take it as such. However, I shall write truthfully about what I see as I shadow you. And I must warn you that I will not allow you or my editor to change what I've written.'

'Is that so?'

'My parents raised me to tell the truth.'

'Which means your articles will expose me if my investigations are slap-dash.'

Thomas noted the way the man gazed at him. He wondered if he'd spoken too forcefully. Would Abberline become angry?

'You, Thomas Lloyd, are a bloody-minded Yorkshireman.' With that, he suddenly threw back his head and laughed out loud.

'Sir, I shall not tolerate you mocking me.'

'I'm not mocking, Thomas, I am laughing because I'm happy and relieved – I know we can talk to one another bluntly, if need be. We're not going to be constrained by what society considers polite or well mannered.'

'My feelings exactly.'

'So, I have something troubling to get off my chest.'

'What's that?'

'This fiancée of yours out in Ceylon. Miss Emma Bright?'

'What of her?'

'Tell her to leave those bloody tea plants to their own devices and come home and marry you.'

Thomas sat up straight, ready to adopt an expression of being deeply offended by such a direct comment on his personal life. However, he felt his stomach muscles quiver, his shoulders began to shake, and a second later he was laughing, too.

'Damn it.' Thomas wiped his eyes. 'I was going to accuse you of being impertinent. But you are absolutely *pertinent*. That's what I think every day. I wish Emma would tell her father that she wants to come back to England.'

'No, she wouldn't *want* to come back to England, Thomas; she would *want* to come back to *you*.'

'I sincerely hope what you say is true.'

'Thomas, I have a distinct feeling that we're going to be the best of friends.'

'I should like that very much.'

Abberline reached inside his coat and pulled out an envelope. 'We have half an hour until our stop. Here's a report on the death of Sir Alfred Denby. There is a photograph of the deceased – brace yourself, the explosion caused some ugly injuries. There is also a letter from the man's brother, insisting that the gunpowder didn't detonate due to careless use of a candle. The man believes that this is a case of murder.'

Thomas noticed the word CONFIDENTIAL on the envelope. 'Are you sure you'd like me to read this?'

'We're now friends, Thomas. I trust you.' Abberline looked him directly in the eye. 'And in this sometimes dangerous line of work, who knows? One day we might have trust each other with our lives.'

CHAPTER 4

THE MAID KNEW she wasn't alone in the woods. A figure stalked her. From the corner of her eye she glimpsed him again and again, yet he'd always vanished by the time she'd spun round.

'Is that you, Jake? Come on … I know it's you.'

But it wasn't Jake, the boy who'd kissed her just twenty minutes ago. She'd liked that kiss, even though it had bruised her lips. The way he'd hugged her when he'd planted that hard, stinging kiss excited her so much she could hardly breathe and her heart had pounded. Jake then invited her to a dance in the village on Saturday night, and now she'd have to ask the housekeeper if she could take time off from work on Saturday instead of Sunday. The maid could imagine the housekeeper peering through those funny little glasses perched on her nose – couldn't she just! Then the frosty woman would declare, 'Oh, a boy, is it? Let me tell you, girl, boys are trouble – they will bring *you* trouble.'

At first, she thought Jake had followed her when she took a shortcut through the wood. But whoever stalked her was no farm lad. The figure was tall, with a strange, long face that was white as milk. Even though the maid had not seen the stranger properly, she was convinced that she'd made out a pair of eyes watching her from the shadows. Just a glimpse of that burning stare had frightened her. For the second time today her chest became so tight she couldn't breathe and her heart thundered until it hurt. But this wasn't the thrill of her true-love's strong arms holding her, this was terror.

The young woman remembered what had happened to a local girl who'd been abducted by a sailor. The brute had done terrible things before cutting his victim's throat. She walked faster. Here the trees crowded together in such a manner that the damp and chilly pathway became so gloomy she could barely see. Her nostrils caught that musty smell of wet earth. Birds cried out as if warning each other of some terrible danger coming ever closer.

A crackle of breaking twigs sounded from behind and she glanced back in terror. A white face – a stark, white face with fiery eyes. Then the face was gone. But the sense of being followed ... stalked ... hunted ... grew stronger.

'Jake? Is that you?'

No reply.

'Stop it, Jake. You're scaring me.'

Although she knew down to the roots of her heart, and the very depths of her blood, that this was no cheerful farm boy. Jake would be working in the fields. He'd think that his sweetheart had returned to the Hall. Not for one moment would he guess that a frightening stranger pursued her.

Suddenly, she yelled with all her might, '*Go away!*'

A ferocious rustle came from her left. Clearly, her pursuer attempted to overtake her without being seen.

But she heard ... *she heard!*

With fear draining her strength away, the maid took a path at random. Soon she realized that this was a wrong turn, possibly a fatally wrong turn, because the path took her even further from the Hall, and the protection of other human beings. Finally, she began to run, because she knew with absolute clarity that the moment grew near when she'd stand face-to-face with the stranger. A man who was deathly white – as if he'd been fashioned from Death itself.

Deeper and deeper into the forest she went ... shadows drowned the path in darkness ... these were the most dangerous moments of her life. And yet, even as panic threatened to overwhelm her, she heard the beautiful music ... no ... she must be imagining those sounds, surely? *Because that's the sound of a flute,* she told herself. *Who would play a flute out here in the forest?* Long, slow haunting notes drifted out of the gloom. A sinuous sound ... mesmerizing ... a melody from a dream.

Then the music stopped. Everything stopped. She couldn't even hear the sound of her own heart. In that silence ... that long, drawn-out silence, when even time itself died away from the natural world, she seemed to inhabit some uncanny realm beyond this one. From behind her, a pair of white hands gently alighted on each of her shoulders. The whiteness of the skin seemed unreal. Although the young maid couldn't turn her head, simply because her muscles refused to work, she could make out from the corner of one eye that one of the gleaming, pearl-white hands was connected to a naked arm.

The hands gently pulled, drawing the young woman backwards, until she felt warm breath on the back of her neck. And in the silent space beneath the trees, there in deep shadow, the young woman shuddered, and she knew that her life would never be the same again.

What happened next amazed and shocked her. Abruptly, the white hands vanished from her shoulders. Without warning, there came a terrific crash as a large object tumbled through the branches. This was followed by a terrific thud as it struck the earth just in front of her.

There on the ground, lying stretched out, and utterly motionless, was a man of perhaps twenty years of age. He was dressed in the clothes of a gentleman. He lay flat on his back, his face turned toward hers. The stranger's red hair gleamed as bright as copper wire. The mouth remained open, clearly revealing a gap in the front teeth. Most noticeable of all, his eyes – they were a vivid, emerald green. Those green eyes stared from the gloom, even though she knew he lay dead. The stranger's chest gave a single heave and a gush of blood spurted from his mouth – a furious river of crimson, surging and bubbling from lifeless jaws.

The maid found she could move again: she began to run, crashing through bushes, searching for a way out. She expected to come face-to-face with the terrifying white phantom at any moment.

At last, she burst into a sunlit clearing to find three men walking there. Without hesitation, she stumbled toward them, while gasping for breath. A young man caught hold of her before she could fall.

'Don't worry, Miss, we have you safe,' said the man.

She looked up into the young gentleman's face. He had bright, copper-red hair; his striking eyes were an emerald green. When he smiled at her, he revealed a distinct gap in the top row of his teeth.

The maid let out a yell of terror. *'I've just seen you back there! You fell from the sky ... I saw you lying dead, and you were all broken!'*

Something inside her head tore free. The maid screamed again ... after that: nothing ...

Nothing but darkness.

CHAPTER 5

THEY ALIGHTED FROM the train at East Carlton. The small, rural station stood at the edge of a village that consisted of cottages with thatched roofs, and in extreme contrast to London these streets were empty, with the exception of an elderly man pushing a wheelbarrow full of potatoes.

Abberline said, 'We're due to be collected by coach at half past eight.' He glanced across at the church clock. 'And it's now twenty-five past the hour. According to Mr Denby's letter we have a fifteen minute drive to Fairfax Manor.'

Thomas Lloyd shielded his eyes against the sun as he scanned what appeared to be the only main road in and out of the village. He could see nothing resembling a coach. Then no doubt life still ambled along at a much slower pace in this rural backwater.

For the past ten minutes or so, Thomas had been mulling over the documents that Abberline had given him to read on the train. What's more, he found it hard to erase the memory of the photograph of Sir Alfred Denby in death. The man's face had been savagely torn by the explosion – his eyes were open, and they appeared to express a mixture of shock and disbelief that his life had reached such a brutal end. The body itself lay partly buried in the debris of the workshop.

Thomas said, 'Nothing in the report suggests that the gunpowder explosion was anything other than an accident. Every morning at six-thirty Sir Alfred collected a small quantity of powder for the cannon, which he then fired at seven sharp as a signal to his employees on the estate to start work in the fields. On the morning of his death, the workshop door remained locked until Sir Alfred unlocked it, just as he'd always done. However, on this occasion he appears to have inadvertently brought the naked flame of a candle too close to the gunpowder.'

Abberline didn't appear convinced by the report's conclusions.

26

'Perhaps the gentleman's rigid observance of his timetable was his undoing? Might not someone have attached a clock to a detonator? That way the explosion could have been precisely timed to occur within a moment of the ever-punctual Sir Alfred stepping through the door.'

'Was there any sign of such a timing device?'

Abberline shook his head. 'Both the police and the coroner were satisfied that Sir Alfred was a victim of fatal mishap and nothing more.'

'However, the brother disagrees.'

'Mr Victor Denby lists a few clues in his letter that suggest foul play. He describes the butler seeing a lurking figure, as he puts it, near the workshop several days previous to the explosion. He also cites the fact that the lock of the workshop had been sprained.'

'So, someone might have forced the lock in order to gain access to the workshop? That would allow them to see how much gunpowder was stored there, and decide that would be an ideal way to dispose of Sir Alfred.'

'And disposed of he was. Nobody could survive a blast of that force.'

'But Mr Denby doesn't mention who would wish to kill his brother.'

'So? The gentleman was an upstanding member of society? An innocent Englishman murdered for no apparent reason – perhaps slain by men who wish to destroy in a completely random fashion?'

'Ah, now you're toying with me. You know something I don't.'

Abberline's eyes twinkled. 'Detectives and journalists approach their work in much the same way. Yes, we look, we listen, we string together facts in order to construct our case, or our newspaper story. But aren't we also like archaeologists? We dig down into the history of our subject. We uncover what has lain hidden for a long time.'

'So you've been digging into Sir Alfred's past?'

'Indeed, I have. His innocence is questionable. Twenty years ago the man may have been involved with the theft of valuable artefacts from Italy. *The Scandal of the Gods of Rome* – you've heard of it?'

'I can't have failed to. The story was in the newspapers. The Royal Family were embarrassed by accusations made by the King of Italy.'

Abberline nodded. 'Gold statues from the time of the Roman Empire were discovered in a cave in Italy – they'd been hidden there fifteen hundred years ago when the country was being over-run by barbarians. Whoever stumbled upon the treasure never reported the find to the authorities. It was only much later that the Italian police learnt that a notorious criminal family, based in Naples, had smuggled out of the country, at least one of the gold statues out of the country, which they sold to a wealthy Englishman.'

'Ah … Sir Alfred?'

'So we believe.'

'But there's no evidence?'

'None.'

'Why was the Royal Family implicated?'

'Rumours reached the Italian king that Sir Alfred had wanted to give to Her Majesty a statue of a gold Faunus – a horned god that resembles the devil.'

'A very generous gift.'

'Generosity be damned. Sir Alfred gambled that he'd be promoted to the peerage after giving Her Majesty such a priceless artefact.' In fact, rumour has it that he achieved his knighthood in a questionable manner.

'Being Lord Denby would have enabled him to become even richer.'

'So we have a greedy man. And one who apparently broke the law by illegally purchasing what amounted to an Italian national treasure.'

'But there is no hard evidence that his involvement with a theft twenty years ago led to his death two months ago?'

'And that's what brings us here: two men in search of that *hard* evidence. Now if I'm not mistaken here is our carriage.'

A cart of decidedly rustic appearance, pulled by a black horse, rumbled along the street. Thomas was surprised to see that the coachman wore the rough smock of a farm worker.

'Mister Abby Line?' sang out the cart's driver.

'Inspector Abberline,' corrected the detective.

The driver scratched his jaw, which was covered with thick, bristly stubble. 'I've been told to get ya'. Hop on, gents. I'll get ya' there quick.'

Abberline raised his eyebrows before climbing onto a bench in the back of the cart. The driver immediately shook the reins and the horse started off before Thomas was on board. He had to run behind and leap on. Abberline caught hold of his arm and helped him to the seat.

'Is this as it should be?' Thomas called out to the driver. 'We were waiting for Mr Denby's coachman.'

'Ha! The coachman left on account of his terrors. I'm the gardener. They told me to pick you two gents up from puffin' Billy.'

'Terrors?' repeated Abberline. 'You say the coachman left on account of his terrors?'

'Aye, sir. The coachman couldn't abide living at the manor house. He'd convinced himself he'd be kill't, too.'

Thomas surmised that their driver meant 'killed' by his use of the word 'kill't'.

'We're here to investigate the death of your former master.'

'Investigate, sir? There's no need to trouble your good selves with that. Everyone hereabouts knows exactly what killed Sir Alfred.'

'He died in the explosion, surely?' said Thomas.

'No, gents. It was the curse that killed Sir Alfred. Just like the curse did for his brothers, too.'

'What curse?'

'You must've heard of the curse? Everyone in these parts has.'

'Perhaps you will tell us,' Abberline said.

'The curse that's killed Sir Alfred and his brothers, sir, is the curse of the Gods of Rome.'

CHAPTER 6

THE MAID SAT in the room that led off from the main kitchen. This was known as the butler's pantry and it's where the butler, housekeeper and senior domestic staff dined. The rest of the staff normally ate in the kitchen. This was the first time the maid had been into the room. She knew she'd only been allowed in because it's where the gentlemen had brought her after she'd fainted in the wood.

The housekeeper peered at the maid through her silver-rimmed glasses with their peculiar little half-moon lenses. 'Laura.' The woman spoke sternly. 'You must not repeat to anyone what you've just told me. Do you hear, girl?'

'But I've already told the gent with red hair, Miss Groom. I said that I'd seen him fall out of the sky, and I saw him lying all dead and broken on the ground.'

'Laura, that's such nonsense. The very man you're speaking about lying dead carried you into the house.'

'I know that, Miss Groom.'

'Then how can you have seen a living, breathing man lying dead on the ground?'

'I don't know, Miss Groom. I just did. It must have been a vision.'

'Domestic servants don't have visions, Laura, only saints have visions. What you're saying is blasphemy.'

'A figure chased me through the forest. I was terrified ... so terrified my wits were scattered. I heard music and had a vision ... or a-a clairvoyance.'

'Laura' – the housekeeper's tone took on a note of warning – 'this foolery of yours must stop."

Laura felt herself getting hot and panicky. She was telling the truth, and she wanted to warn the young man with red hair again. 'I saw a vision of the man's death. He'd fallen out of the sky.'

Miss Groom leaned across the table. She gripped Laura's forearm so fiercely that the girl cried out. 'You will have seen something of the master's work here. You know what it involves. The gentleman with red hair is here to help the master.'

'Which means he is in danger: I must tell him to leave.'

'Good gracious, girl, you'll do no such thing.'

A boy of fourteen thrust his head through a gap in the door. He could barely keep from laughing. 'Seen your phantom again, Laura?'

The housekeeper rounded on the lad. 'Hold your tongue, Daniel.'

'That's what everyone below stairs is saying. Laura got herself chased by a ghost, and it was as pale as morning mist. I reckon we should call it the White Phantom. *Ouch!*'

Miss Groom caught hold of the boy's ear and dragged him to within six inches of her face. 'If I hear you spreading malicious tales about ghosts, I'll thrash the skin off your backside myself, Daniel Jenner. Now, who said you could come in here?'

'*Ouch.* Cook told me. She wants to know if you want more tea.'

'Thank Cook, but tell her we have sufficient.' Miss Groom released the boy's ear and rubbed her fingers together as if they'd become dirty. 'You can go now, Daniel. And remember – no tittle-tattle about ghosts.'

The boy vanished through the door, rubbing his ear as he did so.

The housekeeper gazed thoughtfully out of the window at the Welsh mountains. In the distance, taller than the rest, stood Mount Snowdon. It still wore a coat of frost. And while the other mountains were dull greys and greens, Snowdon was a brilliant white in the sunshine. A ghost mountain – at least that's what it looked like to Laura. She remembered the white figure which had pursued her through the forest that morning and she shivered to the roots of her heart.

'I've a mind to dismiss you, Laura, and send you back to your parents. The master is more forgiving, however. He believes you suffered a nervous shock, and he's told me that you should be allowed to rest for a few days.'

'Thank you, Miss Groom.'

'I don't want to hear any more nonsense about visions and ghosts.'

'I really did see the gentlemen with red hair lying dead on the ground. I remember his green eyes ... the way they were cold and staring and—'

'Listen to me, girl. Don't mention this nonsense again, or I will see to it that you are sent home without references, and you'll never find honest work again. Now, go up to your room. You are to remain in bed until I tell you otherwise. Go on then, child. I'll have broth sent up to you later.'

Laura Morgan climbed the back stairs to the room she shared with two other maids. From there, she looked out of the window and caught sight of the master walking in the company of the red-haired gentleman who'd picked her up from the ground after she'd fallen in a faint.

'I'm so sorry,' she murmured. 'I know that you will die here, but I'm not allowed to warn you again.'

For a moment, she thought she saw a strange face that was white as death. It peered out from the trees at the master and the red-haired gentleman; a second later, it vanished. Icy shivers cascaded through her body and she quickly climbed into bed without getting undressed.

The maid knew that terrible events would happen here soon. Powers beyond her understanding had granted her a glimpse of the future. That's what she believed with all her heart. Yet what could she do to help the doomed gentleman? How could she save him? With savage clarity she remembered the words she'd uttered: *'I've just seen you back there. You fell from the sky ... I saw you lying dead, and you were all broken!'*

CHAPTER 7

THOMAS LLOYD MADE notes about the case that Inspector Abberline was investigating. Or, rather, he attempted to. The cart that he and the detective were riding in had neither springs nor cushioned upholstery to protect them from the violent jolting on the country lane, which seemed to consist of ruts, holes and boulders. More than once, the two men had to grip the sides of the rustic cart to prevent them from being thrown out.

Abberline smiled at Thomas. 'This reminds me of a pleasure steamer I once took from Brighton. The cruise was no pleasure I can tell you. There was very near a hurricane blowing.'

A wheel bounced over a house-brick lying in the road. Their driver swore mightily about inconsiderate people who leave debris on the Queen's highway. After that, a dog raced out of a farmyard in order to bark furiously at them. The startled horse lurched forward, almost tipping Thomas out of the back. The driver cursed again.

'Damn ye, blasted brute!' The man used his whip to lash out in the direction of the dog. The whip didn't frighten the dog in the least and it furiously snapped at the wheels.

'Driver,' Thomas called out, 'we'd very much like to arrive at Fairfax Manor in one piece.'

'Right you are, sir.' The driver took this as encouragement to deploy his whip again. He lashed wildly in the direction of the snarling brute. The leather whipcord came perilously close to striking Thomas rather than the intended target.

A boy whistled from the farmyard. The dog immediately bounded away, wagging its tail, pleased that it had discharged its canine duty. After that, the journey became quieter, even if the cart jolted so much that Thomas's teeth repeatedly clacked together.

'Just a little while, gents,' sang out their driver. 'Soon be there.'

Thomas rolled his eyes. 'Thank heaven. My bones can't stand

much more of this bouncing.'

Abberline's eyes twinkled. 'Perhaps, when time comes to leave, we might enjoy walking back to the station.'

'Indeed so,' Thomas chuckled.

The road became a little smoother and the jolting less violent. Thomas seized the opportunity to jot some notes. *Investigation into death of Sir Alfred Denby. Coroner decided explosion was an accident. My impression is that Abberline doubts this. Abberline mentioned Gods of Rome scandal and Sir Alfred's possible connection thereto. Gold statues were illegally taken from Italy over twenty years ago. So: a connection between theft of statues and death of Sir Alfred? Did someone—*

The cart bumped so violently that the point of his pencil snapped. Thomas sighed. He decided to leave the note-making until this turbulent journey had reached its end, and sat back to admire the view. All around him were meadows, while softly rounded trees, after the harsh, straight lines of London's buildings, were pleasantly easy on the eye. An old man guided a cow down the road.

As the cart passed the herdsman, the driver jerked his thumb back at his passengers. 'Bert, look at these fellers.'

The man stared at Abberline and Thomas as if they were exhibits in a show.

The driver added, 'They're detectives from Scotland Yard. They want to find out what did for poor Sir Alfred, and how he got hisself blown to bits. I told these 'ere detectives what killed the poor old bugger.'

'The curse went and killed him,' grunted the cowman. 'Everyone knows that.'

Thomas shook his head as he murmured to Abberline, 'They're talking as if we're not even here.'

'And something tells me we're going to hear much more about the curse before the day's out.'

The cart finally left the country road for a long driveway that led to a mansion of red brick. Tall, spindly chimneys poked high above the roof. A sign fixed to a gatepost proclaimed:

FAIRFAX MANOR
NO VISITORS WITHOUT PRIOR APPOINTMENT
TRESPASSERS BEWARE

'Seems rather ominous.' Thomas nodded at the sign.

'Ominous or not, we'll do our duty.'

'Do you think Sir Alfred was murdered?'

'That's why we are here, Thomas. Our quest, come hell or high water, is to discover the truth.'

Thomas Lloyd pulled a handle set into a recess beside an imposing door. A bell rang somewhere deep inside the mansion. The windows of Fairfax Manor reflected the April sunshine with such dazzling intensity that it forced Thomas to shield his eyes when he looked up at the building. How many bedrooms does a house like this house have? he wondered, Ten? Twenty? He couldn't recall ever visiting a home of this magnitude before. The owner must be stupendously wealthy.

Abberline, meanwhile, appraised the grounds with those sharp eyes of his, undoubtedly noting specific details that Thomas had missed. This remarkable detective was sharpening up his mind for the coming investigation.

The sound of echoing footsteps approached. Locks and bolts clunked loudly. At last, the door swung open to reveal a tall, thin figure in black. The butler, Thomas saw, was a sombre-faced man of sixty or so, with grey hair and a grey-skinned face of pretty much the same hue.

Abberline spoke briskly, 'I'm Abberline; this is Mr Lloyd. Your master is expecting us.'

'The back,' intoned the butler in a voice that was as grey as his complexion.

'The back?' Abberline shook his head, puzzled. 'I don't understand what you mean?'

'The door at the back of the house.' The butler looked down his grey nose at the men as if they gave off an unpleasant odour. 'Tradespeople, etcetera, must enter via the back door.'

'Be so good as to tell your master that Inspector Abberline is here.'

'Mr Denby is busy this morning. He will speak with you later.'

'He'll talk to me now, damn it. I am here at Mr Denby's request.'

'I have my orders, sir. Mr Denby must not be disturbed.'

'Good grief.' Thomas couldn't believe his ears. They'd travelled all this way only to be treated with the contempt householders' reserve for unwanted door-to-door salesmen. 'Tell Mr Denby we will take the next train back to London if he doesn't let us through this door in the next sixty seconds.'

The butler appeared startled by Thomas's aggressive tone. Clearly, this grey-faced man wasn't used to dissent. 'Very well ... step into the hall. I'll just be a moment.'

Thomas and Inspector Abberline were shown into a lofty hallway. A marble staircase swept upwards into the shadows. Somewhere a clock ticked with a slow, ponderous rhythm.

Abberline said, 'Your threat about us returning to town worked admirably.'

'Do you think I was a little too harsh?'

'Not at all. I wish some of my fellow police officers weren't so overawed by the trappings of aristocracy. They still fear the ruling-classes – something which has ruined many an investigation.'

Ten minutes passed as they stood in that mausoleum of a place. Eventually, the butler glided from the shadows.

'Mr Denby is annoyed at being disturbed,' said the butler in those pompous tones of his. 'However, he will meet you at the workshop, which is the scene of the tragedy that claimed the life of his late brother.'

The butler told them that they'd find the workshop, and Mr Denby, at the rear of the house. After they'd stepped outside he closed the front door, relieved to be shutting these interlopers out. Thomas and Inspector Abberline skirted the formidable structure until they came upon a group of outbuildings.

Thomas murmured, 'Even I can deduce which one is the workshop.' He nodded in the direction of a brick-built building that had clearly suffered extensive damage. Slates were missing from the roof, leaving yawning holes. A gentleman in a long, dark coat and wearing a top hat stood with his back to the building.

When he saw the pair he pulled out a watch, glared at it, then shouted, 'Come along, I don't have all day.'

'The butler didn't like us,' Thomas murmured under his breath, 'and neither does his master.'

'It's not a question of disliking us, it's something else entirely.'

'Well, he's giving an excellent portrayal of someone *pretending* not to like us.'

'Let's have a chat with Mr Denby and then I'll share my suspicions with you.'

Thomas was taken aback by that that mystifying statement. So what had the detective noticed that he hadn't? He began to suspect his journalistic senses weren't as keen as he hoped. Abberline could interpret the tiniest of clues as if he was reading the large print of a newspaper headline.

Inspector Abberline approached the man, raising his hat as he did so. 'Mr Victor Denby. I'm Inspector Abberline; this is my assistant, Mr Lloyd.' Clearly Abberline didn't want to reveal that Thomas was, in fact, a journalist. At least not yet. 'I came here as quickly as I could after receiving your letter.'

Mr Denby, a heavilybuilt man in his sixties, showed no interest in the niceties of handshakes and greetings. Instead, he spoke with curt impatience, 'Ah, Abberline, so you're the Ripper man?'

'Hardly a description I would use of myself, sir.'

'You never caught this Jack the Ripper, then?'

'No.'

'Hmm ... even so, your superiors tell me that you're their best detective.'

'I will do my best to discover what really happened to your brother.'

'Well, Abberline, I'm not discussing anything outside. Come into the workshop ... what's left of it.' The man strode into the building.

Abberline, pausing outside, gazed at the upper windows of the mansion. He spoke in a low voice so Denby couldn't hear, 'Thomas, have you revised your opinion of Mr Denby?'

'Not at all. He despises us. Our very existence on earth seems to anger him.'

'No, he's not angry, Thomas, he's scared. In fact, he's scared for his life.'

'How can you tell?'

'Did you notice the way he repeatedly scanned the trees over there, as if he expected a man with a gun to step out and take a shot at him?'

'I took that as merely impatience.'

'He also made a point of standing with his back to the wall. The man is frightened of who might suddenly appear behind him.'

'So, Denby thinks that whoever killed his brother will return and kill him?'

'Yes, and the man is terrified.'

Denby didn't venture as far as the doorway. Instead, his voice boomed from inside the workshop: 'Well, are coming in here or not?'

The interior of the workshop consisted of bare walls, the only exception being at the far end where one wall had been clad in wooden boards. The floors had been swept clean of debris. On one wall there were black smoke marks. Thomas Lloyd saw that fresh putty lined the window frames, indicating that broken glass had been replaced after the explosion. Even so, reconstruction of the workshop seemed half-hearted. He could see blue sky through holes in the roof.

Victor Denby stood in the corner furthest from the doorway. He seemed calmer now, though his expression was one of impatience. *This is a man who wants to get finished here so he can get back to the house.* Thomas surmised that much from the man's demeanour. Abberline walked the length of the room, examining the walls, floor, and the roof above his head.

'All the original contents have been disposed of,' said Denby. 'You will be familiar with the background to my brother's death. He used to come out here at six-thirty every morning to collect a quantity of gunpowder stored in cupboards fixed to that wall. He then went to a cannon at the front of the house, loaded the powder into the gun, then fired it at seven sharp.'

Abberline examined the scorched wall. 'And that tells the estate staff to begin work?'

'Indeed so. Alfred continued the tradition started by my father.'

'Didn't the workers resent that?' Thomas asked.

'What do you mean?'

'I mean, sir, that some might not like having their lives governed by the firing of a gun.'

Victor Denby scowled. The questions irritated him. 'It's a very large area of farmland and forest, not to mention the gardens. The cannon is an effective way of signalling the start of the working day, and whether the staff resent it or not is neither here nor there. They are paid to work.'

Abberline turned to face the man. 'Were you here at the time of your brother's death?'

'No, I was in living in London. I moved here to take over the running of the estate after my brother was killed.'

'Which bedroom did your late brother occupy?'

'Is it important?'

'Possibly.'

'One on the second floor at the back of the house. You can see the window from here.'

'That's a north-facing room.'

'What of it?'

Abberline went to the doorway in order to study the bedroom windows. 'Surely a south-facing bedroom would be brighter and much more pleasant?'

'This was my brother's home, Inspector; he was free to choose which ever bedroom he wanted.'

'And so picked one that had a perfect view of this workshop?'

'I don't see that is relevant to his death. Do you?'

'I am in the process of accumulating facts,' Abberline told the man. 'It's much too early to draw any conclusions from them.'

'Did you draw any conclusions from the facts you accumulated about the hussies butchered by the Ripper?' Spite glinted in Victor Denby's eye when he said those words.

'I wish I could have solved that case, Mr Denby but it was not to be.'

'Do you think you'll have better luck solving this one?'

Thomas opened his mouth, ready to protest about what Denby was clearly inferring; that Abberline was incompetent. Abberline placed his finger to his lips. A request that Thomas didn't speak.

Victor Denby sniffed, as if the air in the workshop wasn't to his liking. 'I'm a very busy man. I'll leave you gentlemen here to pursue your investigations.'

Abberline spoke politely. 'Sir, I haven't finished asking my questions yet.'

'You ask questions that don't make any sense. Your interest in my brother's choice of bedroom – surely that's hardly relevant, is it?'

'Be patient with me, sir. The more I know, the more I can get to the truth of what happened to your brother.'

'Dash it all, man. Alfred was murdered.'

'By whom?'

'I don't know.'

'How was he murdered?'

'The gunpowder ... a bomb of some sorts ... I don't know exactly how.'

Abberline came back sharply with, 'But I must know *exactly*. I must be able to marshal hard facts. I must have evidence that your brother is the victim of homicide by an individual or individuals that I can eventually identify; otherwise there will be no arrest, no trial and no conviction. Do I make myself understood?'

Denby became angry. 'Do you know to whom you are speaking?'

'I'm speaking to the gentleman who asked me to investigate – a gentleman who is also extremely frightened.'

'Confound it, sir. How dare you?'

'Was Sir Alfred a victim of the curse?'

'Who told you that?'

'That's what local people are saying. Your brother was destroyed by the curse placed on statues known as the Gods of Rome.'

'Lies. Infernal lies and nonsense spouted by local peasants.'

Abberline waited a moment for Denby to calm down. Thomas noticed what Abberline had seen before. Denby's eyes revealed his agitation. He repeatedly shot anxious glances through the windows, as if expecting an unwelcome visitor.

'If we may proceed with the interview?' Abberline spoke with impeccable courtesy.

'Yes, yes, but make it quick.'

'I'd like to know the history of your family.'

Denby stared in disbelief at the detective. 'The history of my family? How in heaven's name can that be of any use to you?'

'It might be of vital importance.'

'This line of questioning is nothing short of impudent.'

Abberline took a deep breath and looked the man in the eye. 'Sir, we must be able to speak frankly to one another. It is essential in police matters that an officer can ask questions freely – questions that might appear blunt, impolite, intrusive and even downright rude. The answers a policeman receives may become the building blocks of his case that leads to a conviction.'

'But really ... how can my family's past have any bearing on my brother's murder?'

'I must cast my net wide and catch as many clues as possible; some will have no relevance whatsoever, some might well unlock the mystery of Sir Alfred's death.'

For a moment, Denby let his guard down. An expression of alarm did appear on his face when he walked to the window and looked out across the lawn. He stiffened, realizing he'd exposed himself to danger. Quickly, he retreated to the corner of the room where two solid walls met, which might offer some protection. The anger vanished now. His shoulders sagged and, when he spoke, it was in a much quieter voice.

'All right, I'll tell you about my family. However, I don't know everything. There are secrets. I have long suspected that certain key facts have been kept from me.' That's when he began to reveal the remarkable story of the Denby bloodline.

The three men stood in the workshop. Brilliant sunshine flooded in through large windows, filling the room with light. This was the scene of the explosion that killed 63 year-old Sir Alfred Denby eight weeks ago. Now the man's brother, dressed in a severe black coat and top hat, revealed the astonishing history of the Denby family. Although he tried to maintain an air of magisterial dignity, Thomas noticed that his stern demeanour often slipped. His eyes darted at the slightest sound. When a gardener passed by the open doorway, Victor Denby stopped dead and froze. He only let out a sigh of relief when he realized that the man was, indeed, a member of his staff. Inspector Abberline was right. Here was an individual who was terrified.

Thomas jotted key facts into his reporter's notebook as Denby spoke.

'The Denby family were blacksmiths. It's said that a Denby man shoed horses for the Roundhead army before the battle of Naseby. It was my grandfather who turned what was a traditional village smithy into a manufacturing business. Not only did he shoe horses, he also employed men to make bridles, stirrups and so on. He was an industrious fellow and he was still shoeing horses in his eightieth year, even though he had nine men working for him.' Denby smiled. 'My grandfather was proud of his workforce; he called them "The Many Nine".'

Abberline nodded. 'I take it that the family back then didn't occupy such a splendid house as this?'

'No, my grandfather lived in a house that went with the old blacksmith's premises down in the village. But he generated enough wealth to buy more houses, which he rented out to local people.'

'So, where did the abundant wealth originate?'

'The abundant wealth, as you put it, came about as a result of my father's genius.' Denby sounded prickled at having to divulge what he clearly considered a private family matter. 'My father inherited my grandfather's business over fifty years ago. This was when England was gripped by railway building fever. Construction companies had an insatiable demand for all manner of ironwork for the new railways – everything from iron wheels to the rails they ran upon. My father was shrewd enough to recognize that demand for all this ironmongery would be worth a king's ransom, so he sold the houses that my grandfather had acquired and invested every penny in a foundry that could produce railway tracks by the mile.'

'The casting of railway lines brought in hard cash?'

'It did indeed.' He puffed out his chest proudly. 'Newspapers called my father Iron Road Denby. Just two years after the first section of rail left the factory my father moved his family into that house.'

Abberline appeared to glance in the direction of the mansion. However, Thomas noticed that the detective's gaze settled on the windowsill instead, where a hammer rested alongside a bag of nails. Thomas endeavoured to see through the detective's eyes. *So, what's significant about that humble hammer and nails that warrants such scrutiny?* Some nails had spilled from the torn bag. They were rusty. A spider had spun its web across the hammer. Was this more evidence that Victor Denby wasn't especially interested in putting right the damage caused by the explosion? After all, the roof had gaping holes where the rain would pour in.

Meanwhile, Victor Denby listed his fathers' achievements with ever-growing pride. 'He bought the leases of several country estates. When my brothers and I were old enough he sent each one of us to these estates and told us to manage them, and make the family even more prosperous.'

'So you and your brothers became country squires?'

'Indeed so. We each occupied our own mansion, such as this one. We either farmed the land ourselves, or rented it out to tenant farmers.'

'You were living in London when your brother died?'

'Yes.'

'You'd left your own country estate for a spell?'

'No.'

'Oh?'

Denby spoke with breezy indifference. 'I lived in Fenton Hall in Devon. It had five thousand acres of farmland. The lease expired, so I had to leave, simple as that.'

'Bear with me while I get this clear in my mind,' said Abberline. 'Your father made his fortune supplying railway track when there was explosive growth in the building of Britain's railway system?'

'Yes.'

'But the railway industry almost collapsed in the 1840s – nearly all construction was halted.'

'My father had already realized that many railway companies had over-stretched themselves and would go bankrupt.'

'So, he invested in country estates, which you and your brothers ran for him?'

'That's correct.'

'But he didn't buy them outright. He merely rented properties, which would then be reclaimed by the owners when the term of the lease expired.'

'That's hardly relevant to the death of my brother.'

'For a man of such keen business instincts, the fact that your father acquired large country estates for such a short term seems ...' – Abberline tilted his head – 'Dare I say, shortsighted?'

'My father was a man of vision, sir. I won't have you speak ill of him.'

'I would not insult a dead man, Mr Denby. I am merely trying to understand why your father invested so much money in country estates that would, one day, have to be surrendered to those who owned the freehold.'

Denby clearly wished to dismiss this line of questioning. Even so, he must have realized that Abberline would persist. 'My father had developed a perfectly well-thought out plan. He bought the leases of six country estates at a comparatively low price. His intention was to make the estates more profitable; then, as a sitting tenant, buy the mansions and the farmland outright when the leases expired. Unfortunately, my father died before he could bring his plan to fruition.'

'Did your oldest brother inherit everything?'

'He did.' The man's nostrils flared angrily. 'My brother, Hubert, had no interest in continuing in my father's footsteps. He inherited every penny, every brick, every blade of grass, but he preferred to take himself off to Africa to engage in missionary work. Hubert hasn't set foot in England in more than thirty years. His solicitor has overall authority of the remaining estates and purse strings. I, and my surviving brothers, are permitted the role of consultants.'

'Thank you,' Abberline said. 'You have been most helpful.'

'I want you to catch the blasted devil who killed my brother.' Even though Denby could hardly be described as friendly, he was no longer hostile toward his visitors from London. 'My apologies, gentlemen, for sending the cart to collect you from the station. Certain circumstances prevent the use of my carriage. Is that everything, gentlemen?'

'Just one more question, Mr Denby. What happened to the contents of this workshop?'

'Oh, that was all blown to smithereens. I had the gardeners clear everything out. It was dumped in the old quarry over yonder.'

'Do I have your permission to search through what's left?'

'By all means – you'll find nothing but bits, though. The explosion left nothing intact. Least of all, my ...'. He gave a regretful sigh. 'To find the quarry, all you need do is use the white gate on the far side of the lawn. A path will take you directly to it. Now, gentlemen, I must return to my work.'

With that, the man hurried back indoors, repeatedly glancing this way and that as he went – a frightened rabbit of a man.

*

Thomas Lloyd closed the white gate behind him. Inspector Abberline waited for him to catch up before they continued along the path toward the quarry.

Abberline asked, 'Do you think you will have enough material for your newspaper story?'

'Yes, but I must confess I didn't understand the purpose of many of your questions.'

'Such as?'

'The significance of why Sir Alfred's bedroom overlooked the workshop.'

'I couldn't help but wonder why the man chose what would be a chilly bedroom on the north side of the house, with the least attractive view of the grounds. What it suggests to me is that he wanted to keep an eye on the workshop at night.'

'Why?'

'You're not asking an old policeman to make wild guesses, are you, Thomas?'

'And why were you so interested in the Denby family history? Surely all this about the brothers being given country estates to manage has no connection with Sir Alfred being killed?'

'Looking in depth at a family's history and present circumstances can be vital. It allowed me to see the family's emotional bedrock, as it were. By emotional bedrock, I mean is the prevailing mood of the family happy? Are they content? Optimistic or pessimistic? Secure or fearful?'

'I'd say that Victor Denby is an extremely disgruntled man, as well as being frightened.'

They headed along a path lined with hawthorn. A deer paused to look at them before bounding away through the bushes.

Abberline watched the deer vanish into the distance. When he spoke again it was in a thoughtful tone. 'Let's try and form a clear picture of the Denby family. The grandfather was a village blacksmith – a hardworking, prudent man by all accounts. He owned a small factory that produced buckles and stirrups, and so on. Then along came his son. The son was ambitious and used the family's wealth to set up a foundry that produced railway track. The blacksmith's son became rich and acquired power and status, too. The man was called Iron Road Denby by the Press and he was suddenly part of the industrial elite. Several years later, there's a slump in demand for railway track. Therefore, he diverted his capital elsewhere and invested in big country estates, no doubt intending to become even richer.'

'But it didn't work out that way?'

Abberline nodded. 'He died before he could complete his strategy, which was to buy the country estates outright. His sons have been left managing land that will soon be taken back by their landlords when the leases expire.'

'I noticed that you were particularly interested in the hammer and nails on a windowsill in the workshop.'

'You noticed them, too? They sent out quite a message, didn't they?'

'The nails were rusty and the hammer was covered in spider's web. It suggests that Victor Denby isn't especially interested in repairing the workshop.'

'And the other matter?'

'What other matter?'

'He couldn't afford to use a builder. His gardener had been replacing panes that had been shattered by the explosion. Now that spring's here the gardener is too busy to continue the repairs.'

'Good heavens, how do you know that?'

'The nails were in a packet that originally contained flower seeds, night scented stock to be precise – that was the description printed on the packet. It must have been the first suitable thing that came to hand when the gardener was told to begin repairing the workshop. Quite simply, the man needed something to carry the nails in.'

'Therefore, Denby isn't as wealthy as he seems.'

'Which brings us back to the importance of gauging the emotional bedrock of a family. The Denby clan were once rich. They are now on their way to becoming poor. This means the sons of the incredibly successful Iron Road Denby won't be happy men. I haven't met the other surviving brothers yet, but I'm inclined to believe that they brood over the family's dwindling fortune and are extremely pessimistic about their future.'

'They might even believe that their decline is attributable to the curse of the Gods of Rome.'

'Quite possibly so. Even modern men can be superstitious about such things.'

'And men can feel a great degree of guilt if their achievements are substantially inferior to those of their fathers.'

'Well put, Thomas. I dare say that Victor Denby and his brothers have dreamt that their father's ghost berates them for permitting the family fortune to dribble away to the point where the gardener ends up having to take on the duties of coachman, builder and goodness knows what else.'

Thomas glanced back at Fairfax Manor. Despite its size, the building's grandeur appeared faded. One of its chimney pots was missing. Rampant ivy covered some of its windows. More evidence of creeping neglect? Undoubtedly so.

Thomas couldn't help but speculate. 'Then the sons of Iron Road Denby might take desperate measures to restore their wealth?'

'And such desperate measures could have crossed over into illegality. What's more, the brothers might have made enemies.'

'You think that one of those enemies planted a bomb that killed Sir Alfred?'

'We shall see, Thomas, we shall see.'

The path reached a slope that led down into an overgrown quarry that was clearly no longer used to obtain stone.

'Hmm ...' Abberline's eyes twinkled. 'This is the interesting part. We get to sift debris from the workshop: we'll be getting our hands dirty – gloriously dirty.'

Inspector Abberline worked methodically. A large door lying at the bottom of the quarry served as a 'finds' table. For a while, he sifted through detritus that domestic staff must have tossed into this huge hole in the ground, along with all the other refuse from Fairfax Manor. Workshop debris was, thankfully, easy to differentiate from food jars, tins and bottles.

Abberline picked a workman's boot from the smelly heap, carefully scrutinized it before setting it down on a pile of empty food tins. 'The gunpowder that Sir Alfred stored in the workshop was, according the police report, kept in a large wall cupboard made from a dark coloured wood.'

'Which means anyone could have looked through a window and discovered that he stored explosive there.'

'That's not possible.'

'But there were plenty of windows in the workshop.'

'What do you notice about the broken glass around your feet?'

'Ah. It's been whitewashed.'

'All the glass fragments are covered with paint, so that suggests all the windows in the workshop were whitewashed.'

'Meaning that nobody could see in. Sir Alfred could do whatever he wanted there in secrecy.'

'Which is altogether mysterious in its own right. Why should collecting a small quantity of gunpowder require such a cloak of secrecy? Why didn't Sir Alfred want people to see what he did in his workshop?'

'A workshop that he could keep watch over at night.'

'Yes. Yes. Yes.' Abberline's eyes blazed. 'You are starting to think like a policeman. Clues are stepping stones to the truth.'

'Are you sure all this broken glass came from the workshop?'

'Pick up a piece; examine it. You'll see black speckles – the black speckles are gunpowder residue.'

'What are we looking for? The remains of a bomb?'

'We're searching for something that suggests Sir Alfred didn't die, because he carelessly placed a candle near a keg of gunpowder. What that "something" might be ...' He shrugged. 'I hope, I'll know it when I see it.'

Abberline stood items of potential interest on the door that he'd laid flat on the ground. These items consisted of such things as a mangled lantern, fragments of a mechanical instrument, and curving pieces of wood that were badly charred. When he lifted a piece of sack to reveal a shoe he gave it close inspection.

'Ah, a high quality piece of footwear; no doubt it belonged to the deceased.' His sharp eyes fixed on the shoe. 'The leather on the upper part has been burnt.'

'Sir Alfred was wearing the shoe when the bomb exploded?'

'The shoe may have come off when the gunpowder detonated – often people are rendered completely naked if they are caught up in an explosion. Or the shoe may have slipped off when the body was dragged from the wreckage.'

'A burnt shoe belonging to a dead man wouldn't be of value to anyone; hence it being dumped here.'

'On the contrary, Thomas, it is immensely valuable to us.' Abberline fixed his attention on the toe of the shoe. 'Look at that.' Using his finger and thumb, he pinched a gleaming fragment from the shoe.

'What is it?' Thomas felt tingles run down his spine. He realized that this search excited him. He felt that, bit by bit, they were getting closer to solving a mystery. And, perhaps, they were nearer to identifying a shadowy figure who'd claimed the life of Sir Alfred Denby. Thomas examined the tiny piece of metal that Abberline handed to him. It appeared to be made from brass. Whatever it was had been twisted out of shape by a huge force. 'And this was embedded in the shoe?' Thomas asked. 'By the force of the blast?'

'Indeed so. See the hole it made in the thick leather at the toe?'

'It's from some mechanism. Part of the bomb?'

Abberline shook his head. 'A part of a lock, I should say.' He walked a few feet to where the smashed remains of a cupboard lay in a bed of nettles. Its door was missing. The hinges had been torn clean out of the woodwork. The oak carcass had been gouged, split, blackened. 'This must be the cupboard where Sir Alfred stored his gunpowder; the powder itself was contained in a small barrel. If he'd opened the cupboard door, and accidentally ignited the gunpowder the blast would have erupted into his face.'

'Killing him instantly.'

'However, the cupboard door must have been shut, or partly shut when the gunpowder detonated. The fragment of lock mechanism in the shoe points to the fact that the explosion occurred as he stood facing this cupboard. Possibly he was in the process of opening the door at the time.'

'You're saying if the door was fully open then the lock mechanism wouldn't have been hurled down into his shoe?'

Abberline gave a single nod.'

Thomas wasn't so sure. 'But he could have opened the doors and inadvertently held the candle too close to the gunpowder.'

'Granted, he might have. However, it seems that Sir Alfred couldn't open the door fully.' He picked up pieces of the cupboard door that had been shattered by the explosion. He carefully arranged the fragments on the ground, so that the pieces were at least roughly in the shape of the door. 'See the small hook that's been screwed into the inside of the door? There's a piece of twine tied to it.'

Thomas frowned. 'So an intruder knows about Sir Alfred collecting gunpowder for the cannon. And they have gone to elaborate lengths to devise a means of detonating the gunpowder when Sir Alfred opened the cupboard. But what mechanism caused the stuff to explode in the man's face?'

Abberline pulled an object out of the grass. 'Possibly this.'

'A pistol?'

'Or what remains of one. And lo-and-behold.' Abberline held up the broken firearm for Thomas to see. 'See what's tied around the trigger?'

'A piece of twine.'

'Twine that exactly matches the other twine tied around the hook that held the cupboard door shut.'

Thomas gazed at the blackened string neatly tied around the trigger. He never got chance to utter what he planned to say next, because a voice thundered down into the quarry, 'You two! If you move so much as an inch, I'll shoot you dead.'

They looked up to see the silhouette of a man holding a rifle. The glare of the sun meant that Thomas couldn't see his face. Thomas lifted his hand to shield his eyes. That's when the stranger took aim and fired.

CHAPTER 8

THE BULLET STRUCK the ground close to Thomas, sending a shower of dirt into the air.

The gunman shouted, 'I blithering well told you not to move! Next time you do that I'll put a round through your skull!'

Abberline adopted a glacial calm. 'Then may we talk?'

'I'm going to bring the police here; you can talk to them!'

'I am a police officer. Mr Denby invited me here.'

Even though the sun's glare made it difficult to see, Thomas saw that the man lowered the rifle. 'My master said that a detective would be coming down from London.'

'This is Inspector Abberline of Scotland Yard.' Thomas felt anger now rather than fear. 'Be sure to point that damn gun *away* from us. Do you hear?'

'It's all right, Thomas.' Abberline's voice was soothing. 'The man was merely doing his duty.'

'His duty? He nearly put a bullet in me.'

'If he'd intended to do that, I'm sure he'd have had no trouble in hitting you between the eyes.'

Thomas intended to reply sharply to that statement, but his mouth had turned dry as dust. He saw how close the bullet had come.

The man with the rifle marched briskly down the slope. 'I'm sorry, sir.' He seemed genuinely regretful. 'I was told to expect visitors calling on my master, only I didn't expect to find them in the quarry.'

'And you are?'

'Brown, sir. The gamekeeper.'

'An ex-army man?'

'Yes, sir. Twenty years in the Devonshire Regiment.'

'Ah, the Bloody Eleven, first-rate men with a heroic tradition,' Abberline said. 'Very well, you know my name. This is Mr Thomas Lloyd. He's assisting me.'

'My master has been most particular in telling me to watch out for trespassers. After his brother was killed he's taken to worrying that he might be next.'

Thomas appraised the gamekeeper. He was a tall, powerfully built man, clean shaven and still possessed the erect bearing of a soldier. He would be an especially formidable bodyguard. Especially so with that rifle.

Abberline spoke conversationally. 'Mr Brown, have you worked for Mr Denby long?'

'Eighteen months. I was on his estate in Devon.'

'Then the lease expired on the property and you eventually found yourself here?'

'That's true, sir.'

'Did Mr Denby seem apprehensive or particularly anxious before the death of his brother?'

'Not that I noticed, sir.'

'Have you heard talk about Sir Alfred's death?'

'About him being blown up? Local folk have ridiculous tales about a curse and Roman gods and some such tomfoolery.'

'You don't believe in curses?'

'No, sir, I do not,' Brown said firmly. 'Would you like me to help you search the quarry?'

'Thank you, but no, Mr Brown. We've found what we were looking for.'

'Very good, sir.' Brown, the dyed-in-the-wool military man, even saluted albeit in a relaxed manner. 'Then I'll continue my rounds, if I may?'

'By all means, Mr Brown. I'm grateful for the information you've given me.'

Brown strode away through the long grass and out of the quarry. Thomas followed Abberline up the slope to the path that led back to Fairfax Manor. White cloud bubbled up over the horizon. Abberline said a few words about April showers being on their way as a cold breeze gusted through the trees. Thomas saw that the policeman carried the remains of the pistol; scorched twine fluttered from the trigger.

Thomas asked, 'Will you tell Mr Denby about what you've found in the quarry?'

'Indeed I will. Sir Alfred was very probably a victim of murder, and there is a real danger that Victor Denby might be the next to die.'

*

The butler – he of the grey hair and grey face – showed Inspector Abberline and Thomas Lloyd into the morning room. Its curtains were drawn shut against the sunlit world outside. Thomas noted a clutter of high-backed chairs, which would have been fashionable in the earlier part of Queen Victoria's reign. Victor Denby rose from a sofa where he'd been reading a newspaper. He wore a dark suit, complete with a stiff, high-necked collar. The man appeared ill-at-ease. Thomas suspected it wasn't just the uncomfortable furniture and clothes that rendered him so.

'Sherry?' offered Denby.

'No, thank you.' Abberline handed Denby the pistol – or, rather, its mangled remains. 'You should see this.'

'An old revolver? What of it?'

'That, to all intents and purposes, is the weapon that killed your brother.'

Denby suddenly became queasy. He quickly handed the gun back to Abberline before pulling a white handkerchief from his breast pocket. He used this to wipe his fingers so thoroughly that an observer might believe that the gun had been covered with blood. Thomas had seen that wasn't the case, of course. It had merely become grimy from lying in the quarry for the last eight weeks or so.

'Uh …' Denby grunted. 'Sit down. Tell me what you now know.'

'You appear very pale, Mr Denby,' Thomas said. 'Would you like me to pour you a sherry?'

'Brandy.' Denby waved his hand at decanters arranged on a side-board. 'A large brandy.'

Abberline sat on a straight-backed chair facing Denby, who remained hunched and pale-faced on the sofa.

Abberline spoke gently. 'Take a moment to compose yourself.'

'I am composed – at least I will be once I've this.' Taking the glass from Thomas, he downed the spirit in one huge gulp. 'You're saying my brother was shot?'

'No. He died in the explosion.' Abberline stood up. 'If we go back to the workshop, I can describe what happened.'

'I'd rather not.' Denby's expression turned to one of fear. The man was clearly afraid to step outside. 'Tell me in here. You can do that?'

'As you wish.' Abberline nodded. 'The killer devised a method to strike the death blow in such a way it would appear to be an accident. What's more, he, or she, made certain that they were nowhere near Sir Alfred when he died. That way the killer wouldn't be linked to the murder.'

'But a pistol? How?'

Inspector Abberline spoke softly. 'I ask you to picture the following sequence of events. The assassin secretly watches your brother. They discover your late brother's habits; that he punctually entered the workshop at six-thirty in order to collect gunpowder for the cannon, which he fires at seven o'clock prompt every morning. At the dead of night, the assassin forces the lock on the workshop door. He ... let us call refer to the killer as "he" for the purposes of this explanation ... he has with him a pistol loaded with a blank round.' Abberline held up the pistol. The twine swung down from the trigger. 'He also has a length of string and a small screw hook. He picks the lock of the door to the powder cupboard. He screws the hook onto the inside of the door. Then he fixes the pistol to the shelf, perhaps with more twine, which is now missing. The gun's muzzle points at the keg of gunpowder. It's likely that the killer also opened the keg and allowed powder to spill out onto the shelf. He then connected the trigger, using a length of twine, to the hook embedded on the inside of the door; this done in such a way that when the door was opened the line pulled the trigger, firing the pistol directly into the gunpowder. The keg contained perhaps five pounds of explosive material – sufficient to cause extensive damage to the workshop ... as well as killing your brother.'

'I knew it was murder,' breathed Denby with an expression of dread. '*I knew.*'

'Do you know anyone who might wish to harm your brother?'

Denby shook his head. 'But my brothers have been dying violent, and unexplained deaths for years.'

'Sir Alfred was the fourth of your brothers whose death has been the subject of an inquest. And an inquest is only held when the coroner must decide whether that death is a result of accident, suicide, manslaughter or murder.'

Denby shuddered. 'The deaths of my brothers were all judged to be accidental. I say otherwise. Some monster ... *an evil, despicable monster* ... has set out to kill every single one of us.' He lurched to his feet. 'I know I shall be next. I've been marked for death! But if the killer steps through that door, he'll rue the day. He won't find me such an easy victim.' Denby reached into his jacket and pulled out a revolver. Unlike the one in Abberline's hand, this one gleamed brightly. He aimed the weapon at the door, as if hoping the murderer would rush into the room. 'I'll kill him!'

Thomas saw the man's finger curl round the trigger. Denby's hand was shaking; his eyes blazed with nothing less than mania. Thomas didn't hesitate. He reached forward, pushed the man's hand down, until the gun pointed at the floor, then he twisted the weapon from his fingers.

'Give it back, damn you!' bellowed Denby. 'How dare you behave so impudently in my home?'

'I'll not give it back, sir. At least not yet.'

'That pistol is mine. I need it to protect my life.'

'I've nearly been shot once today, sir. I don't intend there to be a second time.'

Denby slumped back onto the settee. The man shook so much he could hardly breathe.

'Another brandy please, Thomas.' Abberline held out his hand and Thomas passed him the revolver. Abberline checked that the hammer wasn't cocked before slipping it into his coat pocket. 'We'll sit with Mr Denby for a few moments, while he recovers his composure. After that, I'll explain what we must do next.'

*

Thomas walked around the morning room. He noticed scribbled calculations on at least a dozen sheets of paper that were scattered across a desk. Victor Denby had been totting up household expenses. Even a cursory glance revealed that income exceeded expenditure. A rather desperate looking line beneath one calculation read starkly: *Cut staff by one third.* It had been fifteen minutes since Thomas had taken the pistol from Denby's hand. The man, meanwhile, had downed another brandy, and was much calmer. Abberline took the opportunity to make notes in a small leather-bound book that he'd taken from his pocket.

When Thomas eased back a curtain to look outside he heard Denby groan with alarm. Abberline shook his head as he caught Thomas's eye. Thomas closed the curtain and sat down on a chair.

At last, Victor Denby took a deep breath before shaking himself out of his torpor. 'My apologies, gentlemen. The shock of you confirming that my brother was deliberately murdered struck against my nerves harder than I could have imagined.'

'That's perfectly understandable. A shock like that could unnerve any man.' Abberline returned the notebook to his pocket. 'Do you feel able to continue our conversation?'

'Yes, quite able, Inspector.'

'I ask for your complete co-operation.'

'You have it, sir.' Denby's manner had become almost humble.

'When you capture my brother's murderer you will have saved my life. I see it in such simple terms. Because the devil who took Alfred's life no doubt intends to kill me and my surviving brothers.'

'How many brothers are still alive?'

'Apart from myself, there are three. The oldest brother I have already told you about: he's a missionary in Africa. Then there is Thaddeus: he's sixty-one and has an estate in Scotland. My youngest brother is forty-five. He runs a place in North Wales.'

'What's his name?'

'William Denby.'

'The balloon man?' asked Thomas. 'He once flew across the English Channel, didn't he?'

'These days he's involved with military research. Using balloons to direct artillery fire and for signalling. All hush-hush, though.'

Abberline said, 'I'll visit both men in person, inform them what I've discovered here, and, perhaps more importantly, warn them to keep their guard up.'

'You do believe I and my brothers are in danger?'

'Yes, sir, grave danger.'

'How did we come to find ourselves living this nightmare, Inspector?'

'That's what I shall find out.'

Somewhat unsteadily – a combination of brandy and utter shock – Denby rose to his feet and crossed the room, where he pulled a velvet cord. 'I've rung for the butler. I'll have him send telegrams to my brothers, warning them that they are in danger.'

'I agree, they should be told at the earliest opportunity, even if such a telegram might come as a shock. Oh, and if you would tell your butler that we'll be staying as guests.'

'Really?' Denby reacted with surprise.

'This is where the real work begins. Travelling to and from London would be timeconsuming, and time is now absolutely of the essence. I urgently need to interview all the domestic staff who were here when Sir Alfred was killed.'

'You'll be able to speak to some of them.' Denby sounded like his old blunt self again. 'But not all.'

'Why is that, Mr Denby?'

'It's family policy to transfer a quantity of staff to the other houses every few months. We find it avoids staff becoming overly comfortable and overly complacent. Also, as servants get to know each other too well they begin to form—'

'Romantic liaisons?' asked Thomas.

'No. They form alliances. They begin to pilfer food, drink and ornaments, because they are confident that their fellow servants won't betray them.'

'Interesting,' said Thomas, 'if unorthodox.'

'Nevertheless, it works. Not a great deal is stolen from our houses. Three weeks ago one quarter of the staff from the Scottish house were transported down here. And one quarter of my staff were despatched northwards to Scotland. Keeps 'em on their toes.'

'In that case,' Abberline said, 'I'll interview staff who were present at the time of the explosion, and I'll interview the others when I reach your brothers' properties in Wales and Scotland.'

At that moment, the door opened. The grey butler glided in.

'Sir?' the butler asked with impeccable politeness.

'I'm going to write a number of telegrams. They must be sent today.'

'Of course, sir.'

Victor Denby at least pretended he'd regained his composure. 'Make up two rooms. These gentlemen will be staying overnight as my guests.'

The butler looked down his nose at Abberline and Thomas. 'Should I have rooms in the servants' quarters prepared?'

'Servants quarters?' Denby considered the possibility of ordering just that for a moment, then: 'No. They are important guests. Have rooms made up on the same floor as mine. Tell the cook that there will be two extra for dinner. I'll ring again when the telegrams are ready.'

'Very good, sir. Thank you, sir.' The butler withdrew, bowing as he did so.

Denby's shoulders drooped. Now that the butler had gone he no longer kept up the pretence of being the brusque, authoritarian figure he once was.

His eyes had a beseeching quality when he looked at Abberline. 'You will find that devil of a murderer, won't you, Inspector?'

'I'll do everything in my power to bring him to justice.'

'I pray that you succeed, sir. With all my heart I do.'

CHAPTER 9

THE MAID THOUGHT: this is a world of wonder. I am seeing marvellous things. She glided through the forest. Sunlight pierced the branches. Brightly coloured birds swooped back and forth across the path in front of her. Grass shone a brilliant green. Laura caught the sweet scents of blossom on the trees. Birds sang – a symphony of shimmering notes that resembled the sinuous melody of a flute.

The eighteen-year-old maid followed the figure. The tall, pale shape moved deeper into the forest. Here, gigantic oaks spread their limbs over her, burying her in deep shadow. The young maid felt happy in this hauntingly beautiful place. She wanted to catch up with the figure that possessed a face and hands that glowed as white as pearls. If only she could talk to the stranger. Somehow she knew he had an important message for her. Once she heard the phantom's words she'd be happy and content for the rest of her life.

Laura moved faster, plunging into that realm of shadow beneath the trees. Undergrowth tugged the hem of her nightdress as if the natural world tried to prevent her from pursuing the who was white as death, and who seemed to be enticing her further away from the house – leading her from safety to a place where lives are changed forever.

He's leading me on a dance of death, she thought. But she couldn't turn back – not if she tried with every atom of strength and will-power that her body had to offer. He's leading me on a dance of death, and when he's ready he will stop and turn to face me. *Then I'll know who he really is.* A spring bubbled up through rocks. Falling water made the sound of silver bells – a soft, hypnotic tinkling. Narrows shafts of such dazzling radiance pierced the branches to form pools of sunlight that seemed to burn on the earth like fire. She ran past the skull of a sheep. The path grew narrower. Bushes closed in. Soon she felt branches touching her arms and face.

Laura followed the figure into a deeper darkness. The world grew silent. The birds stopped singing and a deathly hush settled on the place. The white figure stopped dead. Now it was turning ...

... turning toward her ... in order to reveal its stark, white face. She held her breath, ready to fix her eyes on that face and recognize the identity of this spirit.

'Laura!' A man roughly caught her by the arm. 'Laura, we've been looking for you everywhere!'

The man who gripped her wore the livery of a footman. He was red-faced and very, very angry. 'Miss Groom's going to flay your hide for this.' He looked back over his shoulder as he yelled, 'I've found her. Over here!'

Suddenly, more domestic staff appeared: the gardener, another footman, the coachman, and Daniel, the boy who cleaned the boots.

Daniel stared at her in amazement. 'By heck! Laura's not in her clothes! Look, she's wearing her nightdress!'

The gardener tugged off his coat and put it over Laura's shoulders.

The coachman asked, 'Why did you come out here into the forest?'

'I followed *him*.' She pointed at where the white figure had stood, but the path ahead was deserted; the phantom had gone.

Laura sat on the bed while the housekeeper, Miss Groom, told her for the tenth – or was it the twentieth time? – that Laura was a foolish girl. Laura wore a clean nightdress; the other one she'd worn outdoors had become muddy. She must have fallen in the forest, but she neither remembered falling down, nor leaving the house.

Meanwhile, Miss Groom tried to get at the truth. 'What made you go into the wood, and in your nightdress of all things?'

'I don't know.'

'Surely, you must know. You've got a head on your shoulders, haven't you?'

'I lay down in this bed. The next thing I knew I was following a man.'

'What man?' Miss Groom's eyes narrowed behind those strange-looking glasses she wore. 'Did he touch you?'

'No ... and I don't know who it was. He was all strange to look at, even beautiful – so white and shining. Like a spirit, or ... or an angel.'

Miss Groom sighed – an expression of despair as much as frustration. 'I'm so worried for you, child. This morning you fainted in the wood, and you uttered such nonsense about being chased by a ghost.'

'That's what happened, Miss Groom.'

'Tut, child, and worse, much worse, you claimed you had some kind of clairvoyant vision that the gentleman who carried you into the house would fall from the sky and be killed.'

'I did see that happen. I'm not lying.'

'And look at you: face and arms all scratched. I don't know what to do with you, I really don't.'

Laura paced the room, talking quickly as she did so. 'I can see into the future, can't I? That's what's happening. I've been given a gift. I know who will die, and I know how they will be killed. For some reason, God has given me the power of prophecy.'

Miss Groom's palm cracked across Laura's face. 'Do not say such terrible things! You are telling lies about seeing a ghost because you want everyone to think that you are special. But you're not. You are a ridiculous child.'

'I'm not a child. I'm eighteen.'

The housekeeper stormed to the bedroom door. 'You will stay here in the servants' quarters until I say otherwise. But I've half a mind to send you home.'

'Please don't do that, Miss Groom. My parents are old and in poor health. They can hardly support themselves, let alone feed me.'

'Then don't bring shame on them by pretending you see things that aren't there.'

'But I do see them. And I really don't remember leaving this room. It's like I'm walking when I'm asleep.'

Miss Groom glared at her. 'Stay in bed, girl. Do not frighten the girls who share this room with you by telling them any more of your dreadful stories. Do you hear?'

Laura's parents relied on the money, which she sent home to them, and although she knew she was being unfairly treated by the house-keeper, she couldn't risk losing her job, so she nodded. 'Yes, Miss Groom. Please tell the staff how sorry I am for causing them so much trouble and worry.'

'That's more like it. Now stay here and study your own words and actions today … then mend your ways.' She took a key from her pocket. 'I'm not taking the chance of you wandering off again in your nightdress. For all that you were wearing you might as well have been outdoors naked.'

The door slammed shut, leaving Laura alone in the room. The key turned loudly in the lock. Laura wiped a tear from her eye. This morning started so perfectly. She'd been kissed by Jake. They'd made plans for the dance on Saturday night. Now a strange magic had entered her life. She'd encountered the shining figure in the forest.

After that, she'd experienced such a frightening vision when the red-haired man had crashed to the ground in front of her. Now Miss Groom had locked her into the bedroom. Laura was a prisoner. And she was terrified that this was only the beginning of the nightmare.

Laura's prophecy that this was only the start of the nightmare was proved to be correct later that day when she heard voices from outside. The window looked out onto the yard behind Newydd Hall. Already, the evening sunlight fell onto the Welsh mountains and shadows were gathering in the fields.

Laura's heart lurched, for there was her sweetheart, Jake Tregarth. He must have heard about Laura and had come to the house – that much was clear. Now he stood there in the yard. A footman and Miss Groom argued with him. All three were gesturing and voices were raised. Immediately, Laura guessed that Jake wanted to see her, only they were refusing him entry into the house. Of course, such a thing wouldn't be permitted normally – the sweethearts of domestic staff weren't even allowed onto the premises, but Jake must have been so alarmed, when he heard that something strange had happened to Laura, that he'd raced here after finishing work in the fields.

Laura opened the window. 'Jake! I'm here!'

Jake's face lit up when he saw her. 'Laura,' he called out. 'I heard that you were ill … I wanted to see you with my own eyes, but they won't let me into the house.'

'Jake, they've locked me in here. I can't get out!'

He tried to approach the house. The housekeeper and footman held up their hands. Both shouted at him, telling him to go back to the village. Jake, however, had worked the land since childhood. He was much stronger than the footman and he easily shoved the man aside. Miss Groom immediately called for help. The plea was quickly answered by the arrival of three burly, muscular men; they acted with brutal swiftness. Two of the men caught Jake by the arms. The third punched Jake in the stomach; the second punch landed on his jaw. The men holding Jake shoved him roughly and he fell to the ground.

Laura couldn't hear what the men said. However, they pointed at the path that led back to the village: she knew they were telling Jake to leave and not come back.

Jake picked himself up, dusted off his sleeves, and raised his hand to his mouth. Even from here, in the bedroom, Laura saw blood on his fingers. Miss Groom and the men made 'clear off gestures''as if shooing away a troublesome dog.

At last, Jake grudgingly walked away. Before entering the forest, he turned, cupped his hands to his mouth, and shouted: *"Laura, I love you, girl! I'll come back soon! I'll save you!'*

CHAPTER 10

THE CLOCK IN the hallway downstairs delivered its ponderous chimes. Thomas sat at a table in the bedroom that Victor Denby had provided for him. On the twelfth chime, signifying midnight, Thomas laid down his pen. He'd been writing an account of the day's events: meeting Inspector Abberline at the London train station, witnessing the arrest of the pickpocket, followed by the journey here to Fairfax Manor where Abberline had begun investigating the death of Sir Alfred Denby with meticulous care. Thomas had written a detailed account and, as this was a popular newspaper that not only informed its readers, but made a point of entertaining them, too, he had described his own emotions – especially those of astonishment when Abberline had pieced together debris in the quarry that enabled him to accurately formulate his conclusion that Sir Alfred had, indeed, been murdered.

Thomas even drew his own artistic impression of the instrument of Sir Alfred's destruction. That is to say, the way the pistol had been tied to a shelf inside the cupboard where the explosive had been stored. A length of string had been bound to a hook on the inside of the door, and the other end of the string had been tied to the pistol's trigger. When Sir Alfred opened the door, the twine pulled the trigger and … Thomas wrote in large letters beneath his drawing: **BOOM!** Though the editor wouldn't use such an explosive word in the article, it would suggest to the newspaper's artist, who was a far more skilled illustrator than Thomas, that the drawing should be as dramatic and as exciting as possible.

Even though the article would be both dramatic and exciting, Thomas took a great deal of care to portray Inspector Abberline as being the expert detective that he undoubtedly was. What's more, the man exercised a great degree of sensitivity and compassion when dealing with a case as tragic as this. After all, a human being had been murdered. The man's family already grieved that death. Knowing that Sir Alfred had been unlawfully slain would be a terrible shock for the Denby family. Abberline wouldn't increase their distress if he could help it.

Thomas re-read his article. Yes, he was pleased with what he'd done. However, he felt a degree of impatience. Abberline had made both Thomas and his editor promise not to publish until the case had been concluded. Thomas folded the sheets of paper and eased them into an envelope. He always felt a warm glow of satisfaction when he finished a piece of writing that he judged to be good. Of course, the editor would set to work with his red ink! No doubt adding lurid phrases here and there: *Murder most foul! Heinous crimes! Blood carnage!* And other vivid terms would soon pepper the carefully rendered account of the day. Never mind, he told himself. This is the most interesting work I've done in a long while. Who knows? I might be able turn this story into a whole book.

The notion that he might become Abberline's biographer was a pleasing one. The butler – he of the grey visage and grey demeanour – had delivered a whisky and soda to Thomas's room an hour ago. Thomas had postponed the moment of drinking the spirit. This would be his well-earned treat for having finished his article. Thomas turned down the lamp so its brightness yielded to a softer glow. Glass in hand, he took a moment to savour his surroundings as well as the whisky. He'd never before stayed in a house, or a bedroom, as grand as this. His parents were schoolteachers. They occupied the house attached to the school. He'd shared his bedroom with two older brothers, and consequently, because of his junior status, he'd been given a rickety bed, with a mattress that sagged so much in the middle he often dreamt he was being swallowed alive by a gigantic snake.

This bed was huge. Four ornately carved posts supported a canopy from which hung lavish tapestries. He'd found to his discomfort that the drapes were heavy with dust. Just to touch one had released a cloud of particles that sent him into fits of sneezing. On that gargantuan mattress, the butler had laid out a clean nightshirt. Abberline had told Thomas that country houses like this one were accustomed to unexpected guests, so there were always plenty of spare clothes and the necessary accoutrements for upper-class visitors who might arrive not fully equipped for the night. There were was even a silver-backed hair brush and comb set for his use on the dressing table.

'So this is how aristocrats live their lives,' he said aloud, and immediately wondered if Abberline heard him talking to himself from his room across the corridor. He, therefore, sealed his lips lest the detective suspect his new companion of lunacy.

Thomas sniffed his glass. The whisky was much stronger than he was used to. Already his head had that light, swimming sensation engendered by alcohol. Then it had been a long day, too. Evening dinner had been a leisurely, drawn out affair, with the butler serving several courses of rich, buttery food. Glasses of port had followed dinner. After that, there'd been brandy in a room occupied by a billiards table.

Thomas listened for a moment, realizing that something was missing. He nodded. *The sounds of London are missing.* Night and day, he'd hear the rumble of carts on the roads; horses smartly clip-clopping along; the shout of newspaper vendors; men and women talking by the thousand; drunks singing, shouting or fighting; sometimes the urgent sounding of a police constable's whistle. The music of the city was always there. Here, deep in the English countryside, however, there was silence. Only silence. That absence of sound was unsettling. Almost akin to putting a hand on one's chest and suddenly realizing the once reliably beating heart had stopped. The silence, which must be equal to that found in a tomb, unnerved him. He downed the rest of the whisky. And wished he hadn't. His stomach caught fire – or so it felt to him. He poured water into the tumbler from a jug on the nightstand. As he did so, he looked out through the gap he'd left in the curtains. He wanted the light to wake him early, so it wouldn't appear as if he indulged in the lazy habit of sleeping late.

What he witnessed made him freeze. He held his breath as he saw what was taking place down there at the dead of night. A light moved slowly through the workshop where Sir Alfred had died. Thomas watched a glow appear at each window. Someone was down there. They were carrying a lantern as they walked through the workshop. Thomas didn't think twice. He hurried downstairs as quietly as he could, left by the back door, and padded across the yard to the workshop.

The cold night air cleared his head instantly. He now realized that this course of action, to rush down to the workshop, wasn't only impetuous, it was foolhardy. Possibly even dangerous. What if the intruder was Sir Alfred's killer? Might they be armed? Ten seconds from now he might be lying on the ground with a knife blade jammed between his ribs. He should have woken Abberline.

But it was too late now. He could not retreat; he could not behave like a coward.

Thomas Lloyd, a reporter for the *Pictorial Evening News*, took a deep breath, marched into the workshop and shouted as loudly as he could: *'I am a Scotland Yard detective – and you are under arrest!'*

Thomas Lloyd stood panting in the workshop. A figure approached him. The lantern it carried dazzled Thomas so much he couldn't see whether there was just one intruder or several.

The figure lowered the light, allowing Thomas to make out a face.

'That was quite an entrance, Thomas.' Abberline smiled. 'You do realize, however, that it is a crime to impersonate a police officer?'

'I thought you ... uh ... I beg your pardon.' Thomas blushed, feeling stupid.

Abberline slapped the man on the back. 'No pardon need be begged, my friend. That was most heroic of you. I like to see a man do the right thing, even if it did mean taking at least one liberty with the law.'

Thomas took a steadying breath. His heart still pounded like fury. Abberline, meanwhile, turned to study the wall at the far end of the workshop. The man was fully dressed and wearing his coat and hat. Evidently, he hadn't dashed down here on the spur of the moment – as Thomas had just done.

'One detail has been bothering me,' Abberline murmured. 'A humble workshop wouldn't normally be graced with such fine woodwork as this. See? Oak panels entirely cover this end wall from top to bottom.'

'The house was built for a rich man. Might not that wealth be reflected in work-a-day buildings such as this?'

'These oak panels might have once been installed in a drawing room, or a gentleman's study. Very fine craftsmanship.'

'And yet only the end wall is faced with wood. The others are bare brick.'

'Makes one wonder what reason Sir Alfred had for panelling just a single wall so richly, doesn't it?' Abberline set the lantern down. He leaned forwards scrutinizing the woodwork from just a few inches or so.

'What do you see, Inspector?'

''Hmm ... the explosion caused scorch marks; there are pieces of metal embedded in the oak. Although the wood is so hard and so thick, it weathered the blast surprisingly well. But have you noticed that?' Abberline tapped the bottom panel with the toe of his shoe.

Thomas crouched down. 'The blast has pushed the panels

backwards by an inch or so.'

'No ... look again. What do you see?'

Thomas examined where the bottom of the panels met the stone floor. 'Ah, I see ... to be precise, one section which is about six feet wide has been knocked back closer to the wall. Yet the other panels are still in place. Oh!' A shiver of excitement ran down Thomas's spine. 'You think there might be something hidden behind the panels?'

'Shall we take a look for ourselves?'

Thomas pushed the section of panel-work that had been displaced. It refused to budge. 'This thing is solid as iron.'

'There's claw hammer on the windowsill – try that.'

Thomas grabbed the hammer. The only gap where he could insert the claw-part, used to extract nails, was between the floor and the woodwork. He inserted the claw and used the hammer as a lever, aiming to pull the panel forwards. The thing seemed set in stone and still wouldn't move. Presently, his breath shot out white gusts in the cold night air. 'It's no good.'

'If both of us pull together.' Abberline crouched down and gripped the hammer's wooden shaft. Now both men had a firm grip. 'On the count of three. One, two, three, *Pull*.'

A loud scrunching noise, followed by a creak.

'Watch out!' Thomas looked up as a section of oak that was almost eight feet tall toppled forwards.

He leapt to his feet and raised his hands. The falling slab of oak crashed against his palms. It was immensely heavy ... so heavy, in fact, his knees buckled under its weight. Pains shot through his arms to his shoulders.

'Abberline! Get back!'

The detective had been crouching where he'd helped Thomas with the hammer. Now the immense section of oak threatened to crush the man. Abberline scrambled away as Thomas let out a tremendous yell and threw himself back. The panel slammed to the floor. There was an enormous crash that sounded like an explosion in its own right. Dust filled the air.

'Are you all right, Thomas?' The lamplight revealed Abberline's expression of concern. 'You're not hurt?'

'I'm quite unhurt, Inspector. Thank you. The weight of that thing, though – I thought my arms would break.'

'It should be me thanking you, Thomas. That panel would have been the death of me if you hadn't stopped it. You saved my life.'

Both Thomas and Abberline turned to where the section of panel had fallen outwards. The dust had begun to clear and both men stared at what the lamplight revealed.

'I'll be damned,' breathed Thomas in wonder. 'I can see gods.'

Victor Denby took a great deal of persuading to venture out to the workshop in the middle of the night. He only agreed when Abberline suggested that the gamekeeper stand guard outside, armed with the rifle.

'What have you found?' Denby tightened the belt of his dressing gown. The man hated being outdoors. No doubt he expected his brother's killer would be lurking in the shadows. And, equally, Denby expected to be the next victim.

'It's important you see what we've found,' Abberline told him. 'You might be able to explain what it is.'

Denby approached the void that yawned behind the oak panels in the workshop. Every movement was decidedly reluctant. Thomas expected the man to dash back to the safety of the house at any moment. Nevertheless, Denby did as Abberline requested and nervously looked inside.

'Great God in Heaven,' gasped Denby. 'What the dickens have you found, sir?'

'I hoped you could tell us, Mr Denby.'

Denby gulped as if the extraordinary spectacle was too much for him. 'No ... this is monstrous ... absolutely monstrous. Are you suggesting my brother was responsible for this ghastly display?'

'I'm not a man with a classical education. My friend here –' Inspector Abberline nodded at Thoma – is probably better equipped than I to explain.'

Denby wore a dazed expression. What he saw was too much to take in.

'I can't be absolutely sure at this stage,' began Thomas. 'However, concealed behind these panels is a shrine: to be more precise, an altar for the purpose of worshipping pagan gods.'

'My brother was a God-fearing Christian.'

'That may be, Mr Denby,' Abberline said, 'but for some reason he, himself, seems to have believed that he angered the gods of ancient Rome in some way. Perhaps he thought they'd laid a curse on him. This shrine might have been intended to appease them, and encourage them to lift the evil spell.'

'Are you mad, sir?'

'No, I am not.' Abberline moved the lantern in such a way that the light fell on the shelf that had been concealed behind the panel. 'But you, yourself, have heard of the Gods of Rome. Local people believe the curse invoked by those gods resulted in the death of your brother.'

'No ... no .... No ...' Denby's voice became a dry rasp. 'Roman gods. Curses. You don't believe in such things, surely?'

'No, sir, I do not.' Abberline lifted out a statue that was about a foot tall – the carving depicted a man swathed in robes; goat horns protruded from the head. 'But it seems as if your brother did. In fact, he was so frightened of pagan gods, and what they might do, he had this shrine built. '

Thomas said, 'Your brother could gain access to the shrine by opening a section of panelling that had been hinged. Of course, it was all so skilfully constructed that anyone venturing into the workshop wouldn't realize that there was a secret door.'

Abberline nodded. 'And Sir Alfred took the precaution of painting the glass panes white. By doing that nobody could simply look into this building and see him performing his rituals.'

'Rituals? Are you suggesting obscene behaviour?'

Abberline spoke with a swift confidence. 'My friend here tells me that this carving is of Faunus, a deity associated with the great god Pan in Classical mythology. The other figures represent Venus, Mars, Neptune, and the chief god, Jupiter, sometimes known as Jove.' Abberline played the light over the statues, which stood on a shelf that extended back three feet or so to the actual inner-wall. 'There are also bowls. These contain residues of liquid, most likely wine. There are decomposing food-stuffs, such as bread, apples, oranges, and in the largest of the bowls there is a cockerel. See, it's covered with feathers ... the head is missing and there's plenty of dried blood in the bottom of the bowl.'

Thomas added, 'The domestic staff believed your late brother came in here, and locked the door behind him in order to collect gunpowder for the cannon – something he did punctually every morning. We suspect that your brother also opened the secret panel, and prayed to the gods represented by these carved figures.'

'Oh, this too much, gentlemen.' Denby gulped. 'Really too much....'

Abberline picked up a knife from the shelf. 'Your brother's actions aren't for my colleague and me to judge. However, one thing you should know: Sir Alfred sacrificed the cockerel to gods which he believed had the power of life and death over him. See the dried blood on the blade?'

Denby pressed a handkerchief to his mouth. 'Nobody must know about this. Not the newspapers. Not anyone. This blasphemy will bring shame on my family.'

'I intend to keep my investigations absolutely confidential,' Abberline told him. 'For now.'

Denby shook his head, puzzled. 'These statues? Are they the ones known as the Gods of Rome?'

Abberline replaced the knife on the shelf. 'No, these are modern replicas carved from stone, and likely to have little monetary value. The original Gods of Rome are cast from gold.'

Denby wiped sweat from his forehead. 'There was scandal, you know? My brother's name was linked to the theft of Roman statues twenty years ago. Nothing was proved. My brother swore that he had nothing to do with it.'

Thomas asked, 'Would he have told you the truth, if he was in possession of the statues?'

'Of course he would.'

'But he didn't tell you about this shrine,' – Thomas pointed at the stone gods – 'did he, Mr Denby?'

Victor Denby flinched. The insinuation struck a nerve. 'I am tired, and I'm not feeling well. Good night, gentlemen.'

Denby fled back to the house.

'We have stone gods,' Abberline said softly. 'Which begs the question: *w here are* the *golden gods of Rome?*'

CHAPTER 11

THE SUN VANISHED behind the mountains of Wales. The maid saw how the last rays fell upon the tallest peak of all. Snowdon caught the red light – it became a mountain the colour of blood.

An hour had passed since Jake had been beaten in the yard and driven away. Jake had called up to Laura, telling her he loved her, and that he would come back and save her. A maid now entered the room, carrying a mug of warm milk and a piece of bread. The girl seemed frightened of Laura and quickly set the tray down before withdrawing again. Laura heard the key turn in the lock. The sound it made was dreadful. The clunk of the mechanism driving the bolt across signified she was a prisoner.

Night had fallen when she heard raised voices. Suddenly, figures ran across the yard, carrying lanterns. Laura recognized the master, together with men who helped him with his experiments. The figures down in the yard were extremely agitated. She could hear shouts, but no individual words that she could make out. Just then, more figures appeared from the direction of the forest. Four men ran in a tight-knit group. Such a strange way to run, she thought. There was something so unnerving – and so frightening – about this scene. Lamps bobbed as people hurried with them. Splashes of light illuminated outbuildings, trees, and stark, horrified faces. At last, she saw why the four men ran in such a huddle.

They each gripped the handle of a stretcher; the device employed to carry a sick person. On the stretcher lay a figure. She could not see who it was. But it was not moving. It was absolutely still.

Laura pretended to be asleep. The two maids she shared the room with had climbed into bed twenty minutes ago. The pair had worked hard since six o'clock that morning and had fallen fast asleep within moments of their heads touching the pillows. Even so, she'd waited until their breathing settled into a slow, steady rhythm.

Laura sat up in bed. 'Meg? Daisy?'

Neither maid responded to their name, so Laura eased herself out of bed. Earlier, Laura had pretended to be asleep when Meg and Daisy entered the room. Unusually, for such a pair of chatterboxes, neither had spoken, and Laura realized that the incident connected with the figure on the stretcher had left both of them so shocked that they couldn't bring themselves to speak. Laura had opened her eyes by a tiny fraction. Just enough to see Meg place a key in a drawer beneath her clean lace aprons.

Laura didn't risk lighting a candle. Instead, she relied on moonlight filtering through the curtains. She didn't make a sound as she walked barefoot across the floor. Seconds later, she had the key. Silently, she unlocked the door and stepped out into the passageway.

The entire household must have been asleep. There were no sounds whatsoever.

For a moment, she paused. She dreaded what she intended to do, but do it she must. She would prove to everyone that she wasn't a liar. Laura took a deep breath, straightened her back, then with absolute determination she went downstairs.

The maid only lit a candle when she reached the lower floor. After that, she walked along the gloomy corridor that ran at the back of the house. At this time of night, the corridor resembled the entrance to a tomb. She felt so alone down here. The silence had a menacing air. But Laura kept moving. She had to see what lay in the room at the end of this corridor. Her pride compelled her. When a gardener had suddenly died out on the lawn last year he'd been brought to the very same room. Logic dictated that the figure on the stretcher would be delivered there, too.

She walked faster. The sound of a clock in the distance seemed to acquire almost a savage clicking. Darkness swelled in front of her – a living thing, a monstrous thing. Panic and dread crackled along her nerves. Every instinct told her to turn back; to run to the bedroom where Meg and Daisy lay sleeping.

Laura could not do that, however. Not until she saw what she must see with her own eyes.

The clock chimed – a death knell of a sound. Meanwhile, the candle sputtered and threatened to go out: that little bud of fire on the wick barely had the strength to hold the evil darkness at bay. Laura's chest tightened.

Suddenly, she was there. The door knob pressed against her hand – as cold and as hard as a child's skull. She entered a room with white tiles. Cold as a winter's night in here, she thought with a bone-chilling sense of dread. The candle flame shrank back from the horror on the table – or so it seemed to her.

For there, in the centre of the room, was a table and, lying upon it, an object beneath a white sheet. Her bare feet whispered across the floor. She moved as if some stronger force than her controlled her limbs. Laura's hand hovered over the shrouded form. Somewhere outdoors, a dog started to howl. The mournful cry filled the room with shimmering, ghostly echoes.

'Now,' she hissed. 'Do it now.' Her hand quivered above the sheet where the soft material had been moulded by the bump of a nose and deep hollow of the eyes. The shrouded face was still.

But would it remain still? Would the man beneath the sheet react with fury if she disturbed his shroud?

Laura tried to dispel the terrifying image of the dead springing back to life.

'I know who you are,' she breathed, 'and I'm sorry I wasn't allowed to warn you.'

Pinching the fabric between finger and thumb, she pulled back the sheet. There on the table, lying stretched out, and utterly motionless, was the man she'd seen before. Twenty years of age, dressed in the clothes of a gentleman, he lay flat on his back. The man's red hair gleamed as bright as copper wire in the candlelight. The mouth remained open, clearly revealing a gap in the front teeth. She remembered his eyes from last time – both when she saw him in her vision, when he fell out of the sky in front of her, and later when the very same man had found her in the forest. His eyes were green – a vivid, emerald green. Those eyes stared at her even though she knew he was dead – really dead this time.

The stranger's chest gave a single heave and blood spurted from his mouth. She'd seen exactly the same in her vision. The gush of blood – a furious river of crimson, surging and bubbling from lifeless jaws.

That's when the candle went out, and she was alone with the corpse in the darkness.

CHAPTER 12

VICTOR DENBY DIDN'T come down to breakfast. Thomas knew that the discovery of the pagan shrine concealed in the workshop had shaken the man. Therefore, Thomas and Inspector Abberline ate alone in a large room adorned with paintings of the Denby males. Each face wore an expression of sternness and determination – these portraits were statements of their power.

The weather today was breezy. Sunlight chased away April showers only for the clouds to return moments later to spatter the windows with yet more rain. Inspector Abberline commented that spring was late this year, and that frost had already killed a bed of dahlias he'd planted recently.

A maid invited them to help themselves to food from silver tureens on a table. Abberline lifted the lids in turn. The detective seemed to have trouble identifying the food. The cuisine puzzled Thomas, too.

Thomas wrinkled his nose. 'Is this what the rich eat for breakfast?'

'Never dined in a country mansion before?'

'Never.'

'Meals tend to reflect the status of the guests. So I wonder what this breakfast says about us?' Abberline stirred a mound of yellow and green flakes. 'This, I think ... is chopped egg with herb. There's a very strong smell of oregano. Possibly curry has been added as well.'

Thomas lifted a cover. 'And pie. Or what remains of a pie.' He examined the meat beneath its thick, dry-looking crust. 'That's very dark flesh. Game pie, do you think?'

Abberline's moustache bristled as he picked up the plate and sniffed. 'Ah ... a favourite of my grandfather's. Rook pie.'

'Rook?' Thomas glanced outside where black rooks circled trees that contained their nests. 'I've never heard of anyone eating those things.'

'It's a rustic dish from yesteryear. The meat is tough and it's guaranteed to make your jaw muscles ache. Horrible stuff.'

'Have we been served this food as a joke? Or is this the butler's revenge because he clearly doesn't like us?'

Abberline smiled. 'This might sound ungrateful of me ... I suspect we've been served the week's left-overs.'

Thomas persisted in his quest amongst the tureens. At last he was rewarded with the discovery of plain poached eggs, bacon and sausage. 'Ah, this looks edible.'

Both men sat at the long table in the centre of the room to eat. Thomas glanced out through the windows as raindrops struck the glass. The gardener was out there, raking leaves from under a bush. The gamekeeper, whom they'd met at the quarry, patrolled a path that ran alongside the lawn. Thomas had seen the man earlier and guessed that Victor Denby had ordered the man to circle the house, and to watch for intruders. The gamekeeper carried a rifle in the crook of his arm.

'We're well guarded.' Thomas nodded at the window.

'I'll mention to Mr Denby that he consider buying a couple of dogs, too. Hefty brutes with a loud bark should make him feel a little more secure.' Abberline ate a piece of bacon. 'Hmm, not bad.' He chewed thoughtfully for a moment before asking, 'Have you been able to make any progress writing your article?'

'I wrote the first instalment last night. I have a feeling my editor will be pleased.'

'Just remind your editor, if you will, that nothing can be published about the Denby case for the time being.'

'Of course. You'd have no objection to my writing up a news story about how you identified the pickpocket at the station?'

'By all means. The reason why Scotland Yard agreed to you accompanying me is so that the public will have the opportunity to read an honest and accurate account of what a policeman actually does.'

Thomas said, 'Then you will permit me to sit with you when you question the staff?'

'Of course.'

'And to question you, if any aspect of your investigation is unclear?'

'Question me, interrogate, cross-examine. I insist.' He smiled. 'In fact, grill me within an inch of my life, just as these sausages have been grilled to within an inch of theirs.'

'What are your plans for today?'

'The shrine we found last night should be photographed before the statues are removed. I also need to interview the servants who were here when Sir Alfred was killed.'

'May I question witnesses myself?'

'Only when I'm present. Nobody here knows that you're a reporter, and I have to be careful that your questions don't prejudice a court trial – if and when the killer is caught.'

'Understood.'

Abberline pulled a sheet of paper from his jacket. 'I made this copy for you last night.'

'What is it?'

'It's a list of the nine Denby males. Victor Denby believes that an individual, or individuals, plans to slay all the brothers.'

Thomas read the list. 'But the police don't suspect any of the brothers' deaths to be suspicious.'

'No, all are considered to be either fatal accidents or illness. Does anything strike you as odd on that list?'

'No.'

'Take another look and let me hear your thoughts.'

Thomas studied the list again. 'There were nine brothers. Four are still alive. The eldest, Hubert, is a missionary in Africa. Then there is our host, Victor Denby, and Thaddeus, who lives in Scotland, and William, the youngest of the brothers. He's the balloon aviator based in Wales.' Thomas sipped his tea. 'The first to die was Bertram Denby. He fell off a station platform seventeen years ago and was killed by a train.' Thomas paused as he recalled another fact. 'The Gods of Rome scandal, which some have linked to Sir Alfred, occurred twenty years ago.'

'So, the first violent death, even though it's considered an accident, takes place three years after the scandal that embarrassed the British royal family?'

Thomas nodded. 'So, there could be a link?'

'Possibly; however, three years elapse between the theft of Italian treasures and Bertram being struck down by the train.'

Thomas continued, 'The other deaths occur as follows: John Denby drowns as he takes a walk by a river. That's ten years ago. Mortlake Denby dies eight years ago when thrown from a horse. Ah, Joshua Denby.'

'Anything unusual about his death?'

'So far, he's the only one to die at home in bed. Three years ago he succumbed to a blood disorder.'

'Which brings us to the latest death: Sir Alfred Denby, killed by explosion this year.'

'And he is the only brother whom we can state was murdered.'

'Probably murdered, to be more accurate. We need to gather more evidence before using the word "murder" with complete confidence.'

'Do we begin interviewing staff directly after breakfast?'

'Firstly, I'd like to take another look at Sir Alfred's shrine. There still might be more to it than meets the eye.'

This was the first opportunity Abberline had to inspect the shrine by daylight. Thomas helped Abberline move the secret door that still lay on the workshop floor after they'd pried it free of the panelling last night.

Abberline wiped his forehead after they stood the formidable slab of oak against a wall. 'This thing would have shattered my skull if you hadn't caught hold, Thomas. You saved my life, and that's a fact.'

Thomas panted from exertion. 'The explosion not only forced the door inwards by an inch or so, it also snapped the hinges. If you hadn't noticed a section wasn't aligned with the rest of the panels, the shrine might have stayed hidden for years.'

Abberline took out his notebook and swiftly sketched the shrine. 'I've asked the butler to bring in a local photographer, but I'd best make a drawing of what's here. We found the knife just there by the foot of Faunus.' He indicated the bizarre figure with horns protruding from its wavy hair. 'I'd also say that blood from the cockerel had been drizzled over the statue.' He pulled a tape measure from his pocket and handed it to Thomas. 'Would you measure the figures for me, please, and tell me the length of the shelf?'

'The god, Jupiter, is fourteen inches tall, Venus is eleven inches ....'

At that moment, the butler stepped through the door. He looked just as grey in broad daylight as he did indoors. Whether he was being discrete, or simply uninterested, he paid no attention to the shrine adorned with pagan deities. 'The maid told me you'd like to send some telegrams, sir?'

'Thank you, yes.' Once more Abberline reached into his pockets. Thomas wondered if the man had specially deep pockets sewn into the coat, for they seemed to accommodate all the tools of the detective's trade, including a wad of telegram forms. 'There is one to Scotland Yard, and also one to the nearest constabulary, if you could tell me where that is?'

The man's grey lips twitched slightly. 'That would be East Ferry, sir.'

'East Ferry,' Abberline murmured, as he added the destination address to the telegram form. That done, he handed over the forms and coins, which would pay for the sending of the telegrams. 'Thank you, and please despatch them as quickly as you can.'

'Very well, sir. Will there be anything else?'

'If you could arrange for a pot of hot coffee and two cups to be sent out here, that would be most welcome.'

'I'll do so immediately, sir.'

Thomas resumed taking measurements of the objects behind the panelling.

Presently, Abberline said, 'Indulge me, Thomas: what's your theory regarding the pagan altar?'

Thomas gazed at the shelf of Roman gods. They were modern copies of ones he'd seen in the British Museum. Jupiter stood with a thunderbolt in his hand – no doubt frozen in the act of delivering sudden destruction to an errant mortal. 'I'd venture that Sir Alfred Denby had this secret compartment built sometime after the 3rd August, 1881.'

This took Abberline by surprise. 'How on earth did you come by such an accurate date?'

Thomas produced a scrap of newspaper. 'This was wedged between the shelf and the bracket. The carpenter hadn't been careful enough ensuring the brackets were level when he set them into the wall. He used a piece of folded newspaper to lift the shelf at that end.' He unfolded the tightly folded paper and handed it to the detective. 'There's a date printed on the top corner: 3rd August, 1881.'

'We'll make a detective of you yet, Thomas. Go on.'

'Therefore, Sir Alfred has been worshipping at his shrine for almost ten years before his death in February.'

'Although he could have had another shrine elsewhere. He might have been saying his prayers to the goat-horned god for many years before that.'

'He might.'

'If he was raised a Christian, what made this English gentleman bow his head toward heathen deities?'

'I've been thinking about that, Inspector; would you like to hear my theory?'

'By all means.'

'Picture this. Over two decades ago Sir Alfred buys the golden statues known as the Gods of Rome, which have been discovered by chance. Such a find should have been reported to the Italian Government, and, of course, it is illegal to remove antiquities from

Italy without the proper export licence. Sir Alfred smuggles the statues into Britain. All this is done in absolute secrecy. Sir Alfred is ambitious. He plans to gift one of the golden statues to Queen Victoria in the hope he will be given an aristocratic title in return.'

'So instead of remaining Sir Alfred Denby he is elevated to Lord Denby?'

'Which is not only a great honour to serve in the House of Lords, it also puts him in a singular position to become extremely wealthy. An aristocratic title attracts cash like bees to a honey pot.'

'But we know it all goes wrong. The Italian authorities learn that the priceless statues have been discovered, and that one has been offered to the Queen of England, hence the scandal.'

'And yet Sir Alfred was never publicly named as the owner of the statues; moreover, the statues have never been found.'

Abberline scratched his jaw. 'What caused Sir Alfred to believe that Roman gods are real, and should be feared?'

'We can't be sure, but certain events that Sir Alfred experienced made him believe that the gods had cursed him in some way. After all, we do know that the fortunes of the Denby family had begun to falter. Sir Alfred worshipped at his altar in the hope that the gods would lift the curse. If that happened, the Denby family might prosper again.'

'I think you're near the truth, Thomas. Once I met an explorer, who lived in a house full of talismans and magic voodoo dolls. He was a man of science, yet he was terrified that he'd brought some dreadful curse down upon him after he stole a sacred bell from a Chinese temple.'

'Did he break the curse?'

'The curse broke him. He's now confined to an asylum. A demon sits on the end of his bed waiting to eat his soul – or so he tells everyone.'

'Superstition can be a powerful thing. Lucky four leaf clovers, hanging horseshoes from doors.'

Abberline blew into his hands. 'I wonder if our coffee's on its way.'

They had a very long wait for the butler to arrive with a tray, bearing a pot and cups. The coffee was quite cold.

CHAPTER 13

THE TROUBLED MAIDSERVANT, Laura Morgan, had been moved to an attic room of the manor house. Here there was a single bed and a little table with a glass and a jug of water; that's all. Laura stood at a window that looked out toward hills where roaming sheep resembled white speckles against dark heather. A key turned in a lock. Hesitantly, someone opened the door to what was, to all intents and purposes, Laura's prison cell.

'Meg?' Laura felt surprise at the expression of fear on the young maid's face. 'It's only me. Come in.'

The maid, trim in her black dress and white lace apron, nervously entered the room. She carried a tray, bearing bread, cold mutton, pickles, and a Welsh cake studded with raisins. Meg set the tray on the table. That done, she quickly retreated to the door, her eyes averted from Laura, and saying nothing.

'Meg? Have I made you angry?'

Meg shook her head without looking at Laura. She clearly wanted to leave the room as soon as she possibly could.

'Meg, stop.' Laura caught the young maid by the arm.

Gasping with shock, Meg struggled to break free.

'We're friends, aren't we, Meg? I gave you my best boots when yours wore out.'

'Please, Laura … let go.'

'Why won't you talk to me?'

'I'm scared of you.'

'You've no reason to be scared. I'm your friend.'

Meg's eyes were bright with shock; the girl was close to screaming. 'Why did you do that terrible thing last night?'

'I saw men bring a body to the house yesterday. I had to find out who it was.'

'The poor gentleman was dead. What made you go and disturb

him like that?'

'I needed to know if it was the young man with the red hair and green eyes.'

'You've got the devil in you: that's what they're saying below stairs.'

'I haven't.'

'But they say you can see things that aren't there.'

'Meg, who was the dead man?'

'Let me go.'

Meg struggled; the girl wanted to be out of the room with the door locked behind her.

'Meg, I won't let go until you tell me the man's name and where they found him.'

'Then I can go?'

'I swear.'

Tears welled up in Meg's brown eyes. 'It was terrible, Laura. The young gent was Captain Sefton. He'd come to help the master with his work. Yesterday, they sent up one of the balloon things. I hate those balloons, Laura. Surely it's unnatural for a man to ride through the sky like he's become a bird.'

'The master is a good man. He builds flying ships that will defend this country from our enemies.'

'Captain Sefton was up there on a balloon, flying through the air. For some reason he slipped and fell over the side. Oh dear God, Laura, he dropped such a long way. They say he was dreadful to look at. All broken up – his arms and legs twisted around.'

'Where did they find him?'

'On the path that goes from the big clearing in the forest.'

'That's where I saw him fall.'

'You couldn't have. You were locked in the room.'

'No. Yesterday morning, as I walked back from the village, I heard such strange music and a white figure chased after me.'

'Laura, stop it.'

'I was running along the very same path you've just told me about, the one near the big clearing, and *whoosh!* A man fell out of the sky and dropped onto the path not five feet from me. He had red hair, green eyes, and a gap here in his teeth.'

Laura gripped Meg by the arms. She felt the young maid convulse as she gave a loud sob.

'Stop saying these things, Laura. It's not right. They'll send you to a mad house and that'll break my heart.'

'Meg, listen.' Laura spoke tenderly. 'Believe me, please. I saw

Captain Sefton fall out of the sky and be killed.'

'No ...'

'My dear, sweet Meg. For some reason, I've been given the gift to see the future.' She gripped Meg tighter as the girl began to tremble. 'I have visions.'

'You're scaring me, Laura, please stop saying these things.'

'I see the manner in which people end their lives. I have visions of their deaths. ...'

'That's witchcraft.'

'This scares me, too,' she whispered. 'What if I see you, Meg? What if I'm tormented by visions of you lying dead?'

Meg's knees buckled as she fainted. Laura had to hold the maid tightly to stop her falling.

Laura continued, 'Before they sent me here, I worked at Fairfax Manor. It's where Sir Alfred got killed when the gunpowder exploded ... a maid told me that the Denby family have been cursed by something called the Gods of Rome. Meg, I think the curse killed the man with red hair yesterday. What's more, the Gods of Rome are making me have visions of the future.'

Meg's eyes stared dully. Sheer terror had overwhelmed her senses.

Laura murmured, 'I keep asking myself who will be next.' The sounds of a flute came from somewhere faraway. Haunting, sinuous notes glided into the room and into Laura's head, where that slow melody danced deeper and deeper into her soul. 'I don't want to see your dead face in my dreams, Meg. Nor Jake's. Nor the master's. Can you hear the music? There's music when the spirit comes. Pale as death he is. He's one of the Gods of Rome ... can you hear it?'

The door burst open to reveal Miss Groom. 'What on earth's going on here?'

'The music's started. He's approaching ...'

'What have you done to poor Meg?' The housekeeper pulled the maid out of Laura's grasp. 'Oh! The girl's fainted dead away ... if you've hurt her, I shall bring the police.'

A tall man, wearing a long, black coat, stepped into the room. His most striking feature was a bushy beard that was white as snow.

The housekeeper still had to grasp Meg tightly to keep her on her feet. 'I'm sorry about this, Doctor Jones.' She was clearly embarrassed by the situation.

When Doctor Jones spoke it was in a deep, rumbling voice. 'Which one is the lunatic girl?'

'There, standing by the window; she's called Laura Morgan.'

The doctor said, 'Miss Groom, you maintain that the girl sees things that aren't there, and she claims she can perform witchcraft?'

'No, sir. I'm no witch,' Laura protested. 'But I can see the future.'

'She causes the most dreadful trouble, Doctor.' Miss Groom's expression became ferocious. 'Such wickedness. Yesterday, she ran away into the wood, and my staff had to search for her. Last night, she went downstairs to a room where the body of poor Captain Sefton had been left. For some ungodly reason she wanted to touch the corpse. Everyone is shocked by her depraved actions.'

'Leave her to me, Miss Groom. I will make everything all right.' He placed his Gladstone bag on the bed and opened it.

Laura watched as he drew out a jar full of a yellowish powder. Meanwhile, Meg had recovered enough to stand upright by herself. She pressed her hand to her forehead as if afflicted by a fierce headache.

Miss Groom said, 'Laura, you'll cause no more mischief from now on, my girl. No more running off, no more lies about ghosts.'

The doctor poured water from the jug into the glass, then added a spoonful of the yellow powder, which he stirred.

'Drink this,' he told Laura. 'You'll soon feel much better.'

Laura shook her head. 'They're keeping me locked up. I shouldn't be treated like a lunatic.'

Miss Groom spoke firmly. 'Drink the potion, girl, or I'll tell the master that you are beyond helping.'

The doctor handed the glass to Laura. 'Drink, child. The nightmares will vanish.'

Laura knew she had no choice. Her parents' survival depended on her wages. The milky potion had a strange, perfumed odour, and she didn't even know what the drug was. Nevertheless, she drank.

'Lie down on the bed,' directed the man with the white beard. 'Sleep.' He turned to Miss Groom. 'I've administered a powerful sleeping draught. It's an opiate and will render her unconscious.'

'Will it cure her mind?'

'Not a cure, but it will curb the hallucinations for the time being. Perhaps all the girl needs is rest to bring about a cure. I will speak to your master before I leave.'

Laura Morgan tried to tell the doctor that she did not hallucinate – that she was sane. However, the drug was taking effect: already it was beyond her power to move so much as a finger, and she could no longer speak. Her head rolled to one side, so that she gazed in the direction of the window. A white face appeared there. Its skin grew brighter and brighter until it was dazzling and its light seared the room.

But neither Doctor Jones, nor Miss Groom, nor Meg noticed. Laura wanted to shout and point at the figure that hovered there fifty feet above the ground outside the window, yet she couldn't even utter the slightest sound. Nor could she give voice to this premonition: *strangers will come here soon ... there will be more deaths ... many more deaths ....*

CHAPTER 14

THOMAS KNEW THAT trouble had erupted when he heard the woman's scream. This was followed by shouts of: *'MURDER! MURDER!'*

Thomas had been helping Abberline interview staff in a room at the back of the house. When he heard the shouts, he rushed to the window where a shocking sight met his eyes.

'Inspector,' he shouted. 'There's a man lying out there! His face is covered with blood!'

Thomas dashed along the corridor to the back door. Within seconds, he was outside. The man lay flat on his back perhaps twenty yards from the workshop. A rifle lay in the doorway. Thomas immediately identified the fallen man as Brown, the gamekeeper. Blood trickled outwards across the ground. His face was absolutely pale and he didn't move – didn't even appear to be breathing. Domestic staff flooded from the house; there were screams and shouts of panic and distress. He noticed Abberline calling instructions to the butler.

Thomas continued into the workshop. Abberline had arranged for a photographer to take pictures of the shrine before the carvings and bowls were removed. Now the photographer knelt over the smashed remains of his camera. The man shook his head as he gathered the shattered remains of the wooden case to him as if grieving over a dead loved one. The shrine had been attacked, too. Parts of the stone carvings were scattered across the floor.

Thomas ran toward the photographer. The man immediately threw his arm over his face and cried out, 'No! Don't hit me again!'

'Look at me,' Thomas panted. 'My name is Thomas Lloyd. We met earlier.'

The man sagged with relief. 'I thought it was him coming back. Dear God …'

'What happened?'

The photographer remained sitting on the floor, too shaken to stand. Nevertheless, he managed to stammer out an explanation. 'I-I photographed the items on the shelf as you told me to, Mr Lloyd. The gamekeeper came to the door and we chatted about what had been found. Then a second man appeared behind the gamekeeper and *crack!* The stranger hit him with a piece of wood. The poor fellow fell like he'd been struck by a thunderbolt. Then the stranger rushed toward me. He struck me with his fist, and that's the last I knew until just now. My camera, Mr Lloyd ... my camera is in bits.'

'What did the man look like?'

'It all happened so quickly.'

'Try.'

'He wore a dark hat with a large brim and ... and he had a suntanned face. Very suntanned he was. A moustache ... yes, a black moustache.'

'What about his clothing?'

'I'm not sure, other than he was in a yellow coat – bright, mustard yellow.'

'Did he speak to you?'

'No.'

Thomas quickly surveyed the wreckage. The camera, which had been in the form of a brown wooden box on a tripod, had been thoroughly smashed. All the statues had been broken, too. The rotten remains of the cockerel that Sir Alfred had sacrificed to the Roman deities lay on the ground. A large, black fly walked along one stiff wing.

'Can you stand?' Thomas asked the photographer.

'If you give me a moment or two, sir, I'm sure I will.'

Thomas ran back outside. A ring of housemaids and footmen stood around the body of Brown. Abberline crouched beside the man; the detective's fingertips rested on the side of the victim's neck.

Thomas shouted breathlessly, 'Inspector, the shrine's been smashed, and the photographer's been beaten.'

'Is he alive?'

'Yes, he'll be all right.'

The elderly gardener hobbled around the corner of the workshop. 'I've seen 'im! He's yonder! By the barn!'

Thomas didn't hesitate. He shot across the yard with the speed of a greyhound released from its leash.

Abberline called after him in alarm, 'Thomas, for heaven's sake, man, don't get too close! He might be armed!'

Thomas made for the barn that lay along a track some hundred yards from the house. He was perhaps halfway there when he saw a figure flit from a doorway toward a line of bushes. *I've got him,* Thomas thought in triumph. The man's coat flapped open as he ran – it really was a striking mustard yellow.

'Wait!' Thomas yelled. 'You are under arrest!'

At that moment, he no longer thought of himself as a newspaper reporter. No, Thomas Lloyd, was the man who would capture the killer. The intruder moved at a furious pace through bushes into the forest. Thomas ran as fast as he possibly could. He glanced back, but nobody was following at that moment. Then he could hardly expect Abberline to dash with the speed of an athlete – the man was well into middleage.

Thomas had the impression that the one he chased carried a white object. However, the gloom beneath the trees impaired his vision. He could see no detail of the attacker other than he wore a hat and the yellow coat. The pursuit took them by the quarry where Abberline had found the remains of the pistol. Birds flew squawking from the undergrowth as the stranger charged through, trying to make good his escape. Thomas had closed the gap. He was now perhaps twenty yards behind the stranger. The woodland became more overgrown. Barely any light penetrated the branches. Thomas's eyes blurred with exertion to the point the stranger became a yellow smudge.

Pushing aside branches, Thomas tried to close the gap. As he did so, he prepared himself for a fight. After all, the stranger was a violent man. He'd attacked both the gamekeeper and the photographer. He wouldn't surrender quietly. Thomas would have to subdue the killer with his fists.

Thomas crashed onward through the undergrowth. He found himself either jumping over fallen logs, or ducking under low branches. The dampness rising from the ground smelt strongly of forest and the wild animals that dwelt there. He stopped abruptly. Panting, he looked all around him. The soft earth was unmarked by footprints.

'Dash it.' He wiped sweat from his eyes. 'Where is he?'

Thomas held his breath, so the sound of his respiration wouldn't conceal any other noise – such as the furtive approach of the stranger. However, he could hear nothing other than bird song. Neither could he say where the stranger had gone. Thomas ventured to his right, his heart pounding. Dense woodland meant that he couldn't see more than twenty yards in either direction. He retraced his steps to a gully that ran downhill.

Nothing. Not a sign. Tension gave way to frustration.

'He's gone.' Thomas slapped his hand against his thigh. 'I've lost him.'

Ten minutes later, Thomas Lloyd walked back into the yard. He was surprised to find the gamekeeper very much alive and standing by the workshop door. His head was swathed by a thick layer of bandages, and the man swayed, seeming decidedly groggy. Thankfully, he hadn't been murdered as the servants first supposed.

Thomas heard Abberline say, 'Thank you for wishing to help, Mr Brown, but you've had a vicious blow to the head. It would be better if you were to go indoors and rest.'

The gamekeeper, a former soldier, was a proud man. He insisted on doing his duty. 'I wish to tell you what I know, sir, in case I forget.'

'Very well.'

'I didn't see the man who attacked me. He struck me from behind. But there are two things I distinctly remember. One: as I fell, I saw his shoes.'

'Were they in any way distinctive?'

The gamekeeper nodded that bandaged head of his. 'His shoes were unusual. Not like an Englishman's shoes. They were sharply pointed at the toe, and the leather looked very soft. They were reddish in colour – between red and brown, sir, like the way some leaves turn in autumn. Shoes like that must cost a lot of money.'

'And the second thing?'

'The smell … or more properly, sir, the scent. It was the scent of tobacco, but it had a perfumed quality, sir. When I was stationed in Egypt, local men used a particular brand of cigarette that had cloves mixed with the tobacco. It yields a very distinctive aroma.'

'Tobacco mixed with cloves. Reddish shoes.' Abberline nodded his thanks. 'I shall remember that. It's most useful. I'm grateful for your help; now please go and rest. A doctor is on his way and he'll take a look at that wound of yours.'

'I've had worse, sir.'

Despite the injury, the man walked smartly back to the house.

'He's a strong man,' Thomas said. 'And a determined one. He wouldn't rest until he told you what he knew.'

Abberline turned to fix his eye on Thomas.

'I'm sorry, Inspector. I lost the stranger. He escaped me in the wood.'

'I could have been very sorry, too,' Abberline growled. 'You might have been killed, chasing after what must be a dangerous man.'

'He has to be the Sir Alfred's killer. I thought I—'

Abberline erupted with fury. 'You might easily be lying dead out there. What kind of letter would I have had to write to your fiancée? You behaved like a fool!' With that, he stormed back to the house.

Much later that day Abberline had calmed down. Thomas helped him gather up the broken pieces of statue. He also took pains to reassure the photographer that the police would compensate him for the destruction of his camera.

As they placed the debris in boxes, Thomas said, 'He smashed the statues as if expecting to find something inside.'

'There's also one missing. Did you notice that the Faunus has gone? There are no fragments of that particular figure.'

'I did see the stranger carrying an object. It must have been that particular statue.' He coughed. 'I'm sorry, Inspector. Earlier, I acted in haste.'

'You acted bravely. But stupidly. I don't order my men on suicide missions. I won't ask you to do so, either.'

They carried the boxes out into the yard as a cart driven by the gardener rumbled across the stones.

The gardener excitedly pointed at a man in the back. 'This 'ere feller is Zachariah! I found him out on the road. He says he spoke to a stranger this afternoon.'

Zachariah was a wide-eyed man of around seventy, with a straw hat perched on his head.

'Tell the gents, Zachariah. Tell em what he said to you.'

Zachariah took the straw hat from his head, which he fumbled with nervously. 'I was working in the big turnip field. A stranger in a yellow overcoat comes by and he says to me "Where is Fairfax Manor?"'

'That sounds like our man,' Abberline said to Thomas then, turning to the nervous Zachariah, said, 'Yes, sir, please continue.'

'That's all he said, sirs. I'm sorry, sirs.'

'There's no need to be sorry. Thank you for coming to tell me.'

'Tell how he spoke.' The gardener looked gleeful – the man delighted in bringing the witness to Abberline.

'Aye ....' The farmworker took a deep breath. 'He said just those words, sirs: "Where is Fairfax Manor?" He spoke with a foreignness.'

'He wasn't English?'

'No. A foreigner. I could hardly understand him.'

Abberline nodded and turned to Thomas. 'At last, we're starting to build a picture of our suspect. What's more, such a distinctive individual will stand out in a crowd.' Abberline allowed himself a wry smile. 'Your pursuit of the stranger in the yellow coat is far from over, Thomas, in fact I'm convinced that it's only just begun.'

Events flowed at a much faster pace following the attack. A dozen constables arrived from a nearby town. Inspector Abberline put six of them to the task of searching the estate in the company of manservants and gardeners. The lion-hearted gamekeeper insisted on accompanying them with his rifle, even though his head was thickly bandaged. The remaining constables were stationed at various points near the house, whistles at the ready, in case the stranger in the yellow coat returned.

Abberline asked Victor Denby to provide him with shotguns from the gunroom. Denby didn't hesitate and handed out weapons and ammunition immediately. Abberline armed himself with a gun and distributed the others to the police officers. Thomas, meanwhile, stood out on the lawn, scanning the surrounding landscape with a pair of binoculars

A little while later, Inspector Abberline walked up and gave a shotgun to Thomas with the words, 'If you see the man again only fire at him if you need to save your life, or the lives of others. He'll be more use to our investigation alive rather than dead.'

'You suspect he might have been the one who murdered Sir Alfred?'

'I don't rule that out any more than I rule out the very real possibility that for the last twenty years the Denby brothers have been systematically murdered one by one.'

Thomas nodded in the direction of the house. Victor Denby stared out from a window on an upper-floor. 'At least, there's one man who'll be reassured now that he has a guard of armed policemen.'

'The guard won't be a permanent one. Those constables can't be spared their regular duties for long. He'll have to rely on his staff and the gamekeeper for longer term protection.'

Thomas saw the uniformed figures of the policeman walk toward the forest. 'I hope they find our man. However, I fear he'll have fled the area by now.'

'My feelings exactly. Though why he wished to steal a modern replica of a statue is still a mystery.'

'Perhaps to prove to another party that he was there at Sir Alfred's shrine?'

'Which means that our foreign intruder today, who attacked the gamekeeper and photographer, and who wears expensive shoes and smokes cigarettes flavoured with cloves, isn't working alone. What's more, it indicates that our man is answerable to a superior.'

'What happens now, Inspector?'

'We leave.'

'Oh? Our investigation is finished?'

'It has here for now. I need to report back to my superiors at Scotland Yard. No doubt you have your own matters to attend to in London.'

Thomas's heart sank. 'Is this the end of the two of us working together, Inspector?'

'Far from it. I daresay the eldest brother is safe enough out in the wilds of Africa. However, the other surviving brothers in Britain are in danger. Victor Denby has sent them both telegrams, informing them to guard themselves and their homes. If you are willing, I suggest we take the sleeper train to Scotland tomorrow evening.'

'I'll be there.' Thomas Lloyd grinned. 'This adventure is becoming more interesting by the hour. Wild horses won't stop me being on that train with you.'

CHAPTER 15

THOMAS LLOYD WALKED along the busy road. As he did so, he thought: London is a beast. It's a gigantic, monstrous beast that never sleeps. We are the insignificant microbes that live in its belly. A train rumbled along its track; boats on the river sounded their whistles; carts clattered by, street vendors and newspaper sellers shouted at the tops of their voices, dogs in a yard began barking, while pigs in a slaughter house squealed as loudly as the souls of the damned in hell. And, everywhere, huge engines hidden behind factory walls whooshed, thundered and screeched. Steam hammers in foundries pounded relentlessly. Thomas felt their vibrations coming up through the ground to shake his bones. Even after spending just a few hours in the countryside the contrast astonished him. The sheer clamour made his head spin. So, it was with great relief that he closed the door behind him, and climbed the stairs. Thankfully, the tenants of the other rooms would be out at their places of work. He'd be spared the agonies of Billy Wilkins playing his accordion next door. And the truth must be told, Thomas thought, Billy plays the accordion excruciatingly badly.

Mrs Cherryhome, his landlady, bustled from the kitchen. 'Mr Lloyd.' She beamed up at him. 'Mr Lloyd, I'm glad I saw you.'

Thomas paused on the stairs and smiled back. He liked Mrs Cherryhome. A robust woman of fifty-five, she doted on her tenants, as if each and every one of them was a favourite nephew. Her rounded cheeks turned pink with delight.

'A letter arrived this morning.' She picked up an envelope from the hallway table. 'It's very forward of me to say this, but I'm sure it's from your sweetheart. In fact, I swear to the saints it is. I'd know her handwriting anywhere.'

She beamed even more broadly when he came downstairs for the envelope.

'Thank you, Mrs Cherryhome. Yes, it is from Miss Bright.'

'Oh, praise be. I do hate to think of her living on the other side of the world in the company of savages and tigers and all manner of nasties.'

'Emma assures me that the people of Ceylon are most hospitable and kind.'

'That is a relief. I once had a tenant who sailed to Java where he was boiled by cannibals.'

'Emma will be quite safe in Ceylon, Mrs Cherryhome. How's your throat? You told me last week that it was sore.'

'Much better, thank you. I've been taking honey with whisky, that always does me right.'

'I'm glad to hear it.'

'Oh, I'm late, Mr Lloyd. The baker will only have stale bread left if I delay another blessed moment.'

'Good day, Mrs Cherryhome, and take care. The roads are especially busy today.'

'I will, Mr Lloyd, I will. Cheery bye!'

Thomas swiftly climbed the stairs. A letter from Emma! His heart beat faster with excitement and he could barely contain himself from tearing open the envelope there and then. However, he preferred the comfort of his old armchair by his window while he savoured the letter's contents.

On the second floor of the lodging house, Thomas sat in his room and read the letter from his fiancée. Emma spoke of her father's work, cultivating tea plants that would be immune from many of the diseases that often blighted crops, described sunsets over the mountains, the troops of monkeys that flitted about the veranda, and she'd included a sketch of a Hindu temple with its profusion of mysterious carvings. She did not tell him, however, when she and her father would return to England. That saddened him. In fact, he sighed and let his head rest back against the chair. It's time Emma came back to me, he thought. A dutiful daughter is all well and good. But isn't it time she became my wife?

Sounds of traffic flooded through the open window. The April sun shone on the letter that bore the pleasant loops and flourishes of her handwriting, and did he catch the aroma of the scent she wore, rising from the paper? Nevertheless, he realized that he would become gloomy if he sat here for much longer. To take his mind of this frustrating state of affairs, Thomas pulled a sheet of paper from a drawer and sat down at the table. He glanced at the clock on the mantelpiece. The time approached six o'clock in the evening. Just over an hour ago, he and Abberline had gone their separate ways after arriving in London by train. The detective had set off for Scotland Yard; Thomas had gone directly home. Thomas would call on his editor tomorrow at the newspaper's offices then he'd return here to pack for the visit to Scotland. He and Abberline were taking the night train to Edinburgh in order to interview Thaddeus Denby, the 60 year-old brother of Victor – the man who, no doubt, sat behind closed curtains at Fairfax Manor with a loaded pistol in his hand. But then the surviving brothers had every reason to be concerned for their safety. Sir Alfred had been killed eight weeks ago when an intruder fixed a pistol inside a cabinet in such a way that it detonated a cask of gunpowder when the cabinet door was opened.

Thomas's nerves tingled. This case fascinated him. He was thankful to be part of the investigation – and especially thankful now it distracted him from Emma's letter: one that had delighted him so much to open, and one that he'd read feeling progressively gloomier and with increasing disappointment when he realized it contained no word of Emma's return. *Damn Ceylon. Damn those tea plants.* With an effort, he refocused his mind on the case they were investigating.

He wrote on the paper: VICTIMS: DENBY BROTHERS: FIRST BROTHER KILLED NEARLY TWENTY YEARS AGO. MOST RECENT SLAYING: FEBRUARY 1890. A SPAN OF TWO DECADES: A PATIENT KILLER? OR AN INCOMPETENT KILLER? As he saw it, there were two main mysteries here. Once more his pen scratched out letters: ONE. THE MURDERER: WHO IS HE? Beneath that, he added the words: FOREIGN MAN IN YELLOW COAT? Then: TWO. THE GODS OF ROME: ARE THEY CONNECTED TO THE KILLINGS? After a moment's thought, he jotted: POSSIBLY CONNECTED. FOREIGNER WRECKED SHRINE AND STOLE CARVING OF FAUNUS. Thomas returned to the armchair where he rested his head against the comfortable curve of its back. He yawned. The last twenty-four hours had been extraordinary; they'd been exhausting, too. He recalled, with absolute clarity, those dangerous moments when he'd chased the man in the yellow coat deep into the forest. Thomas closed his eyes, and he soon found himself in pursuit of the mysterious stranger again. Although this time it was in his dreams.

Outside, meanwhile, the beast that is London growled and muttered: the eternally restless creature that never slept.

CHAPTER 16

Moonlight shone against the closed curtains in Laura's room. Miss Groom had locked her in here. She was alone. And yet ... and yet ... .

A sound came from the darkness. Breathing, she guessed. The sound wasn't at all loud and possessed a whispery quality. Did someone watch over her as she slept? Miss Groom, perhaps? Or Meg? The respiration changed its rhythm, becoming a little quicker.

Laura tried to turn her face in the direction of the sound. Although it was so dark in the attic bedroom, would she even be able to see who it was? Laura struggled to roll her head on the pillow. She couldn't move. The drug that Dr Jones had administered paralysed her. She couldn't sit up. She couldn't move her head. All she could do was move her eyes. And all she could see of the room was the yellow oblong that revealed where the curtains were, with the moonlight shining on the other side. The table beside her bed resembled a hunched, stunted thing, not unlike a crouching man.

The rising-falling sound of respiration became even faster. There was a snuffling quality – almost animal-like – then a whimper. But very soft ... she had to listen hard to make it out. *I want to see who's there,* she told herself. There is someone in my room. I want to see their face.

Laura wished she could turn her head. However, the drug rendered her as motionless as the tenant of a grave. The breathing sounds abruptly changed to an angry snorting. *How could an animal have got into my room?* The sound grew louder. It's coming closer. Do I keep my eyes open? Do I close them tight? Her sense of dread increased; the breathing grew louder – angrier. She tried her hardest to spring from the bed. But she couldn't move so much as finger.

Then she felt it: the sensation of the creature's breath on her face.

Her heart raced in panic. If the creature bit her she could not fend it off. Her arms lay limp on the bed. All she could do was lie there, a helpless victim. Is this how I am destined to die? She shuddered from head to toe as if icy fingers touched her. Will I meet Death here? Unable to struggle? Unable to cry out?

At last, the opiate that rode those rivers of blood flowing through her heart, couldn't be resisted for a moment longer. Laura's eyelids grew heavy and closed as she felt that inhuman breath against her cheek. Soon, Laura found herself in the embrace of a dream. She moved through a moonlit forest where a white figure glided in front of her, always just ahead, forever eluding her. A tantalizing spirit. A lost soul. A figure leading her into darkness everlasting.

CHAPTER 17

THOMAS LLOYD'S FRIDAY was a busy one. Yesterday, he and Inspector Abberline had been at Fairfax Manor, south of London, now he prepared for the long journey north to Scotland. Thomas knew that Abberline had already despatched a telegram to Thaddeus Denby, informing him they'd take the night train from London to Edinburgh. Thomas had also written a long letter to his fiancée. Reading Emma's letter yesterday had put him in such gloomy spirits. Make no bones about it, he told himself, I wish she'd tell me when she's coming home. Marriage seemed as remote as the man in the moon. Nevertheless, after breakfast, Thomas sat at the table and penned a light-hearted account of his life over the last few days. Of course, he omitted reference to his potentially dangerous pursuit of a murder suspect. He didn't want to worry his fiancée. Although the letter was decidedly lighthearted he did, in fact, write it with a heavy heart. He had to resist the temptation to scrawl in big black letters EMMA, PLEASE COME BACK TO ME! For the human heart is, by turns, a bringer of joy and a torture. He cared deeply about Emma. Being with her brought him happiness, being parted from her inflicted misery.

However, there was so much to do before leaving for Scotland he could dispel some of his gloom with activity. He told his landlady that he'd be away for a few days. When he explained that he'd be travelling to Scotland, she fluttered her hands and said, 'Goodness gracious! Such a long way! I've heard they have snow in July. Be sure to take your warmest clothes, Mr Lloyd. I shall parcel you up some Madeira cake for the journey.'

After thanking her, he took the underground train to Fleet Street where he met his editor. The editor glowed with pleasure when he read Thomas's dramatic account of the investigation of Sir Alfred's death, and the conclusions that Abberline had drawn. He was especially interested in the apparatus constructed from string and a pistol that detonated the keg of gunpowder. 'Fiendish,' the man had murmured, his eyes getting wider by the moment. 'Fiendish and astonishingly cunning.' Thomas had also produced a brief outline for his next report, concerning the discovery of the hidden shrine and its subsequent destruction by a foreign stranger in a yellow coat.

The editor leaned back, exhaling loudly through his bushy moustache. 'I wish we could publish this now, Thomas. We'd increase our circulation and make the other papers green with envy.'

'Inspector Abberline insists that we don't print these reports yet. He doesn't want to alert the killer of Sir Alfred Denby that the death is now considered to be murder.'

'Damn.' The editor's sharp eyes fixed on his young journalist. 'You admire Abberline, don't you, Thomas?'

'Yes, sir. He's a fine detective. A very decent man, too, if I may say so.'

'By all means, portray him as a hero in your newspaper stories, but always remember these facts: Abberline is a policeman, you are a journalist. He will always put the interest of the police force before you, Thomas.'

'What are you suggesting?'

'Abberline will keep information from you. He'll withhold interesting aspects of the case.' A fly crawled across the desk in front of the editor. The man slammed his hand down onto the insect crushing it. 'Don't permit Abberline to conceal juicy titbits from you that will interest our readers. They don't want dull accounts of police procedure, they demand excitement and dramatic chases, such as you've written up here.'

'Then I'll continue to do exactly that, sir.'

'But you could only write about such a thrilling pursuit because you were there and took part. What if you aren't around when Abberline makes a discovery, or interrogates some scoundrel?'

'You want me to spy on him?'

'You're a journalist, aren't you? Observe the great detective in action. Do that openly with his blessing. And do it secretly without him knowing. Give me great stories, Thomas. Help me boost the circulation of our newspaper to new heights.' He scraped the remains of the fly off the palm of his hand with a pen. 'If you help me do that, Thomas, I will put in a word for you. Who knows? There might be promotion waiting just around the corner.'

'Inspector Abberline has been open about his methods; he has shown me friendship.'

'So he will ... until you are of no further use. He still believes that the Press portrayed him as incompetent for failing to catch Jack the Ripper.'

'I don't want to lie to Abberline; neither does my conscience allow me to spy on him.'

'Remember what I said about promotion, Thomas. I know you're engaged to a young lady and plan to be married. Isn't that the case?'

'Yes, sir, but I don't see how that is relevant to what we're discussing now.'

'You can hardly provide a decent home for a new wife on your salary, can you? However, if your stories vividly reveal Abberline as a fascinating human being, flaws and all, then we shall sell more newspapers, you will be promoted, and your salary will be raised to such a level that you can marry Miss Bright. Now, what do you say to that?'

Thomas Lloyd returned to his rooms. Inspector Abberline had told him that he would collect Thomas by hansom cab at six, and that they would go on to Kings Cross Station where they would board a train for Scotland. Meanwhile, the sky darkened. Thunder clouds loomed over London's rooftops. The threat of a storm made horses out in the street fractious. The sound of their whinnying grew louder. Their drivers shouted louder, too, to keep the animals under control.

Thomas checked that he had everything he needed for his journey. He added a fresh notebook and more pencils to his bag. He was determined to write the best possible report of Inspector Abberline's investigation, yet he felt troubled, too. Thomas's editor wanted him to resort to underhand methods. The man had ordered Thomas to spy on Abberline. When Abberline read about the Denby case in the newspaper he'd realize that Thomas had betrayed their friendship. *However ... however ...* Thomas sighed. If his employers were pleased with the stories, he would be promoted. He knew full well that he didn't earn enough to keep Emma in a comfortable home when they married (if and when she came back from Ceylon!). Thomas suspected that in the coming days he would strenuously wrestle with his conscience. *What's more important?* Thomas asked himself. Abberline's trust and friendship? Or money?

The clock on the mantelpiece struck four o'clock. Thomas had just started to polish his boots when a thunderous knock on the door startled him. He opened it to find Abberline standing there.

'Thomas, there's been another death: Thaddeus Denby has been killed.'

*

Thomas had to run to keep up as they rushed from the house. A hansom waited at the side of the road. The horse seemed to sense Abberline's urgent manner: it swung its head and took steps forward. The driver had to rein the animal back, while making repeated cries of 'Whoa ... whoa, there!'

The driver's seat was fixed behind the cab, some six feet above the ground; even so, he deftly leaned forward and opened the twin doors at the front of the vehicle. Abberline indicated that Thomas should climb in first. Abberline followed. The doors clunked shut in front of them as they settled on the upholstered bench that faced the front of the cab. Then – away! Soon they entered the vortex of London traffic: horse-drawn carts, rumbling omnibuses, mules carrying bundles of firewood – and, dodging through this maelstrom of horses and vehicles, men, women and children.

Black clouds gathered, threatening a deluge. The streets were growing darker by the minute as thunderheads marched ever nearer.

Abberline thrust a piece of paper at Thomas. He had to speak loudly over the clatter of wheels: 'A telegram from the head of CID in Edinburgh. At noon today, Thaddeus Denby took a stroll around his house. He was shot clean through the heart. The identity of the killer is unknown.'

'So another of the Denby brothers has been slain?'

'This time there's been no attempt to disguise the attack as an accident.'

'Was the gunman seen?'

'That I have to ascertain.' The hansom lurched violently. Abberline gripped a leather strap that hung down from the roof to steady himself. 'As you'll see from the telegram, details are brief.'

'Are we to take an earlier train to Scotland?'

'I am, Thomas. You will be going directly to Wales. I've told the driver to get you to the station as quickly as possible.'

Quickly as possible turned out to be an alarming dash through crowded streets. Thomas heard the rumble of thunder. A storm was coming; the sky grew ominously dark.

Abberline handed Thomas an envelope. 'That's my letter of introduction for you to hand to Mr William Denby.'

'I'm to call on the balloon man?'

'Indeed you are ... if you are willing, that is?'

'Of course, Inspector. I absolutely want to be part of this investigation.'

'Good man. The Welsh police have been alerted to the fact that there appears to be a plot to execute the Denby brothers.'

'What will be my role?'

'At the start of all this, you asked if you could become my shadow. Now I should very much like you to become my eyes and ears as well. The Denby estate outside Porthmadog is vast and sprawling. It encompasses hills, forests and valleys. William Denby took over the running of the estate when his brother, Joshua Denby, died three years ago. You will recall that Joshua was the only brother to die of natural causes at home. William Denby conducts balloon experiments from his land there.'

'I've read something of his work. He has accomplished some astonishing feats. Once he ascended to the height of two miles – ice formed on the rigging. Last year, he rode in a balloon all the way from England to Russia, a journey of three days.'

'The man is also in danger. There are only two brothers left alive here in Britain: Victor Denby at Fairfax Manor and William Denby at Newydd Hall in Wales.'

'Might the man in the yellow coat be the killer?'

'Possibly. We know the foreign gentleman is as violent as he is determined. After escaping from you he could have caught the train back to London then travelled on to Scotland.'

Thomas frowned. 'But no doubt you had your officers question railway staff at stations that the stranger might have used. A man in such a distinctive yellow coat would be memorable.'

'Indeed he would be. Yet if he was able to change from the yellow coat to an everyday brown or grey, which we see by the thousand, then our suspect, to all intents and purposes, becomes invisible.'

'If the man can change his appearance, and knows how to use the rail network to his advantage, then he might already be on his way to Wales?'

'That's a very real danger. William Denby might be the next to die.'

'But he's been warned? And the police will protect him?'

'William Denby is even more fortunate than that. Because his work for the army is of such importance, a detachment of soldiers are stationed at Newydd Hall. As well as helping him launch his balloons, which require plenty of manpower, they also act as guards.'

A man carrying a tray of loaves dithered in front of the hansom cab. Their driver cursed the ditherer with such fluency that the man gawped in shock. Meanwhile, the storm grew closer. A terrific clap of thunder caused horses in the street to flinch. One white stallion reared up, kicking its front hoofs. Other horses pawed the ground, or lurched forward. Suddenly, there were cries of: 'Whoa, there!' 'Hold your nag!' 'Easy, girl!' Drivers struggled to rein back their animals. A huge dray horse, tethered to a railing, stamped its hoofs so ferociously that sparks shot outwards – flashes of blue fire.

Abberline shook his head. 'There are more than half a million horses in London. At the best of times, they're jittery and unpredictable due to the sheer volume of traffic. I must admit I've wondered what would happen if there was such a violent clap of thunder that it made all those hundreds of thousands of horses bolt at once. It would be a catastrophe of Biblical proportions.'

Thomas hung tight to the handle: the motion of the cab was akin to that of a small boat on a stormy sea. 'You have quite an imagination, Inspector.'

'Imagination be damned. I've seen so much misfortune, and calamity, and downright evil in this city that I don't have to use one atom of imagination.' He tapped the side of his head. 'I only have to remember. And, as I've already told you, I am blessed – or should that be cursed? – with an unusually tenacious memory. I once saw a delivery cart catch fire. It was loaded with kegs of lamp oil. The horse bolted. For all the world, it looked as if a fiery comet went speeding through Piccadilly Circus. Flames spewed out everywhere, setting men and women alight. Burnt human flesh, Thomas.' He shook his head. 'The smell of burning wouldn't leave me. It never has. I only have to catch the acrid smell of burnt bacon and I'm back there again ... in the midst of hell.'

Thomas glanced at the man's eyes, which were fixed into one of those unseeing stares that suggest a person looks inward into recollection, not outwards at their immediate surroundings. Those eyes had seen so much that was violent and cruel. They had also gazed on the victims of Jack the Ripper. They truly had seen hell on earth.

The hansom pulled up outside the entrance of Euston Station, and the driver briskly opened the cab's doors. After dropping Thomas off here, Inspector Abberline would continue on to Kings Cross Station where he'd board his train for Edinburgh.

The detective said, 'As soon as I've completed my work in Scotland I'll come back down to Wales and join you there.' They shook hands, but, as Thomas started to climb down from the cab Abberline caught him by the arm. 'Thomas, you aren't a policeman, so you aren't permitted to interview the domestic staff. But I'd be grateful if you would –' Abberline gave a slight smile, '– chat with them. Perhaps lead them to certain subjects.'

'Such as the Gods of Rome?'

'Exactly.' Abberline touched the brim of his hat. 'God speed and be vigilant. There is a dangerous stranger out there. They won't hesitate in hurting anyone who gets in their way. Beware, Thomas. Beware.'

Friday evening. Thomas Lloyd sat in a carriage packed with men and women as the locomotive hauled the train northwards. The thunderstorm that had begun in London followed the train out into the countryside: bolts of dazzling blue flashed from the clouds. An elderly man sitting opposite Thomas smoked a black cigar, puffing out clouds of the foulest, bitterest smoke that Thomas had ever smelt. Ladies fanned their faces with their hands while exchanging annoyed glances with their travelling companions. Meanwhile, a pair of gentlemen in top hats energetically discussed the merits of investing in gold rather than silver. Thomas Lloyd's seat was a hard one. For some reason, it bulged peculiarly and Thomas shifted constantly, trying to avoid a hard protrusion behind the upholstery that dug into his spine.

He would have preferred to write up his account of the day while it was still fresh in his mind. Especially Abberline's dramatic appearance at Thomas's home to inform him that the Denby brother, who was laird of an estate in Scotland, had been shot dead by an unknown assassin. I wonder if Abberline is enjoying a more comfortable ride than this one, he wondered as what felt like a bony finger jabbed into his back. He suspected a nail had come adrift from the seat's woodwork and that it poked him through the fabric.

The man smoking the evil-smelling tobacco grunted and muttered, 'Blessed thing keeps going out.' He pulled out a match that was as big as a pencil, struck it against the carriage floor, and relit the cigar. All the ladies coughed. One of the men in the top hats declared loudly, 'Gold. Gold will never betray the shrewd investor.'

Lighting flashed. For a split-second the meadows turned blue, and thunder crashed so loudly that the sound hurt the passengers' ears.

'The handclap of doom,' declared the cigar-smoker with relish. '*Memento Mori*. God, Himself, reminding us that we are mortal, and that one fine day we will expire.'

Thomas closed his eyes. The train swayed as it rumbled along its track. As he often did, when alone, he found himself dwelling on certain memories. Barely a day went by when he didn't picture his grandfather's face. Owen Lloyd was a Welshman who had found work in a Yorkshire coal mine and, just as Thomas had been fond of his grandfather, the man had adored his bright-eyed, intelligent grandson who loved to read books. Thomas wished he could speak to the old man again. He'd tell him he was on a journey to the man's homeland. What would his grandfather make of Thomas writing newspaper stories about Inspector Abberline, the greatest detective of the age? He pictured the old man's surprise when he heard that his grandson's words would be read by millions of people throughout Britain and the far flung lands of the Empire.

Thomas's eyes remained closed as he pictured the loveable old fellow's smile of delight. What Thomas wouldn't give to spend another hour in his grandfather's company, but the man had been laid to rest beneath the soft grass of a country churchyard for ten years now – the words Thomas longed with all his heart to speak would forever remain unsaid.

Meanwhile, the rhythm of the train's wheels became almost melodic, and Thomas Lloyd gradually fell into a deep and dreamless sleep.

He woke to find himself alone in the carriage. Night had fallen. He could see nothing of the world outside other than the lights of houses rushing by. The train must have made several stops and his fellow passengers had alighted, including, thankfully, the man with the pungent cigar. He checked his pocket watch. Eight o'clock. Another four hours remained of his train journey to Porthmadog in Wales. Inspector Abberline would, at this moment, be travelling northwards to Scotland.

Finally, Thomas had an opportunity to write up his notes. He moved to a seat by the window: a comfortable one that wasn't armed with a sharp object to irritatingly prod his back. He pulled out paper and a pencil and set to work. He'd no sooner begun writing when a shiver ran down his spine. Nothing less than a revelation had all of a sudden struck him. The man in the yellow coat knew that we'd discovered the hidden shrine. That means the stranger had been keeping watch on the workshop. Had he been spying on us when we opened the secret door? Thomas closed his eyes again; this time to visualize a possible sequence of events that started before the stranger's assault on the gamekeeper and the photographer. *Picture this,* Thomas thought, the stranger keeps watch on the manor. He sees the arrival of Abberline and myself, and observes us from a distance. When he realizes that we have found the shrine in the workshop he chooses his moment to steal one of the carvings. To do this, he knocks both the gamekeeper and photographer unconscious. I give chase. He escapes. The man has anticipated this eventuality and has hidden an overcoat in the forest. The police searched for a man in a striking yellow coat, not an inconspicuous brown or black one. Therefore, the man vanishes as if he's evaporated into thin air.

Thomas understood this important fact: the man suspected of killing Sir Alfred Denby possessed formidable cunning. Thomas opened his eyes again and soon his pencil scratched across the paper as the words flowed. This case fascinated him more and more by the day. If anything, what troubled him the most was that his editor had ordered him to spy on Abberline, and to gather facts that Abberline might wish to remain confidential. Thomas liked the policeman. He had no wish to betray the man's friendship. However, it occurred to Thomas that he might use his time at William Denby's house in Wales to conduct his own investigation, which involved the murder of several brothers linked to gold statues known as The Gods of Rome.

The conductor walked along the passageway that ran by the compartments. 'Change at Crewe for Manchester. Change at Crewe for Wales. Next stop Crewe. All change.'

Yes, he'd adopt a dynamic approach to this case. He'd use his journalistic skills to ask the right questions. Perhaps he would make discoveries of his own? If luck was on his side he might even trace the suspect: the man in the yellow coat – or, rather, the man who once wore the yellow coat. Thomas realized that such a description, *man in the yellow coat*, would be cumbersome. Detectives gave unknown suspects a nickname, so fellow officers knew who they were referring to. Thomas pondered on what he should call the mystery man. Their murder suspect had used explosive to kill Sir Alfred, so how about *The Gunpowder Man*? Thomas shook his head, no; yesterday their suspect had possibly shot and killed the Denby brother in Scotland.

Their suspect, however, had, without a shadow of doubt, stolen one of the carved deities from the workshop. Thomas smiled as he wrote a name: *The God Thief.* Yes, that would do for now. *From henceforth the suspect shall be known as The God Thief.* He liked its resonance; he even allowed himself a broader smile as he pictured a newspaper headline: PICTORIAL REPORTER CATCHES THE GOD THIEF.

Thomas decided to begin his investigation at the earliest possible opportunity. The time had come to start a manhunt of his own.

Thomas Lloyd stepped out of the railway carriage as a church clock struck the chimes of midnight. Instantly, he smelt the tang of the nearby ocean. Gas lights on the main road revealed that buildings here were built of dark stone, giving the impression that the town might have been constructed from the essence of midnight itself.

'Where now?' he asked himself as he left the station. He had the address of William Denby's house; however, he had no means of reaching it other than by foot. But which direction should he take? Porthmadog was a small coastal town. There were no hansom cabs. He doubted that there'd even be a humble cart for hire at this time of night. A cold rain began to fall, transforming the town into a misty, dreamlike place. Voices prompted him to look along a pathway. A pair of men walked toward him. One carried a lantern. Both men wore capes made out of sacks of the kind in which you might carry potatoes. No doubt the sack capes were intended to keep the men dry from the rain, which fell heavier by the moment.

Thomas raised his hat. 'Good evening, gentlemen. Could you please direct me to the nearest hotel?'

They looked Thomas up and down in astonishment, as if he'd stepped over the threshold from some enchanted realm. With an expression of bafflement on his face, one of the caped men spoke some words to the other in a language Thomas didn't understand, though he supposed it to be Welsh. Both men then shrugged and continued walking. Clearly, they understood no English, while he understood no Welsh whatsoever.

'A hotel?' Thomas called after them. 'Or somewhere I might have a room for the night?'

The figures vanished back into the darkness. At somewhat of a loss, Thomas returned to the station; however, the ticket office door had already been locked. No light showed through the windows.

'This is a fine old mess,' he muttered with a sinking heart. Earlier, he'd amused himself with daydreaming about a headline that would read: PICTORIAL REPORTER CATCHES THE GOD THIEF. Now, in his mind's eye, he now another headline: PICTORIAL REPORTED FREEZES TO DEATH IN WALES. There was little he could do other than walk into town and hope he could wake the landlord of some tavern. Either that, or sleep in an alleyway.

Thomas had taken no more than a dozen steps from the station when all of a sudden a coach pulled by four magnificent white horses swept toward him. Light blazed from lamps fixed to the coach itself – this was such an astonishing sight that Thomas stopped dead. Even more surprising was a soldier, dressed in a red coat and armed with a rifle, who sat beside the coachman.

The soldier barked, 'Are you Mr Lloyd?'

'Yes, I'm Thomas Lloyd.'

The driver stopped directly in front of him.

'We're here to take you to Mr Denby's house, sir. Please get into the coach.'

Gratefully, Thomas opened the coach door and settled down into its snug interior. He'd no sooner shut the door when the driver shouted a command to the white horses and away they went.

The rain fell steadily now. Inside the coach, however, behind the closed door and large windows, Thomas was warm and dry. Abberline must have had the foresight to telegraph the arrival time of Thomas's train. As Thomas settled back into the seat, he noticed that on a rack, high on the inner panel of the cabin, was a series of white flasks made from pot. On each one was painted a single word: *Rum*, *Whisky* or *Brandy*. Although he was tempted to take a restorative nip of brandy after his long journey, he decided that such liquid hospitality was reserved for the owner of this luxurious coach.

Thomas checked his pocket watch. Twenty minutes past twelve.

When the time reached one o'clock in the morning, and with the coach still rumbling through wilderness, he said to himself, 'I'm sure Mr Denby won't mind.' He unstoppered the brandy flask and took a few sips.

After that, the journey seemed much more cosy and pleasant. He gazed out of the window, sometimes catching a glimpse of a remote cottage standing high on a mountainside. At other times the coach would plunge into a mysterious forest that looked as if it belonged to a primeval age. On another occasion, he marvelled at the gorgeous cascade of a fast-flowing stream in the darkness.

At last, the coach passed through a gatehouse and he made out a huge mansion that bristled with battlements against the night sky. This was a long way from the busy streets of London. Indeed, this seemed another realm entirely. A land of strange enchantments. A very different world from the one he was accustomed to back in England's sprawling capital city of fourmillion souls.

CHAPTER 18

THE MAID STOOD at the attic window and gazed out into the darkness. She'd been given another draught of the opiate drug earlier in the day. For hours she'd lain on the bed, feeling more like a corpse than a living human being. Dreams and reality had become so intertwined she couldn't separate them. Meg had brought food and drink from time to time, and had wiped Laura's face with a damp cloth while murmuring reassurances. Now Laura supported her weight by placing both hands on the windowsill. The drug had finally lost its power to confine her to the bed, though she still felt dizzy. She looked out in the hope of seeing Jake, the boy who had promised to rescue her.

Huge oaks swayed in the darkness as the storm caught hold and shook them. The winds blew harder and it sounded to Laura as if supernatural beings raced through the forest toward the house. Perhaps spirits were gathering in order to decide who died next? Laura was certain that there would be more deaths. What's more, she was convinced she would have visions of those deaths before they happened. But why was she granted such glimpses of the future? How could she warn those who were destined to die? The housekeeper had locked her in this room? Most of the time, the opiate made her so lethargic she couldn't move a finger let alone utter warnings of death. Perhaps those gruesome visions of the future were Laura's punishment; perhaps she'd committed some wicked act in the past and the spirits wanted her to suffer.

Laura leaned forwards until the cold glass touched the tip of her nose. She heard another noise above the storm winds: the sound of approaching hoofbeats. Suddenly, a blaze of light appeared, and Laura watched as a coach, pulled by four white horses, and carrying shining lanterns, swept along the drive. A footman hurried from the house to the carriage. Quickly, he opened the door and someone passed a large bag to him. After that, a tall figure stepped out. He was a young man, and the way he glanced this way and that suggested that these were unfamiliar surroundings. Indeed, when she caught sight of his face, she saw that he was a stranger. Perhaps he'd come to help the master with his experiments?

The footman led the way to the house, carrying the stranger's bag. The tall man followed behind. Meanwhile, the driver cracked his whip and the white horses pulled the coach away in the direction of the stables.

Laura clenched her fists as if she felt a sudden stab of pain. Suddenly, she was assaulted by another vision – images of such vivid intensity streamed through her head: a figure falling from the sky. Crashing through the roof of a building, shattering slates, and tumbling into a room – this room! Scratches covered his face. Blood smeared his lips.

The red-haired gentlemen had plunged from the balloon. Laura had been granted a vision of his violent death. Had she foreseen how another man would die? Would the victim be the stranger who had just arrived here moments ago?

Laura stumbled back to bed. 'Why are you punishing me?' she cried. 'What have I done wrong? What do you want from me?'

Trembling, she pulled the blanket over her head. Laura feared the worst – terrified what tomorrow would bring.

CHAPTER 19

NEWYDD HALL, WALES, resembled a place of work – part factory, part suite of offices – rather than a gentlemen's country residence. Men walked along corridors with intricate designs drawn on large sheets of paper. One carried a piece of red fabric the size of a bath towel; the man declared with great excitement to a colleague: 'Vulcanized! It's now waterproof. You could fly across the Atlantic with a craft made from this.'

Thomas Lloyd had slept soundly until ten o'clock. The train journey had been interminable then had come the night time drive through the wilderness in a coach drawn by four white horses. This morning he wandered about the big house not knowing where to go. The footman who'd met him from the coach in the early hours took him under his wing.

'Sir, Mr Lloyd, sir. Breakfast finished at eight, but if you go through the green door you'll find coffee and cake.'

'Thank you.' Thomas nodded. 'That should tide me over admirably.'

'Very good, sir. Oh, by the by, lunch is served in the refectory at one sharp.' With that, the man briskly walked away.

Thomas discovered that the room behind the green door was deserted. A coffee pot stood on a warming plate, while slabs of yellow cake occupied a dish beneath a glass cover. Thomas helped himself. The cake, flavoured with lemon, was delicious. As he ate, he gazed through a window which had commanding views of the grounds. The house stood in the bottom of a valley, with hills rising sharply at either side. In the distance, a colossal mountain soared upwards until lost in cloud. Thomas recognized the mountain as Snowdon, the highest in Wales. Lawns stretched out a good couple of hundred yards before ending at dense woodland. A pair of soldiers in red coats, and armed with rifles, patrolled the edge of the tree-line.

The door opened. Thomas turned to see three men enter. The youngest had wispy fair hair and wore a white shirt and dark trousers, the other man was in his forties and was clad in a grey suit; the third man had severely clipped silver hair and wore the uniform of an army officer. All three approached him.

The man in the grey suit smiled in a friendly fashion. 'Good morning, Mr Lloyd. The footman told me you were stoking up on cake and coffee. Capital idea! My name is William Denby.' He held out his hand which Thomas shook.

'Good morning, Mr Denby.'

'Pah! William, please. This –' he indicated the young man with fair hair, '– this is Jack Shaw.' Thomas shook hands with the smiling young man. 'And this warrior of Empire is Colonel Brampton.'

Colonel Brampton gave Thomas the briefest of handshakes.

'Welcome to Newydd Hall,' William said pleasantly. 'I hope you had a tolerable journey, though it's a devil of a long ride up from London.'

Thomas wasn't sure whether to explain he was a reporter that had been assigned to write Abberline's story for the newspapers, or allow them to believe he was a policeman. He needn't have worried about making the decision.

Colonel Brampton spoke sharply. 'I know exactly who you are, Lloyd. You work for the *Pictorial Evening News*. I don't like reporters. I don't want you here. But my superiors wish it otherwise. I thought it only proper you should know my feelings from the start, and to warn you that I won't tolerate any meddling by the Ppress, or there'll be hell to pay.'

After Colonel Brampton had curtly informed Thomas that he didn't like reporters and certainly didn't want them here at the house, he marched away, with the fair-haired young man hurrying to keep up William Denby, meanwhile, remained with Thomas. From time-to-time, men with rolled-up plans under their arms sauntered in to call upon the trestle table where slices of cake and coffee had been set out.

William Denby, thoughtfully sipping his coffee, gazed out at a dozen soldiers who hauled an enormous length of cable from an outbuilding.

'That hawser's two thousand feet long,' William said. 'We're working on how best to tether a balloon, so it can be sent aloft quickly. Colonel Brampton's especially keen to utilize balloons for reconnaissance.'

'I know something of your work, sir. It was fascinating to read how you rose to a height of two miles on a hot summer's day, and how the air grew so cold at that altitude frost formed on the balloon.'

'Ah, those were the days when my balloon research had a peaceful intent. Colonel Brampton intends to put a soldier into one of my balloons and send the fellow five thousand feet into the sky, so that he can tell artillerymen where to target their guns. My balloons have evolved into weapons of war.' He grimaced as if the notion displeased him.

'Surely, that's beneficial, sir. Your inventions will make our nation stronger.'

'And the army gives me a king's ransom to construct bigger and better balloons. Without their money I couldn't afford to keep this house.' He turned to Thomas with a sigh. 'I regret the colonel's snappish manner just now. He shouldn't have been so abrupt with you.'

'Your work is top secret. It's understandable that the army wouldn't welcome a newspaper reporter with open arms.'

William took another swallow of coffee. 'It's not just a question of secrecy. Recently, we had a terrible accident here. One of our team, a Captain Sefton, fell from a balloon – a fall of more than a thousand feet. Everyone was deeply shocked by the accident. The colonel is responsible for the safety of his men and, quite frankly his commanding officers back in London are going to reprimand the man very harshly indeed.'

'I see.'

'They might even send him back to barracks with his tail between his legs, as it were.'

'I beg your pardon, sir.'

'Why on earth do you beg my pardon, Thomas?' His blue eyes twinkled in a friendly fashion.

'I should have expressed my sincerest condolences when we first met. Your brother's murder in Scotland is shocking as it is despicable.'

'Ah ... then Colonel Brampton's outburst would no doubt have thrown you off your train of thought. The colonel does have a disorientating effect on people.'

'Nevertheless, I'm at fault, sir. I should have expressed my regret at the loss of your kith and kin.'

'Thomas, firstly, do not call me "sir". I am William, and sincerely hope we will remain on friendly terms. Secondly, I'm glad you didn't offer your condolences in front of our granite-faced colonel. He doesn't hold with displays of emotion. Visible signs of grief are repulsive to him.'

'As you wish, William.'

'No doubt you're wondering why I don't appear to be expressing sadness over my brother's death. I am shocked by the murder; I freely admit that I am. However, he was twenty years older than me. I scarcely ever met the man, let alone formed a brotherly bond. You know our family's history?'

'Yes, your father became an extremely wealthy businessman.'

'He invested his profits in several country estates. When my brothers were old enough he immediately installed them in mansions, like this one, in order to oversee the running of his properties. My father despatched Thaddeus to his place in Scotland when I was five years old. I've scarcely seen the fellow since.'

Thomas paused as a man bustled through the door, clutching loops of rubber piping. He picked up a slice of cake, gripped it between his teeth, like a dog carrying a bone, then, with his fistfuls of pipes, exited the room.

Thomas waited until the door closed before continuing.

'The colonel knew my identity, so you know why I'm here, and that I'll be joined by Inspector Abberline when he has completed his investigations in Scotland.'

'I have had quite a flurry of telegrams from both the Inspector and from my brother, Victor, at Fairfax Manor.'

'You understand your life is in danger?'

'I do.'

'Detectives have visited you recently?'

'Yes, and they are quite satisfied about my security. The house and grounds are extremely well guarded by armed soldiers.'

'Then you are relatively safe here.'

'Relatively?' William's blue eyes widened. 'You suspect that I'm next on the assassin's list?' He sighed. 'I don't wish to appear flippant, but do you really believe that my brothers have been systematically murdered?'

'Inspector Abberline believes there is evidence to suggest that is so.'

'The inspector is the most respected of detectives. However, I find it hard to accept that an assassin has spent the last two decades stalking my brothers, and slaying them every five years or so.'

'Thaddeus was shot: clearly a case of murder.'

'Does it mean the others were murdered also? I took over this house and its land three years ago when my brother, Joshua, died of illness. A congestion of the blood, or so the doctor recorded on the death certificate.'

'Admittedly, it's a mystifying case,' admitted Thomas. 'However, if Inspector Abberline was here he'd do his utmost to impress on you this fact: *your life is in danger.* A sniper could be hiding in those woods with the express intention of shooting you dead.'

'You speak very frankly, Thomas. Vividly, too.'

'It is necessary, believe me.'

'Then I should also warn my wife and daughter, though it pains me to frighten them.' He sighed. 'I've already told Colonel Brampton that there might be a plot to kill the Denby menfolk. He has, therefore, doubled the guard, and sends out soldiers on horseback to patrol the grounds.'

'Then you will remain indoors?'

'Absolutely not.'

'If you go outside the house, even deploying a hundred soldiers here, or a thousand, cannot guarantee your safety.'

'Thank you for your concern, Thomas.' The man was sincere in his gratitude. 'We have, however, reached a critical stage of our research. Balloon flights must continue, and I must oversee every launch. Though, after what you've just told me, I should disguise my appearance. Perhaps I'll borrow a soldier's tunic – that'll thrown the assassin off my scent, won't it?'

'Perhaps.' Thomas spoke doubtfully.

'I'll test my disguise this afternoon.' He rubbed his hands together, and Thomas realized that William Denby's enthusiastic nature wouldn't easily be suppressed by talk of lurking gunmen. 'I'll give you a tour of the estate. That way you can view my domain. Right.' He clapped his hands together. 'I am due to oversee the production of a thousand cubic feet of hydrogen gas.' Heading for the door, he added cheerfully, 'I'll meet you by the stable block at two. Wrap up warmly. Let's make an adventure of it!'

At precisely two o'clock that afternoon William Denby drove a pony and trap to where Thomas stood near the stable block. The brown and white pony was a small, yet powerful looking animal that was decidedly eager. William repeatedly had to call out 'Whoa, lad', as the pony succeeded in pulling the little cart forward, even though its driver had engaged the brake.

'Climb aboard, Thomas,' sang out William. 'We have a veritable Pegasus here. I think he would fly rather than trot. Whoa, lad.'

Thomas climbed onto the bench beside William. He noted with surprise that William had made an attempt to disguise himself. Instead of wearing the soldier's uniform as he said he would, he'd donned the long, green coat of a coachman, complete with an ancient tricorn hat that appeared to have been nibbled ragged by mice.

'My own wife won't recognize me now, will she?' Laughing, he adopted a rustic accent. 'Hang on tight, sir, while your loyal coachman takes thee on a gallop over yonder hills.'

Thomas opened his mouth to enquire whether the man had brought a revolver for protection, but the pony trotted away so sharply that Thomas was thrown back against the board that formed the seat back.

'You'd best hang on tightly, Thomas, old chap. I wasn't jesting about this animal believing he's mighty Pegasus.'

The pony sped along at something between a trot and a gallop. Thomas gripped the iron framework of the cart's sides. 'We have a fine afternoon,' he said. 'And this is an extraordinary landscape.'

'I've lived in Wales for three years, and every day these mountains amaze me. Such beauty! Do you see Snowdon?' He pointed at the mountain that soared skyward. 'They say you can see five kingdoms from its summit: the kingdom of Ireland, the kingdom of England, the kingdom of the Isle of Man, the kingdom of Wales and, moreover, the kingdom of Heaven.'

'You've flown so high in your airships I daresay you've been closer to the kingdom of Heaven than any mortal man.'

'Ha! So I have, Thomas, so I have!' He pulled the reins back to slow the pony. 'Thrusting little beast, isn't he? His father was a pit pony that spent all his days underground. This one must know that he'll spend all of his in the God-given outdoors. Can't you sense his sheer exuberance?' William Denby seemed to share the animal's lust for life. His speech and movements crackled with energy.

Thomas nodded at the pony. 'He's what my mother would call "a force of nature".'

'Ha! Hold on tight. The road here gets a wee bit bumpy.'

The shaking of the cart became so violent that neither could speak more than two words in a row. They passed through dense woodland. Thomas cast his gaze this way and that, expecting to see the dramatic appearance of a sinister figure with a gun. However, he saw only squirrels, sheep and roe deer. Though the road ran uphill the steepness of the incline did nothing to dampen the pony's enthusiasm. In fact, it showed no sign of tiring as it charged upward to an ancient-looking church.

'If you turn your head back,' William said, 'you'll have a grand view of the house. Can you see the big sheds – the ones with the while walls? That's where we build our ships.' His tone mingled satisfaction and pride. 'We are at the forefront of aviation. One day we will succeed in fixing paddles, driven by an engine, to a balloon ... that will allow us to fly anywhere in the world. We won't be slaves to air currents and wind direction. We shall be masters of the skies.'

'When did your father buy the house?'

'Twenty years ago. As you've already heard, he made vast sums turning Britain into a grid iron with his railways lines. Regrettably, he wasn't so astute when he bought his country estates. Notice how rocky this land is – the hills, the steepness of the valley sides, the marshes down by the river. Barely anything can be grown apart from trees. They are so crooked and twisted that their timber is almost worthless. The land we occupy hereabouts is reasonable for grazing sheep, not much else.' His blue eyes twinkled as he grinned at Thomas. 'Not much good, that is, apart from building and flying my balloons. Whoa, lad.' He coaxed the pony to a dead stop. That done, he sprang down from the cart and quickly tied the reins to a post.

Thomas gazed at the huge mansion. 'Whoever built that must have been astonishingly wealthy.'

'It was built by a cousin of George the Third. He looted half of China to pay for it. He'd be amazed to see the place now ... if we had the power to conjure him from his tomb, that is. The ground floor comprises offices for my staff. Colonel Brampton has his lair there, too.' He shrugged. 'You might have guessed that I don't always see eye-to-eye with the man. The soldiers under his command are good fellows ... salt of the earth, but he runs them ragged.'

'You portray the man as a tyrant.'

'He's overly harsh with his men. Needlessly so, in my estimation.' William shook his head. 'If we saw things from the colonel's point of view I dare say we'd understand his annoyance. Brampton is a senior army officer. What he desires more than anything else, is to lead men into battle, with cannon roaring and regimental flag unfurled. Instead, he is deployed to a country house where dreamers, such as I, try to solve the problems of flight.'

'It is work of national importance.'

'Alas, the colonel will never win a medal in our battle to defeat gravity. And medals are what committed military men like Brampton yearn for with all their soldierly hearts.'

'I see. So, frustrated ambition makes him short-tempered?'

'Indeed, and patience is a valuable commodity in our research. We cannot rush, otherwise there will be more accidents of the kind that claimed poor Captain Sefton.' William pointed at the house. 'See the third floor? That is home to my family; it's comfortable and more than adequate for our needs. Step this way, Thomas.'

Thomas entered the graveyard. The headstones were oblongs of black slate set upright in the ground. The words engraved there were in Welsh. All Thomas could make out were the names of those lying in the earth.

Thomas Lloyd crouched down to read *DYLAN LLOYD* etched beneath a carved skull. 'Some of my ancestors might well be buried here.'

'Perhaps so. Listen to the sound the trees make.'

Thomas heard a whisper in the trees – voices, it seemed, from flesh-less mouths.

'Quite uncanny,' Thomas said. 'Like dozens of people whispering.'

William nodded. 'Locals call the trees that surround this graveyard The Singing Trees. They're supposed to sing the names of the dead who are buried here, and tell stories of what all these people did in life.'

They listened as the breeze blew harder. The whispering rose in volume. There was almost a sense that the trees had noticed the two men standing amid the tombs and were commenting on their visitors. Even the pony twitched its ears and turned to stare at the trees as they sighed as if in agreement.

Thomas said, 'I am already half-believing that the legend of the Singing Trees is true.'

'Ha, there are parts of this landscape that can make you believe in magic. Come on, I wish to show you one grave in particular.'

They walked toward the foot of the church tower where there was a box-shaped tomb in pale stone. This was markedly different from the tablets of liquorice-black slate. What's more, this one bore its inscription in English rather than Welsh.

Thomas read the words aloud, 'Here lies the mortal body of Joshua Gordon Denby. Died 8 December, 1887.'

'My brother: the previous tenant of Newydd Hall. He'd fallen ill six months before he died, which suggests quite powerfully that he wasn't murdered.'

'But the deaths of your other brothers might be a result of foul play.' He didn't mention that Inspector Abberline had discovered that Sir Alfred Denby had triggered a deadly explosion. Nor did he mention the pagan shrine hidden behind the workshop panelling. True, William's brother, Victor, may have told him about those matters in a letter, but Thomas decided he should give Abberline the opportunity to broach those delicate subjects with William.

William turned up his collar against the chill wind. 'We'll ride back along the lane that follows the boundary of my family's property. I find it difficult to say "my property" because I feel as if I'm just the caretaker here.'

Thomas suddenly asked, 'What do you know of the Gods of Rome?' He hoped such a direct question might provoke a candid answer.

William shrugged as he headed back to the cart. 'I don't know much. Other than there was some story about golden statues being found in Italy over twenty years ago. Rumours circulated, suggesting that my brother, Alfred, was somehow involved.'

'Do you believe the rumours?'

'It all happened when I was a very young man. I wasn't much interested. All my time and energy were taken up with balloons.'

'You'll be aware of the curse that's linked to the statues?'

'Of course. After my brother was killed in the explosion two months ago there was a flurry of speculation amongst the servants about the curse.'

'Do you believe there is a curse?'

'The curse is simply a curious myth, just like the story about these trees singing the names of dead people. No, Thomas, I do not believe in curses having the power to destroy human lives.'

The eager pony soon pulled the cart at exhilarating speed into the valley, where a waterfall thundered loudly enough to drown out the rattle of the cart's wheels. Thomas enjoyed the ride. The air refreshed him, making his face tingle pleasantly.

He was gazing up at squirrels, darting along branches, when an object flew from the shadows. That object was a man who bounded onto the cart. The stranger shouted at them in strange accents. Thomas tried to push the man off their vehicle. Instantly, the man shoved Thomas, slamming him back into his seat. Then the attacker launched himself at William Denby.

The pony reacted to the attack by breaking into a gallop, sending the cart bucking along the lane that ran beside the river. Meanwhile, Thomas grimaced in pain. The powerful stranger had thrown him back into his seat with enough force to wind him. Now the man roared with fury at William Denby. This sounded like a foreign tongue, and Thomas couldn't understand a single word. So far, the man hadn't struck William; instead, he'd seized him by the shoulders and bellowed. William not only had to contend with the yelling man, he also struggled to rein back the pony, which hauled the cart at a furious pace.

What happened next happened with astonishing speed. Horses suddenly appeared alongside the cart. Each carried a soldier: one brandished a sabre, another a rifle, the third seized the pony's bridle and brought the animal to a stop. The other two soldiers leapt from the backs of the horses directly onto the cart. Swiftly, they seized the shouting man and hurled him from the cart to the ground. One of the soldiers raised his rifle, ready to smash the man's skull.

William saw that the soldier intended to deliver what would probably be a fatal blow. 'Wait! Don't hit him! Stay your hand!'

'He was attacking you,' the soldier shouted. 'This is your brother's murderer.'

'No, it is not. The man was remonstrating with me. He did not strike me.'

The soldiers hauled the interloper to his feet – the one with the sabre held its point at the man's throat, just in case he renewed his attack.

Thomas saw that the stranger, who'd leapt onto the cart, was no more than eighteen or nineteen years of age. He had a head of unruly, black curls. His eyes were black as coal, too. He spat words that Thomas couldn't understand.

'You will have to speak English, young man,' William told him. 'None of us here understands Welsh.'

The dark-eyed man shook with anger. 'You let her go, see? What you're doing to that poor girl, isn't right, Mr Denby.'

'You recognized me?'

'That I did, you dog. Now you set Laura Morgan free, do you hear?'

The soldier placed the sabre's point against the man's throat: a clear enough warning to take heed. 'You say "sir" when addressing Mr Denby.'

'Not while he keeps a poor girl prisoner, I won't.'

William explained to the soldiers, 'This is a friend of one of my maidservants.' He turned to the man. 'Or, more accurately, she's your sweetheart, isn't she?'

'Laura is my girl. One day, as God is my witness, I shall marry her.'

'Your name's Jake, isn't it? And you live in the village nearby?'

The man nodded. 'Jake Tregarth is my name. You give that name to the police, if you wish.' He lifted his chin – a gesture of defiance. 'I am not afraid, see? Not afraid of you, or your men, even though they beat me to the ground when I came to the house.'

William turned to the soldiers. 'Is this true?'

'He trespassed, sir,' said one of the soldiers, 'demanding to see the girl. He threatened your staff.'

Jake didn't fear the sabre at his throat. 'It isn't right that you keep Laura prisoner. She is a good girl, see, a kind girl.'

'My housekeeper speaks most highly of Laura.'

'Then let her go, sir. It breaks my heart, it does, to picture what your men do to her in that house.'

'Jake, hasn't a member of my staff explained to you about what happened to Laura?'

'No, sir, they haven't said one word, other than ordering me off your land.'

'Jake, may we speak man-to-man without shouting?'

Jake nodded. 'As long as this brute takes the sword from my throat.'

'Very well. Harrison, please put away the sabre. I'm sure Jake will speak civilly from now on.'

'Thank you, sir.' Jake took a deep breath and appeared much calmer when the soldier withdrew the sword. 'What has befallen my Laura?'

'Quite simply she is ill. I'll tell you as plainly and honestly as I can about her condition.'

'Go on, sir.' Jake's eyes glistened.

Thomas realized that although the young man had no fear of the soldiers, he was evidently frightened for his girl.

'Earlier this week, Laura fell sick, something to do with her nerves. She became acutely distressed, and she fainted in the wood. One of my employees brought her back to the house.'

'Her nerves?' Jake visibly gulped. 'You're saying my Laura has become a lunatic?'

'No, Jake. I'm sure it's nothing so serious. Perhaps she's become overwrought in some way. My own doctor has given her medicine that will help her rest.'

'Laura shouted from a window – she told me that she'd been locked in her room.'

'A precaution for her well-being, that's all. Perhaps it was a result of her nervous condition but Laura ran away into the forest. Fortunately, she was found and brought safely back to the house.'

'Then you are not keeping her prisoner?'

Thomas spoke up, 'Mr Denby is a kind and honourable man.'

'Thank you, Thomas.' William smiled at Jake. 'Won't you give Laura a day or two to rest? Then I'd like you to come up to the house so you can see how she is for herself.'

'Bless you, sir.' Jake sounded genuinely grateful. 'I am sorry if I startled you and your companion. I did what I did because I was desperate, see? I had to find out why Laura had been locked away.'

''I understand, Jake.' William held out his hand. This took Jake by surprise. It's highly unlikely that he'd ever been offered a handshake before by a gentleman of William's class. Nevertheless, he clasped William's hand and thanked him again.

Within moments, Jake vanished back into the shadows, the soldiers mounted their horses, and William took up the reins of the little cart. They soon resumed their progress through the wood.

Thomas said, 'Evidently, Colonel Brampton considers your safety a priority. He ordered the soldiers to keep a close eye on you.'

William nodded. 'A wise precaution as it turned out.' He glanced at Thomas beside him. 'Shall we continue our tour?'

'Absolutely. However, I must say that disguising yourself as a coachman hasn't been at all successful. Jake recognized you.'

'Then I should try a little harder. Next time a postman, or a shepherd, or a priest all dressed in black?'

'Perhaps your safety isn't something you should jest about?'

'You're right. This isn't a game, is it? We live in a world where tragedy might lie around the very next corner, isn't that so, Thomas?'

That night, Thomas wrote an account of his first day at Newydd Hall. Or, to be more precise, he wrote two accounts. One would be for his newspaper when Inspector Abberline gave him permission to publish details of the case; the other report of the day's events would be posted to Abberline in Scotland, where the detective was conducting his investigation into the slaying of Thaddeus Denby by an assassin's bullet.

He sat at a small table by the window, re-reading his report by lamplight. Here and there, he made corrections, or added what might prove to be a salient fact. And yet Thomas had very little to say about anything that could help the investigation along. He had made a tour of the sprawling estate here in Wales; he'd visited the grave of

William's brother, who'd died three years ago. William Denby didn't know anything but hearsay about the Gods of Rome; certainly no facts that would prove useful. All in all, the case was becoming even more mysterious and baffling.

Thomas pushed open the window for a breath of fresh air. Winds sighed about the eaves of the house. Stars shone through thinning cloud, revealing the dark, hump-backed shapes of mountains. He leaned out, his hands resting on the window ledge, his head fully out in the cool, night air. His bedroom was located on the third floor. From this height, the ground seemed a long way beneath him. His body suddenly tensed as he saw a face staring up at him – a ghostly, shimmering face at that. A pair of eyes locked onto him with a startling intensity. Thomas had been on the point of shouting a challenge, demanding to know why they stared up at him, when he let out a sigh of relief and chuckled. Fool that I am, he thought. I'm seeing my own reflection. His eye adjusted to the starlight. Dash it all, he'd been gazing into a horse trough for– he'd seen nothing more than the reflection of his own face. The breeze blew harder, causing the eerie mirror-image of his features to disintegrate into ripples.

Quite abruptly, he froze as an idea occurred to him – an idea that was so striking that his skin tingled. He thought: I saw my reflection from an unusual angle and it seemed to be stranger staring up at me. What if I were to look at aspects of this case from a different angle? Would that help?

Thomas continued to stand at the window as he recalled the list of Denby brothers who had died violent deaths. They'd all apparently been killed by accident; the conclusions of the various coroners. So which death stood out? The most unusual death in this catalogue of dead siblings was, Thomas fancied, the one that hadn't aroused any suspicion whatsoever ... the death of Joshua Denby; he'd been claimed by illness in this very house three years ago. At that moment, Thomas heard the sound of soft weeping. Leaning further out of the window, he looked up. Pale hands protruded beyond the window ledge above his. That must be one of the attic rooms, he decided. A servant's room. One of the maids must be in distress for some reason.

Thomas called out gently, 'Hello up there. What's wrong?'

A face appeared some ten feet above his. Against the night sky, it appeared as a striking, pale oval; a pair of glittering eyes looked down at him.

The woman whispered, 'I've seen you before in a dream ... leave this place ... leave tonight ... you are in danger. Death follows you, and he is coming ever closer.'

The face vanished abruptly, leaving him alone. Meanwhile, a cold breeze came down from the mountains to ghost through the forest – it sounded like the long, heartfelt sigh of a lost and despairing soul, or so it seemed to Thomas Lloyd.

The next morning Thomas went downstairs and happened to see William Denby in the conservatory: he was pushing a girl in a wheelchair along a little avenue created by potted ferns. She was around ten years of age, had soft, blonde curls that hung down over her shoulders, and her eyes were the same bright blue as William's. Thomas had planned to mention his encounter with the maid last night, the same one who'd been struck down by mental sickness. She'd peered down at him from the window above his, and her words still resonated: *'I've seen you before in a dream ... leave this place ... leave tonight ... you are in danger. Death follows you, and he is coming ever closer.'* The poor girl must be bewitched by terrifying hallucinations. But meeting William like this, in the company of the invalid child, wasn't the appropriate moment to discuss one of his servants.

'Ah,' William said, 'good morning, Thomas. This is my daughter, Edith. Say "hello" to Mr Lloyd, Edith.'

'Good morning, Mr Lloyd. Are you the newspaper man from London?'

'Indeed I am, Edith.'

The girl's smile was a cheerful one. 'I am very much sorry that I cannot stand to greet you. I'm not as well as I might be this morning. The damp is in my chest again.'

'I'm sorry to hear that, Edith.'

'Will you write about my father's work here?'

'If your father allows it, I would be honoured.'

'He's a brave man, isn't he? To fly through the sky, higher than eagles?'

'He is very brave, Edith. I admire him and I believe millions of other people do so as well.'

This pleased the girl. She grinned up at her father. 'Did you hear that, Papa? Mr Lloyd has declared you famous.'

William smiled back. 'The gentleman is most kind.'

'Kindness be damned. Mr Lloyd speaks the truth.'

'Edith, don't swear in front of guests.'

Edith giggled. 'I will be famous, too, when I fly in my father's balloon. He promises to carry me halfway to heaven.' She giggled again; however, the sound immediately turned to bout of coughing.

William crouched beside her. 'Remember: slow, deep breaths. Try to rest for a while.'

She coughed again. Even so, she gave a mischievous smile. 'Rest be damned.'

He spoke softly. 'Shush there, my dear. Catch your breath.' A woman in a white uniform appeared at the door. 'Ah, Nurse. Will you take Edith to her room? She should have peace and quiet for a while.'

Edith continued to cough, the effect of which seemed to rob the girl of her strength; her head drooped downwards; her shoulders sagged.

After they'd gone, Thomas said, 'I'm sorry to have interrupted you. I hadn't realized there was anyone in the conservatory.'

'Well, you won't have seen us hidden by this jungle.' Denby brushed his hand against the ferns. 'But don't apologize. This area is for my team and guests alike to use. Common ground, as it were. A little public park indoors.'

'Your daughter has a winning personality.'

'And she swears like a grenadier.' William smiled. 'Edith has to spend a lot of time in bed, resting. She hears soldiers talking outside in the gardens. They have, shall we say, an exotic vocabulary.'

'I trust Edith will feel better soon.'

'There are good days and bad days.' He smiled sadly. 'If I have a relentlessly cheerful disposition, it's for the sake of my daughter and wife. The girl is quite poorly, you know.'

'I'm sorry to hear that.' Thomas didn't wish to pry into such delicate matters as the health of the man's daughter so began to make his excuses in order to leave William alone. However, William beckoned him closer.

'Thomas, you'll probably hear this from others, but I'd prefer that you hear it from my lips. Edith had an older sister. Mary had the same condition – a weakness of the lungs. It's a congenital illness, which occurs from time to time in my wife's side of the family. Mary was bedridden for much of her young life. One day, when she was sixteen, I was sitting reading to her. All of a sudden, she sat up very straight and, when she spoke it was with such a note of surprise, "Papa," she said, "I cannot cough". Mary had a tenacious cough, just like Edith's. She needed to cough to clear her lungs. I saw Mary's face grow pale, and I knew at that moment, not only could she no longer cough, she could no longer breathe normally. I carried her outside where the fresh air might revive her.' He sighed as he gazed through the window. 'My lovely, gentle Mary, with her blue eyes and blonde curls, just like

Edith's, slipped away as I held her in my arms.'

'I am so sorry to hear about your loss, William. I truly am.'

'Thank you, Thomas.' He sucked in lungful of air as if he absolutely appreciated the value of this life-giving atmosphere. 'Colonel Brampton orders me to mount guns on the balloon, so we can destroy our enemies from the sky. But you know, Thomas, I am deceiving him. The real reason I press forward with my work on airships is because high altitudes benefit people with lung complaints. I want, with all my heart, to fly little Edith to an altitude where the air is so clear and so pure that she will be healed, and she will not suffer the same fate as her sister. My balloon, God willing, will save Edith's life.'

He continued to stare silently out of the window. No doubt the man lived in that dreadful moment all those years ago when he had carried his daughter Mary outside, and prayed that she would breathe again. After a while, Thomas quietly withdrew from the room.

'Sorry, sir.' The soldier's manner was polite, yet firm. 'I can't allow you into the balloon sheds, sir.'

Thomas had decided to explore the grounds near the house. When he'd approached the large, white buildings the soldier had appeared and held up his hand.

'I'm sorry to have troubled you,' Thomas said. 'The work here is confidential, isn't it?'

'Yes, sir.'

'Have you noticed any strangers hereabouts recently? Particularly foreigners?'

'I couldn't say, sir.' The man remained impeccably polite. 'You would have to make such enquires with the colonel.'

'Of course, good day.' Thomas touched the brim of his hat and retraced his steps.

A gardener hoed soil that had the same fine consistency as pastry crumbs. Thomas strolled toward the man, intending to convey the impression that he was merely enjoying the April sunlight. The gardener, a man of fifty or so with a huge white beard, paused just long enough to say, 'G'morning.'

'Good morning.' Thomas smiled. 'A splendid day.'

'If you say so, sir.'

'Have you worked here long?'

'Five years or more.'

'Your accent indicates you aren't a Welshman.'

'No, sir. It was the old master's intention that staff be transferred from one house to the other every few months.'

'But, of late, you've avoided such removals?'

'The ground is difficult to work here, sir.' He deftly used the hoe to cut out a thistle. 'Gardeners and gamekeepers are kept here on account of their knowledge of the land.'

'I see. So you were here when Mr Joshua Denby took ill and died?'

'Yes, sir. Three years ago, it was. The household was bereft, sir.'

'Was it a long illness?'

'He became afflicted in summer, got took winter.'

'Do you recall the symptoms?'

The gardener's eyes swivelled toward Thomas in surprise. 'Symptoms? I wouldn't know, sir. And it wasn't for the likes of me to know.'

'There must have been talk? You know how servants chatter.'

'I'm a gardener. I'm no chatterer.' Then he said pointedly, 'My work demands so much of me that I've no time for idle gossip.'

Thomas saw what the man implied. 'I shouldn't keep you.' He smiled. 'Though it's been a pleasure to talk to you.'

'Very kind of you, sir.'

An idea suddenly occurred to Thomas. 'You pay such close attention to the flower beds, you'd notice if there was anything amiss about them?'

'Amiss?'

'For example, you'd notice if there were footprints in the soil.'

'You mean left by trespassers?'

Thomas nodded. 'They'd indicate if anyone was hiding amongst the bushes and so on?'

'The colonel asks me to watch out for footprints and the like.'

'Oh?'

'It's them war balloons. The colonel doesn't want foreign spies stealing the master's plans.'

Thomas thanked the gardener and wished him good day. The gardener returned to his never-ending task of hoeing league upon league of flower beds. Thomas noticed that the boy who cleaned the household's boots came toward him at a run.

'Telegram, sir. Telegram!' The boy waved a small envelope.

'Thank you,' Thomas said, as the boy skidded to a halt. 'Best wait, in case I need to send a reply.'

Thomas opened the envelope and pulled out a slip of paper. The message was from his editor at the newspaper. Thomas's article about how Abberline had identified the pickpocket at the London railway station by simply observing the thief's mannerisms had captured the public's imagination. The entire print run of the newspaper had sold out in record time. Readers clamoured for another story about the famous detective. Indeed, the editor, himself, clamoured for more Abberline stories. The message ended with the exclamations : GIVE ME MORE! MORE! MORE!

Such praise – such success! This pleased Thomas, but he couldn't yet deliver reports of the Denby case for publication. What occurred to Thomas was that he could write up the account of Abberline's defeat of the bully who attacked the child because of the spilt milk.

The boy asked, 'Want to telegram a reply, sir?'

He took out a pencil and wrote on the envelope: YOU SHALL HAVE MORE! 'Please have those words telegraphed back to the sender.'

The boy dashed away to the house, thrilled to be given the task of conveying such messages. Thomas decided to return to the house, too. Perhaps he could saunter the corridors until he came upon domestic staff and engage them in conversation. He might be able to extract some valuable nuggets of information regarding Joshua Denby's death. Thomas also found himself thinking about William Denby. The man's character was much deeper and much more complex than he'd hitherto thought. Initially, William's personality had been as bright and breezy as this April morning; however, Thomas hadn't known about the man's sick child. The girl, Edith, was unable to walk. William had confessed in a heartfelt way that another daughter of his had died of the same lung condition when she was sixteen. Moreover, the man had declared that he was exploiting the army's interest in his flight experiments in order to build a balloon that would carry his daughter to an altitude that might alleviate or cure the weakness in her lung. The man would be worried to the very depths of his being about his daughter. He could imagine William and his wife discussing what could be done to alleviate her suffering, and William endeavouring to give Mrs Denby hope with optimistic plans about an altitude cure.

Thomas, deeply immersed in his thoughts, walked with his head down and his fists thrust into his pockets. The notion of a remedy that involved taking the patient aloft in a balloon where the air was purer wasn't so outlandish. He knew many ill people who used the services of mountain-top sanatoriums. Spending time at high altitude, the doctors said, helped ease those suffering from tuberculosis, or bronchitis, or other such maladies of the lung.

He turned the corner of the stable and nearly collided with a figure. 'Penny for your thoughts, Thomas.'

'Inspector?' Thomas couldn't hide his delight at seeing the man.

'Good morning, a boy told me that you were out taking the air.'

'Dash it all, it is good to see you.' He shook the detective's hand warmly. 'Did you learn anything in Scotland about our case?'

Abberline smiled. 'And good to see you, too. I'll tell you about my findings regarding the death of Thaddeus Denby, although to be frank, I discovered very little of value. And what of you? Have you found anything of interest?'

'There's plenty of interest. Here in Wales we have ships that sail through the sky. There is a maidservant who claims she can see into the future. Yet, sadly, there is nothing relevant to the case.'

Abberline fixed his eyes on Thomas – those shrewd eyes, which seemed to read what was on his mind. 'Nothing? Absolutely nothing?'

'There is one oddity – yet it isn't an oddity at all.' Thomas shrugged.

'Let me guess at what's troubling you.'

Thomas laughed. 'I'm sure you never will.'

'Joshua Denby, the man who died peacefully in bed. That's what you find odd.'

'That's precisely what I've been asking myself. How the devil did you know that his death had been on my mind?'

'Because it's been on mine. The truth of the matter is that his death, if it was murder, is crucial to this investigation.'

'How do we prove it was murder?'

'We raise him from his tomb. Joshua Denby's corpse is vitally important. It's evidence!'

CHAPTER 20

'DRINK YOUR MEDICINE.'

Laura knew she had no choice. She took the glass of cloudy liquid from the housekeeper and drank it down. Miss Groom pointed at the bed.

'Hop back in there, girl. Get some sleep.'

'But it's morning, the sun is shining.'

'Sleep will make you better.' Miss Groom primly regarded Laura through those peculiar spectacles with the half-moon lenses. 'What's more, rest will dispel those strange notions of yours.'

Laura sat down on the bed and smoothed out the creases in her nightdress. 'Once I read a story about a pig that spoke our language.'

'That's absurd. Lie down, girl.'

'But what if you were looking at your fingertips and all of a sudden human lips budded there, and they all opened up at once into little mouths, and began to sing a song? You'd go mad, wouldn't you?'

'Hush your nonsense.' Miss Groom hung a nightdress over the back of a chair. 'There's a fresh one for when you wake up.'

'What I'm saying is serious. Just imagine if seeing into the future has such an effect on my mind that it makes me act strangely.'

'The drug should be working by now. Are you sure you drank it all?'

Laura went to the window. Down there in the sunlight, a pair of men stood by the stable block. She'd seen the young man before. He was now in the company of another gent who had a moustache and sideburns – this man was older than the other man. They were deep in conversation.

'Who are those gentlemen, Miss Groom?'

'That's none of your business, Laura. Climb into bed, girl, chop-chop.'

'I've seen them before. I had one of my visions of the future and I

128

saw them. They're not safe here.'

'Laura—'

Laura pounded on the window pane. *'Up here! Listen to me! You're in danger!'*

That was the moment the drug flooded her senses. Brilliant colours burst from the walls. The sky turned red – red as blood – as if the heart of the universe had been torn open.

CHAPTER 21

'WHAT ON EARTH goes on in this place?' Abberline asked, looking up at the attic window.

A girl in a white nightdress pounded on the glass, while shouting in a panicky, frightened way. Thomas couldn't make out the meaning of her cries from this distance.

'That's the maidservant who is ill with her nerves.'

'The poor girl.'

Thomas told the detective about the boy from the village; how he leapt onto the carriage, and the dramatic intervention by the soldiers.

Thomas said, 'Her name is Laura. She is the girl I told you about who insists she is cursed with visions of the future. I saw her leaning out of the window last night. She shouted down to me that I was in danger and must leave at once.'

'I hope they are giving her medical care.'

'William Denby's personal physician is attending to her. I'm sure all is in hand.'

Thomas watched as an older woman drew the unfortunate maid back from the window. Within moments, the screams fell silent. Thomas found himself full of pity for the girl. He couldn't help but wonder how he'd feel if his fiancée became stricken by madness. A condition that warped a person's thoughts in such a ghastly way would seem like demonic possession.

Abberline had been thinking along similar lines. 'Two hundred years ago they would have declared that the girl had the devil inside her. They'd have burned her at the stake.'

They strolled through the gardens for a while. Abberline gazed at the mountains, though clearly he was mulling over the Denby case.

He said, 'William is the last brother to be in charge of one of the family's country estates.'

'Surely there is still Victor Denby at Fairfax Manor?'

'Gone to France. Boarded a ferry yesterday. Scotland Yard telegraphed to say that he'd taken himself off to a secret address.'

'He fears for his life.'

'As I fear for William Denby's.' Abberline thoughtfully stroked his moustache. 'The killer's available prey has been reduced to one.'

Thomas nodded greetings at soldiers who patrolled the grounds. 'At least the man is guarded well. Or rather his work is guarded well, which perhaps amounts to the same thing.'

'Unless we catch our suspect it will only be a matter of time before William Denby is taken, too. We are dealing with a cunning and ruthless assassin.'

They strolled along a series of archways formed by basketwork on which climbing plants grew.

'This will be astonishing in summer,' Abberline murmured. 'Imagine the clematis blooms forming a fragrant tunnel. It would be like a passage to wonderland.'

Thomas decided to ask Inspector Abberline to elaborate on something he'd said earlier. 'You mentioned that Joshua Denby might unlock this mystery?'

'His corpse might do so.'

'You suspect foul play?'

'The other Denby fatalities were judged to be accidental. However, we now suspect otherwise.'

'I learnt from a gardener that Joshua fell sick in the summer and died in the winter.'

'Interesting.'

'What if he did suffer from some illness, but an intruder suffocated him in his sleep?'

'Possibly.'

'One word answers, Inspector. You're hiding what you really think.'

'Speculation can be entertaining, yet it's hardly likely to bring definitive proof.'

'You plan to disinter the man's body?'

'We must, Thomas, we must.'

'He's been three years in the tomb.'

'Viewing the corpse is essential. If I my suspicions are correct, I only have to look into its face.'

Thomas chuckled, although it was such a grim chuckle. 'You don't claim to have supernatural insight, do you?'

'What? Like the poor, unfortunate girl in the attic?' Abberline paused to smell blossom on a bush. 'No, oh no … we are definitely in the realm of science, not the world of witchcraft.' Regretfully, he released his hold on the blossom. Its fragrance masked some of the more pungent realities of life. 'Do you know how to use a camera?'

'Yes.'

'Good. Because it's important that we have a forensically accurate record of what we find in the coffin. I need you to photograph the corpse the instant the lid is removed.'

'Blast it all!' the colonel thundered. *'Get those two men away from here!'*

The man's face turned from pink to fiery red as he glared at Thomas and Abberline in fury. Colonel Brampton stood on the lawn beside a structure some five feet in height, which resembled a cage made from lengths of bamboo. The cage contained a number of glittering cylinders, while extending from the bamboo framework were dozens of thin ropes that formed a neat spider's web pattern on the ground.

Colonel Brampton yelled at a soldier, 'Remove those two men from here immediately!'

William Denby sat cross-legged on the ground nearby. He'd been examining drawings on a sheet of paper.

Inspector Abberline walked swiftly toward Brampton. He didn't seem at all perturbed by the man erupting with anger.

Thomas recognized the cylindrical objects in the bamboo cage. These were war rockets of a type that had been developed by William Hale. In those two-foot-long tubes, gunpowder would have been tightly packed. When ignited, the gunpowder burned at a furious rate, flinging the rocket 2000 yards or more into the faces of the enemy. Each rocket contained an explosive warhead, highly effective at killing both men and cavalry horses. Thomas immediately made the connection between the bamboo frame, containing the rockets, and William Denby's development of the military airship. The blustering, redfaced Colonel Brampton obviously intended to use a balloon to carry the rocket launcher high above the Earth where it could be tested as a weapon of war.

Brampton now appeared more than ready to wage war here on the ground. Furiously, he strode toward Abberline with the intention of blocking the man's way.

The officer bellowed, 'There was a guard standing on that path. How did you get past him?'

Abberline spoke softly in comparison. 'I introduced myself and explained that I had to speak with Mr Denby regarding an urgent matter.'

'I am engaged in military research, which is top secret!'

'And I, Colonel, am investigating the murder of that gentleman's brothers.' Abberline nodded in the direction of William Denby who climbed to his feet.

'This is hardly the place or the time to discuss that with him now.' Brampton turned to the soldier and barked, 'Take these gentlemen back to the house. Now!'

'No, Colonel.' Abberline continued to speak calmly. 'I need a word with Mr Denby. There is something he should know, and it will not wait.'

'I am Colonel Brampton. I am in charge here.'

'You've met Mr Lloyd, I gather. My name is Abberline.'

'Of Scotland Yard. Yes, I know.'

'So, Colonel … will you grant me a few moments alone with Mr Denby?'

'Our work is of national importance. Time is of the essence.'

'Then shall we joust?'

'I beg your pardon?' The colonel was so surprised by this comment that his eyes goggled. 'Joust? What the devil do you mean?'

'Joust.' A twinkle appeared in Abberline's eye; he knew his comment had knocked the soldier off balance, metaphorically speaking. 'Jousting is what knights did in olden times, isn't it? They rode at one another on horseback and tried to unseat their opponent with a lance.'

'Great God in Heaven! You're a senior detective and you talk in riddles.'

'We will joust.' Abberline produced a letter from his pocket. 'Instead of being armed with lances, we are armed with the weapons of our authority. You have the authority of your generals; I have the authority of the Home Secretary.'

Brampton's eyes fixed on the letter. He read the first few lines then stared in astonishment at the signature at the bottom. 'The Home Secretary?' The man almost stammered the words.

'I have the authority to go wherever I please here in order to investigate my case. Of course, you may telegraph your commanding officer should you wish to dispute anything contained in the Home Secretary's letter.'

Brampton clicked his tongue. 'That won't be necessary. Here. Take back your letter ... go where you wish.'

Thomas could almost hear the Colonel thinking: *Go to hell, too, whilst you're about it.*

Abberline approached William Denby and Thomas quickly made the introductions as the men shook hands.

William's eyes twinkled. When they were out of earshot of Brampton he said, 'Not many men stand up to the fiery Colonel Brampton, even fewer get the better of him. You've done both, Inspector.'

'I spoke the truth, Mr Denby. We must move quickly, because there is a dangerous assassin out there.'

'You have my absolute co-operation, Inspector. But, please, call me William. Thomas is, of course, on first name terms with me.'

'As you wish.'

'I wasn't expecting you for several days, Inspector. The last I heard you were investigating my brother's death in Scotland.'

'Your brother appears to have been slain by a marksman, so I realized that I should come here as quickly as possible. There is no doubt in my mind whatsoever, that you are in danger.'

'Thank you for taking my safety so seriously.'

Abberline said, 'I've spoken in such plain terms about the danger, because there isn't time to dress this up in polite phrases. Even as we stand here now, there might be a man aiming a rifle at you.'

'I understand.'

'To continue my plain-speaking, I have to reveal something which will be distressing and painful to you.'

'By all means, speak plainly. I welcome your directness.'

'Your late brother, Joshua Denby.'

'What of him?'

'I need to examine his body.'

'That's not possible.' Shock flitted across William's face. 'He was buried three years ago.'

'Nevertheless, the physical remains must be examined. I need to make urgent arrangements to exhume the body. There is a distinct possibility your brother was murdered.'

Inspector Abberline suggested that they speak somewhere private. Abberline asked if Thomas could be present, too. William had no objection, and soon they were sitting in the drawing room's comfortable armchairs, with sunlight spilling in through tall windows. Abberline dispensed with small-talk and got down to the matter in hand. He explained how Sir Alfred had died. How an ingeniously rigged pistol inside a cupboard had detonated gunpowder, leading to Sir Alfred being killed in what the coroner mistakenly judged to be an accident. Abberline also outlined the facts surrounding the death of William's brother in Scotland. Without a shadow of doubt, murder: a concealed gunman had fired a bullet into the heart of Thaddeus Denby. When William asked questions Abberline answered as conscientiously and as thoroughly as he could.

When William asked if there were any suspects Abberline said, 'Thomas chased an intruder at Fairfax Manor. The individual had been watching us there, and had attacked two men. We don't have a great deal of information about the suspect, other than he is a man of about forty years of age, and that he wore a distinctive yellow coat. Possibly he is from overseas; a witness revealed that he had a strong foreign accent.'

The butler brought in a tray, bearing cups and a teapot. William waited until the man withdrew before saying, 'You told me, Inspector, that you need to unearth my brother, Joshua.'

'What I find in the grave could be vital to solving this case.'

'I understand, although I find the notion distressing. The buried should remain buried.'

Abberline nodded. 'However, it is necessary, William, absolutely necessary.'

Thomas noticed the sadness in William's eyes. The man appeared to be remembering another tragic death and another funeral. This melancholy subject of graves no doubt summoned the raw grief of his daughter's passing and her funeral. Perhaps Thomas was cursed with having too-vivid an imagination, yet he absolutely believed that William saw himself holding his 16 year-old daughter as her lips turned from pink to blue and her eyes grew dull. Thomas tried to dispel morbid images of the girl's funeral. Or imagining the silence of the tomb ... the eternal nothingness ...

William took a deep breath. 'Yes, of course, you must do as you think fit, Inspector. I will ask the colonel for the loan of some of his men. They will open the grave on your command.'

'Thank you, but exhumation of the dead involves an elaborate legal process. I must obtain an order of exhumation from the authorities. The opening of the grave and the lifting of the coffin has, by law, to be carried out as early in the morning as possible, which will probably mean during the hours of darkness. This is to avoid the exhumation becoming a ghoulish spectacle for passers-by. Also, Thomas will be present with a camera. It's essential that he photograph the body the instant the coffin lid is raised.'

'I see.' William grimaced as if a foul taste oozed across his tongue. 'Will you need to bring my brother's remains here?'

'A secure outbuilding is more than adequate. Then a doctor will conduct a detailed examination.'

'Dear God, this is macabre.' William's hand shook as he picked up a tea cup. 'Damned macabre. We've become grave robbers.'

'You, yourself, needn't be present at the exhumation,' Abberline said. 'The process will be conducted with absolute respect. As soon as the examination is complete, your brother will be laid to rest again.'

William took a swallow of tea. 'I have every faith in you, Inspector. Newspapers talk of your compassion and integrity. When you were in pursuit of that devil, Jack the Ripper, you didn't go home after your day's work; you walked Whitechapel's streets, guarding women from the butcher.' William shook off his air of gloom. 'I'll have a room made up for you. Do you require anything else?'

'May I have the use of an office? And a blackboard and easel?'

'Of course.' William pulled a velvet cord by the fireplace. Downstairs, a bell would ring to summon the butler. 'Goodness, I'm the only Denby brother in charge of a country estate now. A sobering thought.'

Abberline sipped his tea. 'You know that your brother, Victor, has left for France?'

'He telegraphed me this morning. The man is scared for his life. I can't blame him for deciding that a dignified retreat is preferable to waiting for the assassin's bullet.'

Thomas asked, 'There are several other country estates owned by the Denby family; who will oversee them now?'

'My eldest brother, Hubert, before leaving for Africa, stipulated that a Land Agent be appointed to manage estate properties if there were an insufficient number of siblings to do the job. Though I suspect those big country houses will lie empty until a new tenant comes along.'

The butler glided into the room. William gave instructions to prepare a guest bedroom for Abberline, and to find a suitable room that would serve as an office. While the tea things were cleared away, and William spoke to his butler, Thomas stood beside Abberline at the window. Abberline's sharp eyes swept the line of trees at the forest's edge. Thomas half-expected to glimpse the flash of a yellow coat. All he did see emerging from the forest was a horse, drawing a cart piled with logs.

Thomas murmured, 'No sign of the God Thief yet.'

'God Thief?' Abberline smiled. 'You gave our suspect a name?'

'He did steal a carved god from the workshop.'

'Ha. Then we'll refer to our suspect as the God Thief until we have his real name. Hmm, now that you've mentioned the carvings it's probably timely to acquaint our host with another facet of this case.'

Abberline waited until the butler withdrew before telling William about the secret pagan shrine devoted to Roman gods, and that apparently Sir Alfred had worshipped there, and had made offerings of food and wine.

William was stunned. He slumped down into an armchair, shaking his head as he did so. 'Good God.' He attempted to smile, but horror shone from his eyes. 'Or perhaps I should exclaim "By Jove". After all, he was chief of the gods, as it were.'

'It must be bizarre to learn that your brother prayed to pagan idols,' Abberline said.

'Did he go mad?'

'I suspect he was involved with stealing the golden statues known as the Gods of Rome. For some reason, he began to fear that the Roman Gods had the power to punish him for the theft. He tried to appease them.'

This revelation hit William. 'My brother was eccentric, but this? It's blasphemous.'

'The intruder, whom Thomas chased, stole a carving of Faunus from the shrine.'

'Ah ...'

'Does that mean something to you?'

'I heard about this Gods of Rome business as a young man. I decided it was all wild rumour and didn't give it much credence. After all, Alfred was never arrested, and the statues were never found. As a child, however, mythology interested me – mainly, because it contained stories about people inventing fabulous ways to fly.' He chuckled. 'There were tales of adventurers tethering birds to chairs and being carried away. There were stranger methods, too, such as gathering dew in jars and waiting for the sun to rise, because it was once believed that the sun had the power to make the morning dew rise into the air. Of all things, when I was a schoolboy, I actually soaked my clothes in dew one morning and waited for the sun to carry me above the treetops.' He shook his head, remembering. 'All I succeeded in doing was catching a cold.'

Abberline smiled at the man's recollection then his face became grave. 'Thomas and I wondered why our suspect would steal the Faunus in particular.'

Thomas placed his fingertips together. 'Let's see, what do I know of Faunus? Hmm, it's such a long time ago since I read those books. I remember that in the ancient world gods often went by different names. Faunus was also known as Pan or Silvanus. He played a flutelike instrument while beautiful nymphs danced. Faunus lived in dangerous, wilderness places – the kind of forest where a man could find himself threatened by wild animals and bandits. Ah ....' William held up his finger as he recalled another fact. 'Faunus had the power to fill human beings with a dread of the unknown. He could make people frightened without them knowing what had frightened them. Faunus's other name is Pan, of course, from which the word "panic" is derived. You could say Faunus is the god of irrational terror. Perhaps your suspect stole the Faunus carving in order to send us a message.'

Thomas asked, 'What could such a message mean?'

Abberline thought for a moment. 'Perhaps our suspect is warning us to be terrified of what we *cannot* see? To be scared of our own shadow.'

'The he is reminding us of the curse of the Gods of Rome,' said Thomas.

They sat there without speaking. Dark clouds covered the sun, and the gloom appeared to forewarn that the days ahead harboured a threat of peril. Thomas recalled the maid's words as she called down from the window in panic (that word again –PANIC: a god-inflicted terror that makes the heart pound and clouds the senses). The girl had shouted: '*Leave this place ... you are in danger. Death follows you, and he is coming ever closer. ...*'

That afternoon brought a change of mood to the inhabitants of Newydd Hall. Warm sunshine bathed the house and gardens. *What makes the place sunnier,* Thomas Lloyd realized, *is that Colonel Brampton isn't here.* The Colonel had announced in that characteristically bad-tempered way of his that he would take the train to Liverpool to discuss confidential matters with a superior, and that he wouldn't return until tomorrow.

Everyone in the house seemed that bit more cheerful after that. Soldiers whistled music hall tunes, guards smiled and nodded at Thomas and Abberline as they examined the grounds. The troops were at ease with themselves now that their commanding officer wasn't breathing fire down their necks.

Abberline, however, remained troubled. He scanned the forest and the Welsh hills. 'A marksman could pick any more of a hundred places to wait until William Denby appeared. A modern rifle, equipped with a telescopic sight, can kill from a quarter of a mile away.'

Thomas nodded. 'However, it will be impossible to keep William indoors. The military are pressing him hard to make more flights.'

'Perhaps that's where the man will be safest: high in the clouds where the assassin can't find him.'

They strolled by a broad terrace at the side of the house. William sat there, between his daughter in the wheelchair, and a lady whom Thomas did not recognise. William beckoned them.

'Inspector. Thomas. Allow me to introduce you to my wife. This is Prudence.'

An attractive woman of forty-five years of age, or thereabouts, dressed in white muslin held out her hand. They exchanged social pleasantries for a while.

William said, 'Thomas has already met Edith, my daughter.'

'Good day again.' Thomas raised his hat to the girl in the chair.

The girl smiled brightly. 'Will you write about this gathering for your newspaper? How will you describe us? Isn't Mama lovely in her white dress? The sunshine demands that we dress cheerfully, don't you agree?'

William laughed. 'Edith, don't bombard the gentleman with questions.'

'I should like to be a newspaper reporter when I grow up,' Edith said. 'I shall write about events from a woman's point-of-view, because men too often interpret the world, and all that occurs upon it, from their perspective.'

Abberline spoke cheerfully. 'Your daughter has such a wise head on her shoulders.'

Prudence tut-tutted. 'Edith, my dear, young ladies do not aspire for careers in any profession, let alone journalism.'

'The world is changing, Mama. Isn't that so, Inspector?'

'Indeed so, yet sometimes I fear it changes too quickly. The minds of men and women appear to lag behind the pace of material progress, and it vexes them.'

Edith's intelligent eyes lit up with delight. 'Haven't I had similar opinions in the past, Papa? Progress is like a torrent that catches hold of men and women and rushes them along so quickly that they are bewildered by the pace of change. Marvellous machines are being invented all the time. Why, only yesterday, I read about a new kind of photographic device that creates a moving picture.'

Prudence appeared discomfited by her daughter's interests. 'I'm sure the Inspector and Thomas are too busy to hear about these flights of fancy.'

Abberline smiled. 'On the contrary, I am very interested.'

Edith beamed. 'Just imagine. If such a camera were used here at this moment, we would see moving pictures of ourselves tomorrow, or ten years from now, and we'd be just as we are now. We would see Thomas nodding his head, just as he does at this moment. I would see my mouth moving as I speak – as it moves now. And we would look at my mother shaking her head, because what I say alarms her.'

The girl's mother still shook her head. 'Your subject matter doesn't alarm me. What does worry me is that you'll tire yourself speaking so much.'

'I feel well this afternoon, Mama.'

William patted his daughter's hand fondly. 'Nevertheless, it wouldn't be wise to over-do things, especially after the way you were coughing this morning.'

Edith gave a regretful sigh. 'Very well. Though I do enjoy discussing this strange and wonderful world we live in.'

'Gracious.' Prudence Denby laughed. 'You are ten years old, but you have the ways of a university professor.'

William kissed his daughter on the cheek. 'And I value her more than can be said.' He turned to Abberline and Thomas. 'Gentlemen, seeing as the colonel is away I'll give you a tour of our workshops. You can witness for yourselves what I've devoted my professional life to these past twenty-five years.'

Edith grinned. 'One day I'll fly up above the clouds with you, won't I, Papa?'

'One day.' He smiled back at his daughter. 'Yes, one day.'

Thomas walked with Abberline and William toward the white sheds that formed the balloon workshops.

William asked, 'Do you know yet when you will open up my brother's grave?'

Abberline said, 'The Burial Act of 1857 stipulates that I must obtain an exhumation licence before I can remove the body. I've written to the Secretary of State in accordance with the rules set out in the Act. If the licence arrives tomorrow, I can exhume the body early the following morning.'

'The exhumation will be respectful?'

'Yes, I guarantee it. Boards will be erected to screen the grave from public view. An official will also be present to oversee the operation; he'll ensure that the rules relating to the removal of the body are followed to the smallest detail.'

They walked in silence for a moment. Eventually, William glanced back at his daughter and wife on the terrace. 'Edith doesn't have friends of her own age. We're rather isolated here, and her lungs are so weak that she can't attend school, so she reads night and day.'

'And thinks a lot, too,' said Abberline. 'She is remarkably intelligent.'

'Prudence worries that Edith thinks too much; however, I encourage my daughter to have an independent mind.'

Thomas smiled. 'I believe she does have the aptitude and the intelligence to become a journalist when she is a grown woman.'

'I wish that could be so.' William's expression became grave. 'Her lungs are becoming weaker. My daughter, Mary, suffered from the same condition, as you know ... she died when she was sixteen. I have to accept the possibility – and it frightens me to say these words – that Edith might not survive beyond the age of eighteen or so.'

William opened the shed door and invited them in. He pointed out what he called the 'Endurance Cabin'. This was a basketwork carriage that would be suspended beneath a balloon when a long distance flight was necessary. There were bunk beds inside the Endurance Cabin, and Thomas recalled what William had admitted that morning, that he intended to carry his daughter on a balloon to a height where the purity of air might heal her lungs. Thomas guessed that this cabin would house the girl for that journey high above the earth. Colonel Brampton, however, undoubtedly believed this would house artillery spotters and the like for military purposes. *Not William, though,* Thomas told himself. *For him, this is the vehicle that will save his daughter's life.*

Later that afternoon, Inspector Abberline interviewed members of domestic staff in the office that William Denby had allocated to him. There was a table that served as a desk, along with a number of straight-backed chairs and a comfortable sofa. Windows overlooked the yard and outbuildings at the back of the house. A blackboard and easel stood in the centre of the room. Abberline chalked headings that he considered significant to the case. He used the name Thomas had given to their only suspect so far: GOD THIEF. Other names included WILIAM DENBY, JOSHUA DENBY (TO BE EXHUMED) and SIR ALFRED

DENBY. Abberline drew white lines that radiated outwards from SIR ALFRED DENBY, like the spokes of a wheel. At the end of most of these lines he added question marks. At the end of one line he wrote: GODS OF ROME. At the end of another: MURDER BY GUNPOWDER.

When he conducted the interviews with footmen, grooms, maid-servants and so on, he turned the easel so the blackboard faced the wall; that meant none of the staff could read what was written there. Because employees were rotated around the Denby country estates every few months, many weren't present at Newydd Hall when Joshua Denby had fallen sick and died. Those that were offered vague state-ments about the master becoming increasingly unwell and weak in the summer of three years ago, and that he expired in the Winter. A doctor recorded the cause of death as congestion of the blood, which could stem from any number of illnesses.

Abberline sighed as he read the death certificate. 'Congestion of the blood is a catchall cause of death. It's only slightly more specific than "died as a result of a visitation from God", which is sometimes still entered on death certificates – it's an elegant sounding phrase meaning the doctor didn't have a clue what killed his patient.'

Thomas decided to ask a question of his own that had been nagging at the back of his mind. 'Inspector, you produced a letter from the Home Secretary earlier. Isn't it unusual to have written authority from such a senior member of government?'

Abberline nodded. 'I allowed William to gain the impression that very important people in high office are concerned about the slaughter of the Denby brothers – they are, of course, just as they are concerned about other crimes – but what really does alarm them are the Gods of Rome. They want me to find those statues.'

'They really are that important?'

'The statues are historical artefacts rightfully belonging to Italy; they're also cast from gold, so immensely valuable. The Italian govern-ment want them back. They are building a museum in Rome. Those golden gods will be the museum's crowning glory.'

'There's more to this than helping the Italians furnish their museum, isn't there?'

'Most astute of you, Thomas. The fact of the matter is, the Gods of Rome scandal embarrassed our royal family and very nearly caused an international incident.'

'The royal family had no involvement in removing the statues from Italy, did they?'

'No. But if they'd accepted stolen goods, as it were, it would have provoked letters of protest from the Italian prime minister, and accusations of depriving Italy of her heritage. Countries have gone to war for less.'

'So, what are you really searching for here, Inspector? The man who killed the Denby brothers, or the golden statues?'

'Both, naturally. However, our prime minster desperately wants me to find those statues. In fact, he's told me that I should do everything humanly possible to get my hands on them.'

CHAPTER 22

Laura climbed out of bed to pour a drink of water from the jug. The powerful opiate she'd been given earlier had begun to leave her body. That slow withdrawal of narcotic left her dry-mouthed, sluggish and somehow jittery – as if she felt she should be doing something important but didn't know what. Laura also tried to open the door. Locked … I'm still a prisoner.

'I'll break out of here,' she said to herself. 'When I do, I'll set fire to the house.' She laughed and it sounded like the laughter of a drunkard. The drug hadn't completely left her yet.

She walked to the window in the hope of seeing Jake. The maid scanned the trees, aching to glimpse his face. Not so much as a sound left her throat, yet tears slowly rolled down her face. What had happened to her? Just last week she'd been a normal maidservant of eighteen. Her working days consisted of beating rugs, scrubbing floors, making up fires, polishing brass – all the usual duties of a maid who served in a country mansion. But something strange had invaded her mind this week. Suddenly, she had visions of the future. She saw how Captain Sefton would meet his death. He'd fallen out of the sky; his body broken by the cruel earth; those green eyes had stared up at her from where he lay; a river of blood had gushed from his mouth.

With a supreme effort, Laura clenched her fists, and willed her gaze to penetrate the gloom that gathered about the trees. Perhaps Jake was out there? Maybe he could see her, even if she couldn't see him? She raised her hand and waved. All the while, her eyes swept back and forth along the treeline, searching for a familiar figure.

Yes … there was a figure. She leaned forwards until her forehead pressed against the cold glass. A man stood beneath a big oak tree right at the edge of the forest. But: *no … it isn't Jake.* Her heart plummeted with disappointment.

'It's another vision,' she told herself. 'A spirit.'

The apparition stared back in her direction. It was too far away to make out its features. However, she didn't *feel* how she usually felt when she saw the white-faced phantom. There was no sense of becoming detached from reality. No unearthly music from a flute. No sense of terror. No panic.

Merely, a stranger gazed at her, that's all. She bit her lip hard. Pain stabbed through her skin. Therefore, the drug no longer numbed her. The world felt real. She could even catch aromas of beef being roasted for dinner. So ... the figure must be real, mustn't it? Why, then, was a man staring at Newydd Hall with such interest.

The man's features were completely invisible to her beneath the brim of his hat. His, coat, though, was striking.

The coat was yellow. Bright yellow.

The figure in the yellow coat raised a hand above its head and waved. Laura Morgan waved back, and thought she saw the man give a single nod to indicate that he'd noticed her. Then he glided back into the shadows and she could see him no more.

CHAPTER 23

THE FOLLOWING MORNING, after breakfast, Inspector Abberline continued interviewing the staff. A laborious task that involved repeating the same questions:

~ *Were you employed here when Joshua Denby fell ill three years ago?*
~ *Were you here at the time of his death?*
~ *Did you notice strangers in the grounds at or around that time?*

After the fifth servant had left the room Abberline exhaled loudly, and turned to Thomas who sat in a chair by the window where he made notes.

'All I can say with certainty,' Abberline said, 'is that that the answers are consistent. But they yield little in the way of useful information.'

Thomas checked his notes. 'So far, none of the staff that who was here during the months of Joshua's illness noticed anything unduly suspicious. They all say the same: that three years ago Joshua Denby fell ill during the summer and died in the winter.'

'And not one member of staff recalls hearing anything about trespassers being seen in the grounds.'

'It seems to me that we'll learn more from Joshua's dead body than the living.'

'For now, that appears to be the case.' Abberline took a piece of chalk and drew a thick, white line beneath the name SIR ALFRED DENBY. 'Most of the brothers, who are now deceased, were content to enjoy lives of leisure. The Denby brothers lived on income from the estates they managed. They spent their time fishing, shooting, playing cards, billiards and the like. None of those men led an industrious life. All were lazy, well-fed idlers, who were waited on by servants. They never married. They didn't even try to earn any more money. All except for ....' Abberline tapped the chalk against the name he'd just underscored.

'Sir Alfred?'

'He's the only one who inherited his father's zeal for profit. I had the opportunity to check the files before leaving London, and it seems Sir Alfred was known to the police. Although never charged with any crime, he had friends who were investigated over a diamond smuggling enterprise more than twenty years ago. No evidence attached itself to Sir Alfred. However, tax records reveal that he earned a substantial income through various business dealings, which weren't connected to farming at Fairfax Manor. What the tax records reveal is that he supplied materials to house-builders.'

A brisk knock sounded on the door. Abberline turned the blackboard to face the wall, so noone else would see what was written there.

Thomas checked names on a list. 'Ah, that'll be the housekeeper.' He opened the door. 'Miss Groom. Thank you for coming along.'

'Good morning,' said Abberline. 'Please do sit down, make yourself comfortable.'

'Thank you, sir.'

Miss Groom was perhaps fifty years of age. The woman was dressed in a black skirt, and a white blouse that had billowing sleeves: the clothing was typical of a housekeeper. On her nose rested a pair of spectacles. The lenses were half-moon shape, and quite small, so she tended to tilt her face downwards in order to peer over the top of the glasses.

Abberline asked the same questions he'd asked the other servants: mainly relating to whether or not she worked here when Joshua Denby took to his sickbed and died.

Miss Groom spoke with the calm assurance of someone accustomed to issuing commands to underlings, and to addressing members of the ruling class. In short, she had a formidable self-confidence. 'Sir, I served the master when he took ill in the July. He'd lost his appetite, he no longer showed any interest in golf, which, until then, he played every day, come rain or shine.'

'As housekeeper you must have seen Joshua Denby on a regular basis?'

'Yes, sir.'

'Would you describe his appearance as he became progressively unwell?'

'He appeared to grow old very fast, as if a day to us was a year to him. His hair used to be thick and dark brown, yet almost overnight it turned white and began to fall away. When I last saw him he was bedridden.'

'Were you here at the house when he died?'

'No, sir. You'll be aware that employees are rotated to different houses?'

Abberline nodded.

She peered over her spectacles at him. 'I transferred to the Scottish house in November. I heard in December that Mr Joshua Denby had been taken from us.'

'Thank you, Miss Groom, you have been most helpful.'

Miss Groom remained seated. 'Wouldn't you like to ask me more questions, sir?'

'Not unless you can think of anything that might be useful.'

'You asked other servants if they saw strangers in the area.'

'Oh, I quite forgot. Yes, did you see anyone, or hear of trespassers hereabouts?'

'A constable's wife in Porthmadog told me that a sailor, an oriental man, had stolen the workings of a valuable clock from a farm up the valley, sir. He was found with a knife with blood on it. They say he'd cut some poor woman's throat.'

'Was the thief arrested?'

'They say he hopped back onto his ship as it left the harbour. They never caught him.'

'Thank you, I'll look into that. What was the constable's name?'

'His name's Isaacs. Henry Isaacs. A tall man with a red beard.'

Abberline glanced across at Thomas. 'Did you make a note of that, Mr Lloyd?'

'Yes, Inspector.'

Abberline thanked the housekeeper again, and she withdrew with a graceful sense of self-assurance.

When she'd closed the door behind her, Thomas smiled. 'Do you believe our murderer is a clock thief from the Far East?'

'Miss Groom is a senior member of staff. She felt it important to provide us with potentially vital information.'

'Even if it's of no use.'

'Oh, it's of use, Thomas. It proves that maids and cooks, and so on, have told one another the questions I ask. Accordingly, they are preparing their answers before they walk through that door.'

'There's nothing suspicious in that, surely?'

'No,' Abberline growled with irritation. 'But they will now begin to compete with one another in order to tell the tallest tale. They want to impress their friends by saying that they gave vital clues to the Ripper detective from Scotland Yard. No doubt, we'll hear about bands of vagabonds roaming the forest, or suspicious men wearing eye-patches, and any number of cock-and-bull yarns about escaped prisoners lurking in barns, or furtive-looking travellers turning up at the dead of night.'

Another knock sounded sharply on the door.

'This will be the footman, Hassop,' Thomas said.

Abberline paced the room. 'Leave him for a moment, I need to think.'

Thomas waited a spell before speaking, 'The investigation maybe progressing slowly, but surely the information we're gathering is useful.'

'The investigation is at a standstill.'

'But when we exhume the body?'

'I'm clutching at straws, can't you see that? I'm hoping Joshua's corpse will reveal vital clues. But what if we find bones that say nothing to us? What then?'

'Inspector, I haven't seen you like this before. Perhaps you should rest for a while before continuing.'

'But I can't rest. Don't you see, Thomas? I can't stop for a moment. What if a bullet ends the life of William Denby? If I died at this very instant it would not matter a jot. There are a hundred detectives who could replace me like that.' He snapped his fingers. 'But William Denby has a brilliant mind. He is unique. His airships could mean life or death for this nation. If William dies, I will be viewed as little better than a traitor who has left England exposed to her enemies.'

'Forgive me, Inspector, but you are one man after all. You cannot be expected to protect William Denby. Not even the soldiers here can guarantee his safety.'

'That's why the colonel has gone to Liverpool. He's going to ask for a detachment of cavalry to be posted here.'

'Even so ... a marksman with a rifle—'

'Don't I know that, Thomas? Don't I know that if even a thousand soldiers guard this house all it takes is one man with a gun? William Denby need only stand at a window and-' The knock sounded at the door again.

'Should I let him in?'

Abberline rounded on Thomas. 'No, damn it, you will not let him in.'

'We can hardly leave him standing out in the corridor.'

'Life and death is in the balance here, and you take me to task over my manners?'

'I did not, I—'

'Thomas!' Abberline's eyes flashed with anger. 'I wanted you to join me on this investigation, because you aren't like other newspaper reporters. You aren't jaded. You don't dig into the mire for the salacious story.'

'I pride myself on seeking the truth.'

'No, damn it, I see a man sitting there who is searching for the master magician who will miraculously solve all crime and put right all wrongs.'

'I beg your pardon?'

'And I beg you to look inside yourself and see the truth. You want me to be that magician who can find thieves and murderers with supernatural ease. But I'm not a magician: I'm a flesh and blood policeman who can only do the best he can. So treat me as a human being, not a worker of miracles!'

'Sir, then look into yourself.' This outburst from a man he admired so much shocked him. 'Tragically, your father died when you were a little boy. I have observed how you talk about the laws of the land and your respect for them.'

'What are you saying, man? Don't be shy – drive your little pointed dagger of *truth* into my back.'

Thomas leapt to his feet. 'Your father died when you were young; you searched for a substitute. The law is something you respect, something you serve, and look up to. The laws of this land are the symbol of authority that replaced your father. Bluntly put: the *LAW* became your father!'

The knock came again. Abberline threw open the door and beckoned in a young blond-haired man in a footman's uniform. The man must have heard raised voices from within the room, but didn't seem unduly concerned. He looked like an actor who had rehearsed his lines and was determined to speak them.

'My name is Hassop, Inspector. I've been a footman in the employ of the Denby family for ten years. I was in service here when Mr Joshua Denby fell ill; however, I was transferred to the Scottish—'

Abberline killed the flow of words with a ferocious glance. 'What rumours did you hear about Joshua Denby?'

'Sir?'

'Did he have women brought here from the town?'

'Women, sir?'

'You know the kind of women, Hassop. Free with their favours.'

'I'm sure that never happened, sir.' Hassop smoothed down his blonde hair. The questions surprised him but he didn't appear perturbed.

Abberline fixed him with a piercing glare. The policeman's eyes became a weapon. 'Tell me Joshua Denby's secrets?'

'Secrets? I'm sure there were no secrets. Mr Denby was a true and honest Englishman.'

'As honest as yourself?'

'Of course, sir.'

'Hassop. Tell me your secret.'

The man stared in shock. 'I ... uh ....'

'I want to know your secret,' Abberline spoke savagely. 'Then I will have the satisfaction of seeing at least one man taken away in chains today.'

Panic made the footman's chest heave as he fought to catch his breath. 'I've done nothing. I am not a criminal.'

'That's a fine gold ring on your finger.' Abberline caught hold of his hand. His fierce grip turned the man's fingers white. 'A large diamond there, too. A diamond ring is unusual to see on the hand of a footman.'

'I've done nothing wrong.'

'Tell me how you acquired the ring.' Abberline released his grip on the hand.

The man gulped. 'Five years ago, I was footman here. Sir Alfred visited Mr Joshua Denby.'

'And you stole the ring?'

'No. I did nothing wrong. Sir Alfred gave me money.'

'What the devil for?'

'Helping him.' His hand shook as he smoothed down his blond hair. 'I ... I had a friend in Porthmadog. His father was a ship's captain. He took cargoes of slate from the quarries hereabouts overseas.'

'How did helping Sir Alfred result in him giving you money?'

'I heard Sir Alfred saying he intended to make enquiries about shipping items into this country.'

'Dare I say that you listened at a closed door, when Sir Alfred had a private conversation with his brother?'

'Yes, sir.' The man appeared so nervous of Abberline that he was prepared to tell him everything. 'He wanted a ship's captain to bring in cargo from somewhere foreign.'

'You're lying.'

'No, sir. The truth is my friend's father shipped brandy into Porthmadog in such a way that it didn't attract the attention of the excise men.'

'The captain was a smuggler?'

'He's dead now ... him and my friend ... drowned at sea, so the truth won't hurt them.'

'I take it then, Hassop, that you introduced Sir Alfred to the captain who smuggled brandy?'

'Sir Alfred gave me ten gold sovereigns. It's the most money I've ever seen in my life.'

'And this happened five years ago?'

'Yes, sir, as God is my witness.'

'Do you know what Sir Alfred shipped into the country?'

'No, sir.'

'Thank you, that's all.'

Hassop all but ran from the room, desperate to escape the detective's savage eyes.

Abberline turned to Thomas. 'What I said to you a few minutes ago was harsh. I am sorry to have hurt your feelings.'

Thomas spoke with icy politeness. 'You clearly felt it necessary, nonetheless.'

'So, will you sock me on the jaw, as the Americans say?'

'Of course not.'

'Then let me buy you a glass of Welsh ale.'

'You want to drink beer with me? After accusing me of being some kind of naïve scribbler?'

'It's almost twelve. The pubs will be open, won't they?'

'What about the interviews?'

'I'm thirsty ... I dare say you are, too. Come on, old chap, grab your coat.'

The butler arranged the transport. A driver, together with a pony and trap, took Thomas and Inspector Abberline into town. April sunshine, meanwhile, gave way to clouds that threatened rain.

Thomas began to wonder about the well-being of Abberline's mind. The man had spoken angrily to Thomas earlier. He'd then conducted a brutal interrogation of the footman. However, Thomas conceded that the harsh questioning had delivered results: the footmen had confessed to arranging a meeting with Sir Alfred Denby and a local mariner who wasn't averse to smuggling brandy.

Now that they were in bustling Porthmadog, Abberline's behaviour continued to perplex Thomas. After being dropped off by the driver of the pony and trap, Abberline walked briskly along the main street as far as the harbour. He'd no sooner set eyes on the ships at anchor then he headed back to a cluster of market stalls. Here, traders sold all manner of items from medicinal concoctions, to fish, to knives and forks, to home-made confectionary. Abberline bought a bag of humbugs and offered one to Thomas. Thomas, meanwhile, still felt anger at what the man had said earlier. Abberline accused Thomas of being unrealistic and cherishing a spurious belief that the detective had near magical powers to solve crimes. Thomas thought the accusation unfair and inaccurate.

Now this. He walked with the detective through the busy town, while sucking the mint humbug. Thomas noticed that men and women nudged each other. Thomas tried to hear what the townsfolk were saying; however, most of them spoke Welsh. Thomas Lloyd could not understand so much as a single word.

'I promised you a glass of beer.' Abberline nodded in the direction of a pub.

Thomas wouldn't be able to drink while he sucked this particularly hard lump of confectionary. Without Abberline seeing, he pulled a scrap of paper from his pocket and transferred the humbug from his mouth to the paper. A moment later, they crossed a floor strewn with sawdust to the bar. The place was crammed with men; lively chatter filled the air, along with a great deal of pungent tobacco smoke. There were sailors here from the port. One suntanned man carried a monkey on his shoulder, its long tail wrapped affectionately around the sailor's neck.

Abberline went to the bar and ordered two pints of beer. Instantly, the clink of tankards, laughter and conversation vanished. The room became absolutely silent. Thomas glanced back at all those eyes staring at them through the fog of tobacco smoke. A man, who'd been sitting on a barrel, lurched to his feet, slopping beer from his mug.

'Look here, then,' boomed the man. 'It's the Ripper copper. They sent him all the way from Scotland Yard, you know.'

Everyone fixed their eyes on Abberline. Nobody moved. Nobody said anything. Even the monkey froze on the sailor's shoulder.

After a pause, perhaps to allow his observations to sink in, the drunk continued in that booming voice, 'I don't know why they sent the Ripper copper here. Inspector Abberline couldn't catch fleas, never mind catch the devil who chopped those bloody women.'

'We came in here to have a drink of beer,' Thomas said, 'that's all.'

The drunk said nothing. He quietly set his mug down. Then he lunged forward, throwing a punch that slammed into Thomas's jaw. Abberline jabbed his fist upwards under the thug's chin. The blow knocked him back into the arms of the men at the far side of the room. Screeching, the monkey leapt onto a lamp that hung from the ceiling.

The drunk roared with fury as he struggled to regain his balance.

The landlord said one word, 'Boys,' and nodded at the door.

Thomas expected the other men in the bar to push the drunk back toward Abberline in order to resume the fight. However, powerful hands seized the drunk. Within seconds, he was propelled through the door and dumped onto his backside in the street.

The landlord went to the door and pointed at the man. 'Stay out of here, Billy, until you've got a sober head back on you again.'

Thomas rubbed his aching jaw.

'Doesn't look to be any damage,' Abberline said.

'A glancing blow. Though I don't mind admitting it damn well hurt.'

Abberline raised his glass. 'To you, Thomas.'

They drank their beer without saying anything more. Thomas could tell that the detective was deep in thought. Meanwhile, the sailor used a piece of bread to coax the monkey down from the ceiling lamp. The landlord's customers returned to their drinks and their conversation, albeit in a quieter way than before. However, they still repeatedly glanced in the direction of Abberline.

Once they'd finished their beer, the two men strolled back to where their driver and the pony and trap waited for them.

After a while, Thomas asked, 'We didn't come into town to taste the local beer, did we?'

'I came to prove what I suspected.' Abberline raised his hat to a group of ladies who watched him walk past.

'And that is?'

'My confidential investigation at Newydd Hall isn't confidential whatsoever. All of Porthmadog knows I'm here.'

'Servants would chat to their friends outside the house. They'd say that a famous detective from Scotland Yard had arrived.'

'Yes, a *famous* detective. I am not boasting when I say this but I do know that my picture has been reproduced in newspapers far and wide.' He sucked in a lungful of air. 'When my superiors assigned me to this case they knew full well that this would happen. They knew that Abberline, the famous – *that is, the famously ill-fated Abberline*

– would become the talk of the town. The men who sent me here knew that my secret investigation would soon become public knowledge.'

'You underestimate your abilities as a detective.'

'Thank you, Thomas. But the fact of the matter is this: there are people high in the government who want someone else to know that the Denby case, which appears to be linked to the Gods of Rome, is being investigated. I must say, Thomas, I believe I have been, as the phrase goes, *set up*. I'm the victim of a conspiracy. A wicked and extremely dangerous conspiracy at that.'

CHAPTER 24

LAURA WAS STANDING at the window of her attic room when she heard the key turn in the lock. The door swung open and in came her friend, Meg. The maid wore her uniform of a black skirt and blouse over which there was a crisp apron in white lace. In her hands, was a pile of neatly folded clothes. Meg smiled brightly at Laura.

'You look better – much like your old self,' Meg said.

'I feel better. The medicine cured me, I'm sure of it.'

'You haven't had any more of those horrible dreams about people falling out of the sky and dying?'

'No, I must have had some sort of fever. It inflamed my nerves, that's all.'

'Miss Groom told me to bring your day clothes; you can go outside later for some fresh air. A footman will walk with you to make sure you don't go and hide yourself in the woods again. Did you hear me, Laura?'

'Hmm?'

'You're so dreamy standing there. Are you sure you don't see anything that you shouldn't?'

'Who are those two men?' Laura pointed through the window. 'The young man with the black hair, and the older one with side-whiskers?'

Meg came to the window. 'Oh, they've caused such a lot of excitement below stairs. The older gent is a detective, and the young man is a news reporter. They're from London.'

'What is the name of the young man?'

'That's Thomas Lloyd. I've seen his name in the *Pictorial*. Isn't he handsome?'

'Why are they here?'

'I don't know if your nerves are up to hearing about it.'

'I've told you, the visions have stopped.'

Laura turned to Meg. She saw a gaunt figure standing behind the maid. It had a white face; its eyes stared with a burning intensity.

Giving no indication that she could see the phantom, Laura spoke calmly, 'There weren't any spirits. I know it was all a nightmare caused by fever.' The music began again: the haunting notes of a flute shimmered on the air. She didn't even flinch when the figure with the white face glided toward her. It raised an arm that seemed to be sleeved in shadow rather than cloth. The figure pointed at the door. It was telling her it was time to leave the room. *Work to be done, Laura. A quest to be embarked upon. A sacred mission.*

Laura managed a friendly smile. 'Tell me about those men.'

Meg didn't see the phantom, nor did she hear the unearthly melody of the flute. The girl smiled. 'It's so exciting. Do you recognize the older man?'

Laura shook her head.

'That's Inspector Abberline of Scotland Yard. He's the detective who tried to catch Jack the Ripper. Remember a ways back, when all those poor women were murdered in London?'

'Yes, I remember.'

The spectre glided forward to rest a pale hand on Laura's shoulder. The other hand pointed at the door again. *Time to leave this room, Laura*, the spectre seemed to be telling her. *Leave and do that which is expected of you.*

'I shall tell you a secret.' Meg's eyes shone with horror and excitement. 'Those men are going to dig the old master out of his grave. Jack said they know how to bring the dead master back to life, and he'll walk back from the graveyard to the house.'

'It's the Curse of the Gods of Rome, isn't it? Everyone knows that the Denby brothers have had an evil spell put on them.'

'Oh, don't talk about the curse, Laura. I'm scared enough as it is. I should hate to see the dead master walk into this house, as if he's alive as you and me.'

The white face set with those burning eyes moved closer ... Laura knew she would scream if that deathly skin should touch her face. The phantom urged her to take action. She was the puppet, and it was the puppeteer: it governed her actions, moved her limbs, and poured visions of violence and death into her brain. The journalist, Thomas Lloyd, was in danger. The phantom showed her visions of the young gentleman falling. With shocking vividness, she saw blood gushing from his head, and his mouth yawning wide in a dreadful scream.

'Meg,' Laura began in a calm voice. 'Thank you for my clothes, but you've forgotten something.'

'Oh?'

'I must have pins for my hair.'

'Miss Groom said nothing about bringing you hair pins.'

'Without my hair pinned up I'll look like a scarecrow.'

'Promise you won't stick the pins into yourself?'

'I even promise not to poke them into Miss Groom's eyes, though she deserves her eyes pricking for locking me in here.'

'Laura! You mustn't talk about sticking pins into people's eyes. That's terrible.'

'So, will you bring me the hair pins?'

'I'll go get some from my room. You start brushing your hair.'

Meg lightly ran to the door. After closing it behind her, she locked it.

'I'm a prisoner again,' she told the white phantom which had been invisible to her friend, just as it had been to the housekeeper and the others. 'But not for long. I know what you want from me. You are telling me to save the life of the newspaperman, Thomas Lloyd. You have a purpose for him, don't you?'

The tall, gaunt creature with the white face stood there without moving.

'Mr Lloyd has a destiny to fulfil, hasn't he? Won't you tell me what you expect from him?'

The phantom moved slowly backwards, melting into the wall as it did so. By and by, the sense of dread that she felt when she was in its presence, melted away, too, and she knew that she would soon begin the most important work of her life.

Meg returned with the pins. Giggling, she handed them over. 'Remember, what you promised? Don't go poking them into old grumpy Groom's eyes.' Meg kissed her friend on the cheek. 'I'm glad you're well, Laura, and the horrors have gone from your head.'

Meg drew the door shut behind her before carefully turning the key in the lock.

Laura Morgan looked through the keyhole, checking that the key had, in fact, been removed. Then she began to bend the hair pins. She'd once unlocked her mother's jewellery box using bent pins when the key had been lost. She was confident she could unlock the door in the same way.

Tonight, she would escape from the room. She would set fire to the master's workshed … she would burn those balloons to ashes. That way, nobody could ever fall from them again and Thomas Lloyd would not die.

CHAPTER 25

THAT AFTERNOON SAW Thomas back at the blackboard. Holding a piece of bright green chalk, he diligently chalked letters as Abberline read out a list of names. These were the known associates of Sir Alfred Denby.

'Is your jaw still hurting, Thomas?' Abberline enquired from where he sat at the table. 'Tell me if you need to rest.'

'I'm all right, thank you. There wasn't much force behind the blow.' Thomas downplayed the injury. Yet although there was only small bruise on his face, the drunkard's punch earlier had jerked his head back sharply enough to leave him with a sore neck.

'Once you've finished the list sit on the sofa ... no, lie on the sofa.'

Thomas nodded and wished he hadn't – moving his head induced a pain like a metal skewer being driven into his neck.

Inspector Abberline read the last three names on the list, 'Jervaise Winterflood, Leonard Guntersson and Horace Brodsworth. I've deliberately taken the names out of alphabetical order, because there's a tendency to attribute a greater importance to those who appear to rank higher on a list, hence the order is deliberately random.' He rose to his feet. 'These are men who were Sir Alfred's friends, or those with whom he had business dealings.'

'Do any of these men have convictions for any criminal offences?'

'Some. I had Scotland Yard check the names against their records. So, if you would add these letters after a name when I read it out. The letter "I" means they were investigated by the police. "C" means they have been convicted. Also, we should mark out those who are no longer alive. In that case add a "D" after the name to signify "Deceased".'

'Ready when you are.'

'Millward "I". Steiger "D". Pickering "A", "C" and "D".'

Abberline methodically worked his way through the list while

159

Thomas chalked the information on the board. It soon became apparent that almost half the men were dead, but then the list did span forty years or so. When Abberline had finished he slipped the paper into a drawer in the table.

Thomas stood back to view the names inscribed in that bright green chalk, together with the accompanying letters. 'Almost a third have been investigated, and there are ... let's see: six men with convictions.'

'Which tells us that Sir Alfred had a large number of acquaintances who weren't averse to breaking the law.'

'You learnt from the footman that Sir Alfred had paid a ship's captain to smuggle goods into the country. It suggests that after he allegedly brought the gold statues into England from Italy twenty years ago, he was still engaged in illegal trafficking.'

'But we'll discover nothing from the captain. If what the footman claims is true, then the captain drowned a while ago.'

'We could interview the men who sailed with him?'

'Question sailors who aided a smuggler?' Abberline smiled. 'I hardly believe we'll have a single word of truth out of them. They'll not risk jail to help us. No, we will have to continue digging deep into the records to uncover more about Sir Alfred.'

'Friends can become enemies.'

'Especially if a man believes his loyalty has been abused.' Abberline clenched his hands behind his back as he gazed out of the window. 'Did I abuse your loyalty earlier, Thomas?'

'Hard words were said, Inspector. But I believe you want me to regard you as the human being that you are, rather than the larger-than-life character portrayed by my newspaper colleagues.'

'I should have spoken frankly with you, but I shouldn't have become angry. This case has me rattled, Thomas. What's more, I'm afraid William Denby will be murdered under our very noses, and there is not a thing I can do to prevent it.'

'And you believed that you, yourself, have been placed in danger.'

Abberline nodded. 'I've been assigned to this case, because it sends out a clear message that the British Government takes the matter so seriously that they've ordered their most famous detective to solve it.'

'You believe the government wish that certain individuals know that you are searching for Sir Alfred's killer?'

'Or for them to suspect that I am, in reality, trying to find the Gods of Rome.'

'You said earlier that this conspiracy could result in you being in danger.'

'I can't help but wonder if there are shadowy figures lurking in government offices, who hope I'm heading for a suitably lethal encounter.'

'Surely, the government don't want you dead?'

'A senior detective, who gives his life during an investigation, would allow them to create a hero. That would send out the loudest message of all that politicians are prepared to sacrifice a famous policeman in the pursuit of truth and justice.'

'If you believe this is so, you will tell your superiors, surely?'

Abberline gave a grim smile. 'Then the head of Scotland Yard would demand my resignation, because I don't have proof of any such a conspiracy. No, Thomas. I will do my job. I will search for both the murderer of the Denby brothers and those statues. I will not be beaten by scheming men who hide in shadowy lairs.' After airing his suspicions so frankly, Abberline gazed out of the window for a moment before murmuring, 'Good heavens, will you look at that?

'A balloon? Dear Lord, there are men in the basket.'

Thomas stood beside Abberline as they watched the huge orange sphere rise from behind the work-sheds. A rope tethered the balloon to a winding wheel, or capstan, which was operated by a dozen soldiers. Slowly, the vessel ascended. When it reached the height of 500 feet or so, the soldiers on the ground stopped paying out the line. The balloon remained fixed at that height. Figures moved about the basket which hung beneath the fabric envelope, containing hydrogen gas – the near-magical vapour that caused the vessel to fly. Presently, a light flashed from the balloon. An answering light flickered from the ground.

'Heliographs,' Thomas whispered in awe. 'They are communicating with one another using Morse code.'

Abberline chuckled – it must be said, a grim-sounding chuckle. 'If I were to receive orders to go up in one of those contraptions I would shudder from head-to-toe. I doubt if my heart could withstand the strain.'

A knock sounded on the door.

'Come in,' called Abberline.

A boy entered with a silver tray on which there was an envelope. 'Letter, sirs.'

'Thank you.' Abberline smiled and nodded. 'Oh, would you ask the butler to come along here when he has a moment?'

After the boy had left, the detective opened the envelope and pulled out a sheet of paper that bore a great deal of black print.

161

'It's the exhumation licence,' he said. 'Later this afternoon, you'd best try and get a few hours' sleep, because we're going to open Joshua Denby's grave tonight. Then we'll find out what secrets his bones can tell us.'

Thomas watched Abberline at work, and he thought: It's as if the man is a locomotive and the throttle's wide open. The engine is racing toward its destination.

The detective added notes to the blackboard. He wrote MARSH TEST in large letters beside the name of Joshua Denby – the man whose skeleton was due to be unearthed in the early hours of the following morning. Abberline returned to the table where he swiftly began writing notes on individual slips of paper. The man almost hummed with energy now. His movements were precise, as if he embarked on a process that he'd rehearsed many times before.

Outside, the orange balloon still strained at its tether; seemingly, it longed to race away across the mountains. Three soldiers in the basket slung beneath the balloon made adjustments to valves and rigging. Thomas caught a glimpse of William Denby on the ground. From time to time, he signalled to the soldiers as they floated 500 feet above the mansion's lawns.

'Can I help in anyway?' asked Thomas.

'Ah ... I've written a number of telegrams.' He gathered up the slips of paper. 'If I'm not here, would you ask the butler to have them sent straight away?' Abberline stood up from the table. 'I need to ask William to loan me some of his soldiers to raise the coffin tonight. He's also providing a camera. I'd like you to acquaint yourself with it today, because I need you to photograph the remains the moment the coffin is opened.'

Thomas nodded. 'You believe Joshua Denby's skeleton might hold an important clue?'

'Possibly a vital clue.'

A rapid tap had no sooner sounded on the door when it swung open. The housekeeper bustled into the room in that no-nonsense way of hers.

'Gentlemen, what can I do for you?' Her manner was briskly efficient.

Thomas noted the way her sharp eyes peered over those half-moon glasses to appraise the state of the room. Not up to Miss Groom's standard of tidiness, he told himself.

Abberline quickly turned the easel around so the blackboard, together with its writing, faced away from her. 'There's been some misunderstanding: I told the boy to ask the butler to come along as soon as he could.'

'Mr Ashton is busy with his duties below stairs, sir. Cases of port have arrived. Mr Ashton insists on cataloguing the bottles and putting them in the wine cellar himself.'

'I have telegrams that must be sent as soon as possible.'

'Of course, I shall see to it straightaway.' Miss Groom advanced toward the table in that self-assured way of hers. 'Would you like the tea tray, sir? There's some very nice Madeira cake.'

'Thank you,' Abberline said as he handed her the slips of paper, 'that would be most welcome.'

'Is there anything else you require, gentlemen?

'No, we have everything we need, thank you ... oh, just one more thing.' Abberline held up a finger. 'Would you arrange for a bedroom to be made available for a new guest? His name is Dr Penrhyn, and he'll be arriving from Bangor University later today.'

'Yes, sir.'

'Doctor Penrhyn will also have scientific equipment, so best send a cart as well as a carriage to collect him from the station. He's expected on the train that arrives at Porthmadog at seven-thirty.'

The woman nodded politely before leaving the room.

'Ha! The formidable Miss Groom.' Thomas smiled. 'Did you notice the way her eyes raked our office?'

'A good housekeeper runs her household like a captain runs his ship. They hate to see so much as a vase one inch out of place.' Abberline picked up a piece of chalk from the floor. 'She'll notice the smallest detail.'

'And woebetide any servant who is slipshod in their duties.'

'I daresay domestic staff shudder and tremble before her wrath.' Abberline checked his pocket watch. 'Four o'clock. We'll begin the exhumation at three in the morning. I'll ask our redoubtable house-keeper to soak some strips of linen in camphor. You'll need to tie the cloth over your mouth and nose before the coffin is opened. And although we can protect ourselves from the smell, there is nothing we can do, alas, to lessen the horrors of what we will see: Uncovering the truth can be a ghastly and terrifying business.'

CHAPTER 26

Work on the exhumation began in darkness as the church clock struck the third chime. A cold wind blew across the churchyard. The trees that surrounded this little realm of bones sounded so much like a chorus of human voices that Thomas raised his lantern to check that there weren't people out there, singing in an eerie, whispery fashion. Thomas recalled his first visit to the churchyard when William had told him about the legend of the Singing Trees – he said that many locals believed that the graveyard trees intoned the names of the dead buried here, and the melancholy stories of their lives.

The wind blew harder, invoking what sounded like a chorus of astonished gasps from the trees: for all the world, it seemed as if those elms and oaks were shocked by what they witnessed taking place here tonight.

Thomas held the lantern high, fixing the scene to memory. He would write an account of these dramatic events at the earliest opportunity. Fifteen lanterns had been set out in a circle around the grave. They splashed their white light over black tombstones that jutted from the ground like a monstrous array of teeth. The only white-stoned tomb lay in the centre of the circle of lanterns. Chiselled onto the box-shaped monument was the name: JOSHUA GORDON DENBY. Abberline was present, of course, together with a representative of the local council who would ensure that the rules of exhumation were adhered to.

Ten soldiers had been assigned to help the inspector with his grisly task. The men were intelligent, resourceful, and they possessed strong arms – all of which they put to good use. Following Abberline's direction, they hammered posts into the ground. To these they attached canvas sheets, which would screen Denby's tomb from the road. After swiftly dismantling the tomb's marble structure they began to dig. It all seemed so dreamlike: the little pool of light in the midst of dark countryside, the gleaming tower of the church, the other-worldly sighs issuing from the trees, the silent figures tirelessly digging soil from the grave pit.

The church clock sounded the passing of five o'clock. Five solemn chimes that shimmered across the fields – a ghostly sound that decayed on the night air. Thomas set the camera onto its tripod. The camera itself was a brown wooden box one foot high, one foot wide and one foot deep. A cumbersome brute and heavy. One of the soldiers darted across to help him as he tightened a brass screw to fix the camera to the tripod.

Abberline nodded at Thomas – a silent encouragement. This was grim business, but it must be done. Important clues might lie hidden in the grave with those cold bones. Thomas felt the chill penetrate his own living body – perhaps Death, itself, giving him a foretaste of the icy eternity of the grave?

Spades crunched the soil, as rhythmic as breathing. *Crunch. Crunch. Crunch.* The Singing Trees were a chorus of whispers. Flickering lanterns sent shadows on a wild dance amid the grave-stones. *Crunch. Crunch. Crunch* ... Thomas's nostrils were filled with the heavy scent of damp earth. *Crunch. Crunch .... Thud!*

'Inspector Abberline, sir,' the soldier said. 'We've reached the coffin, sir.'

Abberline nodded. 'Please bring it up.' He turned to Thomas. 'Be ready with the camera.'

Thomas poured flash powder into a little trough on top of the camera. When ignited this would provide enough illumination for the photograph to be taken. He hoped the breeze wouldn't blow the powder away before it could be used. The church clock ticked away minutes with what seemed deathly slowness.

The soldiers worked with quiet professionalism. They were a close-knit team and barely needed to utter a word to one another in order to understand what their comrades required of them. They put their shovels aside as two men in the bottom of the grave attached ropes to what lay in the pit. Moments, later the two men held up their hands for their comrades to lift them back to the surface. The process went smoothly and swiftly. Six soldiers gripped a rope apiece. Abberline looked down into the grave, nodded and stepped back. The soldiers continued their grim task and began hauling the ropes.

Thomas watched the long box rise smoothly out of its pit. Once clear, the men carried the coffin between them and set it down in front of the camera. Thomas angled the instrument until the lens pointed at the coffin lid. Beneath that rotting wood would be the skull of Joshua Denby.

The local government official stepped forward to wipe dirt from the coffin's name plate. When he was satisfied that the name matched the one on the gravestone, he nodded to Abberline. 'Proceed, Inspector.'

Abberline picked up an iron bar from tools lying on the ground. One of the soldiers unwrapped a parcel of brown paper. From this he handed out what looked like white scarves. These were the linen strips that had been soaked in that strongly aromatic substance known as camphor. Each man tied the fabric over his mouth and nose. Abberline did the same. The soldier passed Thomas a strip of fabric, which he quickly tied in place. The smell of camphor was so intense it stung the inside of his nose, making his eyes water. Nevertheless, he didn't allow its powerful effect to distract him. He gripped the lens cover with one hand and rested his finger on the switch that would ignite the flash powder.

Abberline jammed the sharp end of the bar between the lid and the coffin itself. The man's eyes were bright between the brim of his hat and the white cloth masking his nose and mouth. 'Remember what I said, Thomas. As soon as I remove the lid take the photograph.'

'I'm ready.' Thomas felt his muscles tense.

The soldiers stood in a semi-circle. They seemed to hold their breath in readiness. Even the eerie chorus of the Singing Trees had fallen to the faintest of expectant whispers.

Abberline pried the lid with the iron bar. Nails screeched as they came loose. With a burst of speed, Abberline seized the edge of the coffin lid and hurled it back.

Thomas's gaze locked onto what lay in the coffin. He'd expected bones, a skull, mouldering clothes.

But no …

What he saw shocked him to the depths of his soul. A head lay on a black satin pillow. White hair fanned outwards across that dark fabric. A face … a *whole* face … pale skin. Pink lips. Open eyes staring up into his. Staring with the surprise of a sleeping man suddenly roused from deep sleep.

'*Thomas, the photograph.*'

Thomas Lloyd removed the lens cover. He pressed a switch. The powder ignited, unleashing a searing flash that illuminated what Thomas would remember until his dying day.

The corpse of Joshua Gordon Denby, which had been lying in the ground for three long years, was preserved – perfectly preserved.

CHAPTER 27

CLICK!

The lock turned with shocking loudness. Laura froze as the sound seemed to echo all the way from the attic down to the cellar and back again. Nerves, she thought, her heart pounding, it's just nerves making you imagine the lock was so loud. Even so, she paused a full minute. When she didn't hear the quick footstep of someone coming to investigate the cause of the noise, Laura opened the door. *Success.* Picking the lock with the hair pin had been surprisingly easy. Now she could not delay – not for a moment. The household would be waking soon; she must act quickly.

She'd already dressed in her day clothes. A candle burned in its holder on the floor by the door. Quickly picking it up, she stepped out into the corridor that ran the full length of the attic to the servants' stairwell. Her mouth turned dry, her heart clamoured – what she planned to do horrified her– in fact, made her sick to her stomach– but she must see her plan through. If she didn't, lives would be lost. The master's balloon ships had to be destroyed. If they weren't, Mr Lloyd, the handsome young journalist, would fall from a balloon and be killed. She'd seen his fate in a vision. Now came her chance to save him. Laura had been raised a Christian, and she saw it as her Christian duty to preserve human life, whether it be the life of one dear to her own heart or a stranger.

Laura padded along the night-time corridor, holding the candle high. As she walked, she heard the fluting notes again. They heralded the approach of the spirit which had haunted her of late. She dreaded its appearance. A cold, blue terror filled her. What she wanted to do was flee back to her room and hide shuddering under the bedclothes.

I cannot do that, she told herself. I must be brave. A higher power demands that I preserve the life of Thomas Lloyd. His life is to be saved. He is a man of destiny. She continued, the candle's glow lighting her way. Suddenly a door swung open beside her. One of the maids is awake. They'll raise the alarm! Laura turned to see a man standing there, however. Red hair, green eyes, a gap between his front teeth. Blood seeped over his lips and down his chin. Captain Sefton … his ghost had come to rebuke her … she was certain.

'I'm sorry I couldn't save you,' she whispered. 'I am making amends now. I will destroy the balloons.'

She reached out to touch his face: a gesture of compassion and apology. Her fingers pressed against a cold, hard surface. Captain Sefton had vanished. Instead, a closed door with her hand resting upon it.

'I'm not insane.' The words bubbled from her lips. 'Truly, I'm not.'

That's when she saw a white, spectral figure at the top of the stairs. The phantom pointed down the stairwell. It wanted her to hurry, not to hesitate, not to be distracted: she must fulfil her task. So down the stairs she went. From the kitchen, she collected matches and a heavy glass jar full of lamp oil. She would rely on her night sight now; the candle might be noticed by anyone looking from the house. Whatever happens, she must not be prevented from completing her quest.

Laura opened the back door, and cold, night air blew in at her as if to push her back indoors. Resolutely, she hurried through the fierce breeze toward the work-sheds. Light shone from a building at the stable block. A door opened to reveal a figure wearing a long leather apron. Possibly a mare was about to foal and one of the stablemen had stayed up to watch over the birth. Laura retreated behind a line of bushes lest she be seen. After a few moments, the man returned to the building. She gripped the matchbox in one hand and the jar of lamp oil in the other and hurried toward the work-sheds.

The pale phantom gleamed in the shadows. He, or she, or it, appeared to be watching her. Then creatures from the spirit world must possess other miraculous powers, too. Perhaps it senses the flow of time, she thought, like we can feel the flow of water onto our hands. And what if it sees thoughts and dreams flooding from people's heads, like we can see steam pouring from a locomotive's funnel?

Panic fluttered dangerously inside her. 'I'm not being claimed by madness, am I? Please God, I am still sane, aren't I?'

The phantom raised an arm with an outstretched finger, pointing at the sheds where the master's inventions were stored. It demanded that she execute her plan, and not hesitate for a moment longer. Already lights shone from windows: maids would be donning their uniforms; kitchen skivvies would soon be preparing breakfast for the staff.

Carefully now, she approached the area that servants were forbidden to enter. There would be soldiers on guard. The master's work was secret. She'd been told that the balloons were battleships of the air; they'd win wars; whoever possessed these vessels would become master of the world.

Yet she saw no guards. The way ahead was clear. There was no sound, other than a breeze sighing through the forest. Now the phantom stood by a door that was slightly ajar. Holding the container of lamp oil to her, as snugly as if it were a baby, she entered the shed. The balloons were empty of gas. Fabric envelopes lay limp upon the floor. Everywhere coils of ropes hung from walls. This vast barn of a place was, fortuitously, deserted of people.

In her mind's eye, she saw what she should do. Pull the cork from the glass jar, splash the lamp oil over the balloons, light a match – then: *WHOOSH!* Everything burns ... everything destroyed.

After that she would be content. Thomas Lloyd wouldn't be killed. Perhaps the phantom would be satisfied that she'd completed her task and would leave forever. Laura Morgan could return to her maid work. She would see Jake again. There would be dancing and music and happiness.

She put the box of matches on a table. Then she prepared to pull the cork from the jar.

That's when a figure lunged from the shadows. The phantom? No, she saw a flash of yellow coat. The hands of a living man gripped her by the throat. She felt the heat of them – the fierce, angry heat. A pair of brown eyes glared into hers. With one hand gripping her throat so tightly she couldn't breathe, he tugged the flask from her hand and set it down on the table. The next thing she knew both his hands closed around her throat. Her single thought: *it hurts so much* .... Laura tried to struggle free. She couldn't. Nor could she scream.

Black spots filled her vision. Blood thundered in her ears. The phantom's white face ghosted through the man's head. Briefly, the eerie spirit face became superimposed on her murderer's face, as if he wore a stark mask, pale as death.

Her knees buckled; all her strength gone. She hung limply as he grasped her neck with a savage strength.

'Do not shout,' he hissed in strange accents, 'or I will kill you.'

The man in the yellow coat picked Laura up as if she weighed nothing at all. Swiftly, he carried her from the shed, and away into the darkness of the forest – to a place where her screams would never be heard.

CHAPTER 28

At 6.30 that morning, the soldiers bore the coffin into an outbuilding allocated for use as a laboratory. The men set the heavy casket on stout wooden trestles. Dirt on that grim box had already begun to dry and fall off, as if it had begun to shed its macabre skin.

A man of about forty, with a neatly clipped beard and thick, black eyebrows watched the proceedings. He wore a slaughterman's leather apron over his clothes. Thomas noticed that the man had assembled an apparatus composed of an array of glass pipes on stands, together with beakers of various sizes. Tellingly, there was a table on which were laid a row of tweezers, forceps and scalpels. The tools of the anatomist.

The soldiers bowed their heads at the coffin before respectfully leaving the room.

'Doctor Penrhyn.' Abberline held out his hand, which the doctor shook. 'I appreciate you coming here at such short notice.'

'I am grateful that you asked me to conduct the investigation. Coming from you, this is a great honour, Inspector Abberline.'

'Thank you. Allow me to introduce Mr Thomas Lloyd. He's assisting me in this case.'

Thomas and the doctor shook hands.

Doctor Penrhyn said, 'I can take a specimen from the skeleton whenever you wish.'

'If you'll allow me to examine the remains first, Doctor. Oh, by the way, you'll find more than bones.'

'But I'm told that the body's been in the ground for three years?'

'I think you should see this for yourself.' Abberline nodded to Thomas. 'If you'll help me with the lid? Don't forget to cover your mouth.'

Thomas eased the cloth over the lower half of his face. Once again, pungent camphor aromas flushed through his nostrils to burn his throat. Abberline ensured that his own mouth and nose were similarly protected. Doctor Penrhyn, meanwhile, donned a purpose-made surgical mask.

'Ready, Thomas?'

Thomas nodded. Both men lifted the lid free. Inside that narrow box reposed the corpse of Joshua Denby. The long, grey hair still had the appearance of being neatly brushed. The dead face was white as milk. His eyes were partly open. The man had been buried in evening clothes – it gave the impression of him simply resting before heading out to a formal dinner.

'This is truly remarkable,' breathed the doctor. 'I don't believe I've ever set eyes on a cadaver in this state of preservation after being so long in the ground. See the skin? Soft ... still pliable. Like living skin.'

Thomas's lips gave an involuntary twitch beneath the linen mask as the doctor gently pinched the skin on the back of the corpse's hand.

Abberline examined the face. 'There is very little deterioration of the eyes, too. The iris retains its colour. Pupils are welldefined.'

Then the policeman did something so unexpected, and so shocking, that it made Thomas gulp and clamp his hand to his mouth. Abberline pulled the protective mask from his face, leaned in close over the cadaver, and inhaled deeply through his nose. 'I don't smell anything other than lavender oil, do you, Doctor?'

Doctor Penrhyn removed his mask and sniffed. 'Lavender oil and camphor: the usual method of masking odours of death.'

'What is so significant about the state of preservation?' Thomas asked when his bout of queasiness had passed.

Abberline said, 'It arouses my suspicions somewhat. The doctor's test will prove if those suspicions are correct. However, before the doctor begins work, there's just one more thing.' The man removed his coat and jacket and placed them on a chair. He then rolled up his shirt sleeves.

Thomas's stomach turned somersaults as the Inspector pushed his hands down inside the coffin between the dead flesh and the wooden sides. He pulled out several small cotton bags.

'Potpourri,' he said. 'Put into the coffin at the same time as the body to mask the smell.'

'Nothing unusual there,' Thomas managed to say. Just.

'A penny.' Abberline held up the coin. 'Must have fallen from one of the eyes.'

'How delightfully pagan,' chuckled the doctor. 'Pennies on the eyes to pay the ferryman's fare into the next world.'

'Ah ...' Abberline worked his hand under the corpse's shoulder. 'Interesting. What do we have here?'

He pulled out a black object, the size and shape of a cigarette case. Frowning, he turned it over in his hands. A moment later, he inserted a thumbnail into one side of the object and opened it like a book.

'By Jove, a photograph.' Abberline's face flushed with triumph. 'Look, Thomas. What do you see?'

Thomas stared in astonishment. The photograph was of the tintype kind, meaning it had been formed on a sheet of tin. The image had also been hand-tinted to include a flash of bright yellow on a black and white background.

'It's the Faunus statue,' he exclaimed. 'One of the Gods of Rome – it's gold. Pure gold!'

CHAPTER 29

THE GREY LIGHT of dawn pierced a knothole in the timber wall. Laura Morgan gazed at her surroundings. Spiders had woven billowing veils across the underside of the roof. Serrated saw blades hung from a nail in a plank. She realized that the stranger in the yellow coat had shut her into the woodcutter's hut. When she placed her eye to the knothole she saw trees. She caught a glimpse of the folly, too, the mock ruin of an ancient temple that housed the statue of a Roman goddess.

She thought: If I can see the folly, it means I haven't been taken far from the house. I'm still in the grounds. What if I shout for help? What she saw next immediately crushed all hope of being heard. The man in the yellow coat approached. She saw him clearly through the knothole in the wall. The determined set of his jaw and his hard eyes told her that he would punish her if she shouted. A moment later she heard a bolt being drawn. The door swung open and her abductor strode into the room. He carried a clear glass bottle that appeared to contain water. He set it down on the timber floor beside the door.

'Let me go, please, sir. I won't tell anyone.'

He said nothing. Then he didn't have to. His fierce expression spoke eloquently. This was a brigand who didn't fear people. He would hurt her if she tried to rush past him, or scream in the hope of being heard by the gardeners. He pointed at the bottle.

She protested, 'I'm not drinking from that dirty thing.'

His brown eyes glared into hers. She took a sudden step to the side. Perhaps he interpreted that as her intention to dash for freedom, because he, himself, took a step back toward the door. He pulled open his coat to reveal a pistol attached to the belt around his waist. A warning, clearly. Any attempt at fleeing would be met with a hail of bullets.

'Look at my blouse,' she said. 'You ripped a button clean off. Miss Groom will yell at me for that.'

Saying nothing, he gazed at her with dark, grave eyes.

Suddenly, the words tumbled from Laura's mouth. 'Miss Groom has punished me enough. She locked me into one of the attic rooms. I tell you, sir, and you will listen to me. *You will.* It seems I have been a prisoner all my life. I am eighteen years of age and I've always been a captive of other people one way or another. My mother and father ordered me to do maid-work for the Denby family. I had no choice in the matter, sir. Throughout my life there have always been locked doors, and decisions made on my behalf. It's always, "Laura, we know what's best for you. Laura, do what we tell you to do. Laura, you have no choice in the matter: obey, obey, obey". Let me tell you, sir, I am sick of it.'

He didn't stop her speaking. Those dark eyes of his gazed at her from beneath the brim of his hat.

Laura felt hot, breathless, agitated, yet the words kept coming: 'This week I've been held prisoner in that big house back there. It seems to me that this is my destiny now. I am always confined: my freedom is stolen away from me. The housekeeper locked me up, because I was granted visions of the future. The spirit comes to me and brings me images of what will happen. I foresaw the death of Captain Sefton. I've seen Thomas Lloyd, the newspaper man. And I've seen you! I've seen you, sir, in your yellow coat. You were fighting. You were in a struggle with what seemed like the God of Death himself.'

This time her abductor did react. He crossed himself.

'Now you have locked me into this hut. How long will I be your prisoner, sir? What will you with me? Are you going to murder me? No ... you won't, otherwise the spirit would have shown me a vision of my own death.'

Abruptly, the man stepped out of the hut, closed the door, and drove the bolt across.

She ran to the door where she beat the timbers with her fists. 'I'm not mad, sir. These aren't the words of a lunatic. But I've seen the future. I've seen that men will die!'

CHAPTER 30

THOMAS LLOYD FOLLOWED Inspector Abberline out of the building where the doctor conducted the examination of Joshua Denby's remains. The rising sun shone on Newydd Hall, causing its windows to sparkle so much that the mansion resembled a massive piece of jewellery embedded with dozens of gigantic diamonds. Nobody else was in sight. There was serenity at that early hour.

Abberline examined the photograph he'd found in the coffin. His sharp eyes scrutinized individual details of the image, rather than the picture as a whole.

He handed the photograph to Thomas. 'Be so good as to tell me what you see.'

Mindful that the photograph had been tucked beneath the corpse, Thomas gingerly held it between a finger and thumb. 'A tintype, measuring approximately four inches by six inches.'

'Interesting choice of medium for the image, wouldn't you say? A photograph printed on card would have quickly rotted, but one imprinted on tin will last for years.'

'So, whoever left this in the coffin intended it to remain as a kind of memento for the deceased?'

'Possibly. What else can you tell me about the photograph?'

'It's of a statue – one of the missing Gods of Rome.'

'We can't be certain of that yet.'

Thomas angled the metal sheet so that light fell on it fully. 'A photographic portrait of the deity known as Faunus. The top half is human, or rather human-like, because a pair of ram's horns grow from the forehead. The bottom half of the figure is pure goat – goat legs, goat hoofs, and covered with the fur.' Thomas gazed at the extraordinary figure that the Romans believed was the god of wilderness places. The god's face was that of a young man who wore an expression of delight – well ... perhaps more than delight. This was a vivid expression of excitement, even lust, and the eyes looked downward, as if fixed on the object of his supernatural desire. A goddess, perhaps, or a mortal woman whom he'd bewitched and enticed into the forest. Thomas could almost read the thoughts behind that demonic face: *I shall do what I please with her. She is mine. Nothing on earth can stop me now. I shall enjoy myself. I will immerse myself in pleasure ...*

For a moment, it seemed as if the image had taken control of his senses. Such was the artist's skill that 2000 years ago they'd created something of incredible power. The face was mesmerizing. Thomas took a deep breath and continued, 'The photograph is a black and white depiction, of course. The brick wall in the background is shades of grey. The image of the statue, however, has been hand-tinted with gold paint.'

'It certainly conveys the idea that we are looking at a golden statue ... possibly one of the Gods of Rome, which Sir Alfred Denby is rumoured to have acquired illegally.'

'It's peculiar though, isn't it? The notion that someone hid a picture of a Roman god in Joshua's coffin. Who in their right mind would do that?'

'Perhaps you've hit the nail on the head, Thomas. Perhaps who ever slipped the picture under the corpse wasn't entirely in their right mind.'

'Sir Alfred might be responsible?'

Abberline nodded. 'After all, we discovered the hidden shrine in the workshop. All of this suggests that Sir Alfred became incredibly superstitious and lived in dread of some ancient curse.'

Thomas thought for a moment. 'Do you think Joshua Denby was involved with the statues, too?'

'Possibly.'

Thomas handed the picture back to Abberline. 'Smugglers could have unloaded the statues at Porthmadog harbour. It's entirely feasible that Sir Alfred and Joshua brought them here.' Thomas gazed up at the huge manor house. 'The statues might be hidden somewhere inside.'

'That's something we'll investigate. After all, the photograph's presence in the coffin is almost akin to a message sent to Joshua's ghost.' Abberline gazed at the image of the statue – half man, half goat. 'Picture Sir Alfred creeping into a room the night before Joshua's funeral. The coffin is still open so mourners can pay their last respects. Sir Alfred slips this photograph into the coffin where none will see it. What, then, is Sir Alfred saying to his dead brother? Can we imagine him whispering, "See, Joshua, we succeeded. Here is a photograph of our treasure. Take this image with you to the grave. The gold Faunus is ours now".'

"Do you think Sir Alfred wanted to appease Joshua's ghost for some reason?'

'We might not believe in ghosts, Thomas, but many do. We saw Sir Alfred's shrine where he left offerings to the gods. He must have believed in all kinds of occult creatures, curses and pagan jack-in-a-box imps. He went to a great deal of trouble to ward off ghosts and curses.'

'Will you tell William that the statues might be hidden here?'

'Of course, and we will search the property, though it will be a vast undertaking. After all this time, there's hardly likely to be any outward signs where they are.'

A sudden crunch of footsteps made Thomas glance back. Doctor Penrhyn emerged from the door way, carrying a small bowl. There was something about the man's expression that sent a tingle down Thomas's spine.

'I have the result of the test, gentlemen,' the doctor said. 'You were right to be suspicious, Inspector. I've found poison in the body. Arsenic ... and plenty of it.'

The doctor stood blinking in the sunlight. 'If you'd care to step inside, gentlemen, I'll show you what I've found.'

However, before they could return to the outbuilding, which served as a makeshift laboratory, men emerged from the house in a rush. Thomas could tell that something had happened. Figures gestured to one another, there were shouts, and many a face wore an expression of anxiety.

A footman hurried across the yard. 'Sirs,' panted the man, 'you haven't by chance seen a young woman pass by?'

Abberline shook his head. 'Not a soul.'

'Who is missing?' Thomas asked.

'One of the maids, sir.'

'Laura Morgan, by any chance?'

'You've heard of her, sir?'

Thomas nodded. 'Wasn't Laura confined to her room?'

'Indeed she was, sir, but the creature picked the lock somehow.' The footman seemed more annoyed at having his breakfast interrupted than showing any concern for the missing woman. 'Now she's gone. Likely as not, she's scarpered into yonder woods again.'

Abberline said, 'Then I hope you find her quickly.'

'I hope so, too, sir. Truth is she's lost her wits. It'll be the death of her if she goes wandering out there. Sorry to have troubled you, sirs.'

'Not at all,' Abberline said. 'If you need the help of the local police to find Laura, tell me.'

'Thank you, sir. I'm sure we'll soon have her back – although I expect she'll go to the madhouse after this.'

Moments later, Thomas stood at one side of the open coffin, Inspector Abberline and Doctor Penrhyn stood at the other. The ceiling lamp shone down into that long box with its macabre occupant. Thomas once heard an undertaker saying that he put his "clients into narrow houses": narrow houses being his name for a coffin. The tenant of this "narrow house" gazed out with glassy, unblinking eyes.

Doctor Penrhyn spoke with a brisk air of authority. 'The body has been underground for three years, yet note how well preserved it is; there is virtually no sign of decay. However, records state that the body wasn't embalmed, because the December of 1887 was especially cold.'

Thomas ventured a thought of his own, 'I've heard that victims of arsenic poisoning decay only very slowly after death.'

'Indeed,' said the doctor. 'Arsenic is a preservative. Ironically, it is sometimes the prime ingredient of embalming fluid, and liberally injected into the deceased. Arsenic is also used by taxidermists.'

'Correct me if I'm wrong, Dr Penrhyn,' Abberline began, 'but a person killed by arsenic will only be preserved if the poison has been administered in small doses over a long period of time.'

'That is correct. A single, large dose of arsenic that kills quickly won't have time to be absorbed into every fibre and cell of the human body. Therefore, an individual killed by a single dose won't be granted this wonderful state of preservation you see before you now.' Doctor Penrhyn tucked his thumbs under the shoulder straps of his leather apron and started to talk if addressing his students. 'Arsenic has been used as a poison for centuries. Newspapers often call it Inheritance Powder. There are plenty who tire of waiting for an elderly relative to die so they can inherit their property. Therefore, a spoonful of that lethal powder is added to a coffee here, or a soup there. Is that not so, Inspector?'

Abberline nodded. 'There are at least a dozen known arsenic murders a year.'

Doctor Penrhyn continued, 'Of course, a well-preserved cadaver isn't sufficient evidence of arsenic poisoning *per se*. A certain James Marsh, however, perfected a simple but effective method of establishing the presence of that malevolent Inheritance Powder. I extracted fluid from the body and conducted the Marsh Test with my apparatus.' He nodded at the arrangement of glass tubes and flasks on the table. 'And it reveals the presence of high levels of arsenic. Oh, and I noticed signs of a brick-red mucous in the nasal passages: an indicator of arsenic poisoning, too.'

Thomas said, 'Arsenic can be easily bought in any town or village, so the poisoner wouldn't have had to look far for a murder weapon.'

Abberline gazed at the marble-white face of Joshua Denby, as if the corpse whispered vital clues. 'Doctor, this man fell ill in the summer and died in the winter. There seemed to be no specific cause of death, other than becoming increasingly weak and a general erosion of health. Would that be consistent with someone administering small amounts of arsenic over a period of weeks?'

'Absolutely.' Doctor Penryhn stroked his neatlytrimmed beard. 'If someone wicked enough, and patient enough, decided to put tiny amounts of arsenic into Denby's coffee, for example, it would appear at first that he'd contracted a gastric condition. He'd suffer stomach cramps, looseness of the bowel, then loss of appetite and headaches. Over the coming weeks, as arsenic levels built up inside his body incrementally, he'd begin to suffer drowsiness, convulsions, then, at last, he'd slip into a terminal coma.'

Abberline shook the man's hand. 'Thank you, Doctor Penrhyn. Your work has been invaluable.'

After the doctor had returned to the house to wash and change his clothes, before a well-earned breakfast, Abberline asked Thomas to help him replace the coffin lid and to seal Joshua Denby into his "narrow house" once more. That done, they stepped out into the fresh air. Thomas was grateful. The atmosphere in the outbuilding had become more pungent. He suspected that postponed decay of the flesh wouldn't be postponed for a great deal longer.

Thomas said, 'Joshua Denby is yet another of the Denby brothers to be murdered, isn't he?'

'I believe so, Thomas, and murdered in such a way as to resemble death by natural causes. Only the killer hadn't anticipated that the body would be retrieved in order to conduct the Marsh Test.'

'What I don't understand is why you asked me to photograph the corpse the moment the coffin was opened?'

'Firstly, I needed to preserve an image of the corpse, in case it decayed very quickly after being exposed to the air. Secondly, I wanted the killer to know, if they're still hereabouts, that we'd exhumed the body. And a powerful flash of light from the graveyard that could be seen for miles around should do the trick.'

'You think the killer was watching?'

'The man we're calling the God Thief had spied on us back at Fairfax Manor.'

'Do you think he poisoned Joshua Denby?'

'Extremely unlikely.'

'Oh? But he's our chief suspect.'

'He is *a* suspect. But did he secretly add a few grains of arsenic to Joshua's coffee on a daily basis? No.' Abberline turned to face the warm sun as it rose over the Welsh hills. 'Whoever administered the poison needed to have access to Joshua's meals. In short, Joshua Denby was murdered by someone he knew. And almost certainly by someone who lived under the very same roof.'

Abberline returned to the house. He'd told Thomas that he needed to write to his superiors at Scotland Yard, and to the Home Secretary, informing them about what had been discovered this morning. Abberline also asked Thomas to find William Denby. The man must be told that his brother had been poisoned, and that his death was probably murder. All of which pointed to the inescapable fact that William's life was in danger, as he was the only surviving brother left in Britain. Of the other surviving brothers, one had fled to Europe in fear for his life. The eldest brother was undoubtedly safe from assassination, for he'd vanished into the heart of Africa decades ago to undertake missionary work.

Thomas asked a soldier on guard duty where William could be found. The man directed him to the largest of the work-sheds. Moments later, Thomas entered the vast building that housed the airships. William was busily checking the orange fabric of a balloon envelope. Colonel Brampton had evidently returned early from his visit to Liverpool, for he was here in the shed and glaring in fury at what was scattered on the floor. When he saw Thomas, he rounded on him.

'Mr Lloyd! This area is prohibited to civilians. You must leave immediately.'

'Good morning, Colonel. Inspector Abberline wishes to speak to Mr Denby.'

'Then it can wait,' barked the officer, sharply tapping the swagger stick against his own leg. Clearly, the man wanted to use the stick to give someone a thrashing. 'Having intruders in here last night is bad enough without some scribbler for the Press galumphing about the place.'

William Denby looked up from his work. 'Of course, I shall be glad to see the Inspector immediately.'

'Confound it!' Brampton's chest rose and fell – the man actually panted with fury. 'You know what is planned for next week. We must push on. There is a vast amount to be done before ... *harrumph.*' He made a point of not completing the sentence.

'I have no secrets from either the inspector or Thomas Lloyd,' William said calmly. 'Thomas, the Prince of Wales is to visit us next week. He will watch a demonstration of the balloons.'

'Good heavens.' Brampton's eyes bulged. 'That is confidential information. No one must know that royalty will be—'

'Colonel. If Inspector Abberline is here, he'll hardly fail to notice that Prince Edward himself is strolling around these grounds.'

Thomas approached the two men. 'You say an intruder was here last night?'

'Well, seeing as we are being so candid,' Brampton growled, 'yes, a saboteur intended to destroy the balloons. Undoubtedly an enemy of Great Britain.'

William pointed to a jar of liquid on the table. 'That wasn't there yesterday.'

'What is it?'

'Lamp oil. And see all those matches scattered on the floor? The intruder must have intended to burn the place down.'

Colonel Brampton straightened his tunic. 'I have ordered a search for the saboteur. He'll hang, of course. If we don't shoot the blighter first.'

Crouching, Thomas examined the matches. 'Fortunately, the arsonist was interrupted.'

Brampton gave a dismissive shrug. 'Probably lost their nerve and ran for their lives.'

'William,' Thomas said, 'one of your servants is missing.'

'Laura Morgan. Yes, the poor girl appears to have run away. Everyone's most distressed, she's very popular here.'

'The lunatic girl?' Brampton seemed puzzled that they even deigned to mention her. 'What of it? She's hardly relevant to what happened here last night.'

Thomas shook his head. 'I disagree, Colonel. I think Laura was in this building.'

The colonel made that *harrumph* sound again. 'What earthly reason could the girl have for breaking in here?'

'I can't say,' Thomas replied. 'But I believe she was here, and that she fought with your intruder.'

William's eyebrows rose in surprise. 'What makes you say that?'

Thomas pointed at a small object on the floor. 'Isn't that a button from a woman's blouse?'

Brampton grunted. 'Doesn't prove anything. Might have been lying there for weeks.'

'No, look closely. See this group of matches lying together? The button is lying on top of the matches. The button fell onto them *after* they were tipped out onto the floor.'

'Good grief,' breathed William. 'Thomas is right. Miss Groom will know if the button came from Laura's blouse.'

The colonel grimaced. 'If the girl was here, what does that prove?'

William picked up the button. 'As I said, it suggests that Laura fought with the intruder. The matches were spilled onto the floor *then* a button was torn from her clothes. To go further, I'd say that Laura hasn't chosen to run away. No ... I think she's been kidnapped.'

Brampton frowned. 'Why would a saboteur abduct a maidservant?'

William looked worried. 'Laura would have raised the alarm. She could describe the man. I must admit that I fear for her safety.'

'Then come with me to see Inspector Abberline,' Thomas said. 'He needs to speak to you, and we have important news for him.'

CHAPTER 31

'LAURA ... DON'T BE *frightened, girl ... we want to help you ....*' The man's call shimmered on the morning air.

Laura glanced at her abductor standing there in the centre of the woodsman's hut. His head tilted slightly as he listened to the distant cry.

'*Laura ... where are you, girl?*'

Laura shivered. 'That's Jeffrey, one of the footmen. They're looking for me.'

The man's brown eyes gazed at her from beneath the brim of his hat. When she began to speak again he put his finger to his lips. Once again, she glimpsed the pistol that he wore on his hip – she'd seen photographs of American cowboys wearing a pistol in a similar fashion, tucked into a leather holster at the waist.

'*Laura!*'

This shout appeared much closer than that of the footman. Without hesitation, she rushed to the knothole in the wall and looked out into the bright, sunlit forest. She recognized two men who tended the gardens here at Newydd Hall. They wore rustic smocks and roughly woven straw hats. They called her name as they walked through the trees toward the woodman's hut.

Her kidnapper jammed an eye to a gap in the boards and peered out, for there were no windows in the hut; if it wasn't for knotholes and gaps between the planks, they would be rendered blind to what was happening in the outside world.

The two gardeners approached. Their powerful shouts boomed through the trees, scaring birds into a mass of fluttering wings as they rose into the air. They slashed the underbrush with sticks, perhaps expecting to see her lying there.

'They're coming this way,' Laura hissed. 'They'll find us.'

The man in the yellow coat fiercely gripped her arm before

183

dragging her to the door.

She struggled. 'No. I won't go with you.'

He rested his hand on the butt of the pistol – a clear warning that he'd draw the weapon if she didn't obey.

'No. You won't get me out of that door alive unless you tell me your name.'

The man regarded her with those brown eyes that were so large and solemn looking. He tried tugging her to the door again, but she clung to a metal hook set in the wall.

'No, sir. Tell me your name, or I'll stay.'

He frowned, puzzled by what she demanded. A moment later, however, he said, 'Franco.' His voice had a smoothness and lightness. In no way could it be described as coarse.

'All right, Franco, I'll come with you,' she said. 'But on one condition.'

'You don't make conditions.'

'My name is Laura.'

'Come with me now.'

'I will. But on the understanding you don't hurt those men out there.' She nodded at the pistol. 'If you hurt them, I will find a way to kill you.'

Her words surprised him. In fact, she saw a flash of respect in his eyes.

'I will not kill. You must come now.'

'Laura,' she said firmly.

'Come ... *Laura.*'

Silently, he eased the door open, put his finger to his lips again, and then, holding her tightly by the arm, guided her outside. The two gardeners were at the far side of the hut. For the time being, they wouldn't see Laura and the man. Laura glanced to her right. A group of soldiers, with rifles slung across their backs, were using long wooden poles to move aside weeds in a ditch. They hadn't noticed the pair emerge from the hut.

Franco drew the pistol from its holster.

'Remember,' she whispered. 'Don't hurt anyone.'

He propelled her to the end of the hut where a footpath led into the forest. He moved quickly, pushing her in front of him.

'Laura!'

The footman appeared on the path in front of them. He reacted with confusion when he saw the stranger with Laura. Although he glanced back, clearly wishing to hide in the bushes, he knew he couldn't abandon her. Instead, the young man waved his arms and began yelling, *'Here! Here! Here!'*

Another footman burst through the trees behind him. Both rushed forward – the two instinctively realizing that the odds were in their favour. They'd overpower Laura's kidnapper. That's what they must have been thinking.

Franco raised the pistol, which neither of the men had noticed until now.

'Stop!' Laura yelled at her abductor. 'Don't hurt them!'

Franco fired the pistol above their heads. Both men fled into the bushes, vanishing with the speed of terrified rabbits. Franco pushed Laura ahead of him, urging her to move faster.

He kept repeating the same word, 'Go ... go ... go.'

Meanwhile, the soldiers had reacted to the pistol shot. Glancing back, she saw the soldiers swing the rifles from their backs. Suddenly, there were sharp cracking sounds. A bullet struck a tree, ripping a white furrow across its bark. Soon, however, the pair had vanished from sight into the shadows.

Franco continued to utter the same word over and over: 'Go ... go ... go ...'

We're fleeing from Colonel Brampton's soldiers, she told herself; this turn of events had astonished her. We're running for our lives.

The path took them deep into the forest. Trees towered above her; a thick canopy of branches that blocked out the sun. They moved through a world that dwelt in eternal night, or so it seemed to Laura. The man's yellow coat was the brightest thing in that gloomy realm. His brown eyes constantly scanned their surroundings. He knew the soldiers would be trying to find them.

Laura heard the crunch of her feet on dead leaves; natural scents of the forest prickled her nose; the cold, damp air stroked her skin. For the first time in days, she felt completely connected to the reality of the world. Even the fear she felt of this frightening stranger was a natural fear – anyone else would feel the same emotions in this situation: the fear of being the captive of an armed man. That at any moment he might decide to point the gun at her head, curl his finger around the trigger, and ... *and ... oh ... here it comes again. Even though I hoped I was free of it ...*

Music. Soft, lilting, haunting, shimmering music ... Fluting notes ghosted from the dark heart of the forest. Her muscles tensed. The first violent flickers of panic burst upon her.

The flute's music grew louder. An unearthly fugue blown through the bones of dead men and women. That's the image that came to Laura's mind: flutes that had been carved from the white skeletons of the dead. The notes grew faster, a cascade of sound that frightened her, made her dizzy, *made her want to scream*. She clamped her fists to her ears. When she looked back at the man in the yellow coat he stared in bewilderment.

'Don't you hear it?' she asked in terror. 'The music ... *the music* ... HE IS COMING ... ONE OF THE GODS OF ROME IS COMING ...'

Franco reacted with shock. His eyes opened wide as he spun round, scanning the wild tangle of trees.

The music rose to a crescendo. *Yet, he does not hear it*. That was her last lucid thought before the wave of all-engulfing oblivion swept over her, sending her sprawling to the earth.

The maid awoke. She saw that she was being carried toward a bridge that crossed a stream. Instantly, panic struck her. Because, standing in the middle of the narrow bridge was the white figure. Tall, motionless, unearthly, the creature waited for the man in the yellow coat to carry her to its waiting arms. Events had been leading to her coming to this place – this dreadful place that she never wanted to set eyes on again.

Laura struggled. 'Put me down.'

Franco did as she asked. Of course, he did not see the phantom, or god, or whatever it was, on that bridge. Nor did he hear the music that shimmered on the cold air. A ghostly elegy for ones we have loved and lost. Laura had promised herself that she'd never come back here. *Never ever* ...

But what happened here that was so terrible? She asked herself. Why can't I remember?

Franco spoke softly. 'Laura, why are you scared?'

'The bridge.'

'The bridge? It scares you?'

'Something happened on the bridge....'

Laura's eyes returned to the figure. That elongated white thing grew brighter in the gloom beneath the trees. The white flesh appeared to glow. The music grew louder.

That's when the phantom did something extraordinary. It extended its arms to her. It held out its arms as if it was a distressed child needing its mother. And that's when she remembered.

'We must cross the water, Laura. The soldiers will soon be here soon.'

'No. I can't step onto the bridge.'

'Why not?'

'Because ... I ... remember everything.' Agony lanced her through and through, and tears ran from her eyes.

'Laura. Please ... I can carry you across.'

She shook her head. 'No. Use your pistol. Fire a bullet into my heart.'

'You are still confused.' He regarded her with genuine concern. 'Remember? You fainted.'

'I'm not confused.' She spoke with a clarity that surprised her. 'When I was sixteen I became pregnant. I was not married. My family were ashamed of me. Back then, my father was a gardener here, and he thought he'd lose his job, because his only daughter was going to give birth to a bastard.'

'Laura, if the soldiers see us, they will use their guns again.'

'I will stand between you and them. And I will tear open my blouse and bare my breast. And I will tell them to fire their bullets. I don't deserve to live.'

'Why such melancholy words? You are young. Healthy.'

'I also gave my baby son away. Two years ago, when Charlie was one week old, I came to that bridge with my father ... I walked out halfway across the bridge, and I put my lovely baby boy into the arms of a woman who could not have children of her own. I haven't seen Charlie since.'

'Please, Laura. The soldiers will be here at any moment.'

The man didn't roughly seize her this time. He held out his hand, and waited for her to take it.

She stared at the bridge. The white figure was melting, changing, transforming. The frightening creature was a creature no more. She saw the arms of a baby. She saw its pink mouth as it cried. She saw its eyes. She saw perfect blue eyes, just as she'd seen them when she wrapped her baby snugly in the shawl then put him into the outstretched arms of the stranger.

'Two years ago, sir, I gave my baby away. My father forced me. I was like a prisoner who didn't have the right to say "yes" or "no". He made me give up my son.' She took a deep breath. 'Then I forgot. How can a woman forget that she even gave birth to a child, sir? And forget that she gave that child away? Why was the memory cut from my mind?

'You weren't free to choose, Laura,' he told her gently. 'That means you must not blame yourself for what happened.' He moved his fingers, encouraging her to take his hand.

'No. I will not cross that bridge. I cannot put one foot on it.'

'Then we shall use the path alongside the river. Do not look at the bridge.'

Laura took his hand. His fingers were wet. She looked down at the redness oozing there. 'Franco? A bullet hit you.'

'Yet I am still walking. Now we'll walk together. Si?'

And together, they walked along the path, following the course of the stream.

She did glance back once. A figure stood in the centre of the bridge. For reasons she couldn't fully explain it seemed to resemble a child. Perhaps a child of two years of age. The skin was very white against the gloom beneath the trees. The child gazed at her.

When the ghostly glow began to fade she turned away for the final time, and soon she and the man vanished into the shadows, and the breathless hush that lies beyond the veil of oak and elm.

CHAPTER 32

THOMAS LLOYD FOUND Inspector Abberline standing at the black-board in the room they used as an office. Abberline chalked the words ARSENIC POISONING under the name of Joshua Denby. Quickly, Thomas explained to Abberline that the maidservant, Laura Morgan, didn't appear to have run away after all, but that she'd probably encountered an intruder in one of the sheds that housed the airships.

Abberline nodded as he listened. When Thomas finished he asked, 'Where is William now?'

''He's gone to his office.'

'Has he sent men out to search for the maid and the intruder?'

'Yes, including soldiers armed with rifles.'

'I need to speak to William. Will you tell him I'll be along in a moment?'

Before they left the room, the detective carefully covered the black-board with a cloth to hide what he'd written there from prying eyes.

Abberline followed Thomas into William's office a few moments later. He arrived at precisely the same moment as Colonel Brampton. The colonel reacted angrily when he found that the pair, who he clearly decided were obstacles to his mission, were present.

William had been studying an engineering blueprint; its complex lines depicted an airship bristling with guns – a veritable dreadnought of the sky.

'Really,' exploded Brampton, 'can't this wait, Abberline? Our work has the highest military priority!'

Abberline said, 'Colonel, I must ask for your patience; it's vital that—'

'Confound it, man! No, no, and no again! We demonstrate the airship in front of the Prince of Wales himself, next week. I cannot delay our progress with your rummaging in graveyards and constantly interrupting Mr Denby!'

Inspector Abberline calmly, and in an understated way, said; 'Hold your tongue, Colonel. Don't say another word until I've finished speaking to William here. If you interrupt, I will push you out through that door myself.'

Brampton stared at Abberline; his eyes were wide and round with utter shock.

Before he could so much as splutter in protest Abberline continued, 'Lives hang in the balance. The decisions I make now may determine whether William is alive or dead by the end of today.'

'Colonel,' William said quickly, 'I wish to hear what the inspector has to say.'

Colonel Brampton gave a curt nod. Thankfully, he remained silent.

Abberline said, 'William, I have to tell you that your brother was probably murdered. And murdered by someone close enough to him to administer small doses of poison that would gradually accumulate in the body over several months. When enough of the chemical saturated his organs and bodily tissue, death would occur in such a way that it would seem to be a natural death.' Abberline looked William in the eye as he drove home this important point. 'It is highly likely that three years ago your brother was murdered by someone he knew and trusted.'

'Poisoned, you say? How can you tell?'

'We exhumed Joshua's body, as you know. The corpse was in a state of unusual preservation. This is indicative of poisoning by arsenic over a long period. The arsenic remains in the flesh and staves off decay.'

'I see.'

'Doctor Penrhyn also applied the Marsh Test to samples of physical tissue taken from the body. The test confirms high levels of arsenic.'

William swallowed. 'That is shocking to hear, Inspector. Arsenic? If you hadn't come here nobody would have ever known that my brother was murdered.'

'Although I don't have proof yet regarding all of your deceased brothers, I believe that most, if not all, have been murdered. They were slain in such a way to dupe doctors and police. All the deaths were made to look like accidents bar one.'

'You mean my brother, Thaddeus?'

'He was killed by a single gunshot just a matter of days ago.' Abberline's eyes were drawn to the window, as if expecting to see a sniper aiming a rifle at William's heart. 'If the same person killed your other brothers, then they have changed their method of execution

– because that's what these were: cold-blooded executions, carried out by a calculating and highly resourceful assassin.'

'Who might be under this very roof?'

'Quite possibly.'

Brampton spoke up despite Abberline's prohibition. 'I will double the guard.'

'You could treble the guard,' Abberline intoned gravely. 'You could multiply the guard by a hundredfold, yet William's safety wouldn't be guaranteed. We are dealing with a murderer who moves invisibly. They kill at a time and in a manner that appears to be their prerogative.'

William looked shaken. 'What if the killer fires at me when I am with my family? A stray bullet … a ricochet … my wife or daughter could be taken in a blink of an eye.'

Abberline nodded. 'That's why we must catch the person responsible as quickly as possible.' He turned to Colonel Brampton. 'Give William your revolver.'

This time Brampton didn't disagree with Abberline. He immediately pulled the gun from its holster and handed it to William.

William stared at the gun in his hand. 'The problem is … who is the suspect? If someone steps through that door, how do I know whether he is harmless, or my assassin?'

Brampton spoke up again, 'Find him, Abberline. There isn't a moment to lose.'

'I must have your co-operation, Colonel. Today we will be faced with matters of life and death.'

'You have my co-operation, Inspector.'

'Thank you.'

'However, work must go on. We need to prepare the balloons for royal inspection.'

'Surely you will cancel?'

'Only if the murder suspect isn't found. Until then, we proceed as planned.'

Abberline clearly wished that the soldier would postpone the prince's visit; however, he gave a reluctant nod. 'You must obey your orders, Colonel. Meanwhile, I will do my utmost to find the suspect.'

Suddenly, there was a furious pounding on the door. It burst open to reveal a soldier. The man panted, his chest heaved.

'Colonel, sir! We have seen the girl. A man has taken her. They ran off into the forest before we could catch them.'

Abberline asked, 'Did you see her abductor?'

'Yes, sir.'

'What did he look like?'

'I didn't see his face, sir. He was wearing a hat – large like, a very wide brim. And his coat, sir.'

'Yes?'

'It was yellow ... bright yellow.'

Thomas shouted, 'Abberline, that's our suspect. The God Thief!'

'Colonel.' Abberline headed for the door. 'Have a carriage brought to the front of the house. Get us your best driver, and your fastest horses. It's vital we catch that man!'

'MANHUNT!' The sergeant bellowed the word with enormous power – its sheer loudness hurt Thomas's ears. 'MANHUNT!' He shouted the word again as he waved his men forwards with their rifles. They formed a precise line at the front of the house. 'Only shoot the man if you have to!' roared the soldier. 'He has a girl with him! Don't shoot the girl! I repeat: *Do not ... shoot the bloody girl*. Do you understand?'

They all chorused back, '*Yessir!*'

A footman guided Abberline and Thomas to a waiting carriage. Just seven minutes had elapsed since the soldier had rushed into the house with news that a man in a yellow coat had been seen with Laura Morgan. Soldiers on horseback cantered away along the driveway. The April day had become a whirlwind of movement; horses whinnied, sensing the excitement of the chase. A pair of gamekeepers hurried by with foxhounds on leashes – the dogs knew that the hunt had begun; they pulled forward, eager to track their prey.

Thomas climbed into a two-wheel carriage to sit opposite Abberline. The driver carried a rifle across his lap, as he sat there with the reins one hand and a whip in the other. The huge stallion between the carriage's shafts pawed the ground. Two soldiers on horseback flanked the carriage. A third man galloped up on a white horse. He wore the tweed of a gamekeeper. No sooner had he arrived than William Denby ran from the house. He spoke to the gamekeeper who quickly dismounted. William swung himself up onto the horse.

Abberline called out, 'No, you must stay at the house. You are in danger.'

''I will still be in danger hiding away indoors, won't I, Inspector? I'd much rather be out there with you, looking for the devil.'

'Very well, but take care, sir, take care.'

A footman ran forward to thrust a shotgun into Thomas's hands. He handed him a satchel, too, containing ammunition.

'MANHUNT!' The sergeant's bellow must have been loud enough to rattle the bones of the dead in the cemetery. 'PROCEED!'

The infantry moved off in the direction of the forest.

What came next snatched Thomas's breath away. Their driver cracked the whip and the horse moved with the speed of a race-horse. The carriage thundered away along the drive. The line of men smoothly parted in the centre allowing them to pass through. Thomas clung to his hat. The lawns became a blur.

He noticed Abberline shielding his eyes against the sunlight. The man scrutinized the front of the house.

'Do you see anything, Inspector?'

'It's worth checking if there's anyone watching proceedings out here. The expression on their face might be a useful clue in its own right.'

Thomas looked back at the huge mansion. The house shrank as the horse drew their carriage away at a bone-shaking pace. He could see no one. The windows seemed to stare back at them blankly. That old building was an impassive observer – it had coldly watched genera-tions of men and women live and die, and it didn't care a jot one way or the other who were the quick, and who were the dead.

Three horsemen led the way – two soldiers and William Denby. The forest closed in tight against the road. Soon branches formed a roof above them. The way became dark – a twisting, serpentine route through the trees. Thomas clung tightly to the sides of the carriage to avoid being hurled out. He gripped the shotgun between his knees and prayed that the weapon didn't have a hair-trigger. If a severe jolt caused it to fire, it would blow his head clean off. Ten minutes of hurtling through the gloom made Thomas breathless. His ears were full of the din of wheels against the road. Moreover, his entire body ached.

The driver shouted, 'Whoa!'

Within moments, the carriage had come to a stop. A soldier mounted on a white charger galloped toward them. He pulled up short of the other riders.

'Sir,' he shouted to William, 'the kidnapper has been spotted. He's moving alongside a stream further up this hill. We're going to flush him out.'

William turned to Abberline. 'Stay here. When we've caught our goose, we'll bring him back to you: trussed and ready to roast. Ha!'

William led the other horsemen away, leaving Abberline, Thomas and the driver alone. The driver climbed down from his seat and went to hold the horse by its bridle. The animal had fire in its belly now and wanted to keep running. The driver spoke soothingly to the creature, while stroking its nose.

Abberline appeared uneasy. 'William's got the hunter's spirit on him. I'm afraid he's stopped thinking clearly. If he doesn't keep his wits about him, he could be heading for trouble.'

Thomas checked the shotgun. It was loaded. He rested the weapon across his lap. 'God willing, we'll soon have our prisoner.'

'God willing.' Abberline nodded. 'But what concerns me is that I'm not able to identify something that has been under my very nose.'

'You think you might have missed a clue?'

'An important one. The key to this case might be dangling in front of my eyes, yet for some reason I've not recognized what should be damned obvious.' He sighed with frustration. 'The same happened in the Ripper case two years ago. The day after Mary Kelly had been cut to pieces I stood in a tavern in Whitechapel. A man was by the bar, drinking beer. I'd never seen him before, he was a complete stranger. Yet he smiled and raised his tankard, as if toasting me.'

'He would have recognized you from the newspapers, surely?'

'Thomas. ...' Abberline shuddered as if he'd felt the hand of a murder victim coldly rest upon his shoulder. 'Thomas, the man's smile was *so knowing*. Do you follow what I'm saying? A gloating smile. The stranger looked at me ... and he knew something I didn't. He knew a secret, a profound secret, which I longed with all my heart to know. I could see the truth in his eyes. He had witnessed things that no other living man had seen. At that moment, he enjoyed seeing me there in the tavern – me, a forlorn man, a failed policeman, who could not find the killer of those poor women. Oh, yes, Thomas. I would give every penny I own to know the identity of the murderer.' The breeze rustled through the branches. A furtive whispering. Voices without lips muttering secrets of their own. 'I looked into that stranger's eyes, I saw the knowing smile, and it came so powerfully to me – a revelation of dazzling intensity – the stranger in the tavern knew the Ripper's name. Every instinct told me that fact.'

'Did you speak to him?'

'I was distracted when a constable came in to speak to me. When I looked back, the man had gone. Probably through a side door and into the alley.'

'You can describe him?'

'That's such a peculiar thing. Even though I am blessed, or cursed, with an almost photographic memory, I can't. No. I stared at the stranger from a mere ten paces away. Yet I cannot name an article of his clothing. I can't remember his face. All I do remember – and it's burnt inside of me – is the way he smiled. That and the look in his eye. The amusement. The gratification of knowing secrets that would forever remain hidden from me.'

'The stranger couldn't have been the Ripper. He wouldn't taunt you so brazenly.'

Abberline sighed. 'I wake up at night, and I wonder. Had I been within touching distance of the most notorious murder in the world?' He shook his head. 'You know, my instinct tells me I've seen that same look again recently. A glint in the eye that says: "I'm better than you, Policeman. I know something you don't". But where have I seen it? In whose eye have I seen that expression of gloating? Once again, my usually iron-clad memory is letting me down". Abberline fell silent. A breath of wind stirred the branches again – the oaks whispered to one another.

And, suddenly, there he was. He'd arrived without any fuss, or making the slightest sound during his approach.

'Gentlemen, are you wishing to find me?'

The man in the yellow coat stepped out of the shadows.

The yellow coat blazed like a flame in the gloom beneath the trees. Thomas still sat in the cart opposite Abberline. Both men stared at the stranger. While, emerging from the shadows behind him, was the maidservant, Laura Morgan. She appeared to glide, silent as a ghost. Her expression suggested that here was woman in shock: her eyes were glassy, her face expressionless. Laura never even appeared to notice the carriage, or the men upon it.

The man in the yellow coat was the one and the same one that Thomas had pursued at Fairfax Manor, and whom he'd named The God Thief. The stranger pointed a revolver at Abberline.

'Gentlemen, *pronto:* I need your transport.' His words were strongly accented.

The soldier, who'd been holding the horse, moved so swiftly he was a blur. He flung himself forward, knocking the pistol from the man's hand. The God Thief responded by seizing the soldier by the tunic. He yanked him off-balance, sending him crashing into a tree trunk. The soldier fell sprawling. Thomas saw he'd been knocked cold.

The pistol! Thomas rose to his feet and leapt from the carriage. He shoved the man backwards, away from the pistol lying on the ground.

As he did so, he noticed a hole in the yellow sleeve – a bullet hole? A stab wound? Whatever had caused it, blood streamed from the rip in the fabric. The man was effectively rendered one-handed. Thomas grabbed the man's good arm, and seized him by the collar.

The man's head whipped forward, his forehead striking Thomas on the cheekbone. The blow knocked Thomas off his feet. *Dear God, that hurt.* What's more, when he tried to stand, purple clouds swirled in front of his eyes. His legs wouldn't function, and he sank back down to his knees. Laura watched with a strange blankness of expression. She remained standing there, an unmoving statue, saying nothing, not even blinking.

Abberline launched himself at Thomas's attacker. The God Thief was perhaps twenty years younger than Abberline and he fought like a tiger. A whirling, darting creature. Ferocious. Strong. Completely fearless. Even though limited to the use of one arm, he repeatedly punched Abberline. The detective was driven back until the next blow bounced him against the side of the carriage.

Thomas realized that he would now witness Inspector Abberline's murder. He tried to climb to his feet, but he was so dizzy he slumped back to his knees again.

'Stop....' Thomas managed to croak the word. 'Stop ... enough....'

The God Thief glanced back as Thomas shouted, perhaps expecting Thomas to launch another attack. Thomas, however, was soundly beaten. He felt as if he'd been kicked by a horse.

His attacker spun back to face Abberline – he did so, just as Abberline seized the shotgun from the carriage. Gripping the butt of the gun, he used it as a club. The barrel snapped down with brutal force on the man's injured arm.The man howled. His mouth stretched wide in a massive O. This time the pain struck home. The attacker stumbled back, gasping for air. Abberline turned the gun round, aiming the weapon directly at the man's heart.

Everything happened so fast that Thomas wondered if he was dreaming. Soldiers sprinted through the trees. Horsemen galloped along the road. Everywhere there were milling figures. Strong hands grabbed the figure in the yellow coat. Thomas saw the man's blood dripping onto the soil.

William dismounted from his horse. He pointed a pistol at the man's face.

'You are our prisoner,' William panted. 'You cannot escape.'

The God Thief smiled. 'You really think so?' He spoke in a strong European accent. 'Please look in my pocket.' The smile broadened. '*Si.*

Here in the left pocket of my extraordinary coat. You will find an item there that changes everything.'

Thomas Lloyd thought: We make a strange grouping of people. He'd managed to climb to his feet after being knocked to the ground by the ferocious head-butt. Now he gazed at the people beneath the trees, swaying slightly as he did so. Half-a-dozen soldiers clustered around the man in the yellow coat. Some gripped him by the arms. Others aimed rifles at him. William Denby held a pistol at the man's head. Abberline, meanwhile, dusted himself down after his own fight. That same man had just invited his captors to remove an object from the pocket of his striking yellow coat. The rogue had even smiled as he'd said: *You will find an item there that changes everything.*

Laura Morgan continued to stand there in a trance, her eyes glassily staring into space. Murmuring reassurances, Thomas helped her into the back of the open-topped carriage. When she was seated, he quickly arranged a blanket about her shoulders. Still she'd said nothing. The maid was in a world of her own.

Meanwhile, William Denby reached into the man's pocket. He pulled out an envelope that was smeared redly from the wound. A crimson stain had also formed on the yellow fabric.William handed the envelope to Inspector Abberline. The detective swiftly pulled out a sheet of paper on which was printed an elaborate crest with swirling black lines, topped by a regal crown.

William Denby said, 'We do have our suspect, don't we? The devil that killed my brothers, and planned doing away with me?'

Abberline sighed with frustration. 'No, William, we do not. This letter is from the Italian Embassy in London.' He began to read: '*To whom it may concern. The bearer of this document is a member of the ambassadorial staff of the Kingdom of Italy. I hereby confirm that Signor Franco Cavalli is granted the customary rights and privileges accorded to all members of embassies of all sovereign states, and that Signor Cavalli enjoys full diplomatic immunity.*'

The man in the yellow coat smiled. 'Which means, gentlemen, I am no longer your prisoner. Isn't that so, Inspector Abberline?' The smile broadened. 'Indeed, I know of your fame, *signor*. I much admire your work. *Bravissimo*. A genius. A hero of law and order.'

Abberline gave a curt nod. 'William, let him go. Soldiers, lower your weapons.'

William stared in disbelief. 'We have him! This is your suspect, surely?'

'I don't believe that this gentleman is in any way linked to the deaths of your brothers.'

'But he kidnapped a member of my domestic staff. God alone knows what the brute has done to her. See? A button has been ripped from her blouse.'

'Put your revolver away,' Abberline said firmly. 'You see what is written here. The man has diplomatic immunity. Therefore, I am not allowed to detain him. He is free to go.'

'Thank you, Inspector.' The Italian gave a courteous bow now that the soldiers had released their grip on him. 'If you please?' He held out his hand.

Abberline handed him the paper.

'Inspector.' William's face flushed red with anger. 'I am not going to permit this thug to leave. He kidnapped Laura Morgan. It's clear that he's assaulted her.'

Thomas stepped forward. 'I found the button in the balloon shed. It must have been torn off when Laura struggled with this … gentleman.'

'I am Franco.' The smile hadn't left his face. 'Call me, Franco, please.'

William's jaw had set with absolute determination. 'Look at the girl. She is in shock. Clearly, he has violated her. Who will ever know if I put a bullet in the devil's head? I'll bury him myself under a dung heap.'

'Si.' Franco nodded. 'You could execute me, Signor Denby. However, if you did that you would not hear, from my lips, information that is vital to you.'

'And what is that, pray?' asked Abberline.

'Ah … that is my secret … I will not tell it, unless I have your word as English gentlemen that you will not kill me.'

William lowered the pistol. 'Very well, sir, you have my word.'

'Thank you. I am Italian. A true patriot. I will gladly die for my country. However, I do not wish to surrender this earthly life until my work is complete.'

Thomas snapped angrily, 'And what work is that? Frightening poor maidservants half to death?'

'I would never have harmed her,' he replied. 'Yes, I often employ brutal methods, gentlemen, but I don't kill innocent ladies.'

Abberline nodded. 'The Gods of Rome … that's your work, isn't it? Your quest?'

'Ha, indeed. Bravo, Inspector, you are astute. I did hope you would reach that conclusion before anyone else. Our policemen could learn much from you.'

'That's why you took the carving of the pagan god from the shrine at Fairfax Manor. You wanted to prove to your superiors that you were making progress in your search for the gold statues known as the Gods of Rome.'

William had questions of his own. 'I have given you my word not to put a bullet in your conniving brain. So tell me this secret to which you attach so much importance?'

Franco nodded. 'Of course, you must know. After all, my information might save your life. Though, in truth, it might be beyond saving.'

'Stop playing games,' William said curtly. 'Tell us what you know.'

'I confess. I have been watching you and your house, Signor Denby.' Franco spoke in a matter-of-fact way. 'And in a most discrete fashion, I also observed your late brother, Sir Alfred, at Fairfax Manor.'

'Go on.'

'Coincidentally, I discovered that another man was spying on him. I saw him on several occasions in January this year. I saw the same man here at Newydd Hall. He was spying on you, *signor.*' Franco looked William in the eye. 'He was spying on you – and he carries a rifle. I believe he is an assassin. He will kill you, I'm sure of it.'

Abberline spoke briskly. 'William, ride with the soldiers. Return to the house as quickly as you can.'

'What will happen to this fellow?' He nodded at Franco.

'He has a bullet wound in his arm. With your permission I will see that the injury is dressed.' Abberline turned to Franco. 'And with your permission I would like to ask you some questions.'

'To be interviewed by the world-famous Inspector Abberline of Scotland Yard? It would be an honour, *signor.*' He gave a bow. 'Though I may refuse certain questions. You do understand?'

'You are a professional spy,' Abberline said. 'I'm sure very little of what you say to me will be the truth.'

'This will be a delicious experience, Inspector. I am looking forward to it. Ah ....' Franco turned to gaze at Laura Morgan who sat mute and unmoving in the carriage. 'Two years ago, something very precious was taken from the lady. Take care of her. She has suffered. '

CHAPTER 33

THEY RETURNED TO the manor house. William Denby took Franco Cavalli to have the bullet wound in his arm cleaned and bandaged. Thomas, meanwhile, helped Laura Morgan down from the carriage. Her hands had the chill of a stone tomb.

Laura suddenly gave a sharp intake of breath. 'I saw what nobody else could see ... I saw what's to come. The spirit gave me visions of you fighting the man in yellow. And I know what will happen to you, sir.' She looked directly at Thomas. 'You will be killed, sir. I swear to God, sir, it's true.'

Abberline said gently, 'You will be cared for now. No one will hurt you. You're safe.'

'Thank you, sir.' She swayed.

Abberline put his arm round her shoulders. 'Lean against me, I won't let you fall.'

'You tried so hard to stop those ladies from falling. Inside my head, I see you walking through the darkest part of the city. You tried to save the women, sir, but they were cut to pieces by a smiling man. I see him working with a knife in a room full of blood, and he's always smiling. Later, you stood in the same room, with the poor, butchered girl lying there on the bed.'

The housekeeper, walked across the courtyard toward them. Two young maids accompanied her.

'Here's Miss Groom,' Abberline said in a reassuring voice. 'All is well now, Laura.'

Laura whispered, 'I saw him, sir. In my head, I saw the man they call the Ripper. The smiling man. He wants to torment you ... the smiling man will visit you again. He has a gift for you.'

Miss Groom spoke briskly, 'Come now, girl. Let's get you to bed.'

'Yes, Miss Groom.' Laura allowed the maids to lead her.

The housekeeper nodded at Abberline. 'We'll look after her, sir.

Don't be concerned.'

'With you in charge, madam, I'm sure she is in the best of care.'

Miss Groom smiled, flattered. She raised her hands and made a motion with them as if rinsing them in water. 'Thank you, sir. That's most kind. I treat my staff like they are my own children.'

Laura suddenly stopped dead. She glanced back. 'Sir, I've seen so many things that others can't. I saw a white figure in my room. A ghost man – or perhaps he was one of the Gods of old Rome. Today I saw lost babies in the bulrushes. Nobody else could see them. But I saw them plain. I saw their sad eyes and their hands stretching out.' Tears glistened in her eyes. 'They wanted to be picked up and loved.'

The maids gently coaxed her toward the house.

'I'm sorry about that, sir,' Miss Groom said. 'I fear that the girl has lost her mind.' With that, the woman followed Laura and the maids back to the house.

Thomas turned to Abberline. 'When Laura talked about the room full of blood, she was describing the room where Jack the Ripper killed Mary Kelly, wasn't she?'

'She mentioned a smiling man, too.'

'Of course, she would have read about the Ripper slayings in the newspapers.'

Abberline appeared deep in thought. At last, he sighed. 'Laura claims that there are supernatural beings that we can't see. I have a feeling that all around me are clues that are relevant to the Denby murders. Yet why can't I see them? What am I missing that's so crucial to finding the killer?'

'You, yourself, told me that the assassin is cunning. They make the deaths seem like accidents.'

'Perhaps my eyes are getting too old to see what might be in full view in front of me?' He suddenly walked toward the house. 'Come on, Thomas, it's time we spoke to Signor Cavalli. Perhaps he has witnessed something significant on his spying missions – even though he, himself, might not realize it, he might help us solve this mystery.'

Franco Cavalli sauntered into the room Abberline used as an office. A sling cradled his injured arm. The bloodstained yellow coat hung over the other arm. His large, brown eyes swiftly devoured every detail of his surroundings, including the blackboard covered by the white sheet.

Thomas realized that here was a formidable human being. Cavalli was clearly one of Italy's most effective secret agents. Charisma and intelligence shone from the man's handsome face. Thomas could vouch for the man's strength, too. He doubted if many men would get the better of Cavalli in a fight. If it hadn't been for the bullet in in his arm, he would have easily defeated both William and Inspector Abberline.

'Thomas,' Abberline said, 'would you lock the door please?'

Franco Cavalli raised his eyebrows. 'So, after all ... I am your prisoner, Inspector.' The man spoke with a strong Italian accent. 'I have diplomatic immunity, *si*? To hold me against my will is to offend protocol. This could cost you your rank.'

Abberline said, 'There are just the three of us here: Mr Thomas Lloyd, you, Signor Cavalli, and myself. I don't want us to be disturbed.'

'Then I am free to leave whenever I wish?'

'I will call for a carriage to take you to the station, if that's what you'd prefer.'

'No, *signor*. I relish this opportunity to speak to you. I am certain, Inspector, that I shall learn far more from you than you will from me.' He smiled. 'You are the greatest detective of our age. I am humbled to be in your presence.'

Abberline didn't react to the blatant flattery. He extended his hand toward a chair. 'Please sit down, *signor*.'

'Thank you. A bullet in the arm does, as you English say, take the wind out of one's sails.'

The Italian chose a straight-backed chair near the window. Sunlight flooded over him and he basked in its warmth.

Abberline didn't waste time with small talk. 'Signor Cavalli, what is your purpose here in Britain?'

'I am a spy. My government ordered me to watch the Denby clan. But please call me Franco. We are friends now.'

'You suspect the Denby brothers being involved somehow with the Gods of Rome?'

'There is no "somehow" about it. We know that statues cast from gold were concealed fifteen hundred years ago when barbarians invaded Italy. The emperor ordered that the statues be hidden in a cave. After the Roman Empire fell, the statues' whereabouts were lost. Twenty years ago, a farmer searching for a goat found those fabled gods once more.'

'The find wasn't reported to the authorities?'

'The statues are made of gold, Inspector. The farmer wanted to be rich so he sold them to a criminal family. They sought a purchaser for their treasure. Sir Alfred Denby was the man who bought the statues.

He had them shipped to this country two decades ago.'

'How do you know all this?'

'A *mafiosi*, a man by the name of Aldo D'Silva , faced execution for murder. D'Silva did a deal with the government. In exchange for his life, he told the police all he knew about the Gods of Rome: how they were found, how they were sold, and how the scoundrel, Sir Alfred Denby, smuggled them out of my country. We even know that Denby planned to give the gold Faunus to your queen as a gift. He hoped to be ... how do you put it? Elevated to the aristocracy ... as a reward for his generosity. Being a lord would open doors for Sir Alfred. He would become more powerful, more wealthy.'

'So, you were ordered by your government to find out where the Gods of Rome were hidden, and ... what? Steal them back?'

'Why should I need to steal what, after all, is the property of my people?'

'You believe that the statues are concealed on land belonging to the Denby family?'

'In some basement, or behind a false wall, or some out of the way stable, will be a pantheon of golden gods which were created by the greatest artists of the greatest of all empires: the empire of Rome.'

'You do realize that your spying activities are highly illegal?'

'*Si.*' Franco's smile was as pleasant as ever. 'But I am part of the ambassador's staff. The police cannot prosecute. In fact, I am the innocent victim. I could complain to your superiors that I was enjoying a stroll in the Welsh countryside when British soldiers fired at me for no reason.' He touched his wounded arm. 'A British bullet gashed my flesh. What's more, British policemen pounced on me.'

A knock sounded on the door.

Abberline turned to Thomas. 'Best see who it is.'

Thomas opened the door to reveal a maid in her black dress and white apron. She carried a tray, on which was a glass of golden liquor.

'Sir,' she said politely. 'I've been told to bring this to your visitor. The injured gentleman.'

Franco stood up before giving a low bow. 'Thank you, my lady. Most kind.' He smiled warmly at the maid who blushed bright pink. 'Ah, brandy, the elixir that restores.'

He took the glass from the tray. The maid curtsied.

Abberline spoke to the maid. 'Would you ask the butler to come see me? I would like to ask him a question.'

'I'm sorry, sir. That won't be possible.'

'Oh?'

'A shipment of port has arrived. Mr Ashton lists the bottles in his book, and puts them in the wine cellar himself.'

Thomas rolled his eyes. 'More port? The house must be awash with the stuff.'

Franco chuckled. 'Today, men are shot, men fight with their fists, there is an assassin nearby – he lurks in the dark of the forest – and still the most important task of the day is the laying down of port in the cellar. How delicious ... how British!'

The maid smiled, charmed by the Italian's charisma.

Abberline's expression was unreadable. He merely turned to the maid and said, 'Perhaps you could help me with a small matter?'

'Of course, sir.'

'The butler, Mr Ashton, how long has he served the Denby family?'

'Oh, he's been here ever such a long time.' She smiled. 'He always says that he started work here as a boy cleaning boots. He worked himself up to footman, under-butler, then butler, sir.'

'He'll have worked for the Denby family for at least twenty years?'

'Oooh, yes, sir. More years than that. In fact, he was footman to the old master. That would be Mr William's father.'

Abberline smiled. 'Thank you, what you've told me is extremely useful.'

The maid withdrew from the room. Inspector Abberline opened the drawer in the table and took out a photograph. 'We can speak frankly to one another, can't we, Franco?'

'I am delighted that we converse as friends.'

'Because I would like to show you a photograph I found today. You'll find it of great interest.'

'Oh? Where did you find this photograph?'

'Let us say that it came to us from the underworld.'

'Ha, you are more remarkable than I could have believed, Inspector. If you receive help from the land of the dead, then I am in awe.'

'I will show you this extraordinary photograph,' Abberline told him. 'And you will tell me all you know about the other man who has been keeping watch on this house and Fairfax Manor.'

'I wish I could help, but I simply don't know anything about the other spy.'

'You might not realize it, but a fact that appears insignificant could be the key which unlocks the mystery.'

Franco raised his brandy glass. 'Here's to you, Inspector. And to you, Mr Lloyd. You, Mr Lloyd, must see what I see. Inspector Abberline is an extraordinary policeman. He is the pivot on which this case of murder and theft tips from mystery to enlightenment. We are in the presence of a genius. *Salute!*'

For the next hour Thomas sat quietly listening to Abberline and the master spy, Franco Cavalli, talk. Thomas suspected that there was mutual respect. The Italian was clearly awed by Inspector Abberline. Abberline, himself, recognized that Franco was the consummate professional. Franco explained that he'd travelled to the country estates tenanted by the Denby brothers. He'd kept watch in the hope he'd find evidence that the Gods of Rome were secretly stored at one or more of the houses. However, he'd found no clues to indicate that they were. Abberline asked why Franco had ventured into one of the balloon sheds.

'Simply by chance,' Franco Cavalli answered. 'I have a professional curiosity in all things. When I saw that military airships were being tested here I decided to take a look for myself, make sketches then pass them to my superiors.'

Thomas said sharply, 'They are British balloons, sir. There might come a day when we depend on them to protect our nation.'

'Ah, Mr Lloyd, but what if your warships of the sky fire their guns at Italian cities? Isn't it my duty to protect my nation? The drawings I made will enable our scientists to build airships that will counter yours.'

Thomas held out his hand. 'You may have diplomatic immunity, but I demand you hand over the drawings.'

Franco smiled quite pleasantly. 'As you wish.' He touched his forehead. 'My memory is very good, however. I will remember every detail of what I have seen.' The man pulled sheets of paper from his yellow coat, which he handed to Thomas.

'That is a distinctive coat,' said Abberline.

'Isn't it a wonderful garment? Such a shade of yellow. Buttercup yellow!'

Abberline leaned forwards to examine it more closely. 'What's unusual, too, is that it can be turned inside out. Then people will only see the brown lining.'

'I believe the term for such a garment is reversible, *si*?'

Abberline allowed himself a smile. 'I imagine you ask people for directions to places, even though you know where they are. No doubt you also take a glass of beer in local taverns; therefore ensuring people see a foreigner in a striking yellow coat. Accordingly, witnesses will then give that description to the police.'

'You have a formidable mind, Inspector.'

'When you wish to disappear from view you turn the coat inside out. And, hey-presto, the coat is now a dull, earthy brown, and the police will search fruitlessly for a man in yellow. I see you also have a brown cap in your pocket that no doubt replaces the widebrimmed hat.'

'Exactly. You have learnt the secret of my disguise.' Suddenly the Italian's accent vanished to be replaced with the impeccable tones of an English gentleman. 'Top hole, my man. You really are rather good at this detective lark, aren't you?' Franco smiled. 'I have rehearsed certain phrases so that I further merge with the crowd. I become an English gentleman in a dull coat.'

'Hardly a gentlemen,' Thomas said with a hot burst of anger. 'You mistreated the maid. You kidnapped her.'

'I found her in the building with the airship. She had a jar of oil and matches. The lady intended to burn everything – *foof!*' He waggled his fingers to simulate flames. 'Not only did I believe it necessary to take her away to avoid raising the alarm, I also feared that she would set herself alight. Lamp oil is very dangerous.'

Thomas wouldn't be deflected from what he saw as inhuman treatment of the woman. 'You would have killed her to prevent her describing you.'

'I do not kill innocent men and women, Mr Lloyd. A remote barn would have kept her out of harm's way for a few hours. She would have been released before I vanished back into the night, as it were.'

Abberline held the photograph out for Franco to examine. Thomas saw that it had been sandwiched between two pieces of glass – a wise precaution considering where the photograph had come from.

'This was found in the coffin of Joshua Denby. I had the body exhumed.'

'You must have had your reasons.'

'The Denby brothers are being systematically murdered.'

'Ah ....' Franco nodded. 'The Curse of the Gods of Rome.'

'I don't believe in curses.'

'Nor I, inspector. I believe in greed, fear, vengeance, the lust for power, *amore*, and all those human emotions that drive us to do extraordinary things. Good as well as evil.'

'Do you recognize the photograph's subject matter?'

'It is Faunus, a god of my ancestors. The hand-tinting suggests the statue is made of gold. Therefore, it is one of the Gods of Rome. Do you know where the statue is?'

'Not yet.'

'I see by your eyes that you tell the truth. I believe you.'

'My instinct tells me that you were once a policeman, too.'

'Your instinct is correct. I was ordered to search for our national treasure that was stolen from us. Many Italians believe that our nation will prosper again if the old gods return to Rome.' He handed the photograph back to Abberline. 'Will you inform me if the Faunus is found?'

'Such a communication would have to come from a much higher level.'

Franco nodded. 'Now you want to hear about the man I have seen prowling the Fairfax Manor grounds and here recently?'

'Any description you can give me might prove vital.'

'There is nothing I can give, alas. All I have seen, from a great distance, is a figure dressed in a shapeless, black cape. His hat is always pulled down, hiding the face. He carries a rifle. I don't even know the colour of his hair.'

'You must have seen something that will help me.'

'No, I've seen nothing. He is a figure in a cape. A shapeless blot in shadow.'

'You are an experienced spy, Franco. You don't make general observations – you observe the particular. You remember details.'

'Alas... alas.' The Italian shrugged.

'A man of your calibre ... your expertise ... must have noticed something?' Abberline pressed home his questions. 'You did see a detail that struck you as unusual, didn't you?'

'How do you know that?'

'Because a policeman always spots the unusual detail that nobody else notices.'

'His hand.'

'His hand?'

'His finger, rather ... one finger on his left hand. I tried to observe him through my binoculars. He saw the flash of light on the glass and withdrew. However, I saw his left hand as he pushed a branch aside.'

'And what did you notice?'

'What do you English call it? A wedding band? A wedding ring?'

'Why did that strike you as unusual?'

'Englishmen seldom wear wedding bands when they marry. Italian men, however, do wear a ring when they take a bride.' He gave an apologetic shrug. 'Sorry, Inspector, that is the only specific detail I can offer. Your suspect is married. He wears a gold ring on the third finger of his left hand. You must be disappointed in me.'

'On the contrary. The ring could be important. It could be very important indeed.'

Abberline stood gazing out of the window, his hands clasped behind his back. The man was clearly deep in thought.

Thomas sat quietly on the sofa in the office. He jotted down notes in his book, including the remarkable statement that Franco Cavalli had made, '*You, Mr Lloyd, see what I see. Inspector Abberline is an extraordinary policeman. He is the pivot on which this case of murder and theft tips from mystery to enlightenment ...*'

The Italian's words resonated with Thomas. Abberline was the consummate detective. On numerous occasions he had gathered the subtlest of clues together when investigating other cases; he interpreted them; recognized their significance; he had connected them together in their correct order and solved the puzzle. With that accomplished he arrested the criminal. And yet ... Thomas sensed that Abberline hadn't identified his clues in this particular case. True, they had discovered that Sir Alfred had *not* been accidentally killed in the explosion two months ago. He had been the victim of a device that caused a pistol to fire into a quantity of gunpowder, which resulted in a lethal explosion. Sir Alfred had been murdered. This morning, chemical tests on the body of his brother, Joshua Denby, revealed that the man had been poisoned with arsenic three years ago. A photograph of one of the Gods of Rome had been found in the coffin; probably placed by there by Sir Alfred. That, together with the secret shrine at Fairfax Manor, suggested that Sir Alfred was a superstitious man ... indeed, superstitious to the point of mania.

The words of the secret agent resonated once again: *Inspector Abberline is an extraordinary policeman. He is the pivot on which this case of murder and theft tips from mystery to enlightenment.* Thomas thought: *Yes, he is the pivot, but there is still an insufficient weight of evidence to tip the balance just yet. Abberline is stuck.*

Thomas sketched Franco from memory, although he wouldn't be able to write up this particular aspect of the story for his newspaper. The British secret service was notoriously reluctant to see any news story in print that revealed what they did – or what they failed to do. That included publishing the activities of foreign spies, unless permission was granted by the most senior members of government. Thomas doubted that Franco's search for golden statues smuggled into Britain by a knight of the realm would ever receive clearance for publication.

However, Thomas Lloyd hoped to write a book one day about his time with Inspector Abberline. Perhaps his notes about Franco Cavalli wouldn't be wasted. Meanwhile, Franco had been allocated a room where he could rest before being taken to the railway station at Porthmadog.

Inspector Abberline could have been magically transformed into a statue himself – the man didn't speak, he didn't move. He gazed at the Welsh landscape for fully ten minutes. No doubt the man didn't actually notice the thousands of trees or magnificent mountains. Thomas knew that he gazed on an inner-gallery of mental images: of the secret pagan shrine at Fairfax Manor; at the uncannily preserved face of Joshua Denby. No doubt he brooded over the subtlest of clues; the slightest oddity of human behaviour – or the unwitting slip of a tongue that might betray a wrong-doer.

At last, Abberline inhaled deeply. 'Thomas.' He spoke in a calm, thoughtful voice. 'Thomas, I have set a trap for our suspect.' He turned from the window. '*And it worked.*'

Thomas rose to his feet. 'A trap? What kind of trap?'

'A certain something to make the killer act rashly.'

"You mean to say you've tricked the killer into revealing themselves?'

'I believe we're dealing with more than one individual. There has been a conspiracy to slay the Denby brothers.'

Thomas couldn't keep still. Excitement crackled through him – a searing electricity that made him want to demand to hear the name of the murderers. Yet he forced himself to listen, rather than fire questions at Abberline.

Abberline extended one hand to Thomas, palm upwards. Two strands of cotton, three inches or so in length lay across the palm. 'The trap.' Abberline nodded with satisfaction. 'I suspect one of the killers is here in this house.'

'How do two pieces of thread tell you that?'

'This morning I set my trap. See the cloth covering the blackboard? I threaded one piece of cotton through two small holes at the bottom of the cloth. That meant the flap of the sheet at the front of the black-board was loosely connected to the flap at the back. The other length of cotton I trapped between the door and the door frame when we left this morning. I locked the door and took the key with me.'

'Ah.' Thomas began to understand. 'When you got back, the door was still locked, but?'

'But this piece of white thread was on the floor. I made sure the thread was tightly trapped between the door and its jamb, so it simply wouldn't slip out.'

'Therefore, someone unlocked the door, opened it, the cotton fell to the floor, and then presumably they came in here ... what were they looking for?'

'The intruder wanted to read what was written on the blackboard. Remember, I made a point of turning the blackboard to the wall before we interviewed the domestic staff. Yet I intended the blackboard to be noticeable. No doubt the staff wondered what was written there.'

'But only a person desperate to see what was chalked on the board would risk dismissal by taking a pass key and entering the room.'

Abberline nodded. He lifted the hem of the sheet that covered the board. 'When I returned after Cavalli had been caught I saw that the two flaps of the sheet had been parted – the cotton strand had been pulled out of the corresponding holes. Of course, the thread so loosely connected the two halves of the sheet that anyone lifting it, like so, would never have noticed the thread stretching between front and back ....' Abberline gently raised the part of the sheet that concealed the words on the board. 'Now our intruder could read what's written here. But they wouldn't realize that they've sprung the trap.'

'Did you place any strands of cotton on the drawers?' Thomas approached the table where Abberline kept his notes and the photograph found in the coffin. 'Because it seems to me as if the intruder wanted to search the room.'

'I did. There are pieces of thread between the drawers and surrounding woodwork. None has been disturbed.'

'What does this tell you, Inspector?'

'Someone had a burning need to see what we'd written on the blackboard. Now, Thomas, look at the board closely. What do you notice?'

'Letters have been smudged.'

'How many?'

'Only two. The first two letters of Leonard in the name Leonard Guntersson.'

'Exactly.'

'It's not badly smudged.' Thomas examined the name that had been written in green chalk. 'It's as if the person who came in here touched the letters for some reason.'

'How it looks to me, Thomas, is that the intruder didn't have much time. They knew they were taking a risk. They could be discovered at any moment. The drawers in the table must have been tempting to search for information. However, in order to save precious seconds, the intruder hurried straight to the blackboard.' He pointed at the chalked names. 'Because they suspect that the information they need is right here. That's why they gave this board priority.'

'Leonard Guntersson. He was a known associate of Sir Alfred Denby.'

'We know, also, from police records that he was convicted of dealing in stolen antiquities. He spent twelve months in jail.'

'Can he be linked to the Gods of Rome?'

'Unfortunately not. However, Guntersson had been questioned by the police on numerous occasions about the buying and selling stolen artefacts. More accurately, I should refer to the man as "the late Leonard Guntersson", because he died several years ago, though I don't have a date of death.'

'Do you think our suspect intended to rub out the name, but was disturbed?'

'No. What it indicates,' Abberline said, 'is human nature. If we read something that is important to us ... words that resonate emotionally. We tend to do this.' He lightly touched the board. 'We run our finger along the bottom of the word that is significant. In this case, it's the name Leonard Guntersson. Look closely, the chalk is only smudged at the bottom of the letters L and E.'

Thomas nodded. 'So, an occupant of this house found a pass key this morning. Unlocked the door. Read what was on the board, smudging the letters.'

'And the name that nailed their attention was this one.' Abberline pointed at the name chalked in green. 'Leonard Guntersson, deceased.'

'Do you have a name for the suspect?'

'I hope to have soon.'

Abberline didn't have chance to elaborate. At that very moment a woman's scream reverberated along the corridor outside. A scream of panic, despair, and absolute horror.

CHAPTER 34

THE WOMAN'S SCREAM sent both men running into the corridor. Thomas saw a maid rushing toward the nurse, who looked after Mr and Mrs Denby's daughter.

The maid cried out in panic to the nurse. 'Come quick! Edith's been taken bad ... the child cannot breathe!'

The nurse picked up her skirts and ran toward the maid. 'Has Edith had her medicine?'

'Yes, Nurse! I gave her it myself ... right on the stroke of four o' clock! Edith took two spoons!'

'Where is Edith now?'

'In her bedroom. Oh, please do come quick! I fear for the little mite's life!'

The maid and the nurse ran in the direction of the stairs.

'Poor Edith,' sighed Thomas to Abberline. 'I wish there was something we could do to help.'

'I'm sure the child is in good hands. What's important for us is that we keep to our work. We need to find the individuals who murdered William's brothers before they kill him, too.'

Thomas Lloyd closed the office door behind them. Inspector Abberline returned to the blackboard where he fixed his sharp eyes on the name written there in green chalk: LEONARD GUNTERSSON. He examined where the letters L and E had been smudged.

'The late Mr Guntersson is significant in all this,' Abberline declared. 'Yet for the life of me I don't see how he fits into this case.'

Thomas checked the names in the file that Abberline had brought with him from Scotland Yard. 'There is no date of death, yet it does state that he died of natural causes.'

'It's time to use a trick an old detective taught me ... a trick that utilizes imagination.' Abberline took a piece of chalk and drew a square in the top right hand corner of the blackboard where there were no names. 'The detective insisted that human beings notice more details in the world around them than they realize. He told me that when we are stumped for an answer, which I am now, that it is time to employ his imagination technique. He said that I should draw a picture frame.' He tapped the chalked square on the board. 'Then I should look at it, and visualize a face inside the frame. Sometimes, if we are lucky–' Abberline gave a grim smile – 'our imagination walks hand-in-hand with instinct, and we see the suspect in our mind's eye.'

He took three paces back from the blackboard where he gazed steadily at the chalked outline of the square for a moment. Then he slowly closed his eyes.

Suddenly, he grunted. Opening his eyes, he walked to the board and chalked a name there.

Elsewhere in the house there was commotion. The nurse, the maid, and Edith's parents would be gathering by the girl's bed. Thomas Lloyd had failed to dispel mental images of fraught faces as they watched the child fighting for breath. Her hair would be damp from the hard physical effort of drawing air into her diseased lungs. There would be cries. Anguished shouts. Calls for more medicine. Windows flung open to admit the fresh breeze. Mr and Mrs Denby would pray that their daughter could catch her breath, that the crisis would pass, that she would relax back onto the pillow with her breath coming in easy lungfuls ... not choking ... not a painful gasping for breath.

Here, in the room that served as Inspector Abberline's office, the atmosphere was serene. The detective gazed in wonder at the name he'd written inside the square that he'd just moments ago chalked on the board.

Thomas read the name, 'Miss Groom?'

When Abberline spoke it was with a note of surprise. 'The only face I could visualize in that square was Miss Groom. At first I thought my instinct had duped me. The housekeeper? *No,* I told myself. *It can't be.*'

'You said you used imagination to visualize the suspect's face. Surely, you have simply guessed?'

'No, Thomas ... not a guess. The clues are there. They are slight. In fact, they are the subtlest of clues. But they are there. They exist!' He used the chalk to blaze a white streak beneath the name. 'Miss Groom. She has been employed by the Denby family for sixteen years. Of the domestic staff, only she and the butler would have access to the household pass keys. Therefore, she could have unlocked the door this morning, read what was on the blackboard then locked the door again before going about her duties.'

'Equally, the butler must be a suspect. He has worked for the Denby family since he was a boy. He would have a key to this room, too.'

'But no clues attach to the butler. However, they do attach to Miss Groom. Remember when she came in here yesterday? I'd deliberately kept the blackboard facing outwards so the wording could clearly be seen, instead of turning it to face the wall as I've done in the past. Do you remember what happened?'

'She viewed the room with a great deal of displeasure. She clearly dismissed us as untidy louts.'

'So she did, but she also gave the blackboard, and what what's written upon it, very close attention.'

'I see ... another trap?'

'In a manner of speaking. I wanted to find out if the list of names would be of particular interest to anyone entering our office. She stood absolutely still when she noticed these names. In fact, her body went rigid as she stared at the board. There was no way of knowing which name seized her attention, of course. But, just for a moment, nothing else in the world mattered to her. I then turned the board round so she wouldn't have the opportunity to read more.'

'And, later, she returned to the room to check the names?'

'I believe so. Moreover, we've now identified the name that was important to her.' He pointed at the name printed in green. 'Leonard Guntersson.'

'Miss Groom, therefore, knows him.'

'I think she must. The name means something to her.'

Thomas frowned. 'Is that enough to suggest that she is implicated in the Denby murders?'

'Not in itself. After all, she may have simply been curious about our work.'

'Perhaps she knew Guntersson by chance? Maybe she worked for him in the past?'

'I might agree that in other circumstances all this could be coincidence, and that she was merely being nosy, and that she returned to this room while we were out in order to satisfy her idle curiosity. *However,* she knowingly risked dismissal. William Denby made sure the staff knew that they were forbidden to come in here unless invited by me. No, the truth of the matter is this: Miss Groom has been deceiving us. In fact, she has made it her business to deceive everyone in the house.'

'How so?'

'Recently, we've enjoyed the first days of hot sunshine this year. When I saw her G this morning I noticed that her hands had caught the sun.'

'Really? How can a modicum of /colour point to a woman deceiving people?'

'A housekeeper is conscious of her position. She would keep her hands covered by gloves in hot sunshine. To allow her hands to become reddened by the sun would be unthinkable to her. To her mind, she'd resemble a farm girl.'

'Perhaps she forgot her gloves when she went for a stroll?'

'Formidable women like Miss Groom forget nothing. No. I saw her hands this morning. They were reddened slightly by the sun. Yet she had a pale line here.' Abberline held up his hand. 'A pale mark on the third finger of her left hand.'

'Then she wore a ring when she was outdoors?'

'Miss Groom isn't Miss Groom at all. At very least she is *Mrs* Groom. Yet for some reason she keeps the fact she is married a secret. This deception and her interest in the names on the blackboard are whispering to me that she's implicated in the murders.'

'What do you propose to do now?'

'Confront Miss ... or, rather, Mrs Groom.'

'I'll ring for her.'

'No. If we summon her here she might guess that I know something, and she'll be on her guard. What we need is the element of surprise – *we must catch her off-guard.*'

Thomas Lloyd and Inspector Abberline walked briskly along the corridor to the staircase and descended to the lower floor where there were laundry rooms, store rooms and an assortment of work places staffed by the servants of Newydd Hall. Maids hurried along corridors with baskets full of vegetables, piles of laundry and everything required for the smooth running of the Denby home.

Inspector Abberline asked the maids the same question, 'Have you seen Miss Groom?'

There were startled shakes of the head. They were clearly alarmed that the great Scotland Yard detective needed to find the housekeeper with such breathless urgency.

'Have you seen Miss Groom?' he directed the question at a

footman, carrying a tray of sherry decanters.

'Not today, sir.'

A boy walked along the corridor, pulling a little cart behind him, laden with polished boots.

Abberline stopped the boy. 'Have you seen Miss Groom recently?'

'Last I time I seen her, she came flying down here, kicking out her skirts, and all red faced.' The boy spoke with relish. 'She ran through that cellar door, just like all the damned hounds of hell were biting at her heels.'

'Thank you.' Abberline headed for the door.

Thomas followed Abberline down the steps into a cavernous place of brick arches and dozens of shelves filled with canned food, and jar upon jar of preserved fruits and vegetables. Gas mantles had been turned down; they gave off a dim light that accentuated shadowy corners. A cat, with bright, yellow eyes, sat by a mouse hole in the woodwork. The feline watched the two men hurry by.

Thomas's pulse raced. Electric shocks of excitement snapped along his limbs. *Miss Groom? Part of the murder plot? Apparently so. Bit by bit, the Inspector is accumulating clues that suggest Miss Groom isn't all that she first appeared.*

They'd been hurrying through cellars linked by narrow passageways. A brighter light burned at the far end. Abberline, suddenly pausing, put his finger to his lips.

Has Miss Groom gone to ground here? Is she hiding herself way before she escapes the house altogether? Thomas longed to see the woman's expression when Abberline accused her of slaying the Denby brothers. They approached the cellar room silently. When Abberline reached the door he stood perfectly still. From inside the room came the sound of a faint clink: glass on glass.

Abberline surged forward, thrusting the door open. Thomas followed.

A face looked up at them in shock. The mouth dropped open into a huge O-shape. The eyes went wide, too. A hand moved quickly, covering objects on a table with a towel.

Thomas memorized the scene for his newspaper report. There, sitting at a table, was a blond footman. This was Hassop. He'd admitted that several years ago he'd introduced Sir Alfred to a smuggler in Porthmadog. Now Hassop sat here in the cellar looking decidedly furtive. To go further, he was alarmed to have been found down here.

Abberline spoke quickly, 'Hassop, I'm looking for Miss Groom. Have you seen her?'

When he realized he wasn't the object of the policeman's search he smiled that oily smile of his. 'Not in a while, sir.'

'When did you see her last?'

'Oh … perhaps an hour ago. Maybe two.' He shrugged. 'Can't really say for sure.'

'*Where* did you see her last?' Abberline spoke politely; however, the fuse to the detective's anger was already burning.

'Down here. She'd come into this room for something or other.'

'Your answers are vague, Hassop.'

'I've just had a nap, sir. That must account for my vagueness. I was up working hard when most gentlemen were still lying in their beds.' Hassop smirked. He enjoyed being unhelpful.

'Tell me what Miss Groom wanted from down here.'

'Like I said, sir. This and that.'

'This and that?' Abberline approached the footman. 'Is this *this and that*?'

He plucked the towel from the table. A glass jar contained dark liquid; more dark liquid filled a wine glass. A cigar smouldered on a plate, while, lying on the table, were a dozen photographs the size of playing cards.

Hassop protested. 'This is my personal property. I don't give you permission to touch what's mine.'

Thomas angled his head in order to examine the photographs. 'Naked women? You spend your time down here ogling flesh?'

Abberline picked up the glass, sniffed it. 'And drinking your master's best port … and what's this? Smoking his cigars?'

'No, sir.'

'You've stolen these, Hassop. If you don't answer my questions fully, and in detail, I will have you thrown in gaoll. You'll get six months' hard labour for this.'

'No … I-I-I—' The smirk had gone. Hassop floundered.

'When did you see Miss Groom last?'

The footman stammered – he was scared: 'T-two hours ago.'

'Are you sure?'

'Yes, sir.' He rose to his feet, wringing his hands in anguish. 'She came down here to collect something from a bottle.'

'Tell me exactly what she did after entering this room. And woe betide you if you try and make a fool of me.'

'Miss Groom burst through that door. She was in a tearing hurry. She didn't even speak to me. Anyway, she rushes to the cupboard – that one with the brass handle. She opens the door, takes the cork out of the blue bottle. Then she takes a small bottle from the pocket of her skirt. A tiny bottle, sir. She tips some of the liquid from the big bottle into the little one. Then she puts a stopper in the little bottle and tucks it back into her pocket. As she's closing up the cupboard, I says to her: *What's all the rush for?* She tells me she's late for work upstairs in the master's rooms. And – *whoosh* – off she goes.' The footman's eyes had a searching quality as he looked at Abberline. 'Is that sufficient, sir?' When Abberline didn't reply Hassop's nervousness increased. 'You won't tell the master, will you, sir? I'll be sacked. The workhouse will be the end of me.'

'Think very hard. Did Miss Groom do anything else? Say anything else?'

'I-I don't think so ... you won't tell the master ... it's such a little drop of port—'

'Hassop.' Abberline's voice dropped to a whisper. 'Take a deep breath ... that's it ... now form a picture of Miss Groom in your mind. See her walking in here to the cupboard. Did she do anything that seemed strange, or unusual?'

'No, sir.'

'Are you sure?'

'She filled the little bottle from the big bottle. That's all. Uh ... wait, there was something. The way she moved was all in a rush, like she was late. She checked her watch. It's one of those pinned to the blouse above the breast. So she had to lift the watch in order to see its face.' He sounded pleased now he'd remembered this detail. 'Miss Groom tut-tutted, because she noticed she'd got a dirty mark on her blouse. She took a handkerchief from her pocket and, even though she was late, she took a good moment or two to wipe the mark off the material – it showed up a lot, because the blouse was white.'

'What kind of mark?'

'Dust, I suppose.' The footman shrugged. 'Dust, that's all.'

Thomas spoke up. 'Does your master know about your taste in photographs, too?'

The man's forehead became a mass of ridges as he thought hard. His eyes suddenly blazed in triumph. 'The mark was green – bright green! Paint or chalk!'

Abberline's eyes blazed, too, as he glanced at Thomas. 'Miss Groom it is.'

With that, he crossed the vault to where cupboards lined the wall. He opened the one with the brass handle to reveal a blue bottle standing there. Abberline read the label. Then he pulled out the cork and held the bottle to his nose. Instantly, he recoiled, his eyes watering. 'Camphor.' He replaced the bottle and shut the door.

'Camphor? Miss Groom used that to soak the masks she made for us when we opened the grave.'

Abberline's eyes were on fire. 'There's no time to lose, Thomas! There is to be another murder!'

'Murder?' Thomas followed Abberline through the cellar at a run. 'Miss Groom is planning to kill William Denby?'

'No! It's not William who is going to be the victim ... it's his daughter. Groom is going to murder Edith!'

Thomas followed Abberline out of the cellar. They immediately raced toward a flight of stairs that would take them to the upper floor where William Denby lived with his family.

Abberline panted, 'You see the sequence of events today, don't you? When we were out hunting Cavalli, Miss Groom took her chance. She unlocked the office door in order to confirm that Leonard Guntersson's name was really there, and to find out what was written on the blackboard beside it. She touched the letters, getting chalk dust on her fingers. When she looked at the watch pinned to her blouse some of the green chalk transferred from her fingers to the fabric.'

'But what's her motive? Why is she killing the Denby brothers?'

'That's what I still need to find out. Now let's hope that we're not too late.'

Abberline didn't knock on the apartment door. Pushing it open, he swept along the corridor. 'William? Mrs Denby?'

A maid appeared at a doorway, white with shock. 'Oh, goodness! What's wrong?'

'Where's your mistress?'

'Mrs Denby is with Edith.'

'Which room?'

'That one, sir.'

Abberline ran toward the door, flung it open, and entered the bedroom. Edith lay on the bed. She struggled for breath, her forehead damp with perspiration. Every intake of air had become a grim battle for her. Mrs Denby held a spoon to the girl's lips.

'No!' shouted Abberline. 'Don't give her that – it's poison!'

Mrs Denby gasped with shock. 'Inspector? This is Edith's medicine. The doctor gave it to her. It's the only thing that will save her life.'

'No, Mrs Denby, it will kill her.'

Abberline picked up the brown bottle from the bedside table.

Meanwhile, Edith turned her head slightly at the sound of the commotion. She muttered softly, 'Mother ... I cannot breathe.'

Abberline studied the bottle's label. 'What is this?'

'It's a remedy to help Edith breathe,' Mrs Denby explained. 'It clears her lungs.'

Abberline sniffed the open bottle. Its smell made him flinch. 'There's camphor in this.'

'I believe it's one of the ingredients.'

'Camphor is present in only tiny quantities in medicine. This smells incredibly strongly of the stuff.'

'That may be, Inspector, but Edith has taken this medicine for years.'

'Was Miss Groom here earlier?'

'Yes, she put fresh linen on the bed.'

'She was alone in the bedroom?'

'For a while, yes. Why? What's wrong, Inspector?'

'In small quantities, camphor can be used medicinally, in larger quantities, it is a poison.'

'A poison? I don't understand.'

'Symptoms of camphor poisoning are quickening of the heartbeat. Also, the victim's breathing becomes much slower. Both symptoms together are debilitating. The victim grows progressively weaker. Do those symptoms match those of Edith's?'

Mrs Denby stroked Edith's forehead, trying to soothe the girl. 'Yes, those are the symptoms ... but she does have a lung complaint.'

'What triggered this attack, Mrs Denby, is an excess of camphor in the medicine. Miss Groom added it to the bottle when she was alone in this room. The woman is trying to harm your daughter.'

'Oh, my dear God.'

Abberline called the nurse to the room. 'Go to Dr Penrhyn – he's in a building by the stable block – tell him that Edith Denby is suffering from camphor poisoning. We need him here at once if he is to save this child's life.'

The nurse hurried away to fetch the doctor. Thomas Lloyd knew that Dr Penrhyn would still be finalizing his experiments on the disinterred corpse of Joshua Denby, the brother slain by arsenic. Now the doctor's skill would be put to the ultimate test: to save the life of a human being. He gazed at Edith lying there on the bed. The child's skin was wet from perspiration. The simple act of drawing air into her lungs had become an ordeal. She was exhausted. Her eyelids fluttered, her lips turned blue. The ten year old was barely conscious. Her mother dabbed her forehead with a cloth while murmuring reassurances.

Abberline beckoned a maid who stood at the threshold to the bedroom. 'Guard the doorway to the apartment. Don't let Miss Groom in here. If necessary, do whatever it takes to keep her out.'

Thomas said, 'Inspector, I'll stay here in case Groom comes back.'

'No, I need you with me. The maid can bolt the door after we've gone.' Abberline's sense of urgency crackled in the air. Here was man with a mission – a matter of life and death. He didn't want to waste a second. 'Mrs Denby, where is William?'

'I told him not to do it.' The woman was in tears. 'He's so head-strong. I'm terrified it will be too much for poor Edith.'

'What's he going to do?'

'He's preparing one of the balloons. He intends to carry Edith up where the air is clear. He says altitude alone, will clear her lungs … oh, Inspector, the notion frightens me. I fear it will be the death of my daughter.'

'Mrs Denby, Dr Penrhyn is Edith's best chance of life. Tell him that she has been poisoned, and that he should administer an antidote for an excess of camphor. Also, tell him that your housekeeper added the camphor to Edith's medicine.'

'Yes, Inspector. I understand.'

'I will tell William that Miss Groom is a poisoner, and must be found.' He nodded at the maid. 'Close the door after us. Be sure to drive home the bolts, because Miss Groom still has her keys.'

When they were on the other side of the apartment door, and heard the bolts snap shut, Abberline appeared satisfied that Mrs Denby and her daughter would be safe for now. He hurried downstairs with Thomas at his side.

Thomas Lloyd realized that today had been the most remarkable day of his life. What's more, instinct told him that this extraordinary drama wasn't over yet.

The yard at the back of the house was a whirl of activity. Soldiers ran to the large shed where the balloon was housed. More soldiers hauled a cable across the lawn. William Denby gestured wildly, urging the men to move faster. Thomas thought: This is a father striving to save his daughter. He will move heaven and earth to make her well again.

Yet beyond this vortex of running, shouting, gesturing men were sunlit hills. The forest appeared serene – not a breath of wind blew. Thomas even caught the pleasant scent of lilac blossom on the air. The natural world was at peace. It was only the world of Humanity that had catapulted itself into a hullabaloo of wild frenzy.

LAUNCH THE BALLOON! SAVE THE GIRL'S LIFE! Thomas could almost hear the thoughts of those dozens of men beating the air, just as a drumstick pounds a drum. Colonel Brampton ran to meet Abberline and Thomas as they crossed the yard. The officer's jacket flapped open, he appeared almost dishevelled. His eyes were wide with bewilderment.

'Gentlemen!' shouted Brampton – anxiety flashed in his eyes rather than anger. 'Can you persuade William to stop this madness? He plans to carry his sick daughter high above the Earth. He will kill her!'

Thomas said, 'William believes that the purity of the air will cure her lungs.'

'Yes ... but, dash it all, man, these are military airships. They're not flying sick beds.'

Abberline moved briskly. 'I need to speak to William.'

'God help you, he listens to no one!'

'His daughter has been poisoned. Miss Groom added more camphor to the girl's medicine.'

Brampton stared at Abberline in utter shock. 'Miss Groom has tried to kill the girl?'

Thomas asked, 'Have you seen Miss Groom?'

'No, not recently. Good grief. The Prince of Wales is coming here next week. I must report all this to my commanding officer.'

Abberline spoke drily: 'What your commanding officer will or won't say is the least of our troubles.'

Brampton ran his hands across his scalp, clearly at a loss.

Abberline turned to Thomas. 'See those sentries over there by the fence? Ask them if they've seen Miss Groom, will you? The sooner I arrest that woman the better.'

Thomas hurried in the direction of a pair of soldiers armed with rifles. There were more guards dotted about the perimeter of the yard.

A figure stepped out of from behind one of the sheds. Thomas saw that the man no longer wore his yellow coat. His wounded arm, however, still rested in its sling.

'What is happening, William?' Franco Cavalli asked the question in that nonchalant way of his. 'Have we been invaded by the Russians? Is this war?'

'William Denby's daughter is sick.'

'I am sorry to hear that. But why are they taking the balloon from its shed?'

'I can't speak now, Franco. I need to talk to the sentries.'

'Really? They won't be able to tell you anything. They aren't looking *outwards*. They are looking *inwards* at all these soldiers, being busy as bees round a honey pot. *Si?*'

Thomas continued toward the soldiers.

Franco called after him, 'They have not seen what I've seen. What is obvious.'

Without even glancing back, Thomas quickened his step.

Franco called out again, 'They have not noticed a flash of light from the trees over there. Someone uses a spyglass, or binoculars, or some such device. Sunlight is reflected from a lens.'

'*A lens?*' Thomas spun round to face the Italian. 'Where?'

He pointed. 'That line of trees. A hundred metres to your left.'

Thomas shielded his eyes. Late afternoon sunlight shone brightly along the valley to bathe the trees in a golden glow. Then it came – a silvery flash of light: the same kind of flash when sunlight is reflected.

'My God.' His heart began to pound so furiously it hurt.

The next second he ran toward William. The man helped soldiers attach ropes to a balloon basket on the lawn.

Thomas yelled at the top of his voice: 'GET DOWN! GET DOWN!' Thomas guessed what had reflected the light. The sun had caught the lens of a telescopic sight. 'THERE'S A GUNMAN OUT THERE. GET DOWN!'

The soldiers were well trained and reacted in a blur of speed. Unarmed soldiers ducked behind cover. Sentries grabbed their rifles as they dropped to a crouch; they were instantly ready for any threat that might present itself.

'William!' Thomas bellowed. 'Get down!'

That's when the gunshot rang out. A bullet tore a gash in the lawn just inches from William's feet. Soil exploded upwards. The man was so startled that he lost his balance, and fell sprawling to the ground.

William Denby lay absolutely still, a perfect target for the marksman.

The next bullet would slam into living flesh. The man had just seconds to live.

CHAPTER 35

THOMAS TOOK IN the scene with a single glance. Out here, at the back of the house, the remarkable drama was unfolding in a heartbeat. Franco Cavalli stared in the direction of the trees from where the gunshot had sounded. Abberline ran toward William Denby, yet he was still some fifty paces away. William had stumbled when the bullet had ripped through the lawn just inches from his foot.

Now he lay winded on the grass. He didn't move. The man was the perfect target for the assassin. The next bullet would shatter his skull.

Then an extraordinary thing ... such an extraordinary thing ... Thomas watched a figure, clad in a flapping garment, race across the lawn.

'A woman?' Franco exclaimed. 'Warn her – she'll be killed!'

Thomas watched the figure and, in that moment, realized it was none other than Miss Groom. Her long skirts and her shawl swished as she ran. Without an atom of hesitation, she raced across the lawn to William Denby. Then *the extraordinary* became *the astonishing*. She knelt down in front of her master who lay dazed on the earth after his fall.

She held up her arms as if beseeching God in heaven, and in an astonishingly loud voice cried, 'Don't kill him ... don't you dare!"

If they were prayers, or a plea to the assassin, they went unheeded.

Another loud bang. A rifle bullet screamed through the air. The bullet missed both figures. Then another shot – that missile of lead, racing at 500 miles an hour, slammed into an outbuilding, sending splinters of brick raining down.

Franco hissed, 'He's getting his range. The next shot will kill.'

He snatched a rifle from a soldier, aimed, and fired into the line of beech trees.

Colonel Brampton yelled, 'Damn it! Who gave the order to fire?'

Franco raised the rifle over his head to attract the attention of the troops. 'Men! Look! Do you see gunsmoke drifting out of the trees? Place your shots there. Keep firing. Put the devil off his aim!'

The soldiers gawped at this Italian civilian who had the audacity to give them orders.

Abberline cupped his hands around his mouth. 'Do what he says! FIRE!'

A dozen soldiers – consummate masters of their weapons – aimed their rifles. A series of loud bangs, and a dozen bullets slammed into the trees where a trace of blue gunsmoke still hung in the air. Franco Cavalli fired again; as did the soldiers. More bullets tore at the trees a hundred yards away. Branches fells, white marks appeared on tree trunks where bullet ripped away bark.

Franco gave a roar of exultation. *'Keep firing. Don't let him recover his aim!'*

Thomas glanced across at William. The man had managed to scramble to his feet after hitting the ground hard enough to wind himself. Seizing Miss Groom by the arm, he pulled her toward Abberline. Soon all three retreated behind one of the sheds. The assassin's bullets couldn't reach them now.

The assassin, meanwhile, must have reached the same conclusion. What's more, he would have been forced to shelter behind the thickest of tree trunks to avoid being killed by that bullet storm. The soldiers fired with incredible precision. Round after round slammed into the trees. Leaves showered the dirt, together with twigs and even whole branches.

Abberline emerged from behind the building. He waved his arms over his head.

'Stop firing! He's running!'

Franco whooped with excitement. 'There goes the devil! See, Inspector? The black cloak? He's the same man I saw before! He was at Fairfax Manor!'

Soldiers aimed their rifles at the fleeing assassin. In the shapeless cloak, he resembled a grounded crow, flapping its wings in the useless hope of taking to the skies.

Abberline ran out onto the lawn. *'Stop! Don't fire! I want him in one piece! Do you hear me? Don't kill him! I need that man alive!'*

Night was approaching. Mountains grew darker by the moment. Shadow filled the valley, and servants glided silently through Newydd Hall, lighting lamps, drawing down blinds, and putting more logs on fires as cold air seeped into the house – those ghostly fingers of cold touched Thomas Lloyd's neck as he stood in the corridor. Thomas waited for William to bring him news from the sickroom upstairs.

Thomas vividly recalled those dramatic events of just three hours ago when the gunman had targeted William Denby, and Franco Cavalli and the soldiers fired a salvo of bullets back in his direction. A man in black had fled. However, he'd only made it partway across the meadow beyond the trees when the soldiers caught him. Then, gripping him tightly, they'd brought him back to Inspector Abberline. Meanwhile, Thomas had seized Miss Groom by the wrist. She hadn't struggled. In fact, she appeared to accept this turn of events as her destiny. She said nothing. Not a flicker of emotion crossed her face.

William Denby had raced back to the house. All he longed for at that moment was to be with his wife as Edith Denby struggled to keep death at bay. And for hours that seemed as long as days Edith fought the poison in her blood.

Thomas waited for William to come. He gazed out at the hills as darkness fell: engulfing, drowning, shrouding the living landscape, then glanced at the closed door to Abberline's office. Miss Groom and the assassin were in there. A murmur of voices reached him through the woodwork. He had sensed an air of resignation about the couple. Their fight was done, their battle lost.

Thomas heard a door open in the distance. Feet on the staircase. Echoes coming closer ... then receding, as if being swallowed into the underworld. Thomas felt his muscles tense, because he sensed the moment had come. And, indeed, William appeared at the far end of the corridor. *The man's face is unreadable. So is this bad news? The most tragic news of all?* Thomas took a deep breath; his scalp tingled. He prepared himself to hear the worst.

William stopped dead in front of Thomas. A twitch tugged at one side of his mouth; he'd clearly been under a terrible strain.

For a moment he couldn't speak ... then, at last, the words came rushing out: 'Thomas. Edith is over the worst. She will live.' He shuddered, and seemed close to weeping, though it would be tears of relief. 'Doctor Penrhyn confirms that Edith had been poisoned with camphor. The drug exaggerated the symptoms of the illness, so it appeared as if she suffered an acute attack.' He struggled to keep a grip on emotion. 'Camphor poisoning ... there is no sure antidote. But if the overdose isn't too a large one it can be treated with coffee, of all things. Edith is much better. She is sleeping now and breathing easier.'

'That is wonderful news, William. Wonderful!' Thomas shook the man's hand. 'Perhaps this is a turning point for the better.'

'God willing, Thomas.'

The office door swung open. Abberline stood there. A quiet, magisterial dignity radiated from the man.

Calmly, he asked about Edith. He, too, grasped William by the hand when he heard the good news.

Abberline said, 'Would you step inside, please, William? It's finally time you heard the explanation you've been waiting for.'

Thomas followed William into the office. Inspector Abberline softly closed the door behind them.

Miss Groom and the gunman sat side-by-side on straight-backed chairs. He still wore his long, black cloak that he'd used to mask his physical appearance. Thomas made a mental note of the man's features: he had a square jaw and a broad face; some might say a brutish face. His thick, curly hair was unkempt, while his eyebrows formed striking black arches over a pair of eyes that glared at Abberline. So, there was still a flame of anger in the assassin's heart after all? A pair of burly soldiers stood at the other side of the room. They were there in case the gunman turned violent again. After all, he appeared to be the type who might have formed the habit of brawling in taverns, and settling disputes with the swipe of a razor.

Abberline spoke in an understated way. 'Sitting beside Miss Groom is a man by the name of Jack Durrkar.'

William's eyes burned. 'Miss Groom, you gave poison to my daughter. How could you be so cruel?'

She didn't answer. Her expression hadn't altered once.

Abberline said, 'Miss Groom and this man are responsible for the deaths of three of your brothers, possibly more. To be more accurate, we should refer to Miss Groom as Mrs Durrkar, but for simplicity's sake we'll stick with the name you know her by.'

William wouldn't be denied an answer to his question. Again he asked, 'Miss Groom. Edith is already afflicted with a weakness in her lungs. Why did you make her life worse? What made you put more camphor into her medicine?'

Her eyes flashed with a sudden fire. 'To make you suffer. What's more, I wanted to *see you suffering*. The pain that etched itself into your face brought me such satisfaction.'

'Why?'

She pressed her lips tightly together, saying nothing.

Abberline inhaled deeply. 'I don't know exactly why Miss Groom tormented you by making your daughter appear more ill than she actually is. But I do know that an associate of your late brother, Sir Alfred, was important to her. His name was Leonard Guntersson. He died several years ago.'

Miss Groom glanced sharply at Abberline, though she remained silent.

Abberline continued, 'The clues are small. Yet they do add up to suggest that Miss Groom harbours powerful emotions. Yesterday, I noted that Miss Groom took particular interest in the blackboard which listed names and other items of information. This morning I laid a trap using pieces of cotton – one I threaded through the sheet covering the easel; another thread I nipped between the room door and its frame. I then locked the door. When I returned to the office, the thread that was held in place by the door lay on the rug. Furthermore, someone had disturbed the thread I'd placed in that sheet. An intruder, therefore, had clearly entered the room in order to read what was written on the board. The first two letters in the name Leonard Guntersson were smudged when the intruder touched the board. You'll notice that there is faint mark on Miss Groom's blouse. Green chalk transferred from her fingers to the material when she looked at the watch that is pinned to the blouse.'

'Proves nothing,' Miss Groom said tartly.

'Miss Groom has also been deceiving us all. I noticed that there is a pale mark on the third finger of her left hand. She wears a wedding ring when she meets her husband here. The sun has been much hotter over the last few days. Miss Groom, I believe, dispensed with gloves, because she prefers the intimacy of feeling her bare hand holding the hand of her husband. She married a while ago, but decided for reasons of her own to keep the wedding a secret. Perhaps, more importantly, she wished to keep her husband a secret.'

Durrkar growled, 'Damn foolish game. Holding hands, whisperin' lovin' words ... but that's what she wanted. Like she wanted me to wear this 'ere ring.' He held up his hand. A gold wedding band glinted there.

'Miss Groom,' began Abberline, 'who is Leonard Guntersson? Why is he important to you?'

She remained tight-lipped.

'A former husband?'

'No.'

'He shared your bed?'

'No ... but I loved him. Leonard Guntersson is my father. I say *is*, because he will always be my father, even though he was taken from me seventeen years and eight months ago. Yes. I know precisely how long has passed since he went to his grave. I know it to the days, the hours.' Her eyes were cauldrons of hate.

Durrkar grunted, 'Why bother telling them anything? We're going to the gallows, aren't we?'

'If I am going to hang,' she snarled, 'I will tell them everything. That will give me so much pleasure as I watch Mr Denby's face. I will devour his anguish when I explain how his brothers *really* died. Believe me, gentlemen, I will still be laughing when the noose goes around my neck.' Miss Groom spoke quickly. Her eyes gleamed. She enjoyed this. Oh, yes .... Thomas Lloyd could tell that the woman experienced intense gratification as she confessed her crimes.

CHAPTER 36

'I LOVED MY father,' Mrs Groom told them. 'Leonard Guntersson was a good man. He never committed any crime whatsoever. But he met a scoundrel by the name of Sir Alfred Denby who tricked him into handling stolen antiques. The police arrested my father. Yet there was no evidence to link the stolen valuables to Sir Alfred. My father, however, had innocently placed the antiques in his strong room. After a travesty of a court trial, where the most awful lies were told about my father, he was convicted. That kind-hearted, loving man endured twelve months in a lice-infested cell with diseased convicts. Within weeks of his release my father was dead. His health had been broken by the pit of infection that they call Wandsworth Gaol. I blamed Sir Alfred. The man could have spared my father that year of confinement if he, himself, had confessed to his wrongdoing. Sir Alfred was responsible for my father's death – it was as if he'd pointed a pistol at his heart and pulled the trigger.

'I began to watch Sir Alfred. I'd heard rumours that he'd been involved with statues from Italy. Gold statues, they said. I hoped to find evidence of his crime so I could see Sir Alfred go to prison. But he was too snake-like, too clever. Yet I still followed him ... always at a discrete distance. He didn't know I existed. For weeks I kept watch on him at Fairfax Manor. Then, one morning, I waited at the railway station in East Carlton for a train home to London. It was a gloomy, misty day in November. As I stood on the platform I noticed a man in a top hat in front of me. There was no one else on the platform. My heart gave a leap. "It's Sir Alfred", I told myself. Oh, my heart! I thought it would burst, it was beating so fast. My intention was to accuse him of my father's death. Yet before I could utter a word a goods train came through the station. Steam and smoke covered everything. A grey veil. A shroud. I could hardly see. And I knew the time had come. This was the special time. I stepped forward, and I

230

pushed the man. Sir Alfred fell from the platform and struck the ground in front of the train. The locomotive passed over him and he was killed. Ah ... gentlemen, you look at me strangely. How could the man I killed be Sir Alfred? After all, he died this year in the explosion. No ... I realized what had happened when I read about the accident in the newspaper. I'd killed Sir Alfred's brother by accident. They look so much alike ... the steam and the mist did the rest.

'At first, Inspector, I experienced terrible guilt. I'd pushed an innocent man in front of the train. Thoughts of confessing my crime were uppermost in my mind. However, I felt a compulsion to be in the graveyard on the day of the funeral. My own dear father had died. I know only too well the pain of grief, which tore me apart. So what would be the expression on Sir Alfred's face, and the faces of his brothers, when the man I killed was lowered into his grave? There were so many mourners that another woman in black, wearing a veil, wouldn't be noticed. Sir Alfred stood at the graveside with his brothers. Oh, when the coffin was brought to the grave, what did I see? I saw grief on Sir Alfred's face. His eyes were filled with sadness. No doubt he remembered boyhood games with his brother. He recalled Christmas Days, birthdays, and family gatherings. Now his brother had been broken to pieces and lay cold in a casket. Do you know what I felt, gentlemen?' Her eyes fixed with what Thomas could only describe as hunger on William's face. Overwhelming, ungodly hunger. 'I felt something twist in my heart. As if a key had been turned. My heart actually hurt, yet it was a sweet pain. I pressed my hand to my breast as I felt pressure being released inside my body. Sir Alfred's sadness made me happy. Oh, it sounds cruel of me to say these words. But at last I'd managed to extract at least a modicum of revenge. Sir Alfred caused my father's death; I caused the death of Sir Alfred's brother, and that scoundrel's grief made me feel content with life once more. All this happened many, many years ago, of course. After that, I found employment with the Denby family, using the name Miss Groom. They didn't suspect I was Leonard Guntersson's daughter.'

For the first time in a while, Abberline asked a question, 'And the other brothers who died?'

'All down to me ... well, to be frank, I enlisted the help of my younger brother. But the planning was all mine.' Once more she set her gaze on William. His reaction, his shock, *his horror* fed some hunger in the woman's evil mind. She smiled. 'Mr Denby is appalled. So be it.' Now she didn't stop speaking. Words were now this monstrous creature's weapon of hurt. 'I planned certain *accidents* for the Denby brothers. My brother, Godfrey, became the instrument of my vengeance. Godfrey hid on a river-bank that John Denby favoured for fishing. I'd explained where Godfrey should conceal himself and what he should do. He struck John Denby from behind with a rock. The body floated over a weir where it sustained more injuries. The coroner never suspected that he'd been murdered. Mortlake Denby enjoyed riding. Eight years ago, Godfrey tripped the horse with a rope. Once more, a rock was used to administer the death blow. Once more the coroner's verdict was accidental death. As a senior member of domestic staff I was permitted to attend the funerals. I watched Sir Alfred at every funeral. Each time, his grief eased my grief. His anguish at the loss of a brother was the lotion that soothed away my pain.'

William's face turned crimson with anger. 'The woman is insane.'

'Insane?' echoed Abberline. 'She has carefully planned the murders. They are spaced out over almost two decades. That requires a high level of intelligence, dedication and rational thought. No, not mad.'

'I don't expect you men to understand,' said Miss Groom.

Abberline nodded. 'I agree ... not many human beings could understand how anyone could commit murder in such a calculating way.'

'I did so to heal my broken heart.'

'Why did you poison Joshua Denby? Why didn't you concoct another accident?'

'Four years ago, my brother, Godfrey, caught a chill and died. I had to carry out the act myself. Joshua liked very strong coffee and, as housekeeper, I ensured it was just to his taste. All I need do was add small quantities of arsenic.'

'Because you knew,' Abberline told her, 'that arsenic poison remains in the body, and that the perfect way to kill someone with the stuff is to administer small doses over several months, so it appears the victim has contracted an illness.'

Thomas spoke up. 'But Miss Groom moved to one of the other Denby houses a month or so before Joshua Denby died?'

Abberline walked to the blackboard. 'Joshua had ingested dozens of arsenic doses before Miss Groom left. He was desperately ill. In that weakened state, it only needed for him to catch a cold in order for life to desert him.' He tapped the board. 'The Marsh Test proved he'd been poisoned with arsenic.'

William growled his next words, 'You poisoned my brother, and then you began poisoning Edith.'

Miss Groom gave a curt nod. 'Edith has weak lungs. I read medical books; they told me camphor speeds up the heart, while slowing respiration. When I put small quantities of camphor in Edith's medicine, which also contained camphor, it produced the effect I desired. I orchestrated, what appeared to you, to be a chronic seizure of her lungs.'

Even though William tried to speak, the sheer power of emotion bound the words up inside his throat. He couldn't even utter a snarl of anger.

Miss Groom smiled. 'Your anguish, when your daughter struggled to breathe, was my elixir of life. You were terrified that Edith would die. That terror made me feel wonderful. Moreover, I was in control. I decided when Edith Denby would be well and when she would be ill. I, a woman, a plain housekeeper, had power over Mr William Denby, the great scientist who could make men fly.' She chuckled. 'Oh ... after my brother died I realized another ally would be useful. I visited taverns, drank brandy, and pretended to be a lonely and desperate woman – but one who knew where fabulous golden statues were hidden. I found Jack Durrkar here ... he'd only just been released from prison. He had no home, no money ... all he had was a talent for criminality. I spun him wonderful stories of gold that could be found in one of the country mansions that belonged to the Denby family.'

Jack Durrkar gave a beast-like grunt. 'You witch, you—'

'Once he heard that there was treasure to be found, if only the Denby brothers were dead, he proposed marriage. I accepted.'

'You claim that you tricked me.' Durrkar gave her such an evil look. 'I tricked you. Any man could tell you were mad through and through. A regular Bedlam case. I played along with your silly games with wedding rings, holding hands, secret meetings in the woods. All that sickening make-believe. But, believe me, you witch, once I had that gold I would have seen you off like that.' He clicked his fingers. 'I'd have put you in a sack and drowned you.'

'You haven't the brains to outwit me.' Miss Groom shook her head. 'Fools like you spend half their lives in prison.'

'Ha. Even if my brain doesn't equal yours, we'll still hang the same.'

Abberline opened a table drawer and pulled out two sets of manacles. 'I take it, Durrkar, that you wanted to hurry the process? You didn't see any point in killing the Denby brothers over several years when the job could be done within weeks. Miss Groom told you about Sir Alfred's habit of firing a cannon every morning as signal to his estate staff to begin work.'

'A lovely piece of invention, if I say so myself.' Durrkar leered. 'If the witch here can boast, so can I. I fixed up a pistol in the little closet where Sir Alfred kept his gunpowder. When he opened the door, a string pulled the trigger, and *boom*.'

'You also travelled up to Scotland in order to kill Thaddeus Denby. This time you were so impatient to remove him you used a rifle.'

'I won't deny it – I'll be wearing the hangman's necktie before long, won't I? But you won't find a better man with a rifle in many a mile.'

'Then you came here to Wales with the intention of assassinating Mr William Denby. With two surviving brothers overseas, and unlikely to return any time soon, the Denby mansions would be boarded up. That's when you'd find the gold statues with your wife's help. You'd be a rich man, Durrkar.'

Miss Groom laughed. 'The servants heard all those stories about the Gods of Rome. Everyone from kitchen skivvy, to maid, to gardener, to butler looked for them. You fools, if the statues were on Denby land, don't you they'd have been found by now?'

'You witch!' Durrkar's face turned white with shock. 'You told me that they were hidden in one of the cellars. You said they were likely to be here. Now you tell me that there's no gold! Damn you!' He swung his arm at her face.

Abberline caught the man by the wrist before the blow struck home and snapped on the manacles. The soldiers stepped forward to help him secure the other wrist to the chain.

'You won't find any treasure here, gentlemen.' Miss Groom sat primly in the chair. She was enjoying this. 'I, on the other hand, have my treasure. What I shall value most of all is standing on the gallows, knowing that Mr Denby will have to live with the grief of his daughter's death. I have poisoned her. Yes. My doing, Mr Denby. Now she lies dying … or perhaps she is already dead. You will never know happiness or contentment again. My father's death is avenged.'

Abberline motioned Miss Groom to stand. He fastened one of the iron bracelets to her left wrist. 'Mr Denby, would you tell Miss Groom about your daughter's condition?'

'Gladly. I want to cheat the woman of her sick gratification. Miss Groom–' he spoke with icy calm –' Edith is upstairs. She is recovering. Her respiration is normal again. My daughter will live.'

Miss Groom flinched when she heard those words. 'I poured an ounce of camphor into the medicine. She must be dead now.'

'Doctor Penrhyn acted quickly. He administered coffee, which helps dispel the effects of camphor poisoning. Also, my daughter is much stronger than you believed.'

'No!' Miss Groom struggled. 'No ... you will not cheat me of this.'

The soldiers held her arms as Abberline fixed the second bracelet to her other wrist. With both Miss Groom and Durrkar in chains, the detective nodded at the soldiers. 'There's a police carriage waiting out on the drive. Would you please take them down there? Everyone in this house will sleep better tonight knowing that these two are behind bars.'

The soldiers took the two killers away. Durrkar had been sapped of any inclination to fight and went quietly. Miss Groom cursed and struggled, but she was in chains now. Her war against the Denby bloodline was at an end.

The detective spoke softly. 'Thank you for your hospitality, William. Thomas and I will be leaving at first light tomorrow.'

William thanked him then withdrew. The man's face was a happy one. No doubt he'd hurry upstairs to tell his wife everything. That, and to sit by his daughter's bedside where he'd thank Providence that her life had been spared.

'Thomas,' Abberline began, 'when you return to London tomorrow I daresay you'll have plenty of writing in front of you.'

'That I will, Inspector. This has been a fascinating experience. I'm grateful that you allowed me to become your shadow these past few days.'

'You know, a telegram arrived yesterday. A new case is waiting for me back at Scotland Yard.'

'Oh?'

'You would be most welcome to join me again. To remain my shadow, as it were. Does that interest you?'

Before Thomas could reply, a smiling Inspector Abberline picked up a cloth and wiped the blackboard clean of all that was written there.

CHAPTER 37

Six months later: October, 1890

THOMAS LLOYD AND Inspector Alfred Abberline stepped into the conservatory at Newydd Hall in North Wales. The last time they were here the trees were just coming into leaf; those leaves had now turned from gold to red, and the tops of the mountains were crowned by the first fall of snow.

William Denby, and his wife, Prudence, sat in cane chairs at either side of their daughter. Edith wore her hair in bright, red ribbons. She'd been reading to them from sheets of paper bound together in a homemade book with orange covers.

William jumped to his feet, delighted to see his visitors. 'Good morning, gentlemen. Wonderful to see you again.'

The adults shook hands, exchanged pleasantries, and expressed their delight at being reunited. Thomas noted that Edith Denby watched them with those intelligent eyes of hers. Without a shadow of doubt, the ten year old would be memoriszng this scene.

Thomas smiled at her. 'Are you well, Edith?'

'Quite well, thank you,' she said brightly. With that, she stood up, and walked across the conservatory with her hand extended. 'How was your journey from London?'

Thomas shook her hand. 'The trains were on time, which is a blessing.'

Mrs Denby tut-tutted at her daughter's forthright manner. 'Edith, a nod of the head and a dip of the knee is a perfectly polite way for a young girl to greet a visitor.'

'Mama, I know Thomas ... is it all ight if I call you Thomas? Or would you prefer Mr Lloyd?'

'We are friends, Edith.' He smiled. 'Thomas it is.'

'Thomas, I would like you to see my book.' She held out the volume

236

to him. 'I wrote about the case you and Inspector Abberline investigated here.'

'Thank you.' William took the book, the pages of which were covered with neat handwriting. 'I should be very interested to read it.'

Edith beamed with pleasure. 'You will have seen that I am well again, thanks to you and the inspector. It's true, I have weak lungs and always will, but it was the poison that Miss Groom put into my medicine that made the condition so much worse.'

William smiled fondly. 'Edith doesn't need the wheelchair anymore. She can walk and run.'

Mrs Denby added, 'As long as she doesn't over-tire herself.'

Edith seemed to sparkle with happiness. 'Will you look at my account of the investigation, Inspector Abberline?'

'I'd be delighted to do so. Thank you.'

'I have written the story from the day you arrived here. It's all there: the exhumation of my uncle from his grave, and the cunning way you made Miss Groom reveal herself as the murderer. Oh, I've described the court case, too, and how that scoundrel, Jack Durrkar, cheated the hangman by cutting his own throat. Just imagine! The sharp edge of the razor; it would feel like a nettle sting ... then oblivion ... oblivion everlasting. Isn't Miss Groom going to the gallows next week?'

'Oh, child.' Mrs Denby rolled her eyes in exasperation. 'Why dolls aren't of any interest to you I shall never know. Instead, you write about such horrors as tomb openings, suicides and hangings.'

'That's what happens in real life. Isn't that so, Thomas? And after walking hand-in-hand with death for such a long time I am determined to become part of the world. One day I shall be a newspaper reporter, like Thomas here. Don't look at me like that, Mama. Shall I ask the maid to bring our tea?'

After they'd refreshed themselves with tea and had eaten the most sublime Welsh cakes, William strolled through the gardens with Abberline and Thomas.

Inspector Abberline said, 'Of course, the reason we are here is to tie up some loose ends regarding the investigation.' He smiled. 'We also have a secret motive for visiting you. Both Thomas and I wanted to see Edith with our own eyes now that she has recovered.'

William nodded, smiling, too. 'I've had the best medical men examine Edith. They say that she does have a weakness of the chest, but in her case the condition should slowly improve as she grows older. It was the excess of camphor that Miss Groom administered that caused the severest attacks of breathlessness and weakness.'

'I'm glad to hear that she can look forward to a long life,' Abberline said. 'And, I hope, a happy and productive one.' He paused to gaze at soldiers patrolling near the balloon sheds. 'I must confess to one failing,' he added. 'The statues – the Gods of Rome – have yet to be found.'

'Will they ever?'

'Between you and me, I doubt if they ever will . My belief is that the British Government wishes to enter into treaties with Italy. Theft of the treasure soured relations between the British royal family and the Italian king, so if our government appears to be diligently searching for the statues in order to return them to Rome then a happier relationship would be restored.'

Thomas pointed out, 'Inspector Abberline is famous. So what should have been a secret investigation into the missing artefacts, and their link with the Denby family, would soon be widely known.'

William nodded. 'The Italian spy, the man in the yellow coat, he would have kept watch on you, no doubt, and reported back to his masters.'

'Indeed,' Abberline agreed. 'Signor Cavalli would have reassured the Italian ambassador that the British were being true to their word, and that a senior detective had been assigned to find the treasure.'

'The Curse of the Gods of Rome.' William's smile was wry one. 'Perhaps part of the curse is that they will never be found.'

'What's more, Sir Alfred may have melted the figures down into ingots, which could then be sold to goldsmiths far and wide. A faint trace of the golden gods might even be found in the ring that Thomas wears on his little finger.'

'What you did successfully find were my brothers' murderers. For that, I offer my heartfelt thanks.'

They walked along a wall that sheltered them from the cool breeze. Also walking there were two women. While the pair were still out of earshot, William murmured, 'Ah, there's Laura, Do you remember the girl who believed she had visions of the future?'

'Indeed we do,' Thomas said. 'Has she recovered?'

William sadly shook his head. 'Doctors say that the affliction is permanent. She is lost in her own world now. When the weather is pleasant, a maid will take her for a stroll in the gardens.'

'Then you are keeping her here?' Thomas asked.

'My wife and I agree that we should care for Laura, rather than consign her to an asylum. Her parents are elderly and we still send them her wages.'

'That is most generous,' said Abberline.

'In truth, we are grateful to her. Those visions that plagued her caused her to attempt to destroy the balloons in their sheds. This may seem strange to you, gentlemen, but I absolutely believe that Laura had a vital role in events six months ago. Without her stumbling across Franco Cavalli we would never have caught him. And, ultimately, Cavalli saved my life when he fired the rifle back at Durrkar and spoiled his aim. Laura, alas, will never know how important she is to my family.'

Abberline nodded. 'Laura may have been an unwitting participant, but she was the essential catalyst.'

Thomas shivered a little, and it wasn't due to the coolness of the air. 'Or perhaps she did see more than we can understand?'

'Another mystery for your pen, Thomas.' William doffed his cap as the maid approached, walking arm-in-arm with Laura. 'Ladies.'

Laura's face was pale. Her eyes had the look of someone gazing at a faraway object.

She turned to Thomas. 'Sir, I see your future. The fate of nations will rest upon your shoulders. Your words matter ... they will light an ocean of fire.' Laura's large eyes ranged across the path ahead of them. 'There are so many today. Our gardens are filled with shining people. They watch, listen, wait ... I know that only I can see them ... I shouldn't detain you, sir, but ... what I say is true. The safety of our world will, one day, depend on you.'

Laura continued walking arm-in-arm with the maid. To Thomas, the young woman seemed more ghost than mortal now. An insubstantial wraith. A faint mirage of flesh and blood.

William waited until they were out of earshot. 'We learnt that Laura had a baby. Her father forced her to give the child away when it was just a few days old. The doctor believes that those unhappy events corroded her sanity.'

Thomas saw a figure step out from the woods. 'Isn't that the boy she was going to marry?'

William nodded. 'Ah ... Jake. We've had to explain to him that his sweetheart will never recover, and that it is best for both of them if he continues his life without her. Jake's here to say his final farewell.'

Inspector Abberline took the path back to the house. Thomas and William walked with him. A few minutes later they opened the door and went inside. The sun fell on the hills, and Mount Snowdon shone white in its coat of ice. It looked like a ghost mountain – a mountain, from a different world, or from a different time – or perhaps even from a spirit's dream.